THE SECOND EMPIRE

BOOK FOUR OF THE MONARCHIES OF GOD

PAUL KEARNEY

ACE BOOKS, NEW YORK

THE SECOND EMPIRE

An Ace Book / published by arrangement with
Orion Publishing Group

PRINTING HISTORY
Victor Gollancz hardcover edition / 2000
Ace mass-market edition / April 2002

Visit our website at
www.penguinputnam.com
Check out the ACE Science Fiction & Fantasy newsletter!

ISBN: 0-441-00924-7

ACE®
Ace Books are published by The Berkley Publishing Group,
a division of Penguin Putnam Inc.,
375 Hudson Street, New York, New York 10014.
ACE and the "A" design
are trademarks belonging to Penguin Putnam Inc.

PRINTED IN THE UNITED STATES OF AMERICA

10 9 8 7 6 5 4 3 2 1

For John McLaughlin

WHAT WENT BEFORE . . .

FIVE centuries ago two great religious faiths arose which were to dominate the entire known world. They were founded on the teachings of two men: in the west, St. Ramusio; in the east, the Prophet Ahrimuz.

The Ramusian faith arose at the same time that the great continent-wide empire of the Fimbrians was coming apart. The greatest soldiers the world had ever seen, the Fimbrians had become embroiled in a vicious civil war which enabled their conquered provinces to break away one by one and become the Seven Kingdoms. Fimbria dwindled to a shadow of her former self, her troops still formidable, but her concerns confined exclusively to the problems within the borders of the homeland. And the Seven Kingdoms went from strength to strength—until, that is, the first hosts of the Merduks began pouring over the Jafrar mountains, quickly reducing their numbers to five.

Thus began the great struggle between the Ramusians of the west and the Merduks of the east, a sporadic and brutal war carried on for generations which, by the sixth century of Ramusian reckoning, was finally reaching its climax.

For Aekir, greatest city of the west and seat of the Ramusian Pontiff, finally fell to the eastern invaders in the year 551. Out of its sack escaped two men whose survival was to have the greatest possible consequences for future history. One of them was the Pontiff himself, Macrobius—thought dead by the rest of the Ramusian Kingdoms and by the remainder of the Church hierarchy. The other was Corfe Cear-Inaf, a lowly ensign of cavalry, who deserted his post in despair after the loss of his wife in the tumult of the city's fall.

But the Ramusian Church had already elected another Pontiff, Himerius, who was set upon purging the Five Kingdoms of any remnant of the Dweomer-Folk, the practitioners of magic. The purge caused Hebrion's young king, Abeleyn, to accept a desperate expedition into the uttermost west to seek the fabled Western Continent, an expedition led by his ruthlessly ambitious cousin, Lord Murad of Galiapeno. Murad blackmailed a master mariner, one Richard Hawkwood, into leading the voyage, and as passengers and would-be colonists they took along some of the refugee Dweomer-Folk of Hebrion, including one Bardolin of Carreirida. But when they finally reached the fabled west, they found that a colony of lycanthropes and mages had already existed there for centuries under the aegis of an immortal arch-mage, Aruan. Their exploratory party was wiped out, with only Murad, Hawkwood and Bardolin surviving.

Back in Normannia, the Ramusian Church was split down the middle as three of the Five Kingdoms recognised Macrobius as the true Pontiff, while the rest preferred the newly elected Himerius. Religious war erupted as the three so-called Heretic Kings—Abeleyn of Hebrion, Mark of Astarac and Lofantyr of Torunna, fought to keep their thrones. They all succeeded, but Abeleyn had the hardest battle to fight. He had to storm his own capital, Abrusio, by land and sea, half-destroying it in the process. And in the moment of his final victory, he was smashed down by a stray shell, which blasted what remained of his body into a deep coma.

As Abeleyn lay senseless, administered to by his faithful wizard Golophin, a power struggle began. His mistress Jemilla strove to set up a Regency to govern the kingdom, which would recognise the right of her unborn child—nominally, the King's—to succeed to the throne. Golophin and Isolla, Abeleyn's Astaran fiancée, worked in their turn to curb Jemilla's ambitions. After the weary Golophin's sorcerous powers were restored by the unexpected intervention of Aruan from the West, Abeleyn was roused from his coma, his missing legs replaced by magical limbs of wood.

All across the continent, the Monarchies of God were in a state of violent flux. In Almark, the dying King Haukir bequeathed his kingdom to the Himerian Church, transforming it overnight into a great temporal power. The man at its head, Himerius, was in fact a puppet of the Western sorcerer Aruan, and after a strange and agonising initiation, he had become a lycanthrope like his master.

And in Charibon two of his humbler fellow-clerics, Albrec and Avila, stumbled upon an ancient document, a biography of St Ramusio which stated that he was one and the same as the Merduk Prophet Ahrimuz. The two monks, guilty of heresy, fled Charibon, but not before a macabre encounter with the chief librarian of the monastery city, who also turned out to be a werewolf. They ran into the teeth of a midwinter blizzard, and would have died in the snow had they not been rescued by a passing Fimbrian army, which was on its way east to support the Torunnans in their great battles against the Merduks. The monks finally made their weary way to Torunn itself, there to confront Macrobius with the momentous knowledge they carried.

Further east, the great Torunnan fortress of Ormann Dyke became the focuss of the Merduk assaults, and there Corfe distinguished himself in its defence. He was promoted and, catching the eye of Torunna's Queen Dowager, Odelia, was given the mission of bringing to heel the rebellious nobles in the south of the kingdom. This he undertook with a motley, ill-equipped band of ex-galley slaves which was all the Torunnan King would allow him.

Plagued by the memory of his lost wife, he was, mercifully, unaware that she had in fact survived Aekir's fall and was now the favourite concubine of the Sultan Aurungzeb himself—and bearing his child.

The Merduks finally abandoned their costly frontal assaults and outflanked Ormann Dyke by sea, forcing the fortress's evacuation. The retreating garrison joined up with the Fimbrians who had arrived, too late, to reinforce them, and the combined force would have been destroyed at the North More, had not Corfe disobeyed orders and taken his own command north to break them out of their encirclement. As it was, half of the two armies were lost, and Corfe, thanks to the intrigues of the Torunnan Queen-Mother, became General of the remainder. He and Odelia became lovers, which added to the whispering campaign against him at court, and further prejudiced young King Lofantyr against him.

Lofantyr led the entire remaining Torunnan army into the field in a last-ditch attempt to halt the advancing Merduks, and in a titanic battle north of his capital he lost his wife. Corfe wrenched a bloody victory of sorts out of the débâcle, and once more brought the army home—this time to be made Commander-in-Chief.

The year 551 had ended, and another chapter in Normannia's turbulent history was about to be written. Over the horizon, Richard Hawkwood's battered ship was making its tortured voyage home at last, bearing news of the terrible New World that was stirring in the West.

PROLOGUE

THE makeshift tiller bucked under their hands, bruising ribs. Hawkwood gripped it tighter to his sore chest along with the others, teeth set, his mind a flare of foul curses—a helpless fury which damned the wind, the ship, the sea itself, and the vast, uncaring world upon which they raced in mad career.

The wind backed a point—he could feel it spike into his right ear, heavy with chill rain. He unclenched his jaws long enough to shriek forward over the lashing gale.

"Brace the yards—it's backing round. Brace around that mainyard, God rot you!"

Other men appeared on the wave-swept deck, tottering out of their hiding places and staggering across the plunging waist of the carrack. They were in rags, some looking as though they might once have been soldiers, with the wreck of military uniforms still flapping around their torsos. They were clumsy and torpid in the bitter soaking spindrift, and looked as though they belonged in a sick-bed rather than on the deck of a storm-tossed ship.

From the depths of the pitching vessel a terrible growling roar echoed up, rising above the thrumming cacophony of the wind and the rageing waves and the groaning rigging. It sounded like some huge, caged beast venting its viciousness upon the world. The men on deck paused in their manipulation of the sodden rigging, and some made the Sign of the Saint. For a second sheer terror shone through the exhaustion that dulled their eyes. Then they went back to their work. The men at the stern felt the heavings of the tiller ease a trifle as the yards were braced around to meet the changing wind. They had it abaft the larboard beam now, and the carrack was powering forward like a horse breasting deep snow. She was sailing under a reefed mainsail, no more. The rest of her canvass billowed in strips from the yards, and where the mizzen-topmast had once been was only a splintered stump with the rags of shrouds flapping about it in black skeins.

Not so very far now, Hawkwood thought, and he turned to his three companions.

"She'll go easier now the wind's on the quarter." He had to shout to be heard over the storm. "But keep her thus. If it strengthens we'll have to run before it and be damned to navigation."

One of the men at the helm with him was a tall, lean, white-faced fellow with a terrible scar that distorted one side of his forehead and temple. The remnants of riding leathers clung to his back.

"We were damned long ago, Hawkwood, and our enterprise with us. Better to give it up and let her sink with that abomination chained in the hold."

"He's my friend, Murad," Hawkwood spat at him. "And we are almost home."

"Almost home indeed! What will you do with him when we get there, make a watchdog of him?"

"He saved our lives before now—"

"Only because he's in league with those monsters from the west."

"—And his master, Golophin, will be able to cure him."

"We should throw him overboard."

"You do, and you can pilot this damned ship yourself, and see how far you get with her."

The two glared at one another with naked hatred, before Hawkwood turned and leaned his weight against the trembling tiller with the others once more, keeping the carrack on her easterly course. Pointing her towards home.

And in the hold below their feet, the beast howled in chorus with the storm.

26th Day of Miderialon, Year of the Saint 552.

Wind NNW, backing. Heavy gale. Course SSE under reefed mainsail, running before the wind. Three feet of water in the well, pumps barely keeping pace with it.

Hawkwood paused. He had his knees braced against the heavy fixed table in the middle of the stern-cabin and the inkwell was curled up in his left fist, but even so he had to strain to remain in his seat. A heavy following sea, and the carrack was cranky for lack of ballast, the water in her hold moving with every pitch. At least with a stern wind they did not feel the lack of the mizzen so much.

As the ship's movement grew less violent, he resumed his writing.

Of the two hundred and sixty-six souls who left Abrusio harbour some seven and a half months ago, only eighteen remain. Poor Garolvo was washed overboard in the middle watch, may God have mercy on his soul.

Hawkwood paused a moment, shaking his head at the pity of it. To have survived the massacre in the west, all that horror, merely to be drowned when home waters were almost in sight.

We have been at sea almost three months, and by dead-reckoning I estimate our easting to be some fifteen hundred leagues, though we have travelled half as far as that again to the north. But the southerlies have failed us now, and we are being driven off our course once more. By cross-

staff reckoning, our latitude is approximately that of Ga-brion. The wind must keep backing around if it is to enable us to make landfall somewhere in Normannia itself. Our lives are in the hand of God.

"The hand of God," Hawkwood said quietly. Seawater dripped out of his beard on to the battered log and he blotted it hurriedly. The cabin was sloshing ankle-deep, as was every other compartment in the ship. They had all forgotten long ago what it was like to be dry or have a full belly; several of them had loose and rotting teeth and scars which had healed ten years before were oozing: the symptoms of scurvy.

How had it come to this? What had so wrecked their proud and well-manned little flotilla? But he knew the answer, of course, knew it only too well. It kept him awake through the graveyard watch though his exhausted body craved oblivion. It growled and roared in the hold of his poor *Osprey*. It raved in the midnight spasms of Murad's nightmares.

He stoppered up the inkwell and folded the log away in its layers of oilskin. On the table before him was a flaccid wineskin which he slung around his neck. Then he sloshed and staggered across the pitching cabin to the door in the far bulkhead and stepped over the storm-sill into the companion-way beyond. It was dark here, as it was throughout every compartment in the ship. They had few candles left and only a precious pint or two of oil for the storm-lanterns. One of these hung swinging on a hook in the companionway, and Hawkwood took it and made his way forward to where a hatch in the deck led down into the hold. He hesitated there with the ship pitching and groaning around him and the seawater coursing around his ankles, then cursed aloud and began to work the hatch-cover free. He lifted it off a yawning hole and gingerly lowered himself down the ladder there, into the blackness below.

At the ladder's foot he wedged himself into a corner and fumbled for the flint and steel that was contained in a bottom compartment of the storm-lantern. An aching, maddening time of striking spark after spark until one caught on the oil-soaked wick of the lantern and he was able to lower the thick glass that protected it and stand it in a pool of yellow light.

The hold was eerily empty, home only to a dozen casks of rotting salt meat and noisome water that constituted the last of the crew's provisions. Water pouring everywhere, and the noise of his poor tormented *Osprey* an agonised symphony of creaks and moans, the sea roaring like a beast beyond the tortured hull. He laid a hand against the timbres of the ship and felt them work apart as she laboured in the gale-driven waves. Fragments of oakum floated about in the water around his feet. The seams were opening. No wonder the men on the pumps could make no headway. The ship was dying.

From below his feet there came an animal howl which rivalled even the thundering bellow of the wind. Hawkwood flinched, and then stumbled forward to where another hatch led below to the bottom-most compartment of the ship, the bilge.

It was stinking down here. The *Osprey*'s ballast had not been changed in a long time and the tropical heat of the Western Continent seemed to have lent it a particularly foul stench. But it was not the ballast alone which stank. There was another smell down here. It reminded Hawkwood of the beasts' enclosure in a travelling circus—that musk-like reek of a great animal. He paused, his heart hammering within his ribs, and then made himself walk forward, crouching low under the beams, the lantern swinging in a chaotic tumble of light and dark and sloshing liquid. The water was over his knees already.

Something ahead, moving in the liquid filth of the bilge. The rattle of metal clinking upon metal. It saw him and ceased its struggles. Two yellow eyes gleamed in the dark. Hawkwood halted a scant two yards from where it lay chained to the very keelson of the carrack.

The beast blinked, and then, terrible out of that animal muzzle, came recognizable speech.

"Captain. How good of you to come."

Hawkwood's mouth was as dry as salt. "Hello Bardolin," he said.

"Come to make sure the beast is still in his lair?"

"Something like that."

"Are we about to sink?"

"Not yet—not just yet, anyway."

The great wolf bared its fangs in what might have been a grin. "Well, we must be thankful."

"How much longer will you be like this?"

"I don't know. I am beginning to control it. This morning—was it morning? One cannot tell down here—I stayed human for almost half a watch. Two hours." A low growl came out of the beast's mouth, something like a moan. "In the name of God, why do you not let Murad kill me?"

"Murad is mad. You are not, despite this—this thing that has happened to you. We were friends, Bardolin. You saved my life. When we get back to Hebrion I will take you to your master, Golophin. He will cure you." Even to himself Hawkwood's words felt hollow. He had repeated them too many times.

"I do not think so. There is no cure for the black change."

"We'll see," Hawkwood said stubbornly. He noticed the lumps of salt meat which bobbed in the filthy water of the bilge. "Can't you eat?"

"I crave fresher meat. The beast wants blood. There is nothing I can do about it."

"Are you thirsty?"

"God, yes."

"All right." Hawkwood unslung the wineskin he had about his neck, tugged out the stopper, and hung the lantern on a hook in the hull. He half crawled forward, trying not to retch at the stench which rose up about him. The heat the animal gave off was unearthly, unnatural. He had to force himself close to it and when the head tilted up he tipped the neck of the wineskin against its maw and let it drink, a black tongue licking every drop of moisture away.

"Thank you, Hawkwood," the wolf said. "Now let me try something."

There was a shimmer in the air, and something happened that Hawkwood's eyes could not quite follow. The black fur of the beast withered away and in seconds it was Bardolin the Mage who crouched there, naked and bearded, his body covered in saltwater sores.

"Good to have you back," Hawkwood said with a weak smile.

"It feels worse this way. I am weaker. In the name of God, Hawkwood, get some iron down here. One nick, and I am at peace."

"No." The chains that held Bardolin fast were of bronze, forged from the metal of one of the ship's falconets. They were roughly cast, and their edges had scored his flesh into bloody meat at the wrists and ankles, but every time he shifted in and out of beast form, the wounds healed somewhat. It was an interminable form of torture, Hawkwood knew, but there was no other way to secure the wolf when it returned.

"I'm sorry, Bardolin . . . Has he been back?"

"Yes. He appears in the night-watches and sits where you are now. He says I am his—I will be his right hand one day. And Hawkwood, I find myself listening to him, believing him."

"Fight it. Don't forget who you are. Don't let the bastard win."

"How much longer? How far is there to go?"

"Not so far now. Another week or ten days perhaps. Less if the wind backs. This is only a passing squall—it'll soon blow itself out."

"I don't know if I can survive. It eats into my mind like a maggot . . . stay back, it comes again. Oh sweet Lord God—"

Bardolin screamed, and his body bucked and thrashed against the chains which held him down. His face seemed to explode outwards. The scream turned into an animal roar of rage and pain. As Hawkwood watched, horrified, his body bent and grew and cracked sickeningly. His skin sprouted fur and two horn-like ears thrust up from his skull. The wolf had returned. It howled in anguish and wrenched at its confining chains. Hawkwood backed away, shaken.

"Kill me—kill me and give me peace!" the wolf shrieked, and then the words dissolved into a manic bellowing. Hawkwood retrieved the storm-lantern and re-treated through the muck of the bilge, leaving Bardolin alone to fight the battle for his soul in the darkness of the ship's belly.

What God would allow the practise of such abominations upon the world he had made? What manner of man would inflict them upon another?

Unwillingly, his mind was drawn back to that terrible place of sorcery and slaughter and emerald jungle. The Western Continent. They had sought to claim a new world there, and had ended up fleeing for their lives. He could remember every stifling, terror-ridden hour of it. In the wave-racked carcase of his once-proud ship, he had it thrust vivid and unforgettable into his mind's eye once again.

PART ONE

RETURN OF THE MARINER

ONE

THEY had stumbled a mile, perhaps two, from the ash-laden air on the slopes of Undabane. Then they collapsed in on each other like a child's house of playing cards, what remained of their spirit spent. Their chests seemed somehow too narrow to take in the thick humidity of the air around them. They lay sprawled in the twilit ooze of the jungle floor while half-glimpsed animals and birds hooted and shrieked in the trees above, the very land itself mocking their failure. Heaving for a breath, the sweat running down their faces and the insects a cloud before their eyes.

It was Hawkwood who recovered first. He was not injured, unlike Murad, and his wits had not been addled, unlike Bardolin's. He sat himself up in the stinking humus and the creeping parasitic life which infested it, and hid his face in his hands. For a moment he wished only to be dead and have done with it. Seventeen of them had left Fort Abeleius some twenty-four days before. Now he and his

two companions were all that remained. This green world
was too much for mortal men to bear, unless they were also
some form of murderous travesty such as those which resided in the mountain. He shook his head at the memory
of the slaughter there. Men skinned like rabbits, torn asun-
der, eviscerated, their innards churned through with the
gold they had stolen. Masudi's head lying dark and glistening in the roadway, the moonlight shining in his dead
eyes.

Hawkwood hauled himself to his feet. Bardolin had his
head sunk between his knees and Murad lay on his back
as still as a corpse, his awful wound laying bare the very
bone of his skull.

"Come. We have to get farther away. They'll catch us
else."

"They don't want to catch us. Murad was right." It was
Bardolin. He did not raise his head, but his voice was clear,
though thick with grief.

"We don't know that," Hawkwood snapped.

"*I* know that."

Murad opened his eyes. "What did I tell you, Captain?
Birds of like feather." He chuckled hideously. "What dupes
we poor soldiers and mariners have been, ferrying a crowd
of witches and warlocks to their masters. Precious Bardolin
will not be touched—not him. They're sending him back
to his brethren with you as the ferryman. If anyone escaped,
it was I. But then, to where have I escaped?"

He sat up, the movement starting a dark ooze of blood
along his wound. The flies were already black about it. "Ah
yes, deliverance. The blest jungle. And we are only a few
score leagues from the coast. Give it up, Hawkwood." He
sank back with a groan and closed his eyes.

Hawkwood remained standing. "Maybe you're right. Me,
I have a ship still—or had—and I'm going to get off this
God-cursed country and out to sea again. New Hebrion no
less! If you've any shred of duty left under that mire of
self-pity you're wallowing in, Murad, then you'll realise
we have to get back home, if only to warn them. You're a
soldier and a nobleman. You still understand the concept
of duty, do you not?"

The bloodshot eyes snapped open again. "Don't presume to lecture me, Captain. What are you but the sweeping of some Gabrionese gutter?"

Hawkwood smiled. "I'm a lord of the gutter now, Murad, or had you forgotten? You ennobled me yourself, the same time you made yourself governor of all this—" He swept out his arms to take in the ancient trees, the raucous jungle about them. Bitter laughter curdled in his throat. "Now get off your noble arse. We have to find some water. Bardolin, help me, and stop mooning around like the sky has just fallen in."

Amazingly enough, they obeyed him.

THEY camped that night some five miles from the mountain, by the banks of a stream. After Hawkwood had browbeaten Bardolin into gathering firewood and bedding, he sat by Murad and examined the nobleman's wounds. They were all gashed and scratched to some degree, but Murad's spectacular head injury was one of the ugliest Hawkwood had ever seen. The scalp had been ripped free of the skull and hung flapping by his left ear.

"I've a good sailmaker's needle in my pouch, and some thread," he told Murad. "It may not turn out too pretty, but I reckon I can get you battened down again. It'll smart some, of course."

"No doubt," the nobleman drawled in something approaching his old manner. "Get on with it while there's still light."

"There are maggots in the flesh. I'll clear them out first."

"No! Let them be. I've seen men worse cut up than this whose flesh went rotten for the lack of a few good maggots. Sew them in there, Hawkwood. They'll eat the dead meat."

"God almighty, Murad!"

"Do it. Since you are determined that we are to survive, we may as well go through the motions. Where is that cursed wizard? Maybe he could make himself useful and magick up a bandage."

Bardolin appeared out of the gloom, a bundle of firewood in his arms. "He killed my familiar," he said. "The Dweomer in me is crippled. He killed my familiar, Hawkwood."

"Who did?"

"Aruan. Their leader." He dropped his burden as though it burnt. His eyes were as dead as dry slate. "I will have a look, though, if you like. I may be able to do something."

"Stay away from me!" Murad shouted, shrinking from the mage. "You murderous dastard. If I were fit for it I'd break your skull. You were in league with them from the first."

"Just see if you can get a fire going, Bardolin," Hawkwood said wearily. "I'll patch him up myself. Later, we must talk."

The pop of the needle going through Murad's skin and cartilage was loud enough to make Hawkwood wince, but the nobleman never uttered a sound under the brutal surgery, only quivered sometimes like a horse trying to rid itself of a bothersome fly. By the time the mariner was done the daylight was about to disappear, and Bardolin's fire was a mote of yellow brightness on the black jungle floor. Hawkwood surveyed his handiwork critically.

"You're no prettier than you were, that's certain," he said at last.

Murad flashed his death's-head grin. The thread crawled along his temple like a line of marching ants, and under the skin the maggots could be seen squirming.

They drank water from the stream and lay on the brush that Bardolin had gathered to serve as beds while around them the darkness became absolute. The insects fed off them without respite, but they were too weary to care and their stomachs were closed. It was Hawkwood who pinched himself awake.

"Did they really let us go, you think? Or are they waiting for nightfall to spring on us?"

"They could have sprung on us fifty times before now," Murad said quietly. "We have not exactly been swift, or careful in our flight. No, for what it's worth, we're away. Maybe they're going to let the jungle finish the job. Maybe they could not bring themselves to kill a fellow sorcerer. Or there may be another reason we're alive. Ask the wizard! He's the one has been closeted with their leader."

They both looked at Bardolin. "Well?" Hawkwood said

at last. "We've a right to know, I think. Tell us, Bardolin. Tell us exactly what happened to you."

The mage kept his eyes fixed on the fire. There was a long silence while his two companions stared steadily at him.

"I am not entirely sure myself," he said at last. "The imp was brought to the top of the pyramid in the middle of the city by Gosa. He was a shape-shifter—"

"You surprise me," Murad snorted.

"I met their leader, a man named Aruan. He said he had been high in the Thaumaturgists' Guild of Garmidalan in Astarac a long time ago. In the time of the Pontiff Willardius."

Murad frowned. "Willardius? Why, he's been dead these four hundred years and more."

"I know. This Aruan claims to be virtually immortal. It is something to do with the Dweomer of this land. There was a great and sophisticated civilisation here in the west at one time, but it was destroyed in a huge natural cataclysm. The mages here had powers hardly dreamt of back on the Old World. But there was another difference . . ."

"Well?" Murad demanded.

"I believe they were all shifters as well as mages. An entire society of them."

"God's blood," Hawkwood breathed. "I thought that was not possible."

"So did I. It is unheard of, and yet we have seen it ourselves."

Murad was thoughtful. "You are quite sure, Bardolin?"

"I wish I were not, believe me. But there is another thing. According to this Aruan, there are hundreds of his agents already in Normannia, doing his bidding."

"The gold," Hawkwood rasped. "Normannic crowns. There was enough of it back there to bribe a king, to hire an army."

"So he has ambitions, this shifter-wizard of yours," Murad sneered. "And how exactly do you fit into them, Bardolin?"

"I don't know, Murad. The Blest Saint help me, I don't know."

*We will meet again, you and I, and when we do you will
know me as your lord, and as your friend.* The parting
words of Aruan burnt themselves across Bardolin's brain.
He would never reveal them to anyone. He was his own
man, and always would be despite the foulness he now felt
at work within him.

"One thing I do know," he went on. "They are not content to remain here, these shifter-mages. They are going to
return to Normannia. Everything I was told confirms it. I
believe Aruan intends to make himself a power in the
world. In fact he has already begun."

"If he can make a werewolf of an Inceptine then his words
are not idle," Hawkwood muttered, remembering their outwards voyage and Ortelius, who had spread such terror
throughout the ship.

"A race of were-mages," Murad said. "A man who
claims to be centuries old. A network of shifters spread
across Normannia spending his gold, running his errands.
I would say you were crazed, had I not seen the things I
have on this continent. The place is a veritable hell on earth.
Hawkwood is right. We must get back to the ship, return
to Hebrion, and inform the King. The Old World must be
warned. We will root out these monsters from our midst,
and then return here with a fleet and an army and wipe
them from the face of the earth. They are not so formidable—a taste of iron and they fall dead. We will see what
five thousand Hebrian arquebusiers can do here, by God."

For once, Hawkwood found himself wholly in agreement
with the gaunt nobleman. Bardolin seemed troubled, however.

"What's wrong now?" he asked the wizard. "You don't
approve of this Aruan's ambitions, do you?"

"Of course not. But it was a purge of the Dweomer-folk
which drove him and his kind here in the first place. I know
what Murad's proposal will lead to, Hawkwood. A vast,
continent-wide purge of my people such as has never been
seen before. They will be slaughtered in their thousands,
the innocent along with the guilty. We will drive all of
Normannia's mages into Aruan's arms. That is exactly what
he wants. And his agents will not be so easy to uncover at

any rate. They could be anyone—even the nobility. We will persecute the innocent while the guilty bide their time."

"The plain soldiers of the world will take their chances," Murad retorted. "There is no place on this earth for your kind any more, Bardolin. They are an abomination. Their end has been coming for a long time. This is only hastening the inevitable."

"You are right there at least," the wizard murmured.

"Whose side are you on?" Hawkwood asked the mage. Bardolin looked angry.

"I don't know what you mean."

"I mean that Murad is right. There is a time coming, Bardolin, when it will be your Dweomer-folk ranged against the ordinary people of the world, and you will have to either abet their destruction or stand with them against us. That is what I mean."

"It will not—it must not—come to that!" the mage protested.

Hawkwood was about to go on when Murad halted him with a curt gesture.

"Enough. Look around you. The odds are that we will never have to worry about such things, and we'll leave our bones to fester here in the jungle. Wizard, I'll offer you a truce. We three must help each other if any of us is ever to get back to the coast. The debates of high policy can wait until we are aboard ship. Agreed?"

"Agreed," Bardolin said, his mouth a bitter line in his face.

"Excellent." The irony in Murad's voice was palpable. "Now, Captain, you are our resident navigator. Can you point us in the right direction tomorrow?"

"Perhaps. If I can get a look at the sun before the clouds start building up. There is a better way, though. We must make an inventory. Empty your pouches. I must see what we have to work with."

They tore a broad leaf from a nearby bush and upon it they placed the contents of their pockets and pouches, squinting in the firelight. Bardolin and Hawkwood both had waterproofed tinderboxes with flint and steel and little coils of dry wool inside. The wizard also had a bronze pocket-

knife and a pewter spoon. Murad had a broken iron knife
blade some five inches long, a tiny collapsible tin cup and
a cork water-bottle still hanging from his belt by its straps.
Hawkwood had his needle, a ball of tough yarn, a lead
arquebus bullet and a fishhook of carved bone. All of them
had broken pieces of ship's biscuit lining their pockets and
Murad a small lump of dried pork which was hard as wood
and inedible.

"A meagre enough store, by God," the nobleman said.
"Well, Hawkwood, what wonders can you work with it?"

"I can make a compass, I think, and we can do some
fishing and hunting if we have to also. I was shipwrecked
when I was a boy in the Malacars, and we had little more
than this upon us when we were washed up. We can use
the yarn as fishing line, weight it with the bullet and bait
it with the pork. The blade we can tie to a stave for a spear.
There's fruit all around us too. We won't starve, but it's a
time-consuming business forageing for food, even in the
jungle. We'd best be prepared to tighten our belts if we're
to get back to the coast before the spring."

"The spring!" Murad exclaimed. "Great God, we may
have to eat our boots, but we'll be back at the fort before
that!"

"We were almost a month coming here, Murad, and we
travelled along a road for much of the way. The journey
back will be harder. Maybe they did allow us to escape,
but I still don't want to frequent their highways." He remembered the heat and stink of the great werewolf lying
beside him in the brush, back inside the mountain—

*Would I harm you, Captain, the navigator, the steerer of
ships? I think not. I think not.*

—And shuddered at the memory.

THEY stood watches that first night, taking it in turns to
feed the fire and stare out at the black wall of the rainforest. When they were not on guard they slept fitfully.
Bardolin lay awake most of the night, exhausted but afraid
to sleep, afraid to find out what might be lurking in his
dreams.

Aruan had made a lycanthrope of him.

So the arch-mage had said. Bardolin had had sexual relations with Kersik, the girl who had guided them to Undabane. And then she had fed him a portion of her kill—that was the process. That was the rite which engendered the disease.

He almost thought he could feel the black disease working in him, a physical process changing body and soul with every heartbeat. Should he tell the others? They distrusted him already. What was going to happen to him? What manner of thing was he to become?

He considered just walking off and becoming lost to the jungle, or even returning to Undi like some prodigal son. But he had always been stubborn, proud and stiff-necked. He would resist this thing, battle it for as long as there was any remnant of Bardolin son of Carnolan left in him. He had been a soldier once: he would fight to the very end.

Thus he thought as he sat his watch, and fed the fire while the other two slept. Hawkwood had given him a task: he was to rub the iron needle with wool from one of the tinderboxes. It made little sense to Bardolin, but at least it was something to help keep sleep at bay.

To one side, Murad moaned in his slumber, and once to his shock Bardolin thought he heard the nobleman gasp out Griella's name—the base-born lover Murad had taken aboard ship who had turned out to be a shifter herself. What unholy manner of union had those two shared? Not rape, not love freely given either. A kind of mutual degradation which wrought violence upon their sensibilities and yet somehow left them wanting more.

And Bardolin, the old man, he had been envious of them.

He sat and excoriated himself for a thousand failings, the regrets of an ageing man without home or family. In the black night the darkness of his mood deepened. Why had Aruan let him go? What was his fate to be? Ah, to hell with the endless questions.

He spun himself a little cantrip, a glede of werelight which flickered and spluttered weakly. In sudden fear he sent it bobbing around the limits of the firelight, banishing shadows for a few fleeting seconds. It wheeled like an ecstatic firefly and then went out. Too soon. Too weak. He felt like a man who has lost a limb and yet feels pain in phantom fingers. He drank some water from Murad's bottle, eyes smarting with grief and tyredness. He was too old for this. He should have an apprentice, someone to help bear the load of a greybeard's worries. Like young Orquil perhaps, whom they had sent to the fire back in Abrusio.

What about me, Bardolin? Will I do?

He started. Sleep had almost taken him. For a moment he had half seen another person sitting on the other side of the fire. A young girl with heavy bronze-coloured hair. The night air had invaded his head. He brutally knuckled his aching eye-sockets and resumed his solitary vigil, impatiently awaiting the dawn.

THEY were on their feet with the first faint light of the sun through the canopy. Water from the stream and a few broken crumbs of biscuit constituted breakfast, and then they looked over Hawkwood's shoulder as he set the needle floating on a leaf in Murad's tin cup. It twisted strangely on the water therein, and then steadied. The mariner nodded with grim satisfaction.

"That's your compass?" Murad asked incredulously. "A common needle?"

"Any iron can be given the ability to turn to the north," he was told. "I don't know why or how, but it works. We march south-east today. Murad, I want you to look out for a likely spear shaft. Myself, I reckon I might have a go at making a bow. Give me your knife, Bardolin. We'll have to blaze trees to keep our bearing. All right? Then let's go."

Rather nonplussed, Hawkwood's two companions fell into step behind him, and the trio was on its way.

They tramped steadily until noon, when it began to cloud over in preparation for the almost daily downpour. By that time Murad had his iron knife blade tied on to a stout shaft some six feet long, and Hawkwood was laden with a selection of slender sticks and one stave as thick as three fingers. They were famished, pocked with countless bites, scored and gashed and dripping with leeches. And Murad was finding it difficult to keep the pace Hawkwood set. The mariner and the mage would often have to pause in their tracks and wait for him to catch up. But when Hawkwood suggested a break, the nobleman only snarled at him.

In the shelter of an enormous dead tree they waited out the bruising rain as it began thundering in torrents down from the canopy overhead. The ground they sat on quickly became a sucking mire, and the force of the downpour made it difficult to breathe. Hawkwood bent his chin into his breast to create a space, a pocket of air, and in that second it filled with mosquitoes which he drew in helplessly as he breathed, and spat and coughed out again.

The deluge finally ended as abruptly as it had begun, and for a few minutes afterwards they sat in the mud and gurgling water which the forest floor had become, sodden, weary, frail with hunger. Murad was barely conscious, and Hawkwood could feel the burning heat of his body as the nobleman leaned against him.

They laboured to their feet without speaking, staggering like ancients. A coral-bright snake whipped through the puddles at their feet, and with a cry Murad seemed to come alive. He stabbed his new spear at the ground and transfixed the thrashing reptile just behind the head. It twined itself about the spear in its last agony, and Murad smiled.

"Gentlemen," he said, "dinner is served."

TWO

HAPTMAN Hernan Sequero surveyed the squalid extent of his little kingdom and pursed his lips in disapproval. He rap-rap-rapped his knuckles lightly on the hardwood table, ignoring the bead of sweat that was hovering from one eye-brow.

"It's not good enough," he said. "We'll never be self-sufficient here if these damned people keep on dying. They're supposed to be blasted magicians, after all. Can't they magick up something?"

The men around him cleared their throats, shifted on their feet or looked away. Only one made any attempt to reply, a florid, golden-haired young man with an ensign's bar at his collar.

"There are three herbalists amongst the colonists, sir. They're doing their best, but the plants here are unfamiliar to them. It is a process of trial and error."

"And in the meantime the cemetrey becomes our most thriving venture ashore," Sequero retorted drily. "Very well, one cannot argue with nature I suppose, but it is vexing. When Lord—when his excellency—returns he will not be pleased. Not at all."

Again, the uneasy shuffling of feet, brief shared glances.

There were three men standing about the table besides Sequero, all in the leather harness of the Hebrian soldiery. They were in one of the tall watchtowers which stood at each corner of the palisaded fort. Up here it was possible to catch a breath of air off the ocean, and in fact to see their ship, the *Gabrian Osprey*, as it rode at anchor scarcely half a mile away, the horizon beyond it a far blur of sea and sky at the edge of sight.

Closer to, the view was less inspiring. Peppering the two acres or so which the palisade enclosed were dozens of rude huts, some little better than piled-up mounds of brush. The only substantial building was the Governor's residence, a large timbre structure which was half villa and half blockhouse.

A deep ditch bisected the fort and served the community as a sewer, running off into the jungle. It was bridged in several places with felled trees, and the ground around it was a foul-smelling swamp swarming with mosquitoes. They had dug wells, but these were all brackish, so they continued to take their water from the clear stream Murad had discovered on the first day. One corner of the fort was corralled off and within it resided the surviving horses. Another few days would see it empty. When the last beasts had died they would be salted down and eaten, like the others.

"Fit for neither man nor beast," Sequero muttered, brow dark as he thought of the once magnificent creatures he had brought from Hebrion, the cream of his father's studs. Even the sheep did not do well here. Were it not for the wild pigs and deer which hunting parties brought out of the jungle every few days, they would be gnawing on roots and berries by now.

"How many today then?" he asked.

"Two," di Souza told him. "Miriam di—"

"I don't need to know their names!" Sequero snapped. "That leaves us with, what? Eighty-odd? Still plenty. Thank

God the soldiers and sailors are made of sterner stuff. Sergeant Berrino, how are the men?"

"Bearing up well, sir. A good move to let them doff their armour, if I might say so. And Garolvo's party brought in three boar this morning."

"Excellent. A good man that Garolvo. He must be the best shot we have. Gentlemen, we are in a hellish place, but it belongs to our king now and we must make the best of it. Make no mistake, there will be promotions when the Governor returns from his expedition. Fort Abeleius may not be much to look at now, but in a few years there will be a city here, with church bells, taverns and all the trappings of civilisation."

His listeners were dutifully attentive to his words, but he could almost taste their scepticism. They had been ashore two and a half months now, and Sequero knew well that the Governor was popularly believed to be long dead, or lost somewhere in the teeming jungle. He and his party had been away too long, and with his absence the discontent and fear within the fort was growing week by week. Increasingly, both soldiers and civilians were of the opinion that nothing would ever come of this precarious foothold upon the continent, and the Dweomer-folk were ready to brave even the pyres that awaited in Abrusio rather than suffer the death by disease and malnutrition that was claiming so many of them. At times Sequero felt as though he was swimming against an irresistible tide of sullen resentment which would one day overwhelm him.

"Ensign di Souza, how many of the ship's guns have we ashore now?"

"Six great culverins and a pair of light sakers, sir, all sited to command the approaches. That sailor, Velasca, he wants to complain to you personally about it. He says the guns are the property of Captain Hawkwood and should remain with the ship."

"Let him put it in writing," said Sequero, who like all the old school of noblemen could not read. "Gentlemen, you are dismissed. All but you, di Souza. I want a word. Sergeant Berrino, you may distribute a ration of wine tonight. The men deserve it—they have worked hard."

Berrino, a middle-aged man with a closed, thuggish face, brightened. "Why thank you, sir—"

"That is all. Leave us now."

The two soldiers clambered down the ladder that was affixed to one leg of the watchtower, leaving Sequero and di Souza alone in their eyrie.

"Do have some wine, Valdan," Sequero said easily, and gestured to the bulging skin that hung from a nearby peg.

"Thank you, sir." Di Souza squirted a goodly measure of the blood-warm liquid down his throat and wiped his mouth on the back of his hand. They had been equals in rank, these two young men, until landfall here in the west. Murad had then promoted Hernan Sequero to haptman, making him military commander of the little colony. The choice had been inevitable: di Souza was noble only by adoption, whereas Sequero was from one of the high families of the kingdom, as close by blood to the Royal house as Murad himself. The fact that he was illiterate and did not know one end of an arquebus from another was neither here nor there.

"The Governor's party has been away almost eleven weeks," Sequero told his subordinate. "Within another week or two they should return, with God's grace. In all that time we here have been cowering behind our stockade as if we were under siege. That has to change. I have seen nothing in this country which warrants this absurd defensive posture. Tomorrow I will order the colonists to start marking out plots of land in the jungle. We'll slash and burn, clear a few acres and see if we can't get some crops planted. If things work out, then some of the colonists can be ejected from the fort and can start building homes on their own plots of land. Valdan, I want you to register all the heads of household amongst them, and map out their plots. They will hold them as tenants of the Hebriate crown. We must start thinking of some form of tithe, of course, and you will organise a system of patrols. . . . You wish to say something, Ensign?"

"Only that Lord Murad's orders were to remain within the fort, sir. He said nothing about clearing farms."

"Quite true. But he has been away a lot longer than he

originally anticipated, and we must all show a little initiative now and then. Besides, the fort is overcrowded and rapidly becoming unhealthy. And these damned mariners must do their share. How many soldiers do we have fit for duty?"

"Besides ourselves, eighteen. Hawkwood's second-in-command, Velasca, has a dozen sailors out surveying the coast in two of the longboats. He's also been salvageing timbres and iron from the wreck of the caravel that foundered on the reef. There are a score more still busy making salt and preserving meat and suchlike. For the return voyage. And four of them are in the fort, instructing some of our men in the firing of the big guns."

"Yes. They like to set themselves apart, these sailors. Well, that must change also. Tell Velasca I want a dozen of his men, with firearms, to join our soldiers and place themselves under Sergeant Berrino. We need more men on the stockade."

"Yes, sir. Anything else?" Di Souza's face was completely neutral.

"No—yes. You will dine with me tonight in the residence, I trust?"

"Thank you, sir." Di Souza saluted and left via the creaking ladder. When he had gone Sequero wiped the sweat from his face and allowed himself a mouthful of wine.

He was not yet sure if this place were an opportunity for advancement or the graveyard of his ambitions. Had he stayed in Hebrion he might have been a regimental commander by now. His blood demanded no less. On the other hand, that very blood might have been considered a little too blue for the King's liking, hence his presence here, in this Godforsaken so-called colony. Still, if anyone had ambition, it was his superior, Lord Murad. That one would not have taken part in such a reckless scheme if he had not seen some kind of advantage in it for himself. Better here than at court, then. In the field superior officers had a habit of dying. At court there was only the age-old manoevring for power and rank, none of it counting for much in the presence of a strong king. And Abeleyn was a strong king, for all his youth. Sequero liked him, though he thought him too informal, too ready to lend an ear to his social inferiors.

Was Murad dead? It seemed hard to believe—the man had always seemed to be constructed equaly out of sinew and pure will. But it had been a long time—a very long time. For once in his life, Sequero was unsure of himself. He knew the soldiers were close to mutiny, believing the colony to be cursed, and without Murad's authority to hold them in cheque . . .

A clattering of boots on the ladder, and a red-faced soldier appeared at the lip of the watchtower.

"Begging your pardon, sir, but it's my turn on sentry. Ensign di Souza told me to come on up."

"Very well. I was just finished." What was the man's name? Sequero couldn't remember and felt vaguely irritated with himself. What did it matter? He was just another stinking trooper.

"See you keep your eyes open . . . Ulbio." There. He had remembered after all.

Ulbio saluted smartly. "Yes, sir." And remained the picture of attentive duty as his commander lowered himself down from the watchtower. When Sequero had disappeared he spat over the side. Fucking nobles, he thought. None of them gave a damn about their men.

THE Governor's residence was the only edifice with any pretensions to architecture within the colony. Loopholed for defence like the strongpoint it was, it nonetheless had a long veranda upon which it was almost pleasant to sit and dine of an evening. The wood of the great trees about the fort was incredibly hard and fine-grained, but it made admirable furniture. The sailors had set up a pedal-powered lathe of sorts and that evening Sequero and his guests were able to eat off a fine long table with beautifully turned legs. There was still silver and crystal to eat off and drink from, and tall candles to light the flushed faces of the diners and attract the night-time moths. Were it not for the cloying heat and the raucous jungle they might have been back in Hebrion on some nobleman's estate.

The gathering was not a large one. Besides Sequero and di Souza there were only three other diners. These were

Osmo of Fulk, a fat, greasy and sycophantic wine merchant whose personal store of Gaderian meant it politic to invite him, Astiban of Pontifidad, a tall, grey man with a mournful face who in Abrusio had been a professional herbalist and an amateur naturalist, and finally Fredric Arminir, who hailed originally from Almark, of all places, and who was reputed to be a smuggler.

None of the three men was an actual wizard, so far as Sequero knew, but they all possessed the Dweomer in varying degrees, else they would not be here. He felt a childish urge to make them perform in some way, to do some trick or feat, and he was absurdly gratified when the stout Osmo set weird blue werelights burning at the far corners of the veranda. The insects crowded around them and sizzled to death in their hundreds, whilst the diners were able to eat and drink without continually slapping the vermin from around their faces.

"Something I picked up in Macassar," Osmo explained casually. "The climate there is similar in many ways."

"And you, Astiban," Sequero said. "Being a naturalist, I assume you are rapt with wonder at the wealth of creatures that crawl and flit about us on this continent."

"There is much that is unfamiliar, it is true, Lord Sequero. With Ensign di Souza's permission I have accompanied some of the hunting parties out into the jungle. I have seen tracks there belonging to creatures not seen in any bestiary of the Old World. On my own initiative, I explored the ground beyond our stockade for several hundred yards out into the forest. These tracks approach the fort, and mill about, and then retreat again. It is a pattern I have found a hundred times."

"What are they doing, coming to have a look at us?" Fredric asked, amused.

"Yes, I think so. I think we are being closely watched, but by what exactly I cannot say."

"Are you assigning a rationality to these unknown beasts?" Sequero asked, surprised.

"I do not know if I would go that far. But I am glad we have a stout palisade in place, and soldiers to man it. When the Governor returns from his expedition I am sure he will have learnt much of this continent, which may clarify my findings."

The man sounded like a lecturing professor, Sequero thought irritably. But at least he seemed to think that the Governor would actually return. From the sidelong glances that Fredric and Osmo exchanged, it seemed they did not share his confidence.

Aloud, Sequero said, "We are pioneers. For us the risks are outweighed by the rewards."

"A pioneer you may be, my lord," Astiban said, "but we are refugees. For us it was a place on Captain Hawkwood's ships, or an appointment with the pyre."

"Quite. Well, we are all here now, and must make the best of it."

A solitary gunshot cracked heavily through the thick night air, making them all start in their seats. Di Souza rose. "Sir, with your permission—"

"Yes, yes, Valdan, go and see. Another sentry firing at shadows, I presume."

Then there was a great crashing boom that ripped the darkness apart, and the flash of a cannon firing from the palisade. Men were shouting out there in the darkness. Di Souza pelted off, snatching his sword from where it hung at the front of the veranda and disappearing. Deliberately, Sequero sipped his wine before his wide-eyed guests. "Gentlemen, I am afraid our dinner may well be cut short . . ."

Some unknown beast was bellowing in rage, and there was a flurry of shots, little saffron sparkles. Torches were being lit along the stockade, and someone began beating the ship's bell that was their signall for a full alarm. Sequero rose and buckled on his sword-belt.

"You had best go to your families and make sure they are safe, but I want every able-bodied man on the palisade as soon as possible. Go now."

He finished the last of the Gaderian in his glass as the three men hurried off. It would have been a pity to waste it. There was a regular battle going on out there. He set down the empty glass and strolled off the veranda towards the firing. Behind him, Osmo's blue werelights sputtered and went out.

THREE

"WHAT is it?" Hawkwood asked, waking to find Bardolin standing listening to the night-time jungle.

"Something—some noise far off, towards the coast. Almost I thought it was a cannon firing."

Hawkwood was wide awake in an instant and on his feet beside the wizard. "I knew we were close, but I didn't think—"

"Hush! There it is again."

This time they both heard it. "That's a cannon all right," Hawkwood breathed. "One of my culverins. Perhaps they brought them ashore. God's blood, Bardolin, it can't be more than a few miles away. We're almost home."

"Home," Bardolin repeated thoughtfully. "But why are they firing cannon in the middle of the night, Hawkwood? Tell me that. I don't think it means good news."

They both sat down by the fire again. On the other side of the flames Murad lay like a corpse, mouth open, his face rippled with scar tissue.

"We'll find out tomorrow," Hawkwood said. "A few more miles, and it's finished. We'll board the *Osprey* and get the hell out of this stinking country. Breathe clean air again, feel the wind on our faces. Think of that, Bardolin. Think of it."

The far-off gunfire continued for perhaps an hour, including one well-spaced salvo that sounded exactly like a ship's broadside. After that there was silence again, but by that time Hawkwood had set up his primitive compass and taken a bearing on the sound so that in the morning they could march straight towards it. Then he fell asleep, exhausted.

Bardolin remained awake. They had long since given up the keeping of any kind of sentry, but as the weeks had drawn on he had found himself needing less and less sleep.

Their journey had been incredibly hard—indeed, it had come close to killing them. They had been transformed by it into matt-haired, sunken-eyed fanatics, whose only mission in life was to keep walking, who revered Hawkwood's home-made compass as though it were the holiest relic, who scrabbled for every scrap of anything resembling food and wolfed it down like animals. All the patina of civilisation had been scraped away by day after day of back-breaking toil, and the filth and heat of the rainforest. Many times, they had decided they could go no further, and had become resigned to the idea of death—even inured to it. But odd things had saved them at those critical moments. The discovery of a stream of pure water, finding a freshly killed forest deer, or a medicinal herb which Hawkwood had recognised from his travells in Macassar. Somehow they had lurched from one lucky windfall to another, all the time keeping to the bearing that Hawkwood set for them every morning. And they were going to survive. Bardolin knew that—he had for a long time. But now he also knew why.

When the darkest hour of each night came upon him he lay alone by the fire and fought the disease that was working in him, but each time it progressed a little farther before it receded again.

It came upon him once more this night. It felt like a blest

breath of cold air stealing over him, a chill invigouration which flooded strength into his wasted frame. And then his sight changed, so that he was beginning to see things he normally could not. Murad's heart beating like a bright, trapped bird in his chest. The veins of blood which nestled in his fore-arms pulsing like threads of liquid light.

Bardolin felt his very bones begin to creak, as if they were desperately trying to burst into some new configuration. His tongue circled up and down his teeth, and they had become different; the inside of his mouth felt as hot as an oven, and he had to open it and pant for air. When he did, his tongue lolled out over his lower lip and the sweat rolled off it.

He raised his hands to his eyes and found that his palms had become black and rough. Joints clicked and reclicked. His hearing grew so acute it was almost unbearable, and yet madly fascinating. He could hear and see a whole universe of life twittering in the rainforest around him.

This was it, the most seductive time. When the change felt like a welcome relief, the chance to metamorphosize into something bigger, better, in which life could be tasted so much more keenly and all his old man's aches and weaknesses could be forgotten.

At one instant he writhed there, perfectly suspended between the desire to let the change have its way and his own stubborn refusal to give in. Then he had beaten it again, and lay there as weak as a newborn kitten, the jungle a black wall about him.

"Bravo," the voice said. "I have never seen anyone fight the black disease with such pugnacious determination before. You have my admiration, Bardolin. Even if your struggle is misguided, and futile in the end."

Bardolin raised his exhausted face. "I have not seen you in a while, Aruan. Been busy?"

"In a manner of speaking, yes. You heard the gunfire. You can guess what it means. The ship is intact, though— of that I made sure. My only worry was that the survivors would sail away before you reach the coast tomorrow, so I have whistled up a landward wind which will keep them anchored if they do not want to be run aground."

"How very thoughtful."

"I think of everything. Do you imagine you would have made it this far without my help? Though that mariner of yours is certainly ingenious—and indomitable. I like him. He reminds me of myself when I was young. You are lucky in your friends, Bardolin. I never was."

"My heart bleeds for you."

Aruan leaned over the fire so that the flames carved a molten mask out of his features. "It will, one day. I will leave you now. Keep fighting it if you will, Bardolin, but you harm yourself by doing so. I believe I will summon someone who may be able to clarify your thinking. There. It is done. Fare well. When I see you again you shall have the wide ocean under you." And he disappeared.

Bardolin drank thirstily from the wooden water bottle, sucking at the neck until it was empty. When he felt the cool fingers massage his knotted neck he closed his eyes and sighed.

"Griella, what did he do to you?"

The girl leaned and kissed his cheek from behind. "He gave me life, what else?"

"No-one can raise the dead. Only God can do that."

The girl knelt before him. She was perhaps fifteen years old and possessed of a heavy helmet of bronze-coloured hair which shone rich as gold in the firelight. Her features were elfin, fine, and she hardly reached Bardolin's breast-bone when standing straight.

She was a werewolf, and she had died months ago—before they had even set foot on the Western Continent. What monstrous wizardry had raised her from the ranks of the dead, Bardolin could not imagine and preferred not to guess at. She had appeared several times during their awful journey back from Undabane, and each time her coming had been a comfort and a torment to him—as Aruan had no doubt meant it to be. For Bardolin had come to love her on their westward voyage, though that love filled him with twisted guilt.

"If you only let it happen, Bardolin, I could be with you always," she said. "We have the same nature now, and it is not such a bad thing, the black change. He is not a good man, I know, but he is not evil, either, and most of the time he speaks the truth."

"Oh Griella!" Bardolin groaned. She was the same and not the same. An instinct told him she was some consummate simulacrum, a created thing, like the imps Bardolin had grown as familiars. But that did not make her face any less dear to him.

"He says I can be your apprentice, once you accept your lot. You told me once, Bardolin, that shifters cannot also become mages. Well, you were wrong. How about that? I can be your pupil. You will teach me magic, and I will teach you of the black change."

Bardolin's gaze strayed to where Murad lay in twitching sleep across the fire.

"What about him?" he asked.

She looked confused, then almost frightened. "I remember things. Bad things. There was a fire. Murad did things . . . no, I can't see it." She raised a hand to her face, let it drop, pawed at her mouth, her eyes suddenly empty. In the next moment, she had winked out of sight with the same preternatural swiftness as Aruan.

"Child, child," Bardolin said mournfully. She was indeed some form of familiar, a creature brought to life through the Dweomer. And he felt a furious rage at Aruan for such a perversion. The games he played, with people's lives and the very forces of nature. No man could do such things and be wholly sane.

IN the morning Hawkwood and Bardolin told Murad of the gunfire in the night. He seemed neither surprised nor overjoyed by the news. Instead he sat thoughtfully, picking at the scar which distorted one side of his head.

"When the firing ended it meant that the fort has either beaten off the attack or has been overrun," Hawkwood said.

No-one commented. They were all thinking of the fantastic creatures which had butchered their comrades in Undi. A massed assault by such travesties would be hard for any group of men to withstand, especially since they could only be permanently slain by the touch of iron.

"Let's go," Murad said, rising like some emaciated scarecrow. "We'll find out soon enough."

By midmorning they had glimpsed a line of high ground rising off to their right, broken heights jutting through the emerald jungle like decaying teeth. Hawkwood stopped to study it and then called to the others.

"Look, you know what that is? It's Circle Ridge: *Heyeran Spinero*. My God, we've only a mile or two to go!"

It was almost three months since they had set out, and they were finally back at that stretch of coastline they had explored in the first days of the landing. They went more cautiously now. After all this time, they were almost reluctant to admit any hope into their hearts.

They found the first body close by the clear stream from which the settlement drew its water. A middle-aged woman by her dress, though she had been so badly mauled it was hard to tell. Ants and beetles were already at work upon the carcase in their thousands, and it stank in the morning heat.

Even Murad seemed somewhat shaken. The three men did not look at one another, but continued on their way. Here was the slope they had toiled up on the first day— now a churned-up mire. Things had been discarded in the mud. A powder-horn, a scrap of leather gambeson, a rent piece of linen shirt. And under the bushes at the side of the clearing, two more bodies. These also were civilians. One was headless. Their intestines were coiled like greasy, fly-spotted ropes in the grass.

They trudged down the slope with their hearts hammering in their breasts, and finally the rainforest rolled back and they were stumbling over hewn tree-stumps, cleared space. Before them, the sagging and skewed posts of the stockade stood deserted, and there was a stink of burning in the air, the reek of corruption. Beyond the clearing, they could glimpse the sea through the trees.

"Hello!" Murad shouted, his voice cracking with strain. "Anyone about?"

The gates of the stockade had been smashed flat. A litter of bodies was scattered here, an arquebus trodden into the mud. Blood stood in puddles with a cloud of midges above every one.

"Lord God," Hawkwood said. Murad covered his eyes.

Fort Abeleius was a charnel-house. The Governor's residence had burnt to the ground and was still smouldering. Remnants and wreckage from other huts and buildings were scattered about in broken, splintered piles. And there were bodies and parts of bodies everywhere, scores of them.

Bardolin turned aside and vomited.

Hawkwood was holding the back of his hand to his nose. "I must see if the ship, survived. I pray to God—"

He took off at a run, stumbling over corpses, leaping broken lumber, and disappeared in the direction of the beach beyond the clearing.

Murad was turning over the bodies like a ghoul prowling a graveyard, nodding to himself, making a study of the whole ghastly spectacle.

"The stockade was overrun from the north first," he said. "That split our people in two. Some made a stand by the gate, but most I think fell back to the Governor's residence . . ." He shambled over that way himself, and picked his way through the burnt ruins of the place that he was to have administered his colony from.

"Here's Sequero. I know him by the badge on his tunic. Yes, they all crammed in here'—he kicked aside a charred bone—'and when they had held out for a while, some fool's match set light to the thatch, or perhaps the powder took light. They might have held out through the night otherwise. It was quick. All so quick. Every one of them. Lord God."

Murad sank to his knees amid the wreckage and the burnt bodies and set the heels of his hands in his eyes. "We are in hell, Bardolin. We have found it here on earth."

Bardolin knew better, but said nothing. He felt enough of a turncoat already. There had been over a hundred and forty people here in the fort. Aruan had said the ship would survive. Who manned it now?

"Let's go down to the sea," he said to Murad, taking the nobleman by the elbow. "Perhaps the ship is still there."

Murad came with him in a kind of grieved daze. Together they picked their way across the desolation, gagging on the smell of the dead, and then plunged into the forest once more. But there was that salt tang to the air, and the rush of waves breaking somewhere ahead, a sound from a previous world.

The white blaze of the beach blinded them, and the horizon-wide sea seemed too vast to take in all at once. They had become used to the fetid confines of the rainforest, and it was pure exhilaration to be able to see a horizon again, a huge arc of blue sky. A wind blew off the sea into their hot faces. A landward wind, just as Aruan had promised.

"Glory be!" Bardolin breathed.

The *Gabrian Osprey* stood at anchor perhaps half a mile from the shore. She looked intact, and wholly deserted—until Bardolin glimpsed some movement on her forecastle. A man waving. And then he caught sight of the head bobbing in the waves halfway to the ship. Hawkwood was swimming out to her, pausing in his stroke every so often to wave to whatever crew remained and shout himself hoarse. Bardolin and Murad watched until he reached the carrack and clung to the wales on her side, too weak to pull himself up the tumble-home. A group of men appeared at the ship's rail. Some were sailors, a couple wore the leather vests of soldiers. They hauled Hawkwood up the ship's side, and Bardolin saw one of them embrace his captain.

Murad had sunk down upon the sand. "Well, mage," he said in something resembling his old manner. "At least one of us is happy. It is time to leave, I think. We have outstayed our welcome in this country. Thus ends New Hebrion."

But Bardolin knew that this was not the end of something. Whatever it was, it had only just begun.

FOUR

THE King was dead, his body lying stark and still on a great bier in the nave of Torunn's cathedral. The entire kingdom was in mourning, all public buildings decked out in sable drapes, all banners at half mast. Lofantyr had not reached thirty, and he left no heir behind him.

THE tyredness buzzed through Corfe's brain. He stood in shining half-armour at the dead King's head, leaning on an archaic greatsword and inhaling sweet incense and the muddy smoke of the candles that burnt all around. At the King's feet stood Andruw in like pose, head bent in solemn grief. Corfe saw his mouth writhe in the suppression of a yawn under the heavy helmet, and he had to fight not to smile.

The cathedral was thronged with a murmuring crowd of damp-smelling people. They knelt in the pews or on the flagged floor and queued in their hundreds to have a chance to say goodbye to their monarch. Unending lines of them.

They were not grieving so much as awed by the solemnity, the austere splendour of the dead King's lying-in-state. Lofantyr had not ruled long enough to become loved, and was a name, no more. A figurehead in the ordered system of the world.

Outside it sounded as though a heavy sea were beating against the hoary old walls of the cathedral. Another crowd, less tractable. The surf-roar of their voices was ominous, frightening even. A quarter of a million people had gathered in the square beyond the cathedral gates. No-one was quite sure why—probably they did not truly know themselves. The common people were confused. Palace bulletins stated that the recent battle had been a victory for Torunnan arms. But why then was their King dead and eight thousand of their menfolk lying stark and cold upon the winter field? They felt themselves duped, and were angry. Any spark would set them off.

And yet, Corfe thought, I am expected to take my turn standing ceremonial guard over a dead man, when I am now commander-in-chief of a shattered army. Tradition. Its wheels turn on tyrelessly even in a time like this.

But it gave him a space to think, if nothing else. Two days since the great battle of the Torunnan Plain. "The King's Battle" they were already calling it. Odd how people always thought it so important that a battle should have a name. It gave some strange coherence to what was, after all, a chaotic, slaughterous nightmare. Historians needed things neater, it seemed.

Twenty-seven thousand men left to defend the capital— the Last Army. Torunna had squandered her soldiers with sickening prodigality. An entire field army destroyed in the sack of Aekir. Another decimated in the fall of Ormann Dyke. And even this remaining force had lost nearly a third of its number in the latest round of blood-letting. But the Merduks—how many had they lost? A hundred thousand in the assaults on Aekir, it was reckoned. Thirty thousand more in front of the dyke. And another forty thousand in the King's Battle. How could a single people absorb losses on that scale? Numberless though the hordes of the east might be, Corfe could not believe that they were unaffected by such awful arithmetic. They would hesitate before committing themselves to another advance, another around of killing. That was his hope, the basis for all his half-formed plans. He needed time.

Corfe and Andruw were relieved at last, their place taken with grim parade-ground formality by Colonels Rusio and Willem. Corfe caught the cold glance of Willem as he marched away towards the back of the cathedral. Hatred there, resentment at the elevation of an upstart to the highest military command in the west. Well, that was not unexpected, but it would complicate things. Things were always complicated, even when it came to that most basic of human activities, the killing of one's fellow man.

CORFE was unburdened of his armour by a small regiment of palace servitors in the General's Suite of the palace. His new quarters were a cavernous cluster of marble-cold rooms within which he felt both uncomfortable and absurd. But the general could no longer be allowed to mess with his men, drink beer in the common refectories or pick the mud off his own boots. The Queen Dowager— now Torunna's monarch and sole remaining vestige of royalty—had insisted that Corfe assume the trappings of his rank.

It is a long time, Corfe thought to himself, since I shared cold turnip with a blind man on the retreat from Aekir. Another world.

A discreet footman caught his eye and coughed. "General, a simple repast has been set out for you in your dining chamber. I suggest you avail yourself of it while it is still hot. Our cook—"

"I'll eat later. Have the palace steward sent to me at once, and some writing materials. And the two scribes who attended me last night. And pass the word for Colonel Andruw Cear-Adurhal."

The footman blinked, crinkling the white powder on his temples. Where in the name of God did that fashion begin? Corfe wondered distractedly.

"All shall be as you wish, of course. But General, the palace steward, the Honourable Gabriel Venuzzi, is answerable only to the Monarch of Torunna. He is not under your aegis, if you will forgive me. He is a person of some considerable importance in the household, and were I to convey so—so peremptory a summons, he might take it ill. If you will allow me, I, as senior footman of the household, should be able to answer any questions you might have about the running of the palace and the behaviour expected of all who dwell within it, as guests or otherwise."

This last sentence had inserted within it a sneer so delicate it almost passed Corfe by. He frowned and turned a cold eye upon the powdered fellow. "What's your name?"

The footman bowed. "Damian Devella, General."

"Well, Damian, let's get a few things straight. In future, you and your associate servitors will wipe that white shit off your faces when you attend me. You're not ladies' maids, nor yet pantomime performers. And you will send for this Venuzzi fellow. Now. Clear it with Her Majesty if you must, but get his powdered backside in this room within the quarter-hour, or by God I'll have you and your whole prancing crew conscripted into the army and we'll see if there's even six inches of backbone hidden under all that velvet and lace. Do you understand me?"

Devella's mouth opened, closed. "I—I—yes, General."

"Good. Now fuck off."

Scribes, a writing desk, a decanter of wine, appeared with remarkable speed. Corfe stepped out on to his balcony as behind him the dining chamber was transformed into an office of sorts and members of the household scurried about like ants whose nest has been poked with a stick.

Outside sleet was withering down from the Cimbric Mountains. Corfe could see the vast crowd still milling about in Cathedral Square, their voices meshing into a shapeless buzz of noise. Half of them were Aekirian refugees, still without homes of their own or the prospect of any alteration in their wretchedness. That would change, if he could help it. They were his people too. He had been a refugee like them and could never forget it.

"What's afoot, General?" Andruw's cheery voice demanded. Corfe turned. His friend was dressed in old field fatigues and comfortable boots, but his colonel's braid was

bright and shining-new. It looked as though he had stitched
it on himself. Some of the ice about Corfe's heart eased a
little. It would be a black day indeed that saw Andruw out
of humour.

"Just trying to get a few things done before the funeral,"
he told Andruw. "That crowd means business, even if they
don't know it themselves yet. You brought the papers?"

"They're on the table. Lord, I'll need some sleep tonight.
And some fresh air to blow away the smell of all that ink
and paper. Stacks of it!"

"Think of it as ammunition. Ah—excuse me, Andruw."

A richly dressed man with an ebony staff of office had
been admitted to the room by the footmen with all the pomp
of an eastern potentate. He was very tall, very slim, and as
dark as a Merduk. A native of Kardikia or perhaps southern
Astarac, Corfe guessed.

"Gabriel Venuzzi?"

The man bowed slightly, a mere nod of the head. "Indeed. You, I believe, are General Cear-Inaf."

"The very same. Now listen here Gabriel, we have a
problem on our hands and I believe you may be able to
help me solve it."

"Indeed? I am glad to hear it. And what might be the
nature of this problem, General? Her Majesty has requested
me to give you any assistance in my power, and I of course
must obey her commands to the letter."

"There's your problem, Gabriel. Down there." Corfe gestured at the view from the balcony. Venuzzi stepped over
to the open doors, wincing slightly at the cold air coursing
through them, and glanced out at the murmuring crowds
below.

"I am afraid I don't quite understand you, General. I am
not an officer of militia, merely the head administrator of
the household. If you want the crowd cleared you should
perhaps be addressing some of your junior officers. I do
not deal with commoners."

His hauteur was almost impressive. Corfe smiled. "You
do now."

"Forgive me my ignorance. I still do not follow you."

"That's all right, Gabriel. I don't mind explaining." Corfe

lifted the sheaf of papers Andruw had brought in with him. The two of them had spent the early hours of the morning, before they had done their ceremonial duty in the cathedrals, hunting them up in the storehouse of Palace Housekeeping Records, a musty tomb-like warren dedicated to the storage of statistics.

"I have here records of all the foodstuffs kept in the palace. Not only the palace, in fact, but in Royal warehouses across the entire city and indeed the kingdom. Gabriel, my dear fellow, the household has squirrelled away hundreds of tons of wheat and corn and smoked meat and—and—"

"And stock-fish and hardtack and olive oil and wine," Andruw added. "Don't forget the wine. Eight hundred tuns of it, General."

"And I won't even mention the brandy and salt pork and figs," Corfe finished, still smiling. "Now explain to me, Gabriel, why it is necessary to hoard these stupendous amounts of goods."

"I'd have thought it was obvious, General, even to you," Venuzzi drawled, not turning a hair. "They are Royal reserves, destined to supply the palace on an everyday basis, and also put aside in case of siege."

"All this, to keep the inhabitants of the palace well fed?" Corfe asked quietly.

"Why yes. Certain proprieties must be observed, even in times of war. We cannot"—and here Venuzzi's lean face broke into a knowing smirk—"we cannot expect the nobility to go hungry, after all. Think how it would look to the world."

"It is not a question of going hungry. It is a question of hoarding the means to feed tens of thousands when one has in fact only to supply the wants of a few hundred." There was a tone in Corfe's voice which made everyone in the room pause. His smile had disappeared.

Venuzzi retreated a step from that terrible stare. "General, I—"

"Hold your tongue. In case it had escaped your attention, we are at war, Venuzzi. I am issuing orders for the collection of these hoarded stocks of food and their redistribution

to the refugees from Aekir, and anyone else in Torunn who
has need of them. The orders will be posted up in public
places later today. These scribes have already made out fifty
copies. I need your signature, I am told, before I can start
the process."

"You shall not have it! This is outrageous!"

Corfe stepped closer to the steward. "You will sign," he
said in a voice so soft no-one else in the room heard, "or
I will make a private soldier out of you, Venuzzi. I can do
that, you know. I can conscript anyone I please."

"You're bluffing! You wouldn't dare."

"Try me."

A silence crackled in the room. Venuzzi's knuckles were
bone white around his black staff of office. Finally he
turned, bent over the desk, and seized a quill. His signature,
long and scrawling, was scratched across the topmost set
of orders.

"Thank you," Corfe said quietly.

The steward shot him a look of pure vitriol. "The Queen
shall know of this. You think I am friendless in this place?
You know nothing. What are you but a backwoods upstart
with mud still under your nails? You fool."

Then he turned on his heel and strode out of the room
in a cloud of footmen. The doors boomed shut behind him.

Andruw sighed. "Corfe, a diplomat you are not."

The general bent his head. "I know. I'm just a soldier.
Nothing more." Then he caught his subordinate's eye. "You
know, Andruw, there is a new cemetrey outside the South
Gate. The Aekirians, they created it. There are over six
thousand graves already. Many of them starved to death,
the folk who rot in those graves. While we banqueted in
the palace. So don't talk to me of diplomacy, not now—
not ever again. Just see that those orders are posted all over
the city. I'm off to have a look at the men."

Andruw watched him go without another word.

LATE that night in the capital a group of men met in the
discreet upper room of a prosperous tavern. They wore
nondescript riding clothes: high boots and long cloaks
muddy with the filth of the streets. Some were armed with

military sabres. They sat around a long candlelit tavern table marked with the rings of past carouses. A fire smoked
and cracked in a grate behind them.

"It's intolerable, absolutely intolerable," one of the men
said, a red-faced, grey-bearded fellow in his fifties: Colonel
Rusio of the city garrison.

"They say he is the son of a peasant from down in
Staed," another put in. "Aras, you were there. Is it true, you
think?"

Colonel Aras, a good twenty years younger than anyone
else in the room, looked uncomfortable and willing to
please at the same time.

"I can't say for sure. All I know is he handles those
daemon tribesmen of his with definite ability. Sirs, you
know he had the southern rebels crushed before I even arrived. I'm willing to admit that. Five hundred men! And
Narfintyr had over three thousand, yet he stood not a
chance."

"You almost sound as though you admire him, Colonel."
A silken purr of a voice. Count Fournier, head of the Torunnan Military Intelligence, such as it was. He stroked his
neat beard, as pointed as a spearhead, and watched his
younger colleague intently.

"Perhaps—perhaps I do," Aras said, stumbling over the
words. "In the King's Battle he stopped my position from
being overrun when he sent me his Fimbrians. And then he
threw back the Nalbeni horse-archers on the left, twenty
thousand of them."

"*His* Fimbrians," Rusio muttered. "Lord above! He also
sent you *my* guns, Aras, or had you forgotten?"

"I hope you are not prey to conflicting emotions in this
matter, my dear Aras," Fournier said. "If so, you should
not be here."

"I know where my loyalties lie," Aras said quickly. "To
my own class, to the social order of the realm. To the ul-
timate welfare of the kingdom. I merely point out facts, is
all."

"I am relieved to hear it." Fournier's voice rose. "Gentlemen, we are gathered here, as you well know, to discuss
this—this phoenix which has appeared in our midst. He has

military ability, yes. He has the patronage of our noble Queen, yes. But he is a commoner who prefers commanding savages and Fimbrians to his own countrymen and who is utterly lacking in any vestige of respect for the traditional values of this kingdom. Am I not right, Don Venuzzi?"

The palace steward nodded, his handsome face flushed with anger. "You've read the notices—they're all over the city. He is distributing the Royal reserves at this very moment, breaking open the warehouses and handing the contents out to every beggar in the street who has a hand to lift."

"Such largesse will win him many friends amongst the humbler elements of the population," one of the group said. A short, stocky individual this, with a black patch over one eye and a shaven pate. Colonel Willem, who had been commander of the troops left to garrison the capital when the army marched out to the King's Battle. "A shrewd move, indeed. He has brains, this fellow Corfe."

"Didn't you go to the Queen?" Fournier demanded of Venuzzi. "After all, it's her property he's giving away."

"Of course I did. But she is besotted with him, I tell you. I was told not to cross him."

"He must wield a mighty weapon besides that sword of Mogen's she gave him," Rusio grunted, and the men at the table sniggered, except for Fournier and Venuzzi, who both looked pained.

"She has what she has been hankering after for years," Fournier said icily. "Power in name as well as in fact. She is Torunna's ruler now, no longer the string-puller behind the throne but the occupant of the throne itself. And this Cear-Inaf fellow, he is the fist of the new regime. Mark my words, gentlemen, there are several of us at this table whose heads are about to roll."

"Perhaps literally," Rusio muttered. "Fournier, tell me, will they reopen the investigation into that assassination attempt?"

Fournier coloured. "I think not."

"It was you and the King, wasn't it?"

"What a monstrous accusation! Do you think I would stoop to—?"

"Gentlemen, gentlemen," Willem interjected testily, "enough. We are allies here. There are to be no accusations or recriminations. We must answer this stark question: how do we rid Torunna of this parvenu?"

"Do we want to be rid of him at the moment?" Aras asked nervously. "After all, he is doing a good job of winning the war."

"Good Lord, Colonel!" Rusio snapped. "I do believe you've fallen under this fellow's spell. What are you thinking? Winning the war? We left eight thousand dead on the field a few days ago, including our King. Winning the war indeed!"

Aras did not reply. His face was white as bone.

"It must be legal, whatever else it is," Fournier said smoothly, gliding over the awkward little silence that followed. "And it must not jeopardise the security of the kingdom. We are, after all, in a fight for our very survival at the moment. It may be that Aras is right. This fellow Corfe has his uses—that cannot be denied. And if truth be told, I am not sure the troops would follow anyone else at the moment."

Rusio stirred at this but said nothing.

"So it behoves us to work with him for now. As long as he has the confidence of the Queen he is well-nigh untouchable, but no man is without his weak spots. Aras, you told us he lost his wife in Aekir."

"Yes. He never talks about it, but I have heard his friend Andruw mention it."

"Indeed. That is an avenue worth exploring. There is guilt there, obviously, hence his largesse to the scum of Aekir that we harbour in the capital. And you, Aras, you must work to get closer to him. You obviously admire him, so that is a start. Remember, we are not out to destroy this fellow—we simply feel that he has been elevated beyond his station."

Aras nodded.

"And make sure you recall whose side you are on," Rusio growled. "It's one thing to admire the man, another to let him ride roughshod over the very institutions which bind this kingdom together." A murmur of agreement ran down the table. Willem spoke up.

"Another six hundred tribesmen from the Cimbrics arrived outside the city this evening, wanting to fight under him. Quartermaster Passifal is equipping them as we speak. I tell you, gentlemen, if we do not curb this young fellow he will set himself up as some form of military dictator. He does not even have to rely on the support of his countrymen. What with those savages and his tame Fimbrians at his back, he has a power base completely outside the normal chain of command. They won't serve under anyone else—we saw that at the last planning conference the King chaired, here in the capital. And now he's stirring up the rabble who fled from Aekir when he should be shipping them south, dispersing them. There's a pattern to it all. It's my belief he aims at the throne itself."

"It is disturbing," Fournier agreed. "Perhaps—and this is only a vague suggestion, nothing more—perhaps we should be looking for allies of our own outside the kingdom, a counterweight to this growing army of mercenaries he leads."

"Who?" Rusio asked bluntly.

Fournier paused and looked intently at the faces of the men around the table. Below them they could hear the buzz and hubbub of the tavern proper, but in this room the loudest sound was the crackling of the fire.

"I have received in the last sennight a message brought by courier from Almark, gentlemen. That kingdom is, as you know, now on the frontier. The Merduks have sent exploratory columns to the Torrin Gap. Reconnaissances, nothing more, but Almark is understandably alarmed."

"Almark is Himerian," Rusio pointed out. "And ruled directly by the Himerian Church, I hear."

"True. The Prelate Marat is regent of the kingdom, but Marat is a practical man—and a powerful one. If we agreed to certain . . . conditions, he would be willing to send us a host of Almarkan heavy cavalry in our hour of need."

"What conditions?" Willem asked.

"A recognition that there are grounds for doubting the true identity of the man who claims to be Macrobius."

Rusio barked with bitter laughter. "Is that all? Not possible, my dear Count. I know. I met Macrobius while he still dwelled in Aekir. The Pontiff we harbour here in Torunn is a travesty of that man, admittedly, but he is Macrobius. The Himerians are looking for a way to get their foot in the door, that's all. They failed with war and insurrection and now they'll try diplomacy. Priests! I'd get rid of the whole scheming crew if I had my way."

Fournier shrugged elegantly. "I merely inform you as to the various options available. I, too, do not wish to see Almarkan troops in Torunna, but the very idea that they could be available is a useful bargaining tool. I shall brief the Queen on the initiative. It is as well for her to be aware of it." He said nothing of the other, more delicate initiative which had come his way of late. He was still unsure how to handle it himself.

"Do as you please. For myself, I'd sooner we were hauled out of this mess by other Torunnans, not heretical foreigners and plotting clerics."

"There are not many Torunnans left to do the hauling, Colonel. The once mighty Torunnan armies are a mere shadow of what they once were. If we do not respond in some fashion at least to this overture, then I would not be too sanguine about the safety of our own north-western frontier. Almark might just strike while the Merduks have our attention, and we would have foreign troops on Torunnan soil in any case, except that we would not have invited them."

"Are you saying we have no choice in the matter?"

"Perhaps. I will see what the Queen thinks. For all that she is a woman, she has as fine a mind as any of us here."

"We're getting away from the point of this meeting," Willem said impatiently.

"No, I don't think so," Fournier replied. He steepled his slender fingers and swept the table with hard eyes. "If we are trying to shift this Cear-Inaf from his current eminence it may be best to use many smaller levers instead of one big one. That way the prime movers are more easily kept anonymous. More importantly, Cear-Inaf will find it harder to fight back."

"He's not ambitious," Aras blurted out. "I truly think he fights not for himself but for the country, and for his men."

"His lack of ambition has taken him far," Fournier said drily. "Aras, you have met with him more often than any of us. What do you make of him?"

The young colonel hesitated. "He's—he's strange. Not like most career soldiers. A bitter man, hard as marble. And yet the troops love him. They say he is John Mogen come again. There is even a rumour that he is Mogen's bastard son. It started when they saw him wielding Mogen's sword on the battlefield."

"Mogen," Rusio grunted. "Another upstart bedmate of the Queen's."

"That's enough, Colonel," Fournier snapped. "General Menin, may God be good to his soul, obviously saw something in Cear-Inaf, else he would not have posthumously promoted him."

"Martin Menin knew his death was near. It clouded his thinking," Rusio said heavily.

"Perhaps. We will never know. Do we have any inkling of our current commander-in-chief's plans for the future?"

"It will take time to reorganise and refit the army after the beating it took. The Merduks have withdrawn halfway to the Searil for the moment, so we have a breathing space. There is no word from Berza and the fleet, though. If they succeed in destroying the Merduk supply dumps on the Kardian, we may be left alone until the spring."

"We have some time to work in then. That's good. Gentlemen, unless anyone has a further point to raise, I think this meeting is over. Venuzzi, I take it your people are all in place?"

The steward nodded. "You shall know what he has for breakfast before he has it himself."

"Excellent." Fournier rose. "Gentlemen, good night. I suggest we do not all depart at once. Such things get noticed."

In ones and twos they took their leave, until only Aras and Willem were left. The older officer rose and set a hand on Aras's shoulder. "You have your doubts about our little conspiracy, do you not, Aras?"

"Perhaps. Is it wrong to wish for victory, no matter who leads us to it?"

"No. Not at all. But we are the leaders of our country. We must think beyond the present crisis, look to the future."

"Then we are becoming politicians rather than soldiers."

"For the moment. Don't be too hard on yourself. And do not forget whose side you are on. This Corfe is a shooting star, blazing bright today, forgotten tomorrow. We will be here long after his glory-hunting has taken him to his grave." Willem slapped the younger man's shoulder, and left.

Aras remained alone in the empty room, listening to the late-night revellers below, the clatter of carts and waggons in the cobbled streets beyond. He was remembering. Remembering the sight of the Merduk heavy cavalry charging uphill into the maw of cannon, the Fimbrian pikes skewering screaming horses, men shrieking and snarling in a storm of slaughter. That was how the great issues of this world were ultimately decided: in a welter of killing. The man who could impose his own will upon the fuming chaos of battle would ultimately prevail. Before the King's Battle Aras had thought himself ambitious, a leader of men. He was no longer so sure. The responsibilities of command were too awesome.

"What will it be?" he said aloud to the firelight, the glowing candles.

Either way, he would end up betraying something.

FIVE

HIS wooden heels clicked on the floor like the castanets entertainers danced to. She had tried to make him don shoes, but he seemed fascinated by the sight of his timbre toes tapping on marble. Many times he sagged or slipped and she had to steady him. When she did, the pain speared into her ribs, making her breath come short. He had struck her there with his new knee as she held him down in the midst of Golophin's magicking. But there was no time for trivialities like that. Hebrion had a king again. With her help he was stalking and staggering up and down the Royal chambers like an unsteady lion pacing its cage.

And I have a husband, the thought came to her unbidden. Or will have. A man half human, and the other half—what?

"Unbelievable," King Abeleyn of Hebrion muttered. "Golophin has really surpassed himself this time. But why wood? Old Mercado got himself a silver face. Couldn't I have been given limbs of steel or iron?"

"He was in a hurry," Isolla told him. "They vote on the

regency today. There was nothing else available."

"Ah, yes. My noble cousins, flapping around me like gore-crows looking for a beakful of the Royal carcase. What a shock it'll be when I walk in on the dastards! For I will walk in, Isolla. And in full mail too."

"Don't overdo things. We don't want you looking like an apparition."

Abeleyn grinned, the same grin that had quickened her heart as a girl. He was still boyish when he smiled despite the grey of his hair and the scars on his face. "Golophin may have had to fix my legs, Issy, but the rest of me is still flesh and blood. How do you feel about marrying a carpenter's bench?"

"I'm not a romantic heroine in some ballad, Abeleyn. Folk with our blood marry out of policy. I'll wear your ring, and both Astarac and Hebrion will be the better off for it."

"You haven't changed. Still the sober little girl with the world on her shoulders. Give us a kiss."

"Abeleyn!"

He tried to embrace her and pull her face towards his, but his wooden feet slipped on the stone floor and he went down with a clack and crash, pulling her with him. They landed in a billow of her brocade and silks, and Abeleyn roared with laughter. He kept his grip, and kissed her full on the mouth, one hand cradling the hollow of her neck. She felt the colour flame into her face as she pulled away.

"That put the roses into your cheeks!" he chortled. "By God Issy, you grew up well. That's a fine figure you've got lurking under those skirts."

"That's enough, my lord. You'll injure yourself. This is unbecoming."

"I'm alive, Isolla. Alive. Let me forget Royal dignity for a while and taste the world." His hand brushed her naked collarbone, drifted lower and caressed the swell of one breast where the stiff robe pushed it upwards. A jolt ran through her that dried up the words in her mouth. No-one had ever touched her in that way. She wanted it to stop. She wanted it to go on.

"Well sire, I see you are feeling better," a deep, musical voice said.

They disentangled themselves at once and Isolla helped the King to his feet. Golophin stood by the door with his arms folded, a crooked smile on his face.

"Golophin, you old goat!" Abeleyn cried. "Your timing is as inept as ever."

"My apologies, lad. Isolla, get him to the bed. You've excited him enough for one morning."

Isolla had nothing to say. Abeleyn leaned heavily on her as she helped him back to the large four-poster. Only a two-poster now. The other two were grafted on to the King's stumps.

"My people have to see me," Abeleyn said earnestly. "I can't sit around in here like an ageing spinster. Issy has given me the bare bones of it. Now you tell me, Golophin. It's written all over your face. What's been going on?"

On his own visage, as the humour faded, pain and exhaustion added an instant fifteen years to his age.

"You can probably guess." Golophin poured all three of them wine from the decanter by the King's bed and drained half his own glass in a single swallow.

"It's been only a few weeks, but your mistress Jemilla—"

"Ex-mistress," Abeleyn said quickly, glancing at Isolla. A warmth crept about her heart. She found herself taking the King's hand in her own. It was dry and hot but it returned her pressure.

"Ex-mistress," Golophin corrected himself. "She's proven herself quite the little intriguer. As we speak Hebrion's nobles gather in the old Inceptine abbey and squabble over the regency of the kingdom."

Abeleyn said nothing for a moment. He was staring at his wooden legs. Finally he looked up. "Urbino, I'm thinking. The dry old fart. She'll find it easy to manage him, and he'll wield the most clout."

"Bravo, sire. He's the leading candidate."

"I knew Jemilla was ambitious, but I underrated her."

"A formidable woman," Golophin agreed.

"When is the vote?"

"This afternoon, at the sixth hour."

"Then it would seem I do not have much time. Golophin, call for a valet. I must have decent clothes. And a bath."

The old wizard approached his King and set a hand on the young man's shoulder. "Are you sure you are up to this, lad? Even if Urbino is voted the regency today, all you have to do is make an appearance at any time and he'll have to give it up. It might be better if you rested a while."

"No. Thousands of my people died to put me back on the throne. I'll not let one scheming bitch and her dried-up puppet take it from me. Get some servants in here, Golophin. And I want to speak to Rovero and Mercado. We shall have a little military daemonstration this afternoon, I think. Time to put these bastard conspirators in their place."

Golophin bowed deeply. "At once, sire. Let me locate a couple of the more discreet palace servants. If we can keep your recovery quiet until this afternoon, then the impact will be all the greater." He left noiselessly.

Abeleyn sagged. "Give me a hand here, Isolla. Damn things weigh a ton."

She helped him arrange the wooden legs on the bed. He seemed to find it hard to keep his eyes off them.

"I never felt it," he said quietly. "Not a thing. Strange, that. A man has half his body ripped away and it does not even register. I can feel them now, though. They itch and smart like flesh and blood. Lord God, Isolla, what are you marrying?"

She hugged him close. It seemed amazingly natural to do so. "I am marrying a King, my lord. A very great King."

He gripped her hand until the blood fled from it, his head bent into her shoulder. When he spoke again his voice was thick and harsh, too loud.

"Where are those damn valets? The service has gone to hell in this place."

ABRUSIO had once been home to a quarter of a million people. A fifth of the population had died in the storming of the city, and tens of thousands more had packed up their belongings and left the capital for good. In addition, the trade which was the lifeblood of the port had been reduced to a tithe of its former volume, and men were still working by the thousand to clear the battered wharves, repair bombarded warehouses and demolish those structures too broken to be restored. A wide swathe of the Lower City had been reduced to a charred wasteland, and in this desolation thousands more were encamped like squatters under makeshift shelters.

But in the Upper City the damage was less, and here, where the nobility of Hebrion had their town houses and the Guilds of the city their halls, the only evidence of the recent fighting lay in the cannonballs which still pocked some structures like black carbuncles, and the shallow craters in the cobbled streets which had been filled with gravel.

And here, on the summit of one of the twin hills which topped Abrusio, the old Inceptine monastery and abbey glowered down on the port-city. Within the huge refectory of the Inceptine Order, the surviving aristocracy of Hebrion were assembled in all their finery to vote upon the very future of the kingdom.

T HERE had been a scurry of last-minute deals and agreements, of course, men shuffling and intriguing frantically to be part of the new order that was approaching. But by and large it had gone precisely as Jemilla had planned. Today Duke Urbino of Imerdon would be appointed regent of Hebrion, and the lady Jemilla would be publicly proclaimed as the mother of the crippled King's heir. She would be queen in everything but name. What would Richard Hawkwood have made of that? she wondered, as the nobles convened before her in their maddening, leisurely fashion, and Urbino's face, for once wreathed in smiles, shone down the great table at his fellow blue-bloods.

A crowd had gathered outside the abbey to await the outcome of the council. Jemilla's steward had bribed several hundred of the city dregs to stand there and cheer when the news was announced, and they had, in the manner of things, been joined by a motley throng of some several thousand who sensed the excitement in the air. Jemilla had also thoughtfully arranged for fifty tuns of wine to be set up at various places about the city so that the regent's health might be drunk when the criers went forth to spread the tidings about the change of government. The wine ought to assuage any pangs of uneasiness or lingering royalist feeling left in the capital. Nothing had been left to chance. This thing was here, now, in her hand. What would she do first? Ah, that Astaran bitch Isolla. She'd be sent packing, for a start.

As the hubbub within the abbey died down and the nobles took their places it was possible to hear the clamour of the crowds outside. It had risen sharply. They sounded as though they were cheering. Mindless fools, Jemilla thought. Their country is in ruins about their ears but splash them a measure of cheap wine and they'll make a holiday.

The nobles were finally assembled, and seated according to all the rivallries and nuances of rank. Duke Urbino rose in his space at the right hand of the King's empty chair. He looked as though he was trying not to grin, a phenomenon which sat oddly on his long, mournful face. The horsetrading which had occupied them day and night for the last several days was over. The outcome of the vote was already known to all, but the legal niceties had to be observed. In a few minutes he would be the *de facto* ruler of Hebrion, one of the great princes of the world.

"My dear cousins," Urbino began—and stopped.

The din of the crowds had risen to a roaring pitch of jubilation, but now they in turn were being drowned out by the booming thunder of artillery firing in sequence.

"What in the world?" Urbino demanded. He looked questioningly at Jemilla, but she could only frown and shake her head. No doing of hers.

The assembly listened in absolute silence. It sounded like a regular bombardment.

"My God, it's the Knights Militant—they've come back," some idiot gushed.

"Shut up!" another snapped.

They listened on. Urbino stood as still as a statue, his head cocked to the sound of the guns. They were very close by—they must have been firing from the battlements of the palace. But why? And then Jemilla realised, with a sickening plunge of spirit. It was a salute.

"Count the guns!" she cried, heedless of the shrill crack in her voice.

"That's nineteen now," one of the older nobles asserted. Hardio of Pontifidad, she remembered. A royalist. His face was torn between hope and dismay.

The echoing rumble of the explosions at last died away, but the crowds were still cheering manically. Twenty-eight guns. The salute for a reigning king. What in the world was going on?

"Maybe it's for the new regent," someone said, but Hardio shook his head.

"That'd be twenty-two guns."

"Perhaps he's dead," one of the dullards suggested. "They always fire a salute on the death of a king."

"God forbid," Hardio rasped, but most of the men present looked relieved. It was Jemilla who spoke, her voice a lash of scorn.

"Don't be a fool. You hear the crowds? You think they'd be cheering the death of the King?" It was slipping away— she could feel it. Somehow Golophin and Isolla had stymied her. But how?

The question was soon answered. There was a deafening blare of horns outside and the clatter of many horses. A Royal fanfare was blown over and over. Beyond the great double doors of the refectory they could hear the tramp of feet marching in step. Then a sonorous boom as someone struck the doors from the outside.

"Open in the name of the King!"

A group of timorous retainers belonging to Urbino's household stood there, unsure. They looked to their lord for orders but he seemed lost in shock. It was Jemilla who rapped out, "Open the damn doors then!"

They did so. Those inside the hall stood up as one, scraping back their chairs on the old stone. Beyond the doors were two long files of Hebrian arquebusiers dressed in the rich blue of Royal livery. Banner-bearers stood with the Hibrusid gonfalons a silk shimmer above their heads. And at the head of them all, a tall figure in black half-armour, his face hidden by a closed helm upon which the Hebrian crown gleamed in a spangle of gems and gold.

Wordlessly, the files of arquebusiers entered the room and lined the walls. Their match was lit and soon filled the chamber with the acrid reek of gunpowder. The solitary figure in the closed helm entered last, the banner-bearers closing the doors behind him. The assembled nobles stood as though turned to stone, until a hard voice snapped, "Kneel before your King."

And the figure in black unhelmed.

The aristocracy of Hebrion stared, gaped, and then did as they were bidden. The figure in the black armour was without a doubt Abeleyn IV, King of Hebrion and Imerdon.

He was taller than they remembered, and he looked old enough to be the father of the young man they had once known. No trace of the boy-king remained. His eyes were like two glitters of black frost as he surveyed the kneeling throng. Jemilla remained in her seat by the fire, too paralysed to move, but he did not even glance at her. The chamber stank of fear as much as the burning match. He could have them all shot, here and now, and no-one would be able to lift a finger.

Hardio and a few others who had been against the regency from the first were beaming. "Give you joy of your recovery, sire," the old nobleman said. "This is a glad day for the kingdom."

The severity on the seamed face of the King lifted somewhat: they glimpsed the youth of a few months past. "My thanks, Hardio. Noble cousins, you may rise."

A collective sigh, lost in the noise of the aristocrats getting off their knees. They were to live, then.

"Now," the King went on quietly, "I believe you were gathered here to discuss matters of import that concern my realm." No-one missed the easy emphasis on the *my*, the momentary departure from the Royal *we*.

"We will—if you do not object—take our place at the head of this august gathering."

"By—by all means, sire," Urbino stammered. "And may I also congratulate you on the regaining of your health and faculties."

Abeleyn took the empty throne which headed the long table. His gait was odd: he walked on legs which seemed too long for him, rolling slightly like a sailor on the deck of a pitching ship.

"I was not aware our faculties had ever been lost, Urbino," he said, and the coldness in his voice chilled the room. The nobles were once again aware of the lines of armed soldiers at their backs.

"But your concern is noted," the King continued. "It shall not be forgotten." And here Abeleyn's eyes swept the room, coming to rest at last on Jemilla.

"We trust we see you well, lady."

It took a second for her to find her voice. "Very well, my lord."

"Excellent. But you should not be worrying yourself with the problems of state in your condition. You have our leave to go."

There was no choice for her, of course. She curtsied clumsily, and then left the room. The doors boomed behind her, shutting her away from her ambitions and dreams. Jemilla kept her chin tilted high, oblivious to the roaring jubilation of the crowds outside, the grinning soldiers. Not until she had reached the privacy of her own apartments did she let the tears and the fury run unchecked.

"A very satisfactory state of affairs," Himerius, High Pontiff of the Ramusian Kingdoms of the West, said.

It was a day of brilliant sunshine which blazed off the snow-covered Narian Hills all around and glittered in blinding facets upon the peaks of the Cimbric Mountains to the east. Himerius stood foursquare against the bitter wind which billowed down from those grim heights, and when he exhaled his breath was a white smoke shredded instantly away. Behind him, a group of monks in Inceptine black huddled within their habits and discreetly rubbed their hands together within voluminous sleeves in a futile effort to keep the blood in their fingers warm.

"Indeed, your Holiness," bluff, florid-cheeked Betanza said. "It could not have gone more smoothly. As we speak, Regent Marat is preparing an expeditionary force of some eight thousand men. They should be here in fifteen days, if the weather holds."

"The couriers have gone out to Alstadt?"

"They went yesterday, under escort of a column of Knights. I would estimate that within three months we will have a fortified garrison in the Torrin Gap, ready to repel any Merduk reconnaissance or to serve as a stageing post for further endeavours."

"And what news from Vol Ephrir?"

"King Cadamost will accept a garrison on the Astaran border, but it must not be of Almarkan nationals. Knights Militant only—it is a question of national pride, you understand. Unfortunately, we do not currently have any Knights to spare."

"Almarkan troops are now the servants of the Church as much as the Knights Militant. If it will ease Perigraine's conscience the Almarkans can be clad in the livery of the Knights, but we must install our troops in southern Perigraine. Is that clear, Betanza?"

"Perfectly, Holiness. I shall see to it at once."

"Cadamost shall be made an honourary presbyter, of course. It is the least I can do. He is a faithful son of the Church, truly. But he cannot afford to think of Perigraine alone at a time like this. We must present a united front against the heretics. If Skarp-Hethin of Finnmark is willing to accept Almarkan garrisons, then Cadamost has no reason not to do likewise."

"Yes of course, your Holiness. It is merely a question of prestige. Skarp-Hethin is a prince, and his principality has traditionally been closely allied with Almark. But Perigraine is a sovereign state. Some of the diplomatic niceties must be observed."

"Yes, yes. I am not a child, Betanza. Just get it done. I care not what hoops you have to jump through, but we must have the forces of the Church garrisoned throughout those kingdoms which acknowledge her spiritual supremacy. This is a time of crisis. I will not have the debacle of Hebrion repeated. We lost an entire kingdom to the heretics there because we had insufficient forces on the ground. That must never happen again."

"Yes, Holiness."

"If we are to strike back at the heretics then it can only be

east through the Torrin Gap, and south into East Astarac . . .
Still no word from Fimbria?"

"No, Holiness. Though rumour has it that the Fimbrian
army sent east by the Electors was destroyed along with
the Ormann Dyke garrison at the Battle of the North More."

"Rumour? We base our policy on rumours now?"

"It is difficult to obtain reliable information on the eastern war, Holiness. I have also heard that there has been a
great battle close to the gates of Torunn itself, but of its
outcome we have no word."

"Have we no reliable sources in Torunn?"

"We have, yes, but with the Torunnan capital virtually
under siege it is a slow business getting their intelligence
this far."

Himerius said nothing. His face was drawn and haggard
in the harsh sunlight, but the eyes within it were bright as
gledes. Over the past days he had displayed an astonishing
reservoir of energy for a man of his years, working far into
every night with shifts of scribes and scholars and Almarkan military officers. Privately, Betanza wondered how
long he could keep it up. The Ramusian Church—or this
version of it, at any rate—had in a space of weeks been
transformed into a great empire which now encompassed
not only Almark, but Finnmark, Perigraine and half a dozen
other minor principalities and duckedoms also. Cadamost
of Perigraine, appalled by the carnage in the heretical states
of Hebrion, Astarac and Torunna, had hastened to place his
own kingdom under the protective wing of Charibon. A
loyal son of the Church indeed, Betanza thought, but one
without any balls to speak of.

Betanza himself regarded this sudden transformation of
the Church with mixed feelings. He was Vicar-General of
the Inceptine Order, the second most powerful figure in the
Church hierarchy, but he found himself wondering about
the accumulation of power which was taking place here. If
Torunn had become the focuss of resistance to the Merduk
invasions, then Charibon was now the centre of a huge new
power bloc which stretched from the Malvennor Mountains
in the west to the Cimbrics in the east, and even extended
as far north as the Sultanate of Hardukh, not far from the

foothills of the Northern Jafrar. Only Fimbria, in her hey-day, had ever governed a tract of land so large, and the men who had had this awesome responsibility thrust so precipitately upon their shoulders were clerics, priests with no experience in governance. It made him uneasy. It also seemed not quite right to him that the head of the Ramusian faith in Normannia should spend twenty hours a day dic-tating orders for the levying of troops and the movement of armies. He had not joined the Church to become a gen-eral; he had done his soldiering in the lay world and wanted no more of it.

He looked up and out to where the savage peaks of the Cimbric Mountains brooded, white and indomitable. The snow was blowing in great streaks and banners from their summits, as though the mountains were smoking. The world was on fire; the world he had known as a boy and a young man tottered on the brink of dissolution. If only Ae-kir had not fallen, he found himself thinking. If only Ma-crobius had not been lost.

Such thinking was absurd, of course, and dangerous. They all had to make the best of it. But why did he feel so afraid, so apprehensive of the future? Perhaps it was the change in Himerius. The Pontiff had always been a proud, vain man, capable of ruthless intrigue. But now it seemed that the ambition had left the faith behind. The man never *prayed* any more. Could that be right, in the head of the Church? And that odd light in his eyes occasionally, at night. It seemed otherworldly. Unsettling.

I am tyred, Betanza thought. I am tyred, and I am older than I think I am. Why not step down and walk the clois-ters, contemplate the world beyond this one, and the God Who created it? It is what I donned this habit to do, after all.

But he knew the answer even as he asked the question. He would not stand down because he was afraid of whom Himerius might find to replace him. Already half the Church hierarchy had been reshuffled—Escriban, Prelate of Perigraine, was gone already. He had too independent a mind to sit easily with the New Order. Himerius had in-stalled Pieter Goneril in his place, a nonentity who would do exactly as he was told. And Presbyter Quirion of the Knights Militant, as good a man as ever lifted a sword in the service of the Church, and a personal friend—he was gone too, rotting in some little Almarkan border town. He had lost Hebrion to King Abeleyn, and over a thousand Knights besides. That could not be forgiven.

Charibon has become a Royal court, Betanza thought. We are nothing more than errand-runners for its black-clad monarch. And our faith? What has happened to it?

He found it hard to admit to himself what nagged at him most, and caused him to wake up sweating in the middle of the cold nights. An old scrap of wandering prophecy dreamt up by a madman, but a madman who was nevertheless one of the founding fathers of the Church.

And the Beast shall come upon the earth in the days of the Second Empire of the world. And he shall rise up out of the west, the light in his eyes terrible to behold. With him shall come the Age of the Wolf, when brother will slay brother. And all men shall fall down and worship him.

Betanza had never been much of a reader before he set aside his ducal robes and donned the black habit. In fact, strictly speaking, he had been illiterate. But he had learnt his letters in his years with the Church, and now he found reading to be an occupation he loved. He had shelves of books in his chambers, amongst them certain tomes which, were they found in the possession of a novice, might just consign that novice to the pyre. He had begun collecting them after the strange murder of Commodius the Chief Librarian in the bowels of the great Library of Saint Garaso. There was a chill in his gut as he recalled the lines from *The Book of Honourius*. A madman's ravings or true prescience? No-one could say. And why had Commodius been murdered? Again, no-one knew. His investigations had led nowhere. The two monks who were the prime suspects had disappeared into the night. Oddly, Himerius had seemed unconcerned, more preoccupied with sealing off the catacombs below the library than with tracking down the murderers.

Lord God, it was cold! Would spring never come? What a terrible year.

Himerius had taken to roving the battlements of the cathedral trailed by a gaggle of scribes and subordinates. It helped him think, he said. That was why they were up here now, insects scurrying along the backbone of a slumbering stone giant, Charibon spread out below them like a toy city. The Sea of Tor was still frozen about its margins, and Betanza could see crowds of the local people out fishing on the ice. The winter had been hard on them, and harder still was the billeting in their homes of troops. Lines of soldiers marched into Charibon every day, it seemed. The monastery-city was becoming an armed camp.

Himerius strolled along the battlements dictating to his scribes. Betanza did not move, and only one cleric elected to remain with him. Old Rogien, head of the Pontifical household. His wrinkled face seemed almost transparent in the harsh light, the veins blue at his temples.

"Thinking, Brother?"

Betanza smiled. "I have much to ponder."

"Haven't we all? His Holiness is a man of phenomenal abilities."

"Phenomenal, yes."

"You sound a little disgruntled, Brother."

"Me?" Betanza glanced at the Pontiff's group. They were out of earshot. And he had known Rogien a long time. "Not disgruntled, Rogien. Apprehensive perhaps."

"Ah. Well, in time of war that is every man's right."

"We are not soldiers, though."

"Aren't we? We may not wear mail and wield swords, but we are warriors of a sort nonetheless."

"And Charibon is not a barracks for all the soldiery of Almark."

"But we are on the frontier now, Betanza. They say the Merduks have been sighted even on the eastern shores of the Sea of Tor itself. Charibon was sacked once, by the Cimbric tribes. Would you have it sacked again?"

Betanza grimaced. "You know very well that is not what I mean."

"Maybe I do." Rogien lowered his voice and drew close. "But you will not find me admitting it."

"Why not? Is free speech no longer allowed in Chari-bon?"

Rogien chuckled. "Come now, Betanza, since when has free speech *ever* been allowed in Charibon?"

"You speak of heresy. I speak of policy." Betanza was not amused. But the older monk was unfazed.

"It is all the same these days. If you do not know that yet, then you have not been paying attention. Come now, Brother—you were a duke, a man of power in the secular world. Are you so naive? Relearn the skills which you used before you donned that habit. They will prove invaluable in the days to come."

"Damn it, Rogien, I did not become a monk to become some monastic aristocrat."

"Oh please, Brother. You are a member of the most po-liticized religious order in the world—more than that, you are its head. Don't come the martyred ascetic to me. If you meant what you say you'd be in a grey habit and bare feet, preaching to the poor in some dung-heap town in Astarac."

Betanza could not reply. Rogien was right, of course. But it did not help.

"Come," he said, nodding to the receding backs of the Pontiff and his entourage. "We're being left behind."

"No, Brother," Rogien said coldly. "*You* are being left behind."

SIX

THE old conference chamber of the Torunnan High
Command was a cavernous place, the walls lined with
marble pillars, the fireplaces at each end large enough for
a grown man to stand upright within. The ceiling arched
up into a gloom of ancient rafters all hung with banners
and battle-flags whose bright colours had been dimmed by
age and smoke and dust—and the blood of the men who
had died carrying them in battle. The building dated back
to the Fimbrian Hegemony, but it had not been used in
years, King Lofantyr preferring to meet his generals in
more congenial chambers in the palace. But Queen Odelia,
now ruler of Torunna, had reopened the hall wherein John
Mogen and Kaile Ormann had once propounded their strategies. As the hierarchy of the Torunnan army gathered for
their first conference with the new commander-in-chief, the
ghosts of those past giants seemed to loom heavily out of
the shadows.

The assembled officers were clad in their court dress,

blue for the artillery, black for infantry and deep burgundy for the cavalry. They were an imposing crowd, though an experienced commander might have noted that they were all either very young or very old for their rank. Torunna's most talented officers were all dead. John Mogen and Sibastion Lejer at Aekir, Pieter Martellus at Ormann Dyke, Martin Menin in the King's Battle. What remained was the rump of a once great military machine. Torunna had come to the end of the rope. There were no more reserves to call up, and no-one expected the Fimbrians to send another army to their rescue, not after the first one had been decimated to little purpose up on the North More. It was true that the Cimbric tribes were trickling down out of the mountains to join them in ever increasing numbers, but none of the men present in that historic chamber thought much of the military abilities of those savages, for all that they had accomplished under General Cear-Inaf. They were a freakish anomaly, no more. Their presence at the King's funeral had been in bad taste, it was widely agreed, but the crowds had clamoured to see the famously exotic red horsemen stand guard in rank on scarlet rank as Lofantyr was laid to rest.

The chatter in the chamber was cut short as the general in question entered, and on his arm was the Queen. Odelia seated herself at the head of the long table which occupied the middle of the room and when she had done so the rest of its occupants followed suit, some of them sharing quick, sceptical glances. A woman, at a war council! A few of the more observant men there noted also the way the monarch looked at her most recently promoted general, and decided that palace gossip might be in the right of it after all.

It was General Cear-Inaf who rose to bring the council to order. The Torunnan officers sat dutifully attentive. This man shouldered the burden of the kingdom's very survival. As importantly, he could make or break the career of any one of them.

"You all know me, or know of me," Corfe said. "I served under Mogen at Aekir, and fled my post when the city fell. I served at Ormann Dyke also—as did Andruw and Ranafast here. I commanded the forces which fought at the

North More, and led the withdrawal after the King's Battle. Fate has seen fit to make me your commanding officer, and therefore whatever your personal feelings you will obey my orders as though they were the word of God. That is how an army operates. I will always be open to suggestions and ideas from any one of you, and you may ask to see me in person at any time of the day or night. But my word in any military matter is final. Her Majesty has flattered me with her confidence in the running of this war, and I am to have an entirely free hand. But there will be no more arguments about seniority or precedence in the officer class. Promotion will from now on be won through merit alone, not through family connections or length of service. Are there any questions?"

No-one spoke. They had expected as much. A peasant who had risen through the ranks could hardly be expected to respect the values of tradition or social rank.

"Very good. Now, I have received in the last hour a message from Admiral Berza and the fleet, conveyed by dispatch-galley. He informs me that he has located and destroyed two of the Merduk supply dumps on the shores of the Kardian Sea—"

A buzz of talk, quickly stilled as Corfe held up a hand.

"He writes that the Merduk casualties can be measured in the thousands, and he believes he has sent perhaps three or four million of rations up in smoke. However, his own casualties were heavy. Of the marine landing parties less than half survived, and he also lost two of his twenty-three great ships in the landings. At the time of writing, he has put to sea again to engage a Nalbenic fleet which is purportedly sailing north up the Kardian to secure the Merduk lines of communication. I have already sent him a set of orders which basically gives him free rein. Berza is a capable man, and understands the sea better than any of us here. The fleet will therefore not be coming back upriver to the capital for the foreseeable future."

"But that leaves the line of the river wide open!" Colonel Rusio protested. "The Merduks will be able to cross at any spot they please and outflank us!"

"Correct. But intelligence suggests that the main Merduk

field army has fallen back at least forty leagues from Torunn and is busy repairing the Western Road as far east as
Aekir itself in order to maintain an alternative line of communication free from the depredations of our ships. I believe the enemy is too busy at present to launch another
assault. Andruw—if you please."

Corfe took his seat and Andruw rose in his turn. He
looked a trifle nervous as the eyes of the High Command
swivelled upon him, and cleared his throat whilst consulting
a sheaf of papers in his hand.

"The main army has withdrawn, yes, but our scouting
parties have reported that the Merduks are sending flying
columns of a thousand or so up into the north-west, towards
the Torrin Gap. They are obviously a reconnaissance-in-
force, feeling out a way through the gap to the Torian
Plains beyond. Already people fleeing these raids have
made their way across the Searil and some have even come
as far south as Torunn itself. The Merduk columns are sack-
ing what towns and villages they find as they go and we
have unconfirmed reports that they are constructing a fortress or a series of fortresses up there, to use as stageing
posts for—for further advances. There may in fact be an
entire Merduk army already operating in the north." Andruw sat down, obviously relieved to have got it out without a stumble.

"Bastards," someone murmured.

"Well, there is obviously nothing we can do about that
at the present," Colonel Rusio said impatiently. "We have
to concentrate our efforts here in the capital. The army
needs to be reorganised and refitted before it will be ready
for further operations."

"Agreed," Corfe said. "But we cannot afford to take too
long to do it. What we lack in numbers we must make up
in audacity. I do not propose to sit tamely in Torunn whilst
the Merduks ravage our country at will. They must be made
to pay for every foot of Torunnan ground they try to occupy."

"Hear, hear," one of the younger officers said, and subsided quickly when his seniors turned cold eyes upon him.

"So," Corfe said heavily, "what I propose is that we send

north a flying column of our own. My command suffered less severely than the main body of the army in the recent battle, plus I have just received an influx of new recruits. I intend to take it and clear northern Torunna of at least some of these raiders, then sweep back down towards the capital. It will be an intelligence-gathering operation as much as anything else. We need hard information on the enemy strength and dispositions in the north-west. Thus far we have been relying too heavily on the tales of refugees and couriers."

"I hope, General, that you are not impugning the professionalism of my officers," Count Fournier, head of Torunnan Military Intelligence, snapped.

"Not at all, Count. But they cannot work miracles, and besides, I still need most of them where they are—keeping an eye on the Merduk main body. A larger scale of operation is needed to clean up the north-west. My command will be able to brush aside most resistance up there and reassure the remaining population that we have not abandoned them. That has to be worth doing."

"A bold plan," Colonel Rusio drawled. "When do you intend to move, General? And who will be left in command here in the capital?"

"I shall ride out within the week. And you, Colonel, will be left in charge while I am away. The Queen has graciously approved my recommendation that you be promoted to general." Here, Corfe took up a sealed scroll which had been lying unobtrusively before him, and tossed it to the new general in question.

"Congratulations, Rusio."

Rusio's face was a picture of astonishment. "I have no words to express—that is to say . . . Your Majesty, you have my undying gratitude."

"Do not thank us," Odelia said crisply. "General Cear-Inaf has stated that you merit such a promotion and so we approved it. Make sure you fulfil our faith in you, General."

"Majesty, I—I will do all in my power to do so." Up and down the table, older officers such as Willem watched the exchange with narrowed eyes, and while several officers leaned over in their seats to shake Rusio's hand, others merely looked thoughtful.

"Your job, Rusio," Corfe went on, "is to get the main body of the army back in fighting trim. I expect to be away a month or so. By the time I get back I want it ready to march forth again."

Rusio merely nodded. He was clutching his commission as though he were afraid it might suddenly be wrenched away from him. His lifetime's ambition realised in a moment. The prospect seemed to have left him dazed.

"A month is not long to march an army up to the Thurians and back again, General," Count Fournier said. "It must be all of fifty leagues each way."

"Closer to seventy-five," Corfe retorted. "But we will not have to walk all the way. Colonel Passifal."

The Quartermaster General nodded. "There are a score of heavy grain lighters tied up at the wharves. Each of them could hold eight or nine hundred men with ease. With the wind coming off the sea, as it does for weeks at this time of year, they'll be able to make a fair pace upstream, despite the current. And they are equipped with heavy sweeps for when the wind fails. I have spoken to their crews: they usually make an average of four knots up the Torrin at this time of year. General Cear-Inaf's command could be up amongst the foothills in the space of five or six days."

"How very ingenious," Count Fournier murmured. "And if the Merduks assault us whilst the General and the cream of our army is off on his river outing? What then?"

Corfe stared at the thin, sharp-bearded nobleman, and smiled. "Then there will have been a failure of intelligence, my dear Count. Your agents keep sending back despatches insisting that the Merduks are even more disorganised than we are at present. Do you distrust the judgement of your own men?"

Fournier shrugged. "I raise hypotheses, that's all, General. In war one must prepare for the unexpected."

"I quite agree. I shall remain in close contact with what transpires here in the capital, never fear. If the enemy assaults Torunn in my absence, Rusio will hold them at bay before the walls and I will pitch into their rear as soon as

I can bring my command back south. Does that hypothesis satisfy you?"

Fournier inclined his head slightly but made no reply.

There were no further objections to Corfe's plan, but the meeting dragged on for another hour as the High Command wrestled with the logistic details of feeding a large army in a city already swollen with refugees. When at last they adjourned the Queen kept her seat and ordered Corfe to do likewise. The last of the remaining officers left and Odelia sat watching her young general with her chin resting on one palm whilst he rose and began pacing the spacious chamber helplessly.

"It was a good move," she told Corfe. "And it was necessary. You have taken the wind out of their sails."

"It was a political move," Corfe snarled. "I never thought I'd see the day I handed over an army to a man I distrust merely to gain his loyalty—loyalty which should be freely given, in a time like this."

"You never thought you'd see the day when you'd be in a position to hand out armies," she shot back. "At this level, Corfe, the politics of command are as important as any charge into battle. Rusio was a figurehead for the discontented. Now you have brought him into your camp, and defused their intrigues—for a while at least."

"Will he be that that grateful, then?"

"I know Rusio. He's been marking time in the Torunn garrison for twenty years. Today you handed him his heart's desire on a plate. If you fall, he will fall too—he knows that. And besides, he is not such a pitiful creature as you suppose. Yes, he will be grateful, and loyal too, I think."

"I just hope he has the ability."

"Who else is there? He's the best of a mediocre lot. Now rest your mind over it. The thing is done, and done well."

She rose with her skirts whispering around her, the tall lace ruff making her face into that of a doll—were it not for the magnificent green eyes which flashed therein. She took his arm, halted his restless pacing.

"You should rest more, let subordinates do some of the

running for a change. You are no longer an ensign, nor yet a colonel. And you are exhausted."

He stared at her out of sunken eyes. "I can't. I couldn't even if I wanted to."

She kissed him on the lips, and for a moment he yielded and bent into her embrace. But then the febrile restlessness took him again and he broke away.

"God's blood, Corfe!" she snapped, exasperated. "You can't save the world all by yourself!"

"I can try, by God."

They glared at one another with the tension crackling in the air between them, until both broke into smiles in the same instant. They had shared memories now, intimacies known only to each other. It made things both easier and harder.

"We are quite a team, you and I," the Queen said. "Given half a chance I think we might have conquered the world together."

"As it is I'll be happy if we can survive."

"Yes. Survival. Corfe, listen to me. Torunna is at the end of its strength—you know that as well as or better than I. The people have buried a king and crowned a queen in the same week—the first queen ever to rule alone in our history. We are swamped with the survivors of Aekir and a third of the realm lies under the boot of the invader whilst the capital itself is in the front line."

Corfe held her eyes, frowning. "So?"

She turned away and began pacing the room much as he had done, her hands clasped before her, rings flashing as her fingers twisted them.

"So hear me out and do not speak until I am finished.

"My son was a weak man, Corfe. Not a bad man, but weak. He did not have the necessary qualities to rule well—not many men do. This kingdom needs a strong hand. I have the ability—we both know it—to give Torunna that strong hand. But I am a woman, and so every step I take is uphill. The only reason I am tolerated on the throne is because there are no other alternatives present. The cream of Torunna's nobility died in the King's Battle around their monarch. In any case, Torunnans have never set as much store upon bloodlines as have the Hebrionese, say. But Count Fournier is quite capable of dreaming up some scheme to take power out of my hands and invest it in some form of committee."

Unable to help himself, Corfe interrupted. "That son of a bitch? He'd have to get through the entire army to do it."

Odelia smiled with genuine pleasure, but shook her head. "The army would have no say in the matter. But I am taking the long road to my destination. Corfe, Torunna needs a king—that is the long and the short of it.

"I want you to marry me and take the throne."

Thunderstruck, he sank down on to a chair. There was a long pause during which the Queen appeared increasingly irritated.

"Don't look at me as if I'd just grown an extra head! Think about it rationally!"

He found his voice at last. "That's ridiculous."

She clawed the air, eyes blazing furiously. "Open up your blasted mind, Corfe. Forget about your fears and prejudices. I know how humble your origins are, and I care not a whit. You have the ability to be a great king—more importantly, a great warleader. You could pull the country through this war—"

"I can't be a king. Great God, lady, I even feel uncomfortable in shoes!"

She threw back her head and laughed. "Then decree that everyone must wear boots or go barefoot! Put the petty rubbish out of your mind for a moment, and think about what you could accomplish."

"No—no. I am no diplomat. I could not negotiate treaties or—or dance angels on the head of a pin—"

"But you would have a wife who could." And here her voice was soft, her face grave as a mourner's. "I would be there, Corfe, to handle the court niceties and the damn protocol. And you—you would have the army wholly your own."

"No, I don't understand. We are already there, aren't we? I have the army, you have the throne. Why change things?"

She leaned close. "Because it could be that others will change them for us. You may have won over Rusio today, but you pushed the rest of them further into a corner. And that is when men are at their most dangerous. Corfe, there is no legal precedent in this kingdom for a queen to rule alone, and thus no legal basis."

"There is no law forbidding it, is there?" he asked stubbornly.

"I don't know—no one does for sure. I have clerks rifling through the court archives as we speak, hoping to turn something up. The death of the King has shocked all the office-seekers for the moment—they glimpsed the cliff upon which this kingdom teeters. But sooner or later the shock will wear off, and my position will be challenged. And if they manage to curb my powers even slightly, there is a good chance they will be able to take the army away from you."

"So there it is."

"So there it is. You see now the sense of what I am suggesting? As King you would be untouchable."

He jumped to his feet, stalked across the room with his mind in a maelstrom. Himself a king—absurd, utterly absurd. He would be a laughing-stock. Torunna would be the joke of the world. It was impossible. He reeled away from even the contemplation of it.

And marriage to this woman. Oddly, that disturbed him more than the idea of the crown. He turned and looked at her, to find that she was standing before the fire staring into the flames as though waiting for something. The firelight made her seem younger, though she was old enough to be Corfe's mother. That old.

"Would it be so terrible to be married to me?" she asked quietly, and the prescience of her question made Corfe start. She was a witch, after all. Could she read minds as well as everything else?

"Not so terrible," he lied.

"It would be a marriage of convenience," she said, her voice growing hard. "You would no longer have to come to my bed. I am beyond child-bearing age so there would be no question of an heir. I do not ask you for love, Corfe. That is a thing for the poets. We are talking about a route to power, nothing more." And she turned her back on him and leaned her hands on the mantel as a man might.

Again, that pain in his heart when he looked at her, and imagined the golden hair turned raven, the green eyes grey. Ah, Heria. Lord God, I miss you.

He did not want to hurt this formidable yet vulnerable woman. He did not love her—doubted if he would ever love her or any other woman again. And yet he liked her, very much. More than that, he respected her.

He strode over to the fireplace, stood behind the Queen and placed his hands on hers so that they were standing one within the other. She leaned back into his body and their fingers intertwined, the ornate rings on hers digging into his flesh. Pain, yes. But he did not mind. Nothing good came without pain in this life. He knew that.

"I would have you as a wife," he said, and in that moment he believed he meant it. "But the kingship is too lofty a prize for me. I am not the stuff of Royalty."

Odelia turned and embraced him, and when she drew back she looked strangely jubilant, as though she had won something.

"Time will tell," was all she said.

FIFTY leagues from where Corfe and his Queen stood the new winter camps of the Merduk army were almost complete. Tens of thousands of men were toiling here, as they had toiled ceaselessly in the days since the King's Battle. Their redeployment—it was not a withdrawal, or a retreat—entailed a massive labour. They had felled a fair-sized forest to raise a series of stockades which stretched for miles. They had dug ditches and set up thickets of abatis out to the west, all covered by dug-in batteries of artillery. They had erected tall watchtowers, created roads of corduroyed logs and set up their tents within the new defences. A veritable city had sprung up on the plains west of Ormann Dyke, the new roads leading to it thronged with troops coming and going, supply-waggons, artillery limbers, fast-moving couriers and trudging gangs of Torunnan slaves serving as forced labour. Farther east, nestled within yet more lines of field fortifications, a vast supply depot had been set up, and boxes, sacks and barrels of food and

ammunition were piled in lines half a mile long and twenty
feet high. Crates of blankets and spare uniforms and tents
were stacked to one side by the thousand. Waggons plied
the bumpy log roads between the depot and the camps con-
tinuously, keeping the front-line troops fed and clothed.
Perhaps ten square miles of the Torunnan countryside had
been thus transformed into the largest and most populous
armed camp in the world. Although Aurungzeb, Sultan of
Ostrabar, was commander-in-chief of this mighty host, it
now included large contingents from the sultanates of Nalbeni, Ibnir and Kashdan. The Merduk states had set aside
their differences and were finally combining to settle the
issue with the Ramusians once and for all. They aimed now
at nothing less than the conquest of all Normannia as far
as the Malvennors, and had decided to stop there only because of the dread name of Fimbria.

Aurungzeb himself and his household were not in the winter camps, but had relocated to Ormann Dyke in order to pass
the cold weeks of waiting more comfortably. Ostrabar's Sultan stood this day on the tower from which Martellus the
Lion had once watched the Merduk assaults break upon the
dyke's impregnable defences, and silken Merduk banners
now flew above the Long Walls that Kaile Ormann had
reared up centuries before.

"Shahr Johor," Aurungzeb boomed.

One of the gaggle of soldiers and courtiers who hovered
nearby stepped forward. "My Sultan?"

"Do you know how many of our men died trying to take
this fortress?"

"No Highness, but I can find out—"

"It was a question, not an order. Almost thirty thousand,
Shahr Johor. And in the end we never took it, we only
outflanked it, and forced its evacuation. It is the greatest
fortress in the world, it is said. And you know what?"

Shahr Johor swallowed, seeing the flush creep into his
sultan's swarthy cheeks. "What, Highness?"

But the explosion did not happen. Instead, Aurungzeb
spoke in a low, reasonable tone. "It is utterly useless to us."

"Yes, Highness."

"The Fimbrians, curse their names, constructed it that

way. Approaching it from the east, it is unconquerable. But if by some chance you happen to capture it intact, then it is worthless. All the defences face east. From the west, it is indefensible. Very clever, those Fimbrian engineers must have been."

The courtiers and soldiers waited, wondering if this strange calm were the herald of an unprecedented rage. But when Aurungzeb turned to face them he looked thoughtful.

"I want this fortress destroyed."

Shahr Indun Johor blinked. "Highness?"

"Are you deaf? Level it. I want the dyke filled in, I want the walls cast down and the tower broken. I want Ormann Dyke wiped off the face of the earth. And then, using the same stones, you shall create another fortress, on the *east* bank of the river, facing west. If by some freakish chance the Ramusians ever manage to push back our armies, then we shall halt them here, on the Searil. And we shall bleed them white as they did us. And Aekir, my new capital, it shall be safe. Golden Aurungabar, greatest city of the world. See to it, Shahr Johor. Gather together our engineers. I want a set of plans drawn up for me to see by tonight. And a modell. Yes, a scale modell of how it will look, Ormann Dyke obliterated and this new fortress in its place. I must think of a name . . ."

Shahr Johor bowed, unnoticed, and left the summit of the tower to do his master's bidding. The courtiers who remained looked at one another. Never before had they heard their master speak of anything save advances and victories, and now here he was planning for defeat. What had happened?"

A flabby, glabrous palace eunuch piped up, "My Sultan, do you truly believe that the accursed Unbelievers could ever push our glorious armies back to the Searil? Surely, they are in their death throes. We shall soon be feasting in the palace of Torunn."

Aurungzeb stared moodily out at the ancient fortress below him. "I wish I had your optimism, Serrim. This general of the red horsemen. My spies tell me that he is now commander-in-chief of all the Torunnan forces. He and his

damned scarlet cavalry have saved the Torunnans from destruction twice now."

"Who is this man, lord? Do we know? Perhaps our
agents—"

Aurungzeb snorted with mirth. "He is, by all accounts,
a hard man to kill."

Then his mood soured again. "Leave me, all of you.
No—Ahara, you will remain." He broke into halting Normannic. "Ramusian, you stay here also." And in Merduk
again: "The rest of you, get out of my sight."

The tower cleared of people, leaving two figures behind.
One was a small man in a black habit whose wrists were
bound with silver chains. The other was a slim, silk-clad
woman whose face was hidden behind a jewelled veil. Aurungzeb beckoned the woman over, the thunder on his brow
lifting a little. He twitched aside her veil and caressed a
pale cheek.

"Heart of my heart," he murmured. "How does it go with
you and my son?"

Heria stroked her abdomen. The bulge was visible now.
"We are well, my lord. Batak has used his arts to examine
the child. It is a healthy boy. In five months, he shall be
born." She spoke in the Merduk tongue.

Aurungzeb beamed, encircled Heria's shoulders with one
massive arm and sighed with contentment.

"How I love to hear you use our speech. It must become
your own. The lessons will continue—that tutor has earned
his pay." He lowered his voice. "I shall make you my
queen, Ahara. You are a follower of the Prophet now, and
you shall be the mother of a sultan one day. My heir cannot
have a mere concubine for a dam. Would you like that?
Would you like to be a Merduk queen?" And here Aurungzeb set his huge hands on her shoulders and scrutinized
her face.

Heria met his eyes. "This is my world, now. You are my
lord, the father of my child. There is nothing else. I will
be a queen if you wish it. I am yours to do with as you
will."

Aurungzeb smiled slowly. "You speak the truth. But you
are no slave to me, not any more. A wife you shall be as

well as a queen. We will live in Aurungabar, and our union shall be a symbol." Here the Sultan turned and raised his voice so that the black-garbed man behind them might hear.

"The meeting of two peoples, priest. Would you like that? This way the Ramusians who remain east of the Torrin will see that I am not the monster they—and you—believe me to be."

Albrec shuffled forward, more chains clinking invisibly under his habit. "I think it is a worthy idea. I never thought you were a monster, Sultan. I know that you are not. In the end, a truly great ruler does what is best for his people, not what pleases himself. You are beginning to realise that."

Aurungzeb seemed taken aback by the priest's bluntness. He forced a laugh. "Beard of the Prophet, you are a fearless little madman, I'll give you that. You and your people have courage. Shahr Baraz always told me so. I thought him a sentimental old fool, but I see now he was right."

Heria regarded Aurungzeb with some wonder. She had never before heard him speak of Ramusians with anything resembling moderation. Were the court rumours true then? Was Aurungzeb tiring of war?

He caught her glance, and stepped away towards the parapet.

There was a pause. Finally Heria mustered the resolve to speak.

"My lord, do you really believe this new general of the Ramusians is so dangerous?"

"Dangerous? His army is a broken rabble, his country is led by a woman. Dangerous!" But the words rang hollow somehow.

"Come here, Ahara. Beside me."

She joined him. Albrec stood forgotten behind them.

Together they could look down from the dizzying height of the tower to the battered walls of the fortress and the River Searil beyond, crossed by the new wooden bridges that the engineers had been working on for weeks. On the far side of the river was the great desolation of craters and rubble that had once been the eastern barbican of the fortress. The Ramusian garrison had packed it with gunpowder and destroyed it just as it fell into the hands of the Merduks.

"Look up on the hills to the east, Ahara. What do you see there?"

"Waggons, my lord, dozens of them. And hundreds of men digging."

"They are digging a mass grave to hold our dead." Aurungzeb's face seemed to slump. "Every time we fight the Torunnans, another must be dug."

"Can it go on much longer, lord? So much killing."

He did not reply at once. He seemed tyred—exhausted even. "Ask the holy madman behind you. He has all the answers it seems."

Albrec clinked forward until he too stood on the lip of the parapet. "All wars end," he said quietly. "But it takes more courage to bring them to a close than it does to start them."

"Platitudes," Aurungzeb said disgustedly.

"Your Prophet, Sultan, did not believe in war. He counselled all men to live as brothers."

"As did your Saint," Aurungzeb countered.

"True. They had much in common, the Prophet and the Saint."

"Listen, priest—" the Sultan began heatedly, but just then there was a clatter of boots on the stairway and a soldier appeared on the parapet, panting. He fell to his knees as Aurungzeb glared.

"Highness, forgive me, but despatches have arrived from our forces in the north. Shahr Johor said you were to be informed immediately. Our men have reached the Torrin Gap, Highness. The way to Charibon is open!"

The trouble on Aurungzeb's brow evapourated. "I'll come at once."

And as the soldier leapt up, he followed him off the tower without a backwards glance, his stride as energetic as that of a boy. Heria and Albrec were left behind.

"You are from Aekir?" the little priest asked her at once.

"I was married to a soldier of the garrison, and captured in the sack of the city."

"I am sorry. I thought—I am not sure what I thought."

"Why did you come here, Father—to the Merduks?"

"I had a message I wished them to hear."

"They don't seem to be listening."

Albrec shrugged. "Oh, I don't know. I feel the tide is turning. I think he is beginning to listen, or at least to doubt, Ahara."

"My name is Heria Cear-Inaf. I am still Ramusian, no matter who they make me pray to."

"Cear-Inaf." Albrec knew that name. Somewhere he had heard it before. Where?

"What is it?"

"Nothing. No, nothing." It was somehow important he remember but, as was the way with these things, the more he thought about it the farther it receded.

"The other sultanates are tiring of the war," Heria said quickly. "Especially Nalbeni. They lost ten thousand men in the last battle, and there are rumours that their fleet is being beaten in the Kardian by Torunnan ships. The army is going hungry because its supply lines are overstretched, and the levy, the *Minhraib*, they are discontented and want to get back to their farms. If the Torunnans could win one more battle, I think Aurungzeb would sue for peace."

"Why are you telling me this, Heria?"

She looked around as if they might be overheard. "There is not much time. The eunuchs will come for me soon. He has forgotten about us for a moment, but not for long. You must escape back to Torunn, Father. You have to let them know these things. That new general there—they're all afraid of what he might do next, but it must be quick, whatever it is. He must hit them before they recover their nerve."

Albrec felt a chill about his heart. He remembered meeting the leader of a long column of scarlet-armoured horsemen marching out of Torunn, his eyes as grey as those of the woman who now stood before him.

Who are you?

Corfe Cear-Inaf, Colonel in the Torunnan army.

"Sweet blood of the Saint," Albrec breathed, his face gone white as paper.

"What is it?" Heria demanded. "What's wrong?"

"Lady, you are to come down to the harem at once," a high voice said. They spun around to see the eunuch, Serrim, flanked by a pair of soldiers. "And that Ramusian—he is to go back to his cell."

Heria replaced her veil, her eyes meeting Albrec's in one last, earnest appeal. Then she bowed her head and followed the eunuch away obediently. The Merduk soldiers seized the little priest and shoved him roughly towards the stairs, but he was hardly aware of them.

Coincidence of course, it had to be. But it was not a common name. And more than that, the look in the eyes of them both. That awful despair.

Lord God, he thought. Could it be so? The pity of it.

SEVEN

THE riverfront of Torunn was packed with crowds to see them off, so much so that General Rusio had deemed it necessary to station five tercios of troops there to keep the people back from the gangplanks. The last of the horses had been led blindfolded aboard the boats and the great hatches in the sides of the vessels closed, then re-pitched and caulked while they wallowed at the quays. Corfe, Andruw and Formio stood now alone on the quayside whilst the caulkers climbed back down the tumblehome of the transports and the watermen began the heavy business of unmooring.

General Rusio stepped forward out of the knot of senior officers who had come to see Corfe off. He held out a hand. "Good luck to you then, sir." His face was set, as if he expected to be insulted in some way. But Corfe merely shook the proffered hand warmly. "Look after this place while I'm away, Rusio," he said. "And keep me informed.

You have the details of our march, but we may have to cut corners here and there. Multiple couriers."

"Yes, sir. I'll send the first out in three days, as arranged."

"Lords and ladies," a thick-necked waterman called out, "if'n you don't want to swim upriver you'd best climb aboard." And he spat into the river for emphasis.

Corfe waved a hand at him, and turned back to Rusio. "Keep the patrols out," he said. "By the time I get back I want to know where every Merduk regiment has so much as dug a latrine."

"I won't let you down, General," Rusio said soberly.

"No, I don't believe you will. All right. Andruw, Formio, you heard the man. Time to join the navy."

The trio hauled themselves up one of the high-sided vessels with the help of manropes that had been installed especially for landsmen. They climbed over the bulwark and stood breathing heavily on the deck of the freighter which Corfe jokingly referred to as his flagship.

"All aboard?" the captain roared out from the little poop at the stern of the vessel.

"Aye, sir!"

"Cast off fore and aft. Set topsails and outer jib. Helmsman, two points to larboard as soon as she's under weigh."

"Two points. Aye sir."

A great booming, flapping shadow as the topsails were loosed by the men on the yards high above. The offshore breeze took the sails and bellied them out. The freighter accelerated palpably under Corfe's feet and began to score a white wake through the water. All around them, the other vessels in the convoy were making sail also, and they made a brave sight as they took to the middle of the wide river. The Torrin was almost half a mile in width here at the capital, crossed by two ancient stone bridges whose middle spans were ramps of wood which could be raised by windlass for the passage of ships. They were approaching the first one now, the Minantyr Bridge. As Corfe watched with something approaching wonder, the wooden spans creaked into motion and began rising in the air. Gangs of bridge-raisers were kept permanently employed and worked in shifts day and night to ensure the smooth passage of trade up and down the Torrin. Corfe had always known this, but he had never before been part of it, and as the heavy freighter moved into the shadow of the looming Minantyr Bridge he gawped about him, for all the world like a country peasant come to see the sights of the city for a day.

They passed through the gurgling, dripping gloom under the raised bridge and emerged into pale winter sunlight again. Their captain, a tall, thin man who nevertheless had a voice of brass, yelled out at his crew: "Unfurl the spanker—look sharp now. Ben Phrenias, I see you. Get up on that goddamned yard."

Andruw and Formio were staring around with something of Corfe's wonder. Neither had ever set foot on a boat before and they had thought that the transports which were to take them upriver would be glorified barges. But the grain freighters, though of shallow draught, displaced over a thousand tons each. They were square-rigged, with a sail plan similar to that of a brigantine, and seemed to the landsmen to be great ocean-going ships. They had a crew of two dozen or so though their own captain, Mirio, confessed that they were short-handed. Some of his men had jumped ship and refused to take their vessel north into what was widely seen as enemy-held territory. As it was, the ship-owners had been well-paid out of the shrinking Torunnan treasury, and some of the soldiers who constituted the cargo of the sixteen craft Corfe had hired would be able to haul on a rope as well as any waterman.

Inside these sixteen large vessels were some eight thousand men and two thousand horses and mules. Corfe was bringing north all his Cathedrallers—some fifteen hundred, with the recent reinforcements—plus Formio's Fimbrians and the dyke veterans who had served under him at the King's Battle. It was, he gauged, a force formidable enough to cope with any enemy formation except the main body of the Merduk army itself. He intended to alight from the freighters far up the Torrin, and then thunder back down to the capital slaughtering every Merduk he chanced across and delivering north-western Torunna from the invaders— for a while, at least. Awful stories had been trickling south

to Torunn in the past few days, tales of rape and mass
executions. These things were part and parcel of every war,
but there was a grim pattern to the reports: the Merduks
seemed intent on depopulating the entire region. It was an
important area strategically also, in that it bordered on the
Torrin Gap, the gateway to Normannia west of the Cimbrics. The enemy could not be allowed to force the passage
of the gap with impunity.

And the last reason for the expedition. Corfe had to get
out of Torunn, away from the court and the High Command, or he thought he would go quietly insane.

Marsch appeared out of one of the wide hatches in the
deck of the freighter. He looked careworn and uneasy. It
had taken some cajoling to get the tribesmen aboard the
ships: such a means of transport was entirely inimical to
them, and they feared for the welfare of their horses. Those
who remained out of Corfe's original five hundred had been
galley slaves, and they associated ships with their degradation. The others had never before set eyes on anything
afloat which was larger than a rowboat, and the cavernous
holds they were now incarcerated within amazed and unsettled them.

Corfe could see that the big tribesman was averting his
eyes from the riverbank that coursed smoothly past on the
starboard side of the vessel. He gave an impression of deep
distaste for everything maritime, yet he had greeted the
news of their waterborne expedition without a murmur.

"The horses are calming down," he said as he approached
his commander. "It stinks down there." His face was
haunted, as if the smell brought back old memories of being
chained to an oar with the lash scoring his back.

"It won't be for long," Corfe assured him. "Four or five
days at most."

"Bad grazing up north," Marsch continued. "I am hoping
we have enough forage with us. Mules carry it, but eat it
too."

"Cheer up, Marsch," Andruw said, as irrepressible as
ever. "It's better than kicking our heels back in the city.
And I for one would rather sit here like a lord and watch

the world drift past than slog it up through the hills to the north."

Marsch did not look convinced. "We'll need one, two days to get the horses back into condition when they leave the"—his lips curled around the word—"the *boats*."

"Don't let Mirio hear you calling his beloved *Seahorse* a boat." Andruw laughed. "He's liable to turn us all ashore. These sailors—your pardon, these *watermen*—are a trifle touchy about their charges, like an old man with a young wife."

That brought a grin to all their faces. Corfe detached himself from the banter and made his way aft to where Mirio was standing taking a stint at the helm. The river-captain nodded unsmilingly at him. "We're making three knots, General. Not as fast as I would have hoped, but we'll get you there."

"Thank you, Captain. You mustn't mind my men. They're new to the river, and to ships."

"Aye, well I'll not pretend that I wouldn't prefer to be shipping a hold full of grain instead of a bunch of seasick soldiers and screaming horses, but we must take what comes I suppose. There, we're past the last of the river-batteries and the Royal naval yards."

Corfe looked out towards the eastern bank. The shore—the river was big enough to warrant that name for its banks—was some to two cables away. The walls of Torunn came right down to the riverside here, protected by a series of squat towers which hid countless heavy cannon. Jutting out into the Torrin itself were dozens of jetties and wharves, most of them empty but a few busy with men unloading the small riverboats that plied back and forth across the river here. And sliding behind them now he could glimpse the Royal naval yards of Torunna. Two great ships, tall, ocean-going carracks, were in dry-dock there, their sides propped up by heavy beams, and hundreds of men swarmed over them in a confusion of wood and rope.

"How far is it to the sea?" Corfe asked, peering aft over the taffrail. Behind the *Seahorse* the remainder of the expedition's vessels were in line astern, the foam flying from their bows as they fought upstream against the current.

"Some five leagues," Mirio told him. "In times of storm the Torrin is brackish here, and sometimes ships are blown clear up the estuary from the Kardian."

"So close? I had no idea." Corfe had always thought of Torunn as a city divided by a river. Now he realised that it was a port on the fringe of a sea. That was something to remember. He must talk to Berza when the admiral returned to Torunn with the fleet. If the Merduks could transport armies by sea, then so could he.

THE wind freshened through the day, and Mirio was able to report with visible satisfaction that they were making five knots. The capital had long disappeared, and the transports were moving through the heavily populated country which lay to its west. Farmers here reared cattle, planted crops and fished from the river in equal measure. But while the southern shore seemed prosperous and untouched by war, many houses and hamlets to the north were obviously deserted. Corfe saw livestock running wild, barn doors yawning emptily, and in a few places the blackened shells of burnt villages off on the horizon.

The freighters always moored for the night, for the risk of running into a sandbank in the dark was too great. Their practise was to moor the bows to stout trees onshore and drop a light anchor from the stern to keep the vessel from being swept into the bank by the current. The men could not be disembarked en masse, but on Marsch's insistence Corfe saw to it that a few of the horses and mules were brought ashore in shifts all night and exercised up and down the riverbank. It was also an effective way of posting mobile sentries, and the duty was popular with the men who found their squalid quarters in the depths of the freighters less than congenial.

FOUR days went by. The Torrin arced in a curve until it began to flow almost directly north to south, and then it turned north-west towards its headwaters in the Thurian Mountains. They could see the Thurians on the northern horizon, still blanketed by snow. And to their left, or to larboard, the stern white peaks of the Cimbrics reared up, their heads lost in grey cloud. There were no more farms on the riverbank; this region had been sparsely settled even before the war. Now it seemed utterly deserted, a wilderness hemmed in by frowning mountains and bisected by the surging course of the young river.

The Torrin was barely two cables wide here, and occasionally during the fourth day they had felt the keel of the heavily laden freighter scrape on sunken sandbanks. In addition, the current had become stronger and they averaged barely two knots. On the morning of the fifth day Corfe finally decided to leave the ships behind, to the obvious relief of both soldiers and watermen, and the sixteen huge craft spent an anxious morning edging and nudging their way to the eastern bank before dropping every anchor they possessed in order to hold fast against the efforts of the river to shove them downstream.

What followed was a prolonged nightmare of mud and water and thrashing, cursing men and panicky animals. Each of the freighters possessed floating jetties which could be winched over the side to provide a fairly stable pathway to the shore, but they had not been designed for the offloading of two thousand horses and mules. The animals were hoisted out of the holds by tackles to the yardarms and set down wild-eyed and struggling upon the pitching jetties, with predictable results. By the time the last mule and man was ashore, and the army's supplies were piled in long rows on dry land, it was far into the night. Two men had drowned and six horses had been lost, but Corfe counted himself lucky not to have lost more. The eastern bank was a sucking quagmire of mud and horse-shit for almost a mile, and the troops were hollow-eyed ghosts which staggered with weariness. But they were ashore and essentially intact, having covered over eighty leagues in five days.

THE last of the horses had been settled down for the night and the army's campfires were scattered about the dark earth like some poor counterfeit of the stars overhead. The ground was hard as stone here, a mile from the riverbank, which would make for easy marching, but the cold was difficult to keep at bay with a single blanket, even with

one's feet in the very embers of the fire. Strangely, Corfe
felt less tyred than at any time since the King's Battle, for
all that he had snatched barely four hours' sleep a night on
the voyage upriver. It was the freedom of being out in the
field with his own command. No more conferences or councils or scribbling scribes, just a host of exhausted, chilled
men and animals encamped in the frozen wilds of the north.

The men had meshed together well. They had fought
shoulder to shoulder in the King's Battle, guzzled beer together in the taverns of Torunn and endured the unpleas-
antness of the river journey north. Now they were a single
entity. Cimbric tribesmen, Fimbrian pikemen, Torunnan arquebusiers. There were still rivallries, of course, but they
were healthy ones. Corfe sat by the campfire and watched
them sleep uncomplainingly upon the hard earth, their
threadbare uniforms sodden with mud—and realised that
he loved them all.

Andruw picked his way through the fires towards him,
then dug into his saddlebags. He handed his general a
wooden flask.

"Have a snort, Corfe. It'll keep the cold out. Compliments of Captain Mirio."

Corfe unstoppered the neck and had a good swallow. The
stuff seemed to burn his mouth, and blazed a fiery path all
the way down his gullet. His eyes watered and he found
himself gasping for air.

"I swear, Andruw, you'll go blind one of these days."

"Not me. I've the constitution of a horse."

"And about as much sense. What about the powder?"

Andruw looked back across the camp. "We lost six barrels, and another eight are wet through. God knows when
we'll have a chance to dry them."

"Damn. That eats into our reserves. Well, we've enough
to fight a couple of good-sized engagements, but I want
Ranafast's men made aware that they can't go firing it off
like it's free."

"No problem."

Two more figures came picking their way out of the
flickering dark towards them. When they drew closer Corfe
saw that it was the unlikely duo of Marsch and Formio.

Formio looked as slight as an adolescent beside the bulk of the towering tribesman, his once dapper sable uniform now a harlequin chequer of mud. Marsch was clad in a greasy leather gambeson. He looked happier than he had for days.

"What is this, a meeting of the High Command?" Andruw asked derisively. "Here you two—have some of this. Privileges of rank."

Formio and Marsch winced over the rough grain liquor much as Corfe had done.

"Well, gentlemen?" their commanding officer asked.

"We found those stores that were lost overboard," Formio said, wiping his mouth. "They had come up against a sandbank two miles downstream."

"Good, we need all the match we can get. Marsch?"

The big tribesman threw the wooden flask back to Andruw. "Our horses are in a better way than I thought, but we need two days to"—he hesitated, groping for the word—"to restore them. Some would not eat on the boats and are weak."

Corfe nodded. "Very well. Two days, but no more. Marsch, in the morning I want you and Morin to saddle up a squadron of the fittest horses and begin a reconnaissance of the area, out to five miles. If you are seen by a small body of the enemy, hunt them down. If you find a large formation, get straight back here. Clear?"

Marsch's face lifted in a rare smile. "Very clear. It shall be so."

Andruw was still gulping out of Mirio's flask. He sat, or rather half fell, on his saddle and stared owlishly into the campfire, leaning one elbow on the pommel.

"Are you all right?" Corfe asked him.

"In the pink." His gaiety had disappeared. "Tyred though. Lord, how those boats did stink! I'm glad I'm a cavalryman and not a sailor."

Marsch and Corfe reclined by the fire also. "Makes a good pillow, a war saddle does," Andruw told them, giving his own a thump. "Not so good as a woman's breast though."

"I thought you were an artilleryman, not a horse-soldier,"

Corfe baited him. "Forgetting your roots, Andruw?"

"Me? Never. I'm just on extended loan. Sit down, Formio, for God's sake. You stand there like a graven image. Don't Fimbrians get tyred?"

The young Fimbrian officer raised an eye-brow and then did as he was bidden. He shook his head when Andruw offered the wooden flask to him once again. Andruw shrugged and took another swig. Marsch, Formio and Corfe exchanged glances.

"Do you remember the early days at the dyke, Corfe? When they came roaring down from the hills and my guns boomed out, battery after battery? What a sight! What happened to those gunners of mine, I wonder? They were good men. I suppose their bones lie up around the ruins of the dyke now, in the wreckage of the guns."

Corfe stared into the fire. The artillerymen of Ormann Dyke, Ranafast had told them, had been part of the thousand-man rearguard which had covered Martellus's evacuation of the fortress. None of them had escaped.

A curlew called out, spearing through the night as though lost in the dark. They heard a horse neighing off along the Cathedraller lines, but apart from that the only sounds were the wind in the grass and the crackling of the campfires. Corfe thought of his own men, the ones he had commanded in Aekir. They were a long time dead now. He found it hard to even remember their faces. There had been so many other faces under his command since then.

"Soldiers die—that is what they do," Formio said unexpectedly. "They do not expect to fall, and so they keep going. But in the end that is what happens. Men who have no hope of life, they either cease to fight or they fight like heroes. No-one knows why; it is the way of things."

"A Fimbrian philosopher," Andruw said, but smiled to take some of the mockery out of his words. Then his face grew sombre again. "I was born up here, in the north. This is the country of my family, has been for generations. I had a sister, Vanya, and a little brother. God alone knows where they are now. Dead, or in some Merduk labour camp I expect." He tilted up the bottle again, found it was empty, and tossed it into the fire. "I wonder sometimes, Corfe, if at the end of this there will be anything left of our world worth saving."

Corfe set a hand on his shoulder, his eyes burning. "I'm sorry, Andruw."

Andruw laughed, a strangled travesty of mirth. His eyes were bright and glittering in the flame-light. "All these little tragedies. No matter. I hadn't seen them in years. The life of a soldier, you know? But now that we are up here, I can't help wondering about them." He turned to the Fimbrian who sat silently beside him. "You see, Formio, soldiers are people too. We are all someone's son, even you Fimbrians."

"Even we Fimbrians? I am relieved to hear it."

Formio's mild rejoinder made them laugh. Andruw clapped the sable-clad officer on the back. "I thought you were all a bunch of warrior monks who dine on gunpowder and shit bullets. Have you family back in the electorates, Formio?"

"I have a mother, and a—a girl."

"A girl! A female Fimbrian—just think of that. I reckon I'd wear my sword to bed. What's she like, Formio? You're amongst friends now, be honest."

The black-clad officer hung his head, clearly embarrassed. "Her name is Merian." He hesitated, then reached into the breast of his tunic and pulled out a small wooden slat which split in two, like a slim book.

"This is what she looks like."

They crowded around to look, like schoolboys. Formio held an exquisite miniature, a tiny painting of a blonde-haired girl whose features were delicate as a deer's. Large, dark eyes and a high forehead. Andruw whistled appreciatively.

"Formio, you are a lucky dog."

The Fimbrian tucked the miniature away again. "We are to be married as soon—as soon as I get back."

None of them said anything. Corfe realised in that moment that none of them expected to survive. The knowledge should have shocked him, but it did not. Formio had been right in what he said about soldiers.

Andruw rose unsteadily to his feet. "Gentlemen, you

must excuse me. I do believe I'm going to spew."

He staggered, and Corfe and Marsch jumped up, grasped his arms and propelled him into the shadows, where he bent double and retched noisily. Finally he straightened, eyes streaming. "Must be getting old," he croaked.

"You?" Corfe said. "You'll never be old, Andruw." And an instant later he wished he had never said such an unlucky thing.

EIGHT

GOLOPHIN wiped the sweat from his face with an already damp cloth and got up from the workbench with
a groan. He padded over to the window and threw open the
heavy shutters to let the quicksilver radiance of a moonlit
night pour into the tower chamber. From the height
whereon he stood he could see the whole dark immensity
of south-western Hebrion below, asleep under the stars. The
amber glow of Abrusio lit up the horizon, the moon shining
liquid and brilliant upon the waves of the Great Western
Ocean out to the very brim of the world beyond. He sniffed
the air like an old hound, and closed his eyes. The night
had changed. A warmer breeze always came in off the sea
at this time of the year, like a promise of spring. At long
last, this winter was ending. At one time he had thought it
never would.

But Abeleyn was King again, Jemilla had been foiled,
and Hebrion was, finally, at peace. Time perhaps to begin
wondering about the fate of the rest of the world. A caravel

from Candelaria had put into Abrusio only the day before with a cargo of wine and cinnamon, and it had brought with it news of the eastern war. The Torunnan King had been slain before the very gates of his capital, it was said, and the Merduks were advancing through the Torrin Gap. Young Lofantyr dead, Golophin thought. He had hardly even begun to be a king. His mother would take the throne, but that might create more problems than it solved. Golophin did not give much for Torunna's chances, with a woman on the throne—albeit a capable one—the Merduks to one side and the Himerians to the other.

Closer to home, the Himerian Church was fast consolidating its hold over a vast swathe of the continent. That polite ninny, Cadamost, had invited Church forces into Perigraine with no thought as to how he might ever get them out again. What would the world look like in another five years? Perhaps he was getting too old to care.

He stretched and returned to the workbench. Upon it a series of large glass demi-johns with wide necks sat shining in the light of a single candle. They were all full of liquid, and in one a dark shape quivered and occasionally tapped on the glass which imprisoned it. Golophin laid a hand on the side of the jar. "Soon, little one, soon," he crooned. And the dark shape settled down again.

"Another familiar?" a voice asked from the window. Golophin did not turn round.

"Yes."

"You Old World wizards, you depend on them too much. I think sometimes you hatch them out for companionship as much as anything else."

"Perhaps. They have definite uses, though, for those of us who are not quite so . . . adept, as you."

"You underestimate yourself, Golophin. There are other ways of extending the Dweomer."

"But I do not wish to use them." Golophin turned around at last. Standing silver in the moonlight by the window was a huge animal, an eldritch wolf which stood on its hind legs, its neck as thick as that of a bull. Two yellow lights blinked above its muzzle.

"Why this form? Are you trying to impress me?"

The wolf laughed, and in the space of a heartbeat there was a man standing in its place, a tall, hawk-faced man in archaic robes.

"Is this better?"

"Much."

"I commend you on your coolness, Golophin. You do not even seem taken aback. Are you not at least a little curious about who I am and what I am doing here?"

"I am curious about many things. I do not believe you come from anywhere in the world I know. Your powers are . . . impressive, to say the least. I assume you are here to enlighten me in some fashion. If you were going to kill me or enslave me you could have done so by now, but instead you restored my powers. And thus I await your explanations."

"Well said! You are a man after my own heart." The strange shape-shifter walked across the chamber to the fireplace where he stood warming his hands. He looked around at the hundreds of books which lined the circular walls of the room, noted one, and took it down to leaf through.

"This is an old one. No doubt much of it is discredited now. But when I wrote it I thought the ideas would last for ever. Man's foolish pride, eh?" He tossed the aged volume over to Golophin. *The Elements of Gramarye* by Aruan of Garmidalan. It was hand-written and illuminated, because it had been composed and copied in the second century.

"You can touch things. You are not a simulacrum," Golophin said steadily, quelling the sudden tremble in his hands.

"Yes. Translocation, I call it. I can cross the world, Golophin, in the blink of an eye. I am thinking of announcing it as a new Discipline. It is a wearying business, though. Do you happen to have any wine?"

"I have Fimbrian brandy."

"Even better."

Golophin set down the book. There was an engraving of its author on the cover. The same man—Lord above, it was the same man! But he would have to be at least four centuries old.

"I think I also need a drink," he said as he poured out

two generous measures of the fragrant spirit from the decanter he kept filled by the fire. He handed one to his guest and Aruan—if it truly could be he—nodded appreciatively, swirled the liquid around in the wide-necked glass and sipped it with gusto.

"My thanks, brother mage."

"You would seem to have discovered something even more startling than this *translocation* of yours. The secret of eternal youth, no less."

"Not quite, but I am close."

"You are from the uttermost west, the place Bardolin disappeared to. Aren't you?"

"Ah, your friend Bardolin! Now there is a true talent. Golophin, he does not even begin to appreciate the potential he harbours. But I am educating him. When you see him again—and you will soon—you may be in for a surprise. And to answer your question: yes, I come from the west."

Golophin needed the warmth of the kindly spirit in his throat. He gulped it down as though it were beer.

"Why did you restore my powers, Aruan? If that is who you are."

"You were a fellow mage in need. Why not? I must apologise for the . . . abrupt nature of the restoration. I trust you did not find it too wearing."

It had been the most agonising experience Golophin had ever known, but he said nothing. He was afraid. The Dweomer stank in this man, like some pungent meat left to rot in a tropical clime. The potency he sensed before him was an almost physical sensation. He had never dreamt anyone could be so powerful. And so he was afraid—but absolutely fascinated too. He had so many questions he did not know where to begin.

"Why are you here?" he asked at last.

"A good idea. Start out with the most obvious one. Let us just say that I am on a grand tour of the continent, catching up on things. I have so much to see, and so little time! But also, I have always had a liking for Hebrion. Do you know, Golophin, that there are more of the Dweomer-folk here in this kingdom than in any other? Less, since the purges orchestrated by the Mother Church, of course, but still an impressive number. Torunna is almost wholly deserted by our people now, Almark never had many to begin with—too close to Charibon. And in Fimbria there was some kind of mind-set which seemed to militate against our folk from the earliest times. One could hypothesize endlessly on the whys and wherefores, but I have come to believe that there is something in the very bones of the earth which causes Dweomer-folk to be born, an anomaly which is more common in some locations than others. Were your parents mages?"

"No. My father was an official in the Merchants' Guild."

"There—you see? It is not heredity. There is some other factor at work. We are freaks of nature, Golophin, and have been persecuted as such for all of recorded history. But that will change."

"What of Bardolin? What have you done with him?"

"As I said, I have begun to unlock his powers. It is a painful procedure—such things have never been easy—but in the end he will thank me for it."

"So he is still alive, somewhere out in the west. Are the myths true then? There is actually a Western Continent?"

"The myths are true. I had a hand in creating some of them. Golophin, in the west we have an entire world of our own, a society founded on the Dweomer. There is something back there in the very air we breathe—"

"There are more of you then?"

"I am the only one of the original founders who survived thus far. But there are others who came later. We are few, growing fewer. That is why I have returned to the Old World. We need new blood, new ideas. And we intend to bring with us a few ideas of our own."

"Bring with you? So you mages from the west are intent upon returning to Normannia!"

"One day, yes. That is our hope. My work at present is the preparation of the world for our coming. You see now why I am here? We will need friendly voices raised on our behalf in every kingdom, else our arrivall might result in panic, even violence. All we wish, brother mage, is to come home."

A sudden thought shook Golophin. "One moment—the wolf image. That was a simulacrum, yes?"

Aruan grinned. "I wondered when that question would come up. No, it was not. I am a shifter, a sufferer of the black disease, though I no longer see it as an affliction."

"That is impossible. A mage cannot also be a lycan-thrope."

"Bardolin thought so also. He knows better now. I am a master of all Seven Disciplines, and I am busy creating more. What I am here tonight to ask, Golophin, is whether you will join us."

"Join you? I'm not sure I understand."

"I think you do. Soon I will no longer be a furtive night visitor, but a power in the world. I want you to be my colleague. I can raise you very high, Golophin. You would no longer be the servant of a king, but a veritable king yourself."

"Some might think your ambitions a little too wide-ranging. How are you going to manage this?"

"Time will tell. But it is going to happen. The lines are being drawn all over the continent, though not many are aware of them yet. Will you join us, Golophin? I would consider it an honour to have a man such as you in our camp. Not merely a powerful mage, but a keen mind used to the intricacies and intrigues of power. What do you say?"

"You are very eloquent, Aruan, but vague. Do you fear to tell me too much?"

Aruan shrugged. "You must take some things on trust, that is true. But I cannot relate to you the details of a plan which is still incomplete. For now, it would be enough if you could at least consider yourself our friend."

The lean old wizard stared at his visitor. Aruan's face was angular and autocratic, and there was a cruelty lurking there in the eyes. Not a kindly, nor yet a generous coun-tenance. But Golophin sensed that in this, at least, he was speaking the truth. Imagine: an entirely new world out there beyond the endless ocean, a society of mages living without fear of the pyre. It was a staggering concept, one that sent a whole golden series of speculations racing through Gol-ophin's mind. And they wanted to come back here, to the

Old World. What could be wrong with finding a home for such . . . such castaways? The knowledge they must have gathered through the centuries, working in peace and without fear! The ancient wizard had a point: how many more decades or centuries of persecution could the Dweomerfolk take before they were wiped out altogether? At some point they had to stand together and halt it, turn around the prejudices of men and demand acceptance for themselves. It was a glittering idea, one which for a second made Golophin's heart soar with hope. If it were only possible!

And yet, and yet—there was something deeply disturbing here. This Aruan, for all his surface charm, had a beast inside him. Golophin could not forget that one, desperate mind-scream he had heard Bardolin give thousands of leagues away.

Golophin! Help me in the name of God—

The terror in that cry. What had engendered it?

"Well?" Aruan asked. "What do you say?"

"All right. Consider me friendly to your cause. But I will not divulge any of the secrets or strategies of the Hebrian crown. I have other loyalties too."

"That is enough for me. I thank you, Golophin." And Aruan held out a hand.

But Golophin refused to shake it. Instead he turned and refilled his glass. "I suggest you leave now. I have to be on my way back to the city very soon. But"—he paused—"I wish to speak with you again. I possess an inquisitive mind, and there is so much I would know."

"By all means. I look forward to it. But before I go, I will show my goodwill with a gift . . ."

Before Golophin could move, Aruan had swooped forward like a huge dark raptor. His hand came down upon Golophin's forehead and seemed fixed there, as though the fingers had been driven like nails through the skull. Golophin's glass dropped out of his hand and shattered on the stone floor. His eyes rolled up to show the whites and he bared his teeth in a helpless snarl.

Moisture beaded Aruan's face in a cold sheen. "This is a great gift," he said in a low voice. "And a genuine one. You have a subtle mind, my friend. I want it intact. I want

loyalty freely given. There." He stepped back. Golophin fell
to his knees, the breath a harsh gargle in his throat.

"You will have to experiment a little before you can use
it properly," Aruan told him. "But that inquisitive mind of
yours will find it a fascinating tool. Just do not try to cross
the ocean with it in search of your friend Bardolin. I cannot
allow that yet. Fare thee well, Golophin. For now." And he
was gone.

Panting, Golophin laboured to his feet. His head was
ringing as though someone had been tolling a bell in his
ears for hours. He felt drunk, clumsy, but there was a weird
sense of well-being burning through him.

And there—the knowledge was there, accessible. It
opened out before him in a blaze of newfound power and
possibilities.

Aruan had given him the Discipline of Translocation.

NINE

WILD-EYED, filthy and exhausted, the prisoners were herded in by Marsch's patrol like so many cattle. There were perhaps a dozen of them. Corfe was called to the van of the army by a beaming Cathedraller to inspect them. He halted the long column and cantered forward. Marsch greeted him with a nod.

The prisoners sank to the cold ground. Their arms had been bound to their sides and some of them had blood on their faces. Marsch's troopers were all leading extra horses with Merduk harness: compact, fine-boned beasts with the small ears and large eyes of the eastern breeds.

"Where did you find them?" Corfe asked the big tribesman.

"Five leagues north of here. They are stragglers from a larger force of maybe a thousand cavalry. They had been in a town." Here Marsch's voice grew savage. "They had burnt the town. The main body had waggons full of women amongst them, and herds of sheep and cattle. These"—he

jerked his head towards the gasping, prostrate Merduks—
"were busy when we caught them."

"Busy?"

Again, the savagery in Marsch's voice. "They had a woman. She was dead before we moved in. They were taking turns."

The Merduks cowered on the ground as the Torunnans and tribesmen, glaring, gathered about them.

"Kill the fuckers," Andruw said in a hiss which was wholly unlike him.

"No," Corfe said. "We interrogate them first."

"Kill them now," another soldier said. One of Ranafast's Torunnans.

"Get back in ranks!" Corfe roared. "By God, you'll obey orders or you'll leave this army and I'll have you march back to Torunn on your own. Get back there!"

The muttering knot of men moved apart.

"There were over a score of them," Marsch went on as though nothing had happened. "We slew eight or nine and took these men as they were pulling on their breeches. I thought it would be useful to have them alive."

"You did right," Corfe told him. "Marsch, you will escort them down the column to Formio. Have the Fimbrians take charge of them."

"Yes, General."

"You saw only this one body of the enemy?"

"No. There were others—raiding parties, maybe two or three hundred each. They swarm over the land like locusts."

"You weren't seen?"

"No. We were careful. And our armour is Merduk. We smeared it with mud to hide the colour and rode up to them like friends. That is why we caught them all. None escaped."

"It was well done. These raiding bands, are they all cavalry?"

"Most of them. Some are infantry like those in the big camp at the King's Battle. All have arquebuses or pistols, though."

"I see. Now take them down to Formio. When we halt for the night I want them brought to me—in one piece, you

understand?" This was for the benefit of the glowering Torunnans who were standing in perfect rank but whose
knuckles were white on their weapons.

"It shall be so." Then Marsch displayed a rare jet of
anger and outrage.

"They are not soldiers, these things. They are animals.
They are brave only when they attack women or unarmed
men. When we charged them some threw down their weapons and cried like children. They are of no account." Contempt dripped from his voice. But then he rode close to
Corfe and spoke quietly to his general so that none of the
other soldiers overheard.

"And some of them are not Merduk. They look like men
of the west, like us. Or like Torunnans."

Corfe nodded. "I know. Take them away now, Marsch."

ALL the rest of the day, as the army continued its slow
march north, the prisoners were cowering in Corfe's
mind. Andruw was grim and silent at his side. They had
passed half a dozen hamlets in the course of the past two
days. Some had been burnt to the ground, others seemed
eerily untouched. All were deserted but for a few decaying
corpses, so maimed by the weather and the animals that it
was impossible to tell even what sex they were. The land
around them seemed ransacked and desolate, and the mood
of the entire army was turning ugly. They had fought Merduks before, met them in open battle and striven against
them face to face. But it was a different thing to see one's
own country laid waste out of sheer wanton brutality. Corfe
had seen it before, around Aekir, but it was new to most
of the others.

Andruw, who knew this part of the world only too well,
was directing the course of their march. The plan was to
circle around in a great horseshoe until they were trekking
back south again. The Cathedrallers would provide a mobile screen to hide their movements and keep them informed as to the proximity of the enemy. When they
encountered any sizeable force the main body of the army
would be brought up, put into battle-line, and hurled forward. But so far they had not encountered any enemy for-

mation of a size which warranted the deployment of the
entire army, and the men were becoming frustrated and
angry. It was four days since they had left the boats behind,
and while the Cathedrallers had been skirmishing con-
stantly, the infantry had yet to even see a live Merduk—
apart from these prisoners Marsch had just brought in.
Corfe felt as though he were striving to manage a huge
pack of slavering hounds eager to slip the leash and run
wild. The Torunnans especially were determined to exact
some payment for the despoliation of their country.

They camped that night in the lee of a large pine wood.
The horses and mules were hobbled on its edge and the
men were able to trudge inside and light their first campfires
in two days, the flames hidden by the thick depths of the
trees. Eight thousand men required a large campsite, some
twelve acres or more, but the wood was able to accom-
modate them all with ease.

Once the fires were lit, rations handed out and the sentries posted, Formio and four sombre Fimbrians brought the
Merduk prisoners to Corfe's fire. The Merduks were shoved
into line with the dark trees towering around them like
watchful giants. All about them, the quiet talk and rustling
of men setting out their bedrolls ceased, and hundreds of
Corfe's troopers edged closer to listen. Andruw was there,
and Ranafast and Marsch and Ebro—all the senior officers
of the army. They had not been summoned, but Corfe could
not turn them away. He realised suddenly that if it came
down to it, he trusted the discipline of his own Cathedrallers and the Fimbrians more than he did that of his fellow
countrymen. This night they were not Torunnan professional soldiers, but angry, outraged men who needed something to vent their rage upon. He wondered, if it came to
it, whether he would be able to stop them degenerating into
some kind of lynch mob.

He walked up and down the line of prisoners in silence.
Some met his eyes, some stared at the ground. Yes, Marsch
had been right: at least four of them had the fair skin and
blue eyes of westerners. They were no doubt part of the
Minhraib of Ostrabar, the peasant levy. Ostrabar had once
been Ostiber, a Ramusian kingdom. The grandfathers of

these soldiers had fought the Merduks as Corfe's Torunnans were fighting them now, but these men had been born subjects of the Sultan, worshippers of the Prophet, their Ramusian heritage forgotten. Or almost forgotten.

"Who amongst you speaks Normannic?" Corfe snapped.

A short man raised his head. "I do, your honour. Felipio of Artakhan."

Felipio—even the name was Ramusian. Corfe tried to stop his own anger and hatred from clouding his thinking. He fought to keep his voice reasonable.

"Very well, Felipio. The name of your regiment, if you please, and your mission here in the north-west of my country."

Felipio licked dry lips, looking around at the hate-filled faces which surrounded him. "We are from the sixty-eighth regiment of pistoleers, your honour," he said. "We were infantry, part of the levy before the fall of the dyke. Then they gave us horses and matchlocks and sent us out to scout to the north up to the Torrin Gap."

"Scouting, is it?" a voice snarled from the blackness under the trees, and there was a general murmur.

"Be silent!" Corfe cried. "By God, you men will hold your tongues this night. Colonel Cear-Adurhal, you will take ten men and secure this area from further interruption. This is not a God-damned court-martial, nor yet a debating chamber."

Andruw did as he was ordered without a word. In minutes he had armed men, swords drawn, stationed about the prisoners.

"Go on, Felipio," Corfe said.

The prisoner studied his feet and continued in a mumble. "There is not much more to tell, your honour. Our Subhadar, Shahr Artap, he commanded the regiment, gave us a speech telling us that this was Merduk country now, and we were to do as we pleased . . ." Sweat broke out on Felipio's forehead and rolled down his face in shining beads of stress and terror.

"Go on," Corfe repeated.

"Please your honour, I can't—"

Andruw stepped forward out of nowhere and smashed

the man across the face with a mailed fist, bursting open his nose like a plum and ripping the flesh from one cheek-bone.

"You will obey the General's orders," he said, his voice an alien growl which Corfe could scarcely recognise.

"That's enough, Andruw. Step back."

Andruw looked at him. There were tears flaming in his eyes. "Yes sir," he said, and retreated into the shadows.

Another murmuring from the surrounding men. The night air crackled with suppressed violence. The firelight revealed a wall of faces which had gathered around despite Corfe's orders. Naked steel gleamed out of the dark. Corfe met Formio's eyes, and held the Fimbrian's gaze for a few seconds. Formio nodded fractionally and walked away into the trees.

"On your feet, Felipio."

The squat Merduk rose unsteadily, his face a swollen, scarlet mess through which bone gleamed. One eye was already closed.

"How far north did your regiment go—clear up to the gap?"

Felipio nodded drunkenly.

"Are there any other Merduk forces up there? Is it true your people are building forts?"

Felipio did not answer. He seemed half conscious. Corfe watched him for a moment, then moved down the line of prisoners to the next fair-skinned one.

"Your name." This one was little more than a boy. He had pissed in his pants and his face was streaked with tears and snot. Not too young to rape, though. Corfe seized him by the hair and drew him upright.

"Name."

"Don't kill me, please don't kill me. They made me do it. They took me off the farm. I have a wife at home—" He started sobbing. Corfe reined in an urge to strike him, to let loose his own fury and hatred and beat his stupid young face into a bloody morass of flesh and broken bone. He lowered his voice and whispered in the blubbering boy's ear.

"Talk to me, or I will hand you over to *them*." And he gestured to the press of silent men.

"There are other regiments up north," the boy bleated. "Four or five of them. They are building a big camp, walls and ditches. Another big army is coming north . . . they are going to—to the monkish place by the shores of the sea. That's all I know, I swear it!"

Corfe released him and he sagged, hiccuping and crying. So the Merduks were going to launch an expedition against Charibon, and they were fortifying the gap. Something worth knowing, at last. He turned away, deep in thought. As he did a large group of men advanced out of the shadows, the wall of faces dissolving into a crowd which surged forward.

"We'll take care of them from here, General."

"Get back in ranks!" His bellow made them pause, but one stepped forward and shook his head. "General, we'd follow you to hell and back, but a man has his limits. Some of us have lost families and homes to these animals. You have to leave the scum to us."

At once another knot of figures appeared, with Formio at their head. Sable-clad Fimbrians with their swords drawn. Cimbric tribesmen in their scarlet armour. They positioned themselves with swift efficiency about Corfe and the Merduks as though they were a bodyguard. Formio and Marsch stood at Corfe's shoulders.

"The General gave you an order," Formio said evenly. "Your job is to obey. You are soldiers, not a mob of civilians."

The two bands of armed men faced each other squarely for several moments. Corfe could not speak. If they began to fight one another he knew that the army was doomed, irrevocably split between Fimbrian and Torunnan and tribesman. His authority over them hung by a straw.

"All right, lads," Andruw said breezily, materialising like a ghost from the surrounding trees. "That's enough. If we start into them, then we're no better than they are. They're criminals, no more. And besides, are you willing to see the day when a Torunnan officer is obeyed by Fimbrians and mountain savages and not by his own countrymen?

Where's your pride? Varian—I know you—I saw you on the battlements at the dyke. You did your duty then. Do it now. Do as the General says, lads. Back to your bivouacs."

The Torunnans shifted their feet, looking both embarrassed and sullen. Corfe moved forward to speak to their ringleader, Varian. Thank God Andruw had remembered his name.

"I too lost a home and family, Varian," he said quietly. "All of us here have suffered, in one way or another."

Varian's eyes were hot blazes of grief. "I had a wife," he croaked, hardly audible. "I had a daughter."

Corfe gripped his shoulder. "Don't do anything that would offend their memory."

The trooper coughed and wiped his eyes roughly. "Yes, sir. I'm sorry. We're bloody fools, all of us."

"So are all men, Varian. But we were husbands and fathers and brothers once. Save the hatred for a battlefield. These animals are not worthy of it. Now go and get some sleep."

Corfe raised his voice. "All of you, back to your lines. There is nothing more to do here, nothing more to see."

Reluctantly, the throng broke up and began dispersing. Corfe felt the relief wash over him in a tepid wave as they obeyed him. They were still his to command, thanks to Formio and Andruw. They were still an army, and not a mob.

IN the middle watch of the night he did the rounds of the camp as he always did, exchanging a few words with the sentries, looking in on the horses. He took his own mount, an equable bay gelding, from the horse-lines and rode it bare-back out of the wood and up to the summit of a small knoll which lay to the east of the camp. Another horseman was there ahead of him, outlined against the stars. Andruw, staring out upon a sleeping Torunna. Corfe reined in beside him, and they sat their horses in silence, watching.

On the vast dark expanse of the night-bound earth they could see distant lights, throbbing like glow-worms. Even as Corfe watched, another sprang up out on the edge of the horizon.

"They're burning the towns along the Searil," Andruw said.

Corfe studied the distant flames and wondered what scenes of horror and carnage they signified. He remembered Aekir's fall, the panic of the crowds, the inferno of the packed streets, and wiped his face with one hand.

"I'm sorry I lost my head back there for a time," Andruw said tonelessly. "It won't happen again." And the anger and despair ate through the numbness in his voice as he spoke again. "God's blood, Corfe, will it ever end? Why do they do these things? What kind of people are they?"

"I don't know, Andruw, I truly don't. We've been fighting these folk for generations, and still we know nothing about them. And they know as little about us, I suspect. Two peoples who have never even tried to understand one another, but who are simply intent on wiping each other out."

"I've heard that in the west, in Gabrion and Hebrion, the Sea-Merduks trade and take ship with Ramusian captains as though there were no barriers between them. They sail ships together and start businesses in partnership with each other. Why is it so different here?"

"Because this is the frontier, Andruw. This is where the wheel meets the road.

"I stood ceremonial guard in Aekir once, at a dinner John Mogen was giving to his captains before the siege. I think that if anyone had some understanding of the Merduks, he did. I think he even admired them. He said that men must always move towards the sunset. They follow it as surely as swallows flit south in wintertime.

"Originally the Merduks were chieftains of the steppes beyond the Jafrar, but they followed the sun and crossed the mountains, and were halted by the walls and pikes of the Fimbrians. The Fimbrians contained them: we cannot. That is the simple truth. If we are not to fight one another into annihilation, then one day we shall have to broker a peace and make a compromise with them. Either that, or we will be swept into the mountains and end our days the leaders of roving homeless tribesmen, like Marsch and his people."

"I must talk to Marsch. That mountain savage bit . . . I have to tell him—"

"He knows, Andruw. He knows."

Andruw nodded. "I suppose so." He seemed to be having trouble finding the words he wanted. Corfe could sense the struggle in him as he sat his horse and picked at its mane.

"They shamed us back there, Formio and Marsch and their men. There they were, foreigners and mercenaries, and they stood by you while your own people were almost ready to push you out of the way. Those men were at the dyke with us—they saw us there. A few even served under you in the barbican. There's no talk around their campfires tonight. They have failed you—and themselves."

"No," Corfe said quickly. "They are just men who have been pushed too far. I think none the worse of them for it. And this army is not made up of Fimbrians and Torunnans and the tribesmen. Not any more. They're my men now, every one of them. They've fought together and they've died together. There is no need to talk of shame, not to me."

Andruw grimaced. "Maybe . . . You know, Corfe, I was ready to slit the throats of those prisoners. I would have done it without a qualm and slept like a baby afterwards. I never really hated before, not truly. In a way it was some huge kind of game. But now this—this is different. The refugees from Aekir, they were just faces, but these hills . . . I skylarked in them when I was a boy. The people up here are my own people, not just because they are To-runnan—that's a name—but because I know how they live and where. Varian hasn't seen his wife and child in almost a year, and he doesn't know if they're alive or dead. And there are many more like him throughout the troops that came from the dyke. They sent their families out of the fortress at the start, back here to the north, or to the towns around Torunn. They thought the war would never come this far. Well, they were wrong. We all were."

"Yes," Corfe said, "we were."

"Are we doomed, do you think? Madmen fighting the inevitable?"

"I don't know. I don't care either, Andruw. All I know

is how to fight. It's all I've ever known. Perhaps one day it will be possible to come to some kind of terms with the Merduks. I hope so, for the sake of Varian and his family and thousands like them. If it does not prove so, however, I will fight the bastards until the day I die, and then my ghost will plague their dreams."

Andruw laughed, and Corfe realised how much he had missed that sound of late.

"I'll just bet it will. Merduk mothers will frighten children yet unborn with tales of the terrible Corfe and his red-clad fiends."

"I hope so," Corfe smiled.

"You think that snot-nosed boy was telling the truth about the Merduks marching on Charibon?"

"Possibly. It could be misinformation, but I doubt it. No, I think it's time the army went hunting. The quickest road to the gap from Ormann Dyke lies two days' march east of here. Tomorrow that's where we're going, with the Cathedrallers out in front under you and Marsch."

"Any guesses on the size of the army we're looking for?"

"Small enough for us to take on, I should think. The Sultan still believes the Torunnan military to be penned up in Torunn, licking their wounds, and Charibon has never been well defended. We may be outnumbered, but not by much, I hope."

"We can't stay out too long. We carry only enough rations for another three weeks."

"We'll go on half rations if we have to. I will not allow them to send an army through the gap. I've no more love for the Ravens of Charibon than the next man, but I'm damned if I'll let the Merduks waltz over Normannia like they owned it already. Besides, I have this feeling, Andruw. I think the enemy is slowing down. We've blunted their edge. If they find they have to fight for every yard of Torunnan soil, then they may end up content with less of it."

"An open battle will do the men good."

"This is war we're talking about, Andruw. A battle that will kill and maim great numbers of the men."

"You know what I mean, Corfe. They need to taste blood again. Hell, so do I."

"All right, I take your point." Corfe turned his horse around with a nudge of his knee. "Time to get some sleep."

"I think I'll stay here and think a while," Andruw said.

"Don't think too much, Andruw. It doesn't do any good. Believe me, I know." And Corfe kicked his mount into a canter, leaving Andruw to stare after him.

ALBREC'S cell was sparse and cold, but not unbearably so. To a monk who had suffered through a Ramusian novitiate it seemed perfectly adequate. He had a bed with a straw pallet which was surprisingly free of vermin, a small table and rickety chair and even a stub of candle and a tinderbox. There was one small window, heavily barred and set so high up in the wall that he had no chance of ever seeing out of it, but at least it provided a modicum of light.

He shared his cell with sundry spiders and an emaciated rat whose hunger had made it desperate. It had nibbled at Albrec's ears in the first nights he had been here, but now he knew to set aside for it some morsel of the food which was shoved through a slot in the door every day, and it had come to await the approaching steps of the turnkey more eagerly than he. The food was not appetising—black bread and old cheese and sometimes a bowl of cold soup which had lumps of gristle bobbing in it—but Albrec had never been much of an epicure. Besides, he had much to occupy his mind.

Every so often his solitary reveries were interrupted by a summons from the Sultan, and he would be hauled out of the cell, to the grief and bewilderment of the rat, and taken to the spacious chambers within which Aurungzeb had set up his household. The eunuchs would fetter him ceremoniously—more for effect than anything else, he thought—and he would stand in a discreet corner awaiting the pleasure of the Sultan. Sometimes he was left forgotten for hours, and was able to watch with avid fascination the workings of the Merduk court. Sometimes Aurungzeb was dining with senior army officers, or venerable mullahs, and Albrec would be called upon to debate with them and expound his theory on the common origin of the Saint and the Prophet. The Sultan, it seemed, liked to shock his guests with the little infidel. Not only were Albrec's words, often translated by the western concubine, Heria, inflammatory and blasphemous, but his appearance was agreeably bizarre. He was a court jester, but he knew that his words and theories shook some of the men who listened to them. Several of the mullahs had demanded he be executed at once, but others had argued with him as one might with a learnt adversary—a spectacle that Aurungzeb seemed to find hugely entertaining.

He thought about Avila sometimes, and about Macrobius, and could not help but wonder how things were in the Torunnan capital. But for some reason he thought mostly about the cavalry officer he had once briefly encountered outside the walls of Torunn. Corfe Cear-Inaf, now the commander-in-chief of all the Torunnan armies. The Sultan seemed obsessed by him, though to the Merduks he was known only as the leader of the scarlet cavalry. They had not yet learnt his name. Albrec gained the impression that the Merduk army in general existed in a state of constant apprehension, awaiting the descent of the terrible red horsemen upon them. Hence the current emphasis on fortification.

And Heria, the Sultan's chief concubine, pregnant by him and soon to become his queen—she could very well be this Corfe Cear-Inaf's lost wife. Albrec locked that knowledge deep within himself and resolved never to divulge it to anyone. It would wreck too many lives. It might even tip the balance of the war. Let this Torunnan general remain nameless.

And yet—and yet the despair in her eyes was so painful to behold. Might she not take some comfort from the fact that her husband was alive and well? On this matter Albrec was torn. He was afraid he might inflict further pain on someone who had already suffered so much. What good would it do her anyway? The situation was like some ethics problem set for him during his novitiate. The choice between two courses of action, both ambiguous in their outcome, but one somehow more spiritually correct than the

other. Except here he held in his hands the power to make
or break lives.

A clamour of keys and clicking locks at his door announced another summons. The rat glanced once at him
and then bolted for its hole. It was not mealtime. Albrec
sat on the edge of his bed. It was very late; unusual for him
to be wanted at this hour.

But when the door swung open it was not the familiar
figure of the turnkey who stood there, but a Merduk mullah,
a richly dressed man with a beard as broad as a spade, and
the cloaked and veiled figure of a woman. They entered his
cell without a word and shut the door behind them.

The woman doffed her veil for a brief second to let him
see her face. It was Heria. The mullah sat down upon Albrec's solitary chair without ceremony. His face was familiar. Albrec had spoken to him before at a dinner.

"Mehr Jirah," the mullah said. And in heavily accented
Normannic: "We talk four—five days—" He looked ap-
pealingly at Heria.

"You and Mehr Jirah spoke last week," she said
smoothly. "He wished to speak to you again, in private.
The guards have been bribed, but we do not have much
time and his Normannic is sparse, so I will interpret."

"By all means," Albrec said. "I appreciate his visiting
me."

The mullah spoke in his own tongue now, and after a
moment's thought Heria translated. Albrec thought he
sensed a smile behind the veil.

"First he asks if you are a madman."

Albrec chuckled. "You know the answer to that, lady.
Some have labelled me an eccentric, though."

Again, the speech in Merduk, her interpretation of it.

"He is an elder in the *Hraib* of the Kurasin in the Sultanate of Danrimir. He wants to know if your claims about
the Prophet are mere devilment, or if they are based on any
kind of evidence."

Albrec's heart quickened. "I told him when we spoke
before that they are based on an ancient document which I
believe to be genuine. I would not make such claims if I
did not believe in my soul that they are true. A man's be-

liefs are not something to make a jest out of."

When this was translated Mehr Jirah nodded approvingly. He seemed then to hesitate for a long while, his head bent upon his breast. One hand stroked his voluminous beard. At last he sighed and made a long speech in Merduk. When he had finished Heria stared at him, then collected herself and rendered it into Normannic in a voice filled with wonder.

"The Kurasin are an old tribe, one of the oldest of all the Merduk *Hraib*. They had the privilege of being the first of the eastern peoples to hear the preachings of the Prophet Ahrimuz, almost five centuries ago. They hold a tradition that the Prophet crossed the Jafrar Mountains from the west, alone, on a mule, and that he was a pale-skinned man who did not speak their tongue but whose holiness and learning were self-evident. He dwelled with the Kurasin for five years before travelling on northwards to the lands of the Kambak *Hraib*. In this way the True Faith came to the Merduk peoples: through this one man they deemed a Prophet sent by God, who came out of the west."

Albrec and the mullah looked at one another as Heria finished translating. In the Merduk cleric's eyes was a mixture of fear and confusion, but Albrec felt uplifted.

"So he believes me then."

Merduk and Normannic. A long, halting speech by Mehr Jirah. Heria spoke more swiftly now. "He is not sure. But he has studied some of the books which were saved from the Library of Gadorian Hagus in Aekir. Many of the sayings of St Ramusio and the Prophet Ahrimuz are the same, down to the very parables they used to illustrate their teachings. Perhaps the two men knew each other, or Ramusio was a student of Ahrimuz—"

"They were one and the same. He knows that. I can see it in his eyes."

When this was translated there was a long silence. Mehr Jirah looked deeply troubled. He spoke in a low voice without looking at Albrec.

"He says you speak the truth. But what would you have him do about it?"

"This truth is worth more than our lives. It must be declared publicly, whatever the consequences. The Prophet said that a man's soul suffers a kind of death every time he tells a lie. There have been five centuries of lies. It is enough."

"And your people, the Ramusians, will they wish to hear the truth also?"

"They are beginning to hear it. The head of my faith in Torunn, Macrobius, he believes it. It is only a matter of time before men start to accept it. This war must end. Merduks and Ramusians are brothers in faith and should not be slaying one another. Their God is the same God, and his messenger was a single man who enlightened us all."

Mehr Jirah rose.

"He will think upon your words. He will think about what to do next."

"Do not think too long," Albrec said, rising also.

"We must go." The Merduk opened the cell door. As he was about to leave he turned and spoke one last time.

"Why were we chosen to do this thing, do you think?"

"I do not know. I only know that we were, and that we must not shirk the task God has assigned us. To do so would be the worst blasphemy we could commit. A man who spends his life in the service of a lie, knowing it to be a lie, is offencive to the eyes of God."

Mehr Jirah paused in the doorway, and then nodded as Heria interpreted Albrec's words. A moment later he was gone.

"Will he do anything?" Albrec asked her.

"Yes, though I don't know what. He is a man of genuine piety, Merduk or no. He is the only one out of all of them who does not despise me. I'm not sure why."

Perhaps he knows quality when he sees it, Albrec found himself thinking. And out of his throat the words came tumbling as though without conscious volition.

"Your husband in Aekir. Was his first name Corfe?"

Heria went very still. "How do you know that?"

A rattle of metal up the corridor beyond Albrec's cell. Men talking, the sound of boots on stone. But Heria did not move.

"How do you know that?" she repeated.

"I have met him. He is still alive. Heria"—the words rushed out of him as someone outside shouted harshly in Merduk—"he is alive. He commands the armies of Torunna. He is the man who leads the red horsemen."

The knowledge had almost a physical heft as it left him and entered her. He believed for an instant that she would fall to the floor. She flinched as if he had struck her and sagged against the door.

The turnkey appeared on the threshold. He looked terrified, and plucked at Heria's sleeve whilst jabbering in Merduk. She shook him off.

"Are you sure?" she asked Albrec.

He did not want to say it for some reason, but he told the truth. "Yes."

A soldier appeared at the door, a Merduk officer. He pulled Heria away looking both exasperated and frightened. The door was slammed shut, the keys clicking the lock into place again. Albrec slumped down on the bed and covered his face with his hands. Blessed Saint, he thought, what have I done?

TEN

IT was spring when they first sighted the Hebros Mountains on the horizon, and Hawkwood bent his head at the tiller and let the tears come silently for a while. Around him others of the crew were more vocal, loudly thanking God for their deliverance, or sobbing like children. Even Murad was not unmoved. He actually shook Hawkwood's hand. "You are a master-mariner indeed, Captain, to make such a landfall."

Hebrion loomed up steadily out of the dawn haze, the mountains tinted pink as the sun took them. They had weathered North Cape five days ago, beat before a passing storm in the Gulf of Hebrion, and were now sailing up Abrusio's huge trefoil-shaped bay with a perfect south-west breeze on the larboard quarter. They had been away almost eight months, and the brave *Osprey* was sinking under them at last, every able-bodied man taking a shift at the pumps. But the water was almost over the orlop and Bardolin had

had to be rechained in the master's cabin or he would have drowned in the bilge.

Fair winds almost all the way, and apart from the one squall which had almost sunk them they had had a swift passage, and the accuracy of their landfall was indeed nothing short of miraculous. Hawkwood was burnt dark as mahogany by the sun, and he stood at the tiller in rags, his beard and unkempt hair frosted by salt and sea wind, his eyes two blue flashes startling in so swarthy a face. With the aid of his cross-staff, the accumulated lore of a lifetime at sea and a string of good luck, he had brought the *Osprey* home at last after one of the longest voyages of recorded history. And surely one of the most disastrous.

The seventeen survivors of the expedition at liberty stood on deck and stared as the carrack wheeled smoothly round to north-north-east and the familiar shoreline slid past on the larboard side. There was still snow on the Hebros, but only a light dusting of it, and the sun was warm on their naked backs—not the punishing hothouse heat of the west, but a refreshing spring warmth. They could see Abrusio's heights rising up out of the haze ahead, and one of the soldiers cried out, pointing at the little flotilla of fishing yawls off the port beam as though they were some marvell.

Abrusio. They saw now the ruined expanses of the Lower City, the devastation of the docks, and the frantic rebuilding work that was going on there, thousands of men at work on miles of scaffolding. Hawkwood and Murad looked at one another. They had missed a war or some great natural disaster in their time away, it seemed. What other surprises were waiting for them in the old port-city?

"Back topsails!" Hawkwood cried as the *Osprey* slid through the sparsely populated wharves, all of which seemed damaged in some way or other. The Inner Roads were almost deserted of vessels, though the Hebrian naval yards were crammed full of warships, most of which were under repair.

"Stand ready with the bow-line there!"

The carrack slowed as the sails were backed and spilled their wind. Half a dozen men stood at the beakhead, ready

to leap ashore with the heavy mooring ropes and make
them fast to the bollards there. A small crowd had gathered
on the quayside. Men were shading their eyes and pointing
at the battered ship, some arguing with each other and shaking their heads. Hawkwood smiled. There was a slight jar
as the *Osprey* came up against the rope buffers at the lip
of the wharves.

"Tie her off lads. We're home."

Men leapt overboard and made the ship fast. Then they
embraced each other, laughing, weeping, jumping up and
down like a crowd of bronzed ragamuffins gone mad.

"Your Excellency," Hawkwood said with heavy irony,
"I have brought you home."

The nobleman stared at him, and smiled. "Excellency no
more. My title expired with the colony, as did yours, master
Hawkwood. You will die a commoner after all."

Hawkwood spat over the carrack's side. "I can live with
that. Now get your aristocratic backside off my ship."

Nothing in Murad's eyes. No shared comradeship, no
sense of achievement, nothing. He turned away without another word and walked off the ship. The *Osprey* was so
low in the water that one no longer had much of a climb
down from the ship's rail to the wharf. Murad continued
walking, a grotesque, tatterdemalion figure which drew a
battery of stares from the crowd that was gathering. None
of them dared accost him, though, despite their consuming
curiosity. The last Hawkwood saw of him he was negoti-
ating the burnt expanse of what had been the Lower City,
his face set towards the heights whereon Hebrion's Royal
palace loomed up out of the dawn haze.

Done with him at last, Hawkwood thought, and thanked
God for it—for a whole host of things.

"Is that the *Gabrian Osprey*? Is that really her?" someone
shouted out from the buzzing throng on the wharf.

"Aye, it's her. Come home from the edge of the world."

"Ricardo! Ricardo Hawkwood! Glory be to God!"

A short, dark man in rich but soiled garments of blue
and yellow pushed through the crowd. He wore the chain
of a port captain. "Richard! Ha, ha, ha! I don't believe it.
Back from a watery grave."

Hawkwood climbed over the ship's rail, and staggered as the unmoving stone of the wharf met his feet. It seemed to be gently rising and falling under him.

"Galliardo," he said with a smile, and the short man clasped his hand and shook it as though he meant to wring it off. There were tears in his eyes.

"I had a mass said for you these six months past. Oh God, Richard, what has happened to you?"

The press of bodies about Hawkwood was almost unbearable. Half the dock workers in the area seemed to have gathered about the *Osprey* to look and wonder and hear her storey. Hawkwood blinked away his joy at landfall and tried to make himself think.

"Did you find it, Richard?" Galliardo was babbling. "Is there indeed a continent out in the west?"

"Yes, yes there is, and it can rot there as far as I'm concerned. Listen, Galliardo, she's about to sink at her moorings. Every seam in her has sprung. I need men to man her pumps and caulkers to stop her holes, and I need them now."

"You shall have them. There's not a mariner or carpenter in the city would not give his arm to have the privilege of working on her."

"And there's another thing." Hawkwood lowered his voice. "I have a . . . a cargo I need offloaded with some discretion. It has to go to the Upper City, to the palace."

Galliardo's eyes were shining with cupidity. "Ah, Richard, I knew it. You've made your fortune out there in the west. A million in gold, I'll bet it is."

"No, no—nothing like that. It's a . . . a rare beast, brought back for the King's entertainment."

"And worth a fortune, I'll wager."

Hawkwood gave up. "Yes, Galliardo. It's priceless."

Then the port captain's face grew sombre. "You don't know what happened here in Abrusio. You haven't heard, have you?"

"No," Hawkwood said wearily. "Listen, you can tell me over a flagon of beer."

Galliardo laid a hand on his arm. "Richard, I have to tell you. Your wife Estrella, she is dead."

That brought him up short. Slender, carping little Estrella. He'd hardly thought about her in half a year.

"How?" he asked. No grief there, only a kind of puzzled pity.

"In the fires, when they torched the Lower City. During the war. They say fifty thousand died at that time. It was hell on earth."

"No," Hawkwood said. "I have seen hell on earth, and it is not here. Now get me a gang of caulkers, Galliardo, before the *Osprey* settles where she lies."

"I'll have them here in half a glass, don't worry. Listen, join me in the Dolphin as soon as you can. I keep a back room there, since the house went."

"Yours too? Lord, Galliardo, has no-one any good news for me?"

"Precious little, my friend. But tidings of your return will be a tonic for the whole port. Now come—let me buy you that beer."

"I must fetch my log and rutter first."

Hawkwood reboarded the carrack and made his way along the familiar companionway to the stern cabin. Bardolin sprawled there, a filthy mass of sores and scars, his eyes dull gleams in a tangle of beard and hair. Blood crusted his chains, and he stank like a cage in a zoo.

"Home at last, eh Captain?" he whispered.

"I'll be back soon, Bardolin, with some helpers. We'll get you to Golophin by tonight. He lodges in the palace, doesn't he?"

Bardolin stirred. "No, don't take me to the palace. Golophin has a tower in the foothills. It's where he carries out his researches. That's where you must take me. I know the way; it's where I served most of my apprenticeship."

"If you say so."

"Thank you, Captain, for everything. At one time all I wished for was death. I have had time to think. I begin to see now that there may be some value in living after all."

"That's the spirit. Hang on here, Bardolin. I'll be back soon."

Hawkwood tentatively laid a hand on the chained man's shoulder, then left.

"You have a worthy friend there, Bardolin," Griella said. She materialised before him like a ghost.

"Yes. He is a good man, Richard Hawkwood."

"And he was right. It is worth going on. Life is worth living."

"I know. I can see that."

"And the disease you live with—it is not an affliction, either. Do you see that?"

Bardolin lifted his head and stared at her. "I believe I do, Griella. Perhaps your master has a point."

"You are my master now, Bardolin," she said, and kissed him on his cracked lips.

MURAD'S town house had survived the war intact but for a few shot-holes in the thick masonry of the walls. When the heavy door was finally opened under his furious knocking the gatekeeper took one look at him and slammed it shut in his face. Murad broke into a paroxysm of rage, hammering on the door and screaming at the top of his lungs. At last the postern door opened to one side, and two stout kitchen lads came out cracking their knuckles. "No beggars, and no madmen allowed at this house. Listen you—"

Murad left them both groaning and semi-conscious in the street and strode through the open postern, pushing aside sundry servants and bellowing for his steward. The kitchen staff scattered like a flock of geese before a fox, the women yelling that there was a maniac loose in the house. When the steward finally arrived, a cleaver in his hand, Murad pinioned him and stared into his eyes. "Do you know me, Glarus of Garmidalan? Your father is a gamekeeper on my estates. Your mother was my father's housekeeper for twenty years."

"Holy God," Glarus faltered. And he fell to his knees. "Forgive me, lord. We thought you were long dead. And you have . . . you have changed so—"

Murad's febrile strength seemed to gutter out. He sagged against the heavy kitchen table, releasing the man. The cleaver clanged to the floor. "I am home now. Run me a bath, and have my valet sent to me. And that wench there"—he pointed to a cowering girl with flour on her hands—"have her sent at once to the master bed-room. I want wine and bread and cheese and roasted chicken. And apples. And I want them there within half a glass. And a message sent to the palace, requesting an audience. Do you hear me?"

"Half a glass?" Glarus asked timidly. Murad laughed.

"I am become a naval creature after all. Ten minutes will do, Glarus. God's blood, it is good to be home!"

TWO hours later, he was admiring himself in the full-length mirror of the master bed-room, and the weeping kitchen maid was being led away with a blanket about her shoulders. His beard and hair had been neatly trimmed and he wore a doublet of black velvet edged with silver lace. It hung on him like a sack, and he had to don breeches instead of hose, for his legs were too thin to be revealed without ridicule. He supposed he would put weight on, eventually. He was hungry, but the food he had eaten had made him sick.

His valet helped him slide the baldric of his rapier over his shoulder, and then he sipped wine and watched the stranger in the mirror preen himself. He had never been a handsome man, though there had always been something about him which the fair sex had found not unattractive. But now he was an emaciated, scarred scarecrow with a brown face in which a lipless mouth curled in a perpetual sneer. Governor of New Hebrion. His Excellency. Discoverer of the New World.

"The carriage is ready in the court-yard, my lord," Glarus ventured from the door.

"I'll be there in a moment."

It was barely midmorning. Only a few hours ago he had been a beggar on a sinking ship with the scum of the earth for company. Now he was a lord again, with servants at his beck and call, a carriage waiting, a king ready to receive him. Some part of the world had been put back to rights at least. Some natural order restored.

He went down to the carriage and stared about himself avidly as it negotiated the narrow cobbled streets on the way to the palace. Not too much evidence of destruction in this part of the city, at least. It was good of Abeleyn to see him so promptly, but then the monarch was probably afire with curiosity. Important that Murad's own version of events in the west was the first the King heard. So much was open to misinterpretation.

Glarus had told Murad of the war, the ruin of the city and the King's illness while he had pounded his seed into the rump of the whimpering maid. A lot had been happening, seemingly, while he and his companions had been trekking through that endless jungle and eating beetles in order to survive. Murad could not help but feel that the world he had come back to had become an alien place. But the Sequeros were destroyed, as were the Carreras. That meant that he, Lord Murad of Galiapeno, was now almost certainly closest by blood to the throne itself. It was an ill wind which blew nobody any good. He smiled to himself. War was good for something after all.

The King received him in the palace gardens, amid the chittering of cicadas and the rustling of cypresses. A year before, Murad had sat here with him and first proposed the expedition to the west. It was no longer the same world. They were no longer the same men of that summer morning.

The King had aged in a year. His dark hair was brindled with grey and he bore scars on his face even as Murad did. He was taller than he had been, Murad was convinced, and he walked with an awkward gait, the legacy of the wounds he had suffered in the storming of the city. He smiled as his kinsman approached, though the lean nobleman had not missed the initial shock on his face, quickly mastered.

"Cousin, it is good to see you."

They embraced, then each held the other at arm's length and studied the other man's face.

"It's a hard journey you've been on," Abeleyn said.

"I might say the same of you, sire."

The King nodded. "I expected word from you sooner. Did you find it, Murad, your Western Continent?"

Murad sat down beside the King on the stone bench that stood sun-warmed in the garden. "Yes, I found it."

"And was it worth the trip?"

For a second, Murad could not speak. Pictures in his mind. The great cone of Undabane rising out of the jungle. The slaughter of his men there. The jungle journey. The pitiful wreck of Fort Abeleius. Bardolin howling in the hold of the ship in nights of wind. He shut his eyes.

"The expedition was a failure, sire. We were lucky to escape with our lives, those of us who did. It was—it was a nightmare."

"Tell me."

And he did. Everything from the moment of weighing anchor in Abrusio harbour all those months ago through to mooring the ship again that very morning. He told Abeleyn virtually everything; but he did not mention Griella, or what Bardolin had become. And Hawkwood's part in the tale was kept to a minimum. The survivors had pulled through thanks to the determination and courage of Lord Murad of Galiapeno, who had never despaired, even in the blackest of moments.

The birds sang their homage to the morning, and Murad could smell juniper and lavender on the breeze. His storey seemed like some cautionary tale told around a sailor's fireside, not something which could actually have happened. It was a bad dream which at last he had woken from, and he was in the sunlit reality of his own world again.

"Join me for lunch," the King said at last when Murad was done. "I also have a tale to tell, though no doubt you've heard a part of it already."

The King rose with an audible creaking of wood, and the pair of them left the garden together, the birds singing their hearts out all around them.

THE message was brought to Golophin in the palace by a breathless boy straight from the waterfront. He had eluded every footman and guard and was bursting with news. The *Gabrian Osprey* had returned at last, and her captain was having some precious form of supercargo sent to his tower in the hills. It would be there around mid-afternoon. Captain Hawkwood would like to meet with him this evening, if it was convenient, and discuss the shipment.

The whole dockside was in a high state of excitement. The surviving crew members of the *Osprey* were being feted in every tavern that still existed in the Lower City, and they were telling tales of strange lands, stranger beasts, and rivers of gold!"

Golophin gave the boy a silver crown for his pains and halted in his tracks. He had an idea he knew what Hawkwood's cargo was. He snapped to an eavesdropping palace attendant that he wanted his mule saddled up at once, and then repaired to his apartments in the palace to gather some books and herbs that he thought he might need.

Isolla found him there, packing with calm haste.

"Something has come up," he explained. "I must leave for my tower at once. I may be gone a few days."

"But haven't you heard the news? Some lord who went off to find the Western Continent has come back. He's to be the star of a levee this afternoon."

"I had heard," Golophin said with a smile. "Lord Murad is known to me. But a friend of mine is . . . is in trouble. I am the only one who can help him."

"He must be a close friend," Isolla said, obviously curious. She had not thought Golophin close to anyone except perhaps the King himself.

"He was a pupil of mine for a time."

A pageboy knocked and poked his head around the door. "The mule is saddled and ready, sir."

"Thank you." Golophin slung his packed leather bag over one thin shoulder, clapped his broad-brimmed hat on his pate, and kissed Isolla hurriedly. "Watch over the King while I'm away, lady."

"Yes, of course. But Golophin—"

And he was gone. Isolla could have stamped her foot with frustration and curiosity. Then again, why not indulge herself? Much though she liked Golophin, she sometimes found his air of world-weary superiority infuriating.

She would miss the levee and the explorer's tales, but something told her that Golophin's urgent errand was tied into the arrival of this ship from the west.

Isolla strode off to her chambers. She needed to change into clothes more suitable for riding.

ELEVEN

THE army woke up in the black hour before the dawn, and in the frigid darkness men stumbled and cursed and blew on numbed fingers as they strapped on their armour and gnawed dry biscuit. Corfe shared a mug of wine with Marsch and Andruw while the trio stood and watched the host of men about them come to life.

"Remember to keep sending back couriers," Corfe said through teeth clenched against the cold. "I don't care if there's nothing to report; at least they'll keep me updated on your location. And don't for God's sake pitch into anything large before the main body comes up."

"No problem," Andruw said. "And I won't teach your grandmother how to suck eggs, either."

"Fair enough." The truth was that Corfe hated to send the Cathedrallers off under someone else's command— even if it were Andruw. He was beginning to realise that his elevated rank entailed sacrifice as well as opportunity. He shook the hands of Marsch and Andruw and then

watched them disappear into the pre-dawn gloom towards
the horse-lines. A few minutes later the Cathedrallers began
to saddle up, and within half an hour they were riding out
in a long, silent column, the sunrise just beginning to
lighten up the lowering cloud on the horizon before them.

By midmorning the remainder of the army, some six and
a half thousand men in all, was strung out in a column half
a league long whose head pointed almost due east. In the
van rode Corfe, surrounded by the fifteen or so cuirassiers
who were all that remained of Ormann Dyke's cavalry regiment. His trumpeter, Cerne, had insisted on remaining with
him, and Andruw had ceremoniously left behind a further
half-dozen of the tribesmen as a kind of bodyguard. Behind
this little band of horsemen marched five hundred Torunnan
arquebusiers followed by Formio's two thousand Fimbrians, and then another group of some three thousand arquebusiers under Ranafast. After them came the mule train of
some six hundred plodding, bad-tempered, heavily laden
animals, and finally a rearguard of almost a thousand more
Torunnans.

For the first few miles of their advance they could actually glimpse the Cathedrallers off close to the horizon: a
black smudge in an otherwise grey and drear landscape.
But towards noon the country began to rise in long, stony
ridges across the line of march which slowed their progress
and obscured their view of the terrain to the east. By early
afternoon the cloud had broken up and there were wide
swathes of sunlight come rushing across the land, let slip
by fast-moving mare's-tails high above their heads. At the
eastern limit of sight, they could see black bars rising
straight into the air and then leaning over as they were
taken by the high altitude winds. The smoke from the towns
aflame along the River Searil. The infantry stared at the
smoke as they marched, and the winding column of men
toiled along in simmering silence.

Camp was made that night in the shelter of a tall ridge.
Sentries paced its summit and Corfe allowed the men to
light fires, since the high ground hid them from the east
and south. It was bitterly cold, and the sky had cleared

entirely so that above their heads was a vast blaze of stars, the larger winking red and blue.

A courier came in from Andruw at midnight, having been five hours on the road. The Cathedrallers were bivouacked in a fireless camp some four leagues south-west of the river. They had destroyed three roving bands of Merduk scavengers at no loss to themselves, and were now turning south-east, parallel with the Searil. There was a large town named Berrona there which seemed not to have been sacked yet, but from the increasing numbers of the enemy that Andruw was encountering, he thought that their main body must not be too far away and Berrona would be too plump a target for the Merduks to pass by.

Corfe sat by his campfire for a few minutes whilst the courier snatched a hasty meal and some of the cuirassiers rubbed down his horse for him and saddled up another to take him back.

Squinting in the firelight, Corfe scrawled a reply. Andruw was to scout out the environs of Berrona with one or two squadrons only, keeping the rest of his men out of sight. The main body would force-march to his location in the morning. Corfe estimated it was some thirty-five miles away, which would be a hard day's going, but his men would manage it. Then they would await the turn of events.

If the army was to return to Torunn in any kind of fighting condition, then this was the only chance Corfe had to bring a large Merduk force to battle. Another two days, three at most, and they would have to head for home, or start cutting rations even past the meagre amount they were subsisting on at present. And that would almost certainly mean that the horses would start to fail, something which Corfe could not afford to let happen.

The weary courier was sent on his way again. He would reach Andruw just before dawn, with luck, having ridden seventy miles in a single night. How he found his way in a region wholly unknown to him, over rough ground, in the dark, was a mystery to Corfe. He and Andruw had taken a series of maps north with them, only to discover that they were years out of date. Northern Torunna, in the shadow of the Thurians, had always been a wilder place than the south of the kingdom. It had few roads and fewer towns, but strategically it was as vital as the lines of the Searil and Torrin rivers. One day, when he had the time, Corfe would do something about that. He would make of the Torrin Gap a fortress and build good roads clear down to the capital for the passage of armies. The Torunnans hitherto had relied too much on what the Fimbrians had left behind them. Ormann Dyke, Aekir, Torunn itself and the roads which connected them—they were all legacies of the long-vanished empire. It was time the Torunnans built a few things of their own.

THE army was on the march again before dawn. Corfe and his Cathedraller bodyguards rode ahead of the main body, leaving old Ranafast in charge behind them. They passed isolated farmsteads that had been burnt out by Merduk marauders and once came across a lonely church which had inexplicably been spared the flames, but within which the enemy had obviously stabled their horses for some considerable time. The charred remains of two men were bound to a stake in the churchyard, the blackened stumps of their legs ending in a mound of dead embers and ash. Corfe had them buried and then rode on.

They halted at noon to rest the horses and wait for the infantry to come up. Corfe gnawed salt beef and bit off chunks of hard army biscuit while ceaselessly searching the eastern horizon for signs of life. Around him the tribesmen talked quietly in their own tongue to each other and their horses.

A solitary horseman appeared in the distance and the talk ceased. He was riding at full, reckless gallop, yanking up his mount's head when it stumbled on loose rock, bent low in the saddle to extract every ounce of speed out of the beast. A Cathedraller, his armour winking like freshly spilt gore. Corfe waved at him and he changed course. A few minutes later he had come to a staggering halt in front of them, his horse spraying foam from its mouth, nostrils flared and pink, sides heaving. He leapt off his steed and proffered a despatch case.

"Ondruw—he send me," he gasped.

"Good man. Cerne, give him some water. See to his horse and get him a fresh one." Corfe turned away and shook out the scroll of tattered paper Andruw had scrawled his despatch upon.

> *Merduk main body sighted three leagues south of Berrona. Some fifteen thousand men, plus two thousand cavalry out to their front. All lightly armed. My position half a league north of the town, but am withdrawing another league to the north to avoid discovery. Looks like they intend to enter Berrona this afternoon. Citizens still unaware of either us or the Merduks. How soon can you come up?*
>
> *Andruw Cear-Adurhal*
> *Colonel Commanding*

Corfe could sense the desperate plea in Andruw's words. He wanted to save the town from the horror of a Merduk sack. But men can only march so fast. It would be nightfall before the army was reunited, and Corfe did not intend to launch the men into a night attack after a thirty-five-mile march, against a superior foe. What was more, he could not even afford to let Andruw warn the townsfolk of the approaching catastrophe—that would give away the fact that there was a Torunnan army in the region, and when his men came up in the morning they would find the Merduks prepared and ready for them.

No, it was impossible. Berrona would have to take its chances.

There had been a time when he might have done it, when he had less braid on his shoulders and there was not much more at stake than his own life. But if he crippled this army of his, Torunna would be finished. He scribbled a reply to Andruw with his face set and pale.

> *Hold your new position. Do not engage the enemy under any circumstances. Infantry will be with you tonight. We will assault in the morning.*
>
> *Corfe Cear-Inaf*
> *Commander-in-Chief*

There. It gave Corfe a sick feeling in his stomach to hand the return despatch to the courier, and as the man set off again he almost thought better of it and recalled him. But it was too late. The tribesman was already a receding speck soon lost to view. It was done. He had just consigned the citizens of Berrona to a night of hell.

"WHAT are we to do with the prisoners?" Ranafast asked as the endless column of trudging men filed past.

The infantry had come up, and after the briefest of rests was on the move again. The sun was already westering, and they still had a long way to go to effect the rendezvous with Andruw and the Cathedrallers. But not a single man had dropped out, Ranafast and Formio had informed Corfe. The news that they were about to pitch into the Merduk raiders had filled the troops with fresh energy, and they stepped out with a will.

"Let them go," Corfe said. "They're nothing but a damned nuisance."

Ranafast stared at him, dark eyes glittering over a hawk nose and an iron-grey beard which looked as though it had been filed to a point.

"I can have the men take care of them," he said.

"No. Just set them free. But I want to talk to them first."

"Sir, I have to protest—"

"I won't make the men into murderers, Ranafast. We start slaughtering prisoners out of hand, and we're no better than they are. The men will have plenty of chances to kill themselves a Merduk tomorrow, in open battle. Now have the prisoners sent to me."

"I hope you know what you're doing, General," Ranafast said.

The captives were a miserable looking bunch, guarded by a couple of Fimbrians who regarded their charges with detached contempt. They cowered before Corfe as though he were their executioner. Part of him was longing to order their deaths. He held no illusions about what they had been doing up here in the north, but at the same time he was thinking of the peasant army he had slaughtered down at

Staed. Narfintyr's tenants, small farmers forced to take up arms for a lord they barely knew and who regarded them as expendable chattel. It had sickened Corfe, the slaughter of such poor ignorant wretches, and these Merduks were the same. They had been conscripted into the Sultan's army, leaving families and farms behind. Some of them did not even possess Merduk blood. He would kill men like these in their nameless thousands in the days and months to come, but that was the unavoidable consequence of war. He would not stain his conscience with their cold-blooded murder. He had enough blood on his hands already.

"You are free to go," he told them. "On the condition that you do not rejoin the Merduk army, but instead try to find your way home to your families. I know you did not join this war by choice, but because you were forced to. So be on your way in peace."

The men gaped, then looked at one another, jabbering in Merduk and Normannic. They were incredulous, too astonished to be happy. Some reached out to touch his stirruped feet and he backed his horse away from them.

"Go now. And don't come back to Torunna ever again. If you do, I promise that you will die here."

"Thank you, your honour!" the man Corfe recognised as the battered Felipio shouted out. Then the Merduks broke away, and as a group began running towards the long shadows of the Thurian Mountains in the north, as if trying to get away before Corfe changed his mind. The marching Torunnans watched them go, some of them spitting in disgust at the sight, but not a man protested.

Corfe turned to Ranafast, who still sat his horse nearby.

"Am I a bloody fool, Ranafast? Am I going soft?"

The veteran smiled. "Maybe, lad. Maybe you are just becoming something of a politician. You know damn well those bastards are going to try and rejoin their comrades— they've nowhere else to go. But if they make it, the news that the Torunnans treat their prisoners well will spread like a wildfire in high summer. If the Merduk levy thinks it will receive quarter when it lays down its arms, then it may not fight quite so hard."

"That's what I was hoping, I suppose, though I'm still

not convinced of it. But I've come to a conclusion, Ranafast: we can't win this war through force alone. We need
guile also."

"Aye, we do. Doesn't taste too good in the mouth
though, does it?" And Ranafast wheeled his horse away to
rejoin the army column. Corfe sat his own mount and
watched the freed Merduks running madly up into the foothills until they were mere dots against the snow-worn bulk
of the Thurian Mountains on the horizon before them. For
a crazed, indecipherable moment, he almost wished he were
running with them.

CATHEDRALLER scouts guided them in that night. The
weather had deteriorated into a face-stinging drizzle
which was flung at them by winds off the mountains, but
the wind would at least muffle the sound of their marching
feet and clinking equipment. The men had their heads down
and were dragging their feet by that time, and in the blus-
tery darkness half a dozen pack-mules had somehow broken free from their handlers and been lost, but in the main
the army was intact, the column a trifle ragged perhaps, but
still whole. Andruw had found a level campsite some five
miles north of the town. There was a stream running
through it, a boon to both horses and men, but as the weary
soldiers filed into the bivouac their heads lifted and they
peered intently at the southern horizon. There was an orange glow flickering in the sky there. Berrona was burning.

Andruw greeted Corfe unsmilingly, his face a pale blur
under his helm marked only by two black holes for eyes
and a slot for a mouth.

"Their cavalry entered the town several hours ago," he
said. "They took the men off to the south. Now they're
having a little fun with the women."

Corfe rode up close until their knees were touching. He
set a hand on Andruw's shoulder.

"We can't do it—not tonight. The men are done up.
We'll hit them at dawn, Andruw."

Andruw nodded. "I know. We must be sensible about
it." His voice was cracking with strain.

"Have you scouted out the main body?"

"They're still bivouacked to the south. Their camp is full of the loot and women from half a dozen different towns. These lads have been having a fine old time of it up here in the north. It must seem like a kind of holiday for them."

"It ends tomorrow morning with the dawn, I promise you. Now get the officers together. I want you to tell us all you know about the dispositions of these bastards."

Andruw nodded and started to move his horse away. Then he halted.

"Corfe?"

"Yes?"

"Promise me something else."

Andruw's voice was thick with grief but it was too dark for Corfe to read his face. "Go on."

"Promise me that tomorrow we will take no prisoners."

The wind and the subdued clamour of an army settling down for the night filled the silence that stretched between them. Politics, strategy, his talk with Ranafast; they rose like a cloud in Corfe's mind. But smouldering there under all the rationalisations were his own anger, and his friend's grief. When Corfe finally responded, his voice was as raw as Andruw's had been.

"All right then. Tomorrow there will be no quarter. I promise you."

TWELVE

THE town of Berrona had always been an unremarkable place, tucked away on the north-western border of Torunna not far from the headwaters of the River Searil. Some six thousand people dwelt there in the shadow of the western Thurians, their only link with Torunna proper a single dirt road which snaked away to the south across the foothills. With the fall of Ormann Dyke, they had become technically behind the Merduk lines, but thus far in this winter of carnage and destruction they had remained untouched. They were too far out of the way, closer to Aekir than to Torunn, and cradled by the long out-thrust spurs of the Thurian Mountains so that the war had passed them by and was a matter of tall tales and rumours, no more. A few of the survivors of Aekir's fall had somehow made their way there and had been welcomed, holding forth to packed audiences in the inns of the town and chilling the listeners with tales of war and atrocity. *Get out of here*, the Aekirians said. *Cross the Torrin river while there is still time*. But the townsfolk, though they shuddered appropriately at the stories of horror the refugees had to tell, could not believe that the war would touch them. *We are too out of the way,* they said. *Why would the Merduks want to come this far north when the armies are fighting way down on the plains about the capital? We will sit the war out and see what happens.*

The Aekirians, shocked, broken travesties of the prosperous city-dwellers they had once been, merely shook their heads. And though they were invited to stay with genuine compassion by the folk of Berrona, they refused and resumed their weary flight west towards the shrinking Torunnan frontier.

But the people of the town were proved right, it seemed. As midwinter passed and the new year grew older they were indeed forgotten and left undisturbed. They hunted in the hills as they had always done in the dark months, bored fishing holes in the ice that crusted the Searil and ate into their stores of pickles and dried meat and fish and fruit. And the world left them alone.

"HORSES, Arja! Look! Men on horses!"

The girl straightened, pressing her fists into the hollow of her back as though an old woman, though she was not yet fifteen. She shaded her eyes against the glare of sunlight on snow and peered out across the white hills to where her younger brother was pointing with quivering excitement.

"You're imagining again, Narfi. I can't see a thing." She bent to knot the rawhide rope about the firewood she had gathered, dark hair falling about her face. But her brother Narfi tugged at her sleeve.

"Look now! I'll bet you can see them now! Anyone could."

Sighing, she slapped his hand away and stared again. A dark bristle of movement, like a spined snake, off in the distance. They were so far away it was impossible to tell if they were even moving. But they were definitely men on horses, a long column of them riding half in shadow, half in sunlight as the scudding winter clouds came and went before the wind. Even as she watched, Arja saw the fleeting sparkle as the sun glittered off a line of metal accoutrements. Lance points, helmets, breastplates.

"I see them," she said lightly. "I see them now."

"Soldiers, Arja. Are they ours, you think? Would they let me up on a horse?"

Arja abandoned the firewood and grasped her brother's arm roughly. "We have to get home."

"No! I want to watch. I want to wait for them!"

"Shut up, Narfi! What if they're Merduks?"

At the word "Merduks" her brother's round face clouded. "Dada said they wouldn't come here," he said faintly.

His sister dragged him away. When she glanced back over her shoulder she could see that they were bigger. The dark snake had broken up into hundreds of little figures, all glittering in long lines. And farther away—back where the cloud and the distance rendered all things hazy—she thought she saw more of them. It looked like the line of a faraway forest undulating along the slopes and hollows of the hill. An army. She had never seen one before but she knew instantly what it was. A big army. She gulped for air, prayers flitting through her head like a tumble of summer swallows. They would ride on past. No-one ever came to Berrona. They would pass by. But she had to tell her father.

THAT afternoon the column of horsemen rode into the town as though they were triumphal warriors returning home. There were hundreds of them, perhaps even thousands, all mounted on tall bay horses and clad in outlandish armour, their lance points gay with silk streamers and a pair of matchlock pistols at the pommel of every saddle. The silent townsfolk lined the streets and some of the riders waved as they rode past, or blew kisses to the more comely of the women. They came to a halt in front of the town hall and there the leading riders dismounted. The town headman was waiting for them on the steps of the hall, pale as snow but resolute. One of the more gorgeously caparisoned horsemen doffed his helm to reveal a brown smiling face, his eyes as dark as sloes.

"I bring greetings in the name of Aurungzeb my Sultan

and the Prophet Ahrimuz, may he live for ever," he cried
in a clear, young voice. His Normannic was perfect, only
a slight accent betraying its origins.

"Ries Millian, town headman," the white-faced figure on
the steps said, his voice wavering with strain. "Welcome to
the town of Berrona."

"Thank you. Now please have all the people in this town
assemble in the square here. I have an announcement to
make."

Millian hesitated, but only for a moment. "What is it you
wish of us," he asked.

"You will find out. Now do as I say." The Merduk officer
turned and rapped out a series of commands to his men in
their own language. The column of horsemen split up.
Some two hundred remained in the square before the town
hall whilst the rest splintered into groups of one or two
dozen and set off down the side streets, the hooves of their
horses raising a clattering din off the cobbles.

The headman was conferring with other men of the town
in whispers. At last he stepped forward. "I cannot do as
you say until I know what you intend to do with us," he
said bravely, the men behind him nodding at his words.

The Merduk officer smiled, and without a word he drew
his tulwar. A flash of steel in the thin winter sunlight, and
Ries Millian was on his knees, choking, his hands striving
in vain to close his gaping windpipe. Blood on the cobbles,
squirts and gouts of it steaming like soup. The headman
fell on his side, twitched, lay still. In the crowd a woman
shrieked, rushed forward and cast herself on to the body.
The Merduk officer gestured impatiently and two of his
men lifted her away, still shrieking. In full view of the
crowd that had gathered, they stripped her, cutting the
clothes from her body with their swords and slicing flesh
from her limbs as they did so. When she was naked, they
bent her over and one thrust his scimitar up between her
legs with a grunt, until only the hilt of the weapon was
visible. The woman went silent, collapsed, and slid off the
end of the blade. The Merduks grinned and laughed. He
who had killed her sniffed his bloody sword and made a
face. They laughed again. The Merduk officer wiped his

tulwar off on the headman's carcase and turned to the paralysed huddle of men Millian had been conferring with.

"Do as I say. Get everyone here in the square. Now."

THE day drew on into an early winter evening, but for the folk of Berrona it seemed that it would never end.

The Merduks had cleared out the town house by house, stabling their horses in the humbler dwellings. The menfolk had been separated from the women and children and marched away south over the hills by several hundred of the invaders. Then there had been the sound of gunfire, crackling out into the cold air endlessly. It had gone on for hours, but none of the women could or would agree on what it meant. A few of the local shepherds had been dragged in by the invaders, bloody and terrified. They said that there was a huge Merduk army encamped out in the pastures to the south of the town, but few of the people believed them or had time to consider the ramifications of such a phenomenon. Their own tragedy filled their minds to overflowing.

Arja had seen some women dragged off into empty houses by groups of the laughing soldiers. There had been screams, and later the Merduks had emerged restrapping their armour, smiling, talking lazily in that horrible language they had. One woman, Frieda the blacksmith's wife who was held to be the prettiest in the town, had been stripped and forced to serve wine to the Merduk officers as they lounged in the headman's house. Her husband they had searched out and trussed up in a corner so that he was forced to watch as they finally raped her one by one. In the end they had killed her. But they blinded and castrated the blacksmith before leaving him a moaning heap on the floor. No-one had dared help him, and he had bled to death beside the violated corpse of his wife. Arja knew this because some of the other women had been treated in the same manner as Frieda and then released. They had seen it happen.

Perhaps fifty of the women of the town had been herded up and were now in the town hall. They were the young, the pretty, the well-shaped. Outside, night was drawing in

and the Merduks had lit bonfires in the streets, piling them
high with furniture from the empty houses. They were sack-
ing the town, looting anything of value and destroying what
they could not carry away. Many buildings had been burnt
to the ground already, and it was rumoured the Merduks
had locked most of the old people inside them first.

Arja had not seen her father since the men had been
taken away. Her brother, though barely eight years old, had
been taken along with him. Now she was alone with a
crowd of women and girls, imprisoned in the dark. A few
of the women were sobbing quietly, but most were silent.
Occasionally there were whispered conversations, most of
them consisting of speculation on the fate of their husbands
and fathers and brothers.

"They are dead," one woman hissed. "All dead. And
soon we will be too."

"No, no," another said frantically. "They have taken
away the men to work for them. Why would they kill their
labourers? The men are digging defences out beyond the
town. Why kill those who can work for you? It makes no
sense."

This straw of hope seemed to cheer many of the women.
"It is war," they said. "Terrible things happen, but there has
to be a sense to it all. Soldiers have their orders. So we are
under the Merduks now—they have to eat too. We will
adjust. We can be useful to them."

A scraping and thudding as the double doors of the town
hall were opened. It was full night outside, but the saffron
light of the bonfires flickered in and the sky was orange
and red with distant flames as the outskirts of the town
blazed. The women could see the black silhouettes of many
men outlined by the flames. Some held flasks and bottles,
others naked swords. There was no talk of usefulness now.

Some screamed, some were dully passive. The Merduk
troopers walked amongst them looking into their faces and
running their hands up and down their bodies as though
testing the mettle of an auctioned horse. When they found
what they wanted they took the woman by the wrist or the
hair and dragged her outside. When half the women had
been taken, the doors were closed again and those who

remained huddled in a corner embracing each other, bereft of speech.

Shrieks in the night. Men laughing. Arja cowered with the rest, her mind a white furious blank. Every sensation seemed to be dragged out, as in some hideous dream. She could not believe that this day had happened, these things. It was all utterly beyond anything she had ever known or imagined before, a window into another world she had not known could exist. Was this what war was like, then?

What seemed like hours passed, though they had no way of telling the passage of time, and their estimation of what constituted hours and minutes seemed to have been skewed and twisted until all frames of reference were useless in this new universe.

The screams died away. No-one slept. They sat with their arms about one another and stared at the black doors, awaiting their opening.

And at last the clumps and scrapes as their turn came and the portals of the town hall swung wide once more. Arja was almost relieved. She felt that she had been stretched so taut in the black time of waiting that soon she must snap like a green stick bent too far.

The selection procedure was swifter this time. A shadow which reeked of sweat and beer and urine seized Arja's arm and drew her outside into the hellish light of the bonfires. There were waggons parked in the square filled brimfull of naked women who hid their faces with their hair. Some had blood matting them. A few bodies, contorted out of all humanity, sprawled upon the cobbles with their innards piled like glistening heaps of mashed berries around them. In one of the bonfires what looked like the trunk of a small tree burnt, but the sickening stink of its burning was not that of charring wood.

Arja's captor plucked at her clothes. He was a small man, and to her surprise he was not dark-skinned or dark-eyed. He looked like a Torunnan and when he spoke it was in good Normannic.

"Take them off. Quickly."

She did as she was bidden. All over the square women were undressing whilst a crowd of several hundred men

watched. When she had stripped down to her undershirt she
could go no further. The numbness was eaten through and
she felt a moment of pure, incapacitating panic. The
Torunnan-looking Merduk chuckled, swigged from a bottle
and then ripped her undershirt from her back so that she
stood naked before him.

Some of his comrades gathered with him, eating her up
with their eyes. When she tried to cover herself with her
hands they slapped them away. They were laughing, drunk.
Some had their breeches unbuttoned and their members
lolled and shone wetly in the firelight. Again, the panic beat
great dark wings about Arja's head. Again, a sense of the
unreality of it all.

The soldiers spoke together in the Merduk tongue, as
easy and unforced as men who have met in an inn after a
long day's work. Two of them grabbed her by the arms.
Two more forced her knees apart. And then the little
Torunnan-like trooper took his bottle and thrust it up between Arja's thighs.

She screamed at the agony, struggled impotently in the
grasp of the four soldiers who held her. The small trooper
worked the bottle up and down. When he pulled it out at
last the glass was red and shining. He winked at his fellows
and then took a long draught from the bloody neck, smack-
ing his lips theatrically.

They bent her over a pile of broken furniture, splintered
wood piercing her breasts and belly. Then one mounted her
from behind and began thrusting into her torn insides.
There was only the pain, the blooming firelight, the hands
grasping hers so tightly they were numb. Something soft
was pushed against her lips and she pulled her head back
from the smell, but her hair was grasped and a voice spoke
in Normannic: *open up*. She took the thing into her mouth
and it grew large and rigid and was pushed back down her
throat until she gagged. They thrust into her from both di-
rections. Warm liquid cascaded down her naked back and
the men cursed and laughed. Liquid pulsed into her mouth,
salty and foul. The thing in there softened again and slid
out between her lips. She vomited, the taste of her bile
somehow cleaner, though it scalded her lips and tongue.

The hands released her and she slumped on to the hard cobbles. They were cold and wet beneath her. It is over, she thought. It is done.

Then another knot of soldiers strode up, pushing aside the first group, and she was seized upright once again.

THE dawn air was full of the smell of burning, the blue winter horizon smudged with smoke. The mobs of horsemen took their time to rub down their mounts, assemble in the square and root in their saddlebags for breakfast. Finally a series of orders was shouted out and the troopers mounted. Their horses were burdened with wineskins, flapping chickens, bolts of cloth and clinking sacks. Their officers were already outside the town, on a hill to the south. With them was a gaggle of splendidly accoutred senior commanders from the Merduk main body, their banner-bearers holding up bravely flapping silk flags in the freshening wind.

Finally the heavily burdened cavalry formed up and filed out of the gutted wreck of Berrona. Some were sullen and heavy-headed. A few were nodding in the saddle, and yet others seemed to be still drunk with the excesses of the night. They pointed their horses' noses to the south, where less than two miles away a vast Merduk camp sprawled across the land. They rode with the rising sun an orange blaze in their left eyes and the town smouldering behind them. Near the rear of their meandering and straggling column half a dozen waggons trundled and jolted along, drawn by mules, cart-horses and plodding oxen. A conglomeration of naked, bleeding and sodden humanity crouched in the waggons, silent as statues. Around them some of the soldiers of the Sultan, light at heart, began singing to welcome the dawn of the new day.

Arja had her head bent into her knees to shut out the world. She and the other women of the town—those who had survived—huddled together for warmth and comfort in the beds of the waggons. Some of them were sobbing soundlessly, but most were dry-eyed and seemed almost to be elsewhere, their minds far away. Thus it hardly registered upon them when the Merduks stopped singing.

The waggon halted. Men were shouting. Arja lifted her head.

The Merduk column had coalesced into a formless crowd of mounted men who milled about in disorder. What was happening? Some of the Merduks were throwing their garnered loot from their saddles in panic. Others were fumbling for the matchlocks at their pommels. Officers were yelling, frantic.

Then Arja saw what had caused the transformation. On the hillside behind the burnt-out wreck of Berrona a long line of men had appeared, thousands of them. They were still a mile away, but they were coming on at a run. Black-clad soldiers, some carrying guns, others with shouldered pikes. They advanced with the drilled remorselessness of some terrible machine.

"The army is here!" one of the women called out gladly. "The Torunnans have come!" A nearby Merduk trooper hacked her furiously about the head with his scimitar and she toppled over the side of the waggon.

A few minutes of chaos as the Merduks hovered, indecisive. Then the whole body of cavalry took off to the south in a muck-churning, frenzied gallop. The waggons were left behind along with a litter of discarded plunder.

It was painful to regain interest in the world, almost like coming alive again in some agonising wrench of rebirth. Arja raised herself to her bloody knees the better to see what was happening. Tears coursed down her face.

The ground under the wheels of the waggons seemed to shake with a subterranean thunder. It was both a noise and a physical sensation. The Torunnans were bypassing the burnt-out streets of the town, their formation dividing neatly and with no loss of speed. But they would never catch up with the fleeing Merduk cavalry—they were all on foot. Arja felt a hot blaze of pure hatred flare up in her heart. The Merduks would get away. They had killed her father and her brother, and they would get away.

The thunder in the ground grew more intense. It was an audible roar now, as though a furious river were coursing under the stones and heather of the hills.

—And then they burst into view with all the sudden fury

of an apocalypse. A great mass of cavalry erupted in a long line from behind a ridge to the south, at right angles to the fleeing Merduks. Arja heard a horn call ring out clear and free above the awesome rumble of the horses. The riders were armoured in scarlet, and singing as they came.

The Merduks looked over their right shoulders, and even at this distance Arja could see the naked terror on their faces. They kicked their mounts madly, tossing away booty, weapons, even helmets. But they were not fast enough.

The red horsemen ploughed into the mob of Merduk cavalry like a vermilion thunderbolt. She saw dozens of the lighter enemy horses actually hurled end over end by the impact. A thrashing Merduk trooper was lifted high into the air on the end of a lance. The enemy seemed to simply melt away. The red tide engulfed them, annihilating hundreds of men in the space of heartbeats. Only a few dozen Merduks broke free of the murderous scrum of men and horses, to continue their manic flight south towards their main camp. More were running about on foot, screaming, but the heavily armoured scarlet cavalry hunted them down like rabbits, spearing them as they ran or trampling them underfoot. Then there was another horn call and at once the horsemen broke off the pursuit and began to re-form in a neat line. A black and crimson banner billowed above their heads bearing some device she could not quite make out. The whole engagement had taken not more than three or four minutes.

The Torunnan infantry were running past the waggons now, panting men with sweat pouring down their faces and their eyes glittering like glass. They kept their line as though connected by invisible chains, and as they ran a great animal growl seemed to be coming from their throats. One man hurriedly seized Arja's hand as he passed by and kissed it before running on. Others were weeping as they ran, but all kept their ranks. The smoke from their lit match hung in the air after they had passed, like some acrid perfume of war. As they reached the ranks of the cavalry ahead, the horsemen split swiftly in two and took up position on their flanks. Then the united formation advanced again, at a fast march this time, and began eating up the

ground between them and the Merduk camp with the calm
inexorability of a tidal wave.

It seemed to Arja in that moment one of the most glorious things she had ever seen.

THIRTEEN

THE ceremony was a simple one, as befitted the steppes where it had ultimately originated. It took place in the open air, with the Thurians providing a magnificent backdrop of white peaks on the northern horizon. The ruins of Ormann Dyke's Long Walls glowered nearby like ancient monuments, and the Searil river rushed foaming to the west.

Two thousand Merduk cavalry, caparisoned in all the finery they possessed, surrounded an isolated quartet of figures, making three parts of a hollow square about them. On the fourth side a special dais had been constructed and canopied with translucent silk. The wind twisted and turned the fine material like smoke, giving glimpses of the Royal concubines seated on scarlet and gold cushions within, the eunuchs standing to their rear like pale statues. A host of gaudy figures clustered around the foot of the dais, fleeting flashes of winter sunlight sparkling off an emperor's ransom in gems and precious metals. To the rear of the sur-

rounding cavalry, a dozen elephants stood, painted out of
all recognition, hung with silk and brocade and embellished
with gold and leather harness. On their backs were wide
kettle-drums and a band of Merduk musicians gripping
horns and pipes. As the ceremony began the kettle-drums
rumbled out with a sound like a distant barrage of artillery,
or thunder in the mountains. Then there was silence but for
the wind hissing over the hills of northern Torunna.

Mehr Jirah stood before Aurungzeb, Sultan of Ostrabar,
and Ahara, his concubine. The Sultan held the reins of a
magnificent warhorse in his right hand and a worn and
ancient-looking scimitar in his left. He was dressed in the
plain leather and furs of an ancient steppe chieftain. Ahara
was clad as soberly as Aurungzeb, in a long woollen cloak
and a linen veil.

Mehr Jirah cried out loudly in the Merduk tongue, and
the two thousand cavalry clashed their lances against their
shields and roared out in affirmation. Yes, they would accept this union, and they would gladly recognise this
woman as their Sultan's First Wife. Their Queen.

Then Aurungzeb put the reins of his warhorse in Ahara's
hand and set the scimitar which had been his grandfather's
at her feet. She stepped over it lightly, and the whole host
cheered, the musicians on the backs of the elephants blasting out a cacophony of noise. Mehr Jirah offered a bowl
of mare's milk to the couple and they sipped from it in
turn, then kissed. And it was done. Aurungzeb, the Sultan
of Ostrabar, had a new wife: one with a child growing in
her belly who would one day be the legitimate heir to the
throne.

THEY had cleared a new set of apartments for her in the
tower of Ormann Dyke. Their windows looked east
over the River Searil towards Aekir and the Merduk lands
beyond. She sat at the window for a long time whilst a
small army of maids and eunuchs hurried back and forth
lighting braziers, moving furniture, setting out arrays of
sweetmeats and wines. Finally she became aware that
someone stood behind her, watching. She turned from the
view, still dressed in the sombre steppe costume in which

she had been married, and found Serrim, the chief eunuch, standing there, and beside him a tall Merduk in leather riding breeches, a silk tunic and a wide sash about his middle with a knife thrust into it. He was weather-worn and gaunt, his beard as hoary as sea salt. His eyes were grey like her own but he was staring out of the window over her shoulder and did not meet her appraisal. He looked to be in his sixties but his carriage was that of a much younger man.

"Well?" Heria asked. Serrim had been a bully when she was a mere concubine. Now that she had been catapulted into the Merduk nobility he had quickly become a sycophant. She disliked him the more for it.

"Lady, His Majesty has sent Shahr Baraz to you to be your personal attendant."

The lean Merduk hauled his gaze from the window and met her eyes for the first time. He bowed without a word.

"My attendant? I have plenty of those already." Shahr Baraz looked as though he belonged on a horse with a sword in his hand, not in a lady's chambers.

"He is to be your bodyguard, and is to attend you at all times."

"My bodyguard," Heria said wonderingly. And then something stirred from her memory. "Was it not Shahr Baraz who commanded the army which took Aekir? I thought he was an old man—and—and no longer with us."

"This is the illustrious khedive's son, lady."

"I see. Leave us, Serrim."

"Lady, I—"

"Leave us. All of you. I want the chamber cleared. You can finish your work here later."

A procession of maids left the room at once. The eunuch padded off with them, looking thoroughly discontented. Heria felt a brief moment of intense satisfaction, and then the cloud came down again.

"Would you like some wine, Shahr Baraz?"

"No, lady. I do not indulge."

"I see. So you are my bodyguard. Who do you intend to protect me from?"

"From whomsoever would wish to harm you."

She switched to Normannic. "And can you understand this tongue?"

The Merduk hesitated. A muscle twitched in his jaw. There was a long, livid scar there that ran from one cheek into his beard.

"Some words I know," he replied in the same language.

"Do you understand this, then? That I believe you are nothing more than a spy set here by the Sultan to keep watch over me and report my every move?"

"I am not a spy," Shahr Baraz said heatedly.

"Then why would the Sultan place the capable son of such an illustrious father in such a menial position?"

His grey eyes had flared into life. His Normannic was perfect as he replied, "To punish me."

"Why would he want to punish you?"

"Because I am my father's son, and he thinks my father failed him before this fortress."

"Your father is dead, then?"

"No—I don't know. He disappeared into the mountains rather than return to court to be . . . to answer for his actions."

She switched back to Merduk. "Your Normannic is better than you think."

"I am no spy," he repeated. "Even the Sultan would not ask me to be that. My family have served the House of Ostrabar for generations. I will not fail the Sultan's trust— nor yours, lady. I swear it. And besides"—here a glint of humour pierced his sternness—"the harem is full of spies already. The Sultan has little need of another."

She actually found herself liking him. "Have you family of your own?"

"A wife and two daughters. They are in Orkhan."

Hostages for his good behaviour, no doubt. "Thank you, Shahr Baraz. Now please leave me."

But he stood his ground stubbornly. "I am to remain with you at all times."

"All times?" she asked with one raised eye-brow. Shahr Baraz flushed.

"Within the bounds of propriety, yes."

She felt a pang of pure despair, and abandoned the game.

"All right." The prison walls were still intact, then. She might be able to order about a flock of flunkeys, but her position was essentially unchanged. She had been a fool to think otherwise.

Heria turned to regard the view from the lofty window once more. The pain was there of course, but she kept it at bay, skirted around it as a man might avoid a bottomless quagmire in his travells. Somewhere over the horizon in the east the ruins of Aekir stood, and somewhere in those ashes were the remains of another life. But the man with whom she had shared that life was still alive. Still alive. Where was Corfe now, her one and only husband? Strange and terrible that the knowledge he lived and walked and breathed upon the earth was a source only of agony. She could take no joy in it, and she scourged herself for that. She bore another man's child, a man who now called her wife. She had been ennobled by the union, but would live what remained of her life behind the bars of a jewelled cage. While her Corfe was alive—out there somewhere. And leading the fight against the world she now inhabited.

She wanted to die.

But would not. She had a son in her belly. Not Corfe's child, but something that was precious all the same—something that was hers. For the child she would stay alive, and she might even be able to do something to aid Corfe and the Torunnans, to help those who had once been her own people.

But the pain of it. The sheer, raw torment.

"Shahr Baraz," she said without turning round.

"Lady?"

"I need . . . I need a friend, Shahr Baraz." The tears scalded her eyes. She could not see. Her voice throbbed with a beat like the sob of a swan's wing in flight.

A hand touched the top of her head gently, resting there only for a second before being withdrawn. It was the first touch of genuine kindness she had received for a very long time, and it broke some wall within her soul. She bowed her head and wept bitterly. When she had collected herself she found Shahr Baraz on one knee before her. His fingers tapped her lightly on the fore-arm.

"A Merduk queen is not supposed to weep," he said, but his voice was gentle. He smiled.

"I have been a queen for only a morning. Perhaps I will get used to it."

"Dry your eyes, lady. The kohl is running down your face. Here." He wiped the streaked paint from her cheeks with his thumb. Her veil fell away.

"A man who touches one of the Sultan's women will have his hands cut off," she reminded him.

"I will not tell if you do not."

"Agreed." She collected herself. "You must forgive me. The excitement of the morning . . ."

"One of my daughters is about your age," Shahr Baraz said. "I pray she will never have to suffer as I believe you have. I would rather she lived out her days in a felt hut with a man she loved than—" He stopped, then straightened. "I will have your maids sent in, lady, so that you may repair yourself. It is inappropriate that I should be here alone with you, even if I am an old man. The Sultan would not approve."

"No. If you want to do something for me, then have the little Ramusian monk sent here. I wish to speak with him. He is imprisoned in the lower levels of the tower."

"I am not sure that—"

"Please, Shahr Baraz."

He nodded. "You are a queen, after all." Then he bowed, and left her.

A queen, she thought. So is that what I am now? She remembered the hell of Aekir at its fall, the Merduk soldier who had raped her with the light of the burning city a writhing inferno in his eyes. The terrible journey north in the waggons, John Mogen's Torunnans trudging beside them with their necks in capture-yokes. Men crucified by the thousand, babies tossed out in the snow to die. All those memories. They made part of her mind into a screaming wilderness which she had walled off to keep from going mad.

She was alone in the room. For a blest moment she was alone. No gossiping maids or spying eunuchs. No gaggle of concubines intriguing endlessly and bitching about petty slights and imagined neglects. She could stand at the window and look at what had once been her own country, and feel herself free. Her name was Heria Cear-Inaf and she was no queen, only the lowly daughter of a silk merchant, and her heart was still her own to bestow where she pleased.

"Beard of the Prophet, what does this mean? Are you here alone? God's teeth, this will not do! Where is that scoundrel Baraz? I'll have him flogged."

The Sultan of Ostrabar strode into the chamber like a gale, accompanied by a knot of his staff officers. He was dripping with jewells and gold once more, and a rich, fur-lined cloak whirled about him like a cloud. Silver tassels winked on the pointed toes of his boots.

Heria refastened her veil hurriedly.

"Shahr Baraz is off running an errand for me, my lord. Do not blame him. I wanted to see if he were truly mine to command."

Aurungzeb boomed with laughter. He bristled a kiss through her thin veil that bruised her lips. "Well done, wife! That family needs humbling. They take too much of the world's troubles upon themselves. Have you tumbled to my jest, then? The officers' quarters are buzzing with it. A Baraz as a lady's maid! Keep him on the tips of his toes—it will do him good. But you are still in your bridal gown! Get those ancient rags off your back. Tradition is all well and fine, but we cannot have my First Wife looking like a beggar off the steppe. Where are your attendants? I'll kick Serrim's fat arse next time I see him."

"They are preparing my wardrobe," Heria lied. "I sent them all off to do it. They are so slow."

"Yes, yes, you must be firm with them, you know. Have a few of them flogged, and they'll start to jump right smartly." Aurungzeb embraced her. The top of her head came barely to his chin, though she was tall for a woman.

"Ah, those beautiful bones! I do not know how I shall keep myself from them till the babe is born." He nuzzled her hair, beaming. "I must be off, my Queen. Shahr Johor, hunt out those damn maids. My wife is here alone like a mourner. And get the furniture sent up—the things from

Aekir we had shipped." Aurungzeb looked around the
room. It had been part of Pieter Martellus's chambers in
the days when the dyke had been Torunnan, and was as
bare as a barracks.

"Poor surroundings for a woman, though it's better than
a tent out in the field. We'll have to prettify the place a
little. I may just let this tower stand, as a monument. I must
be off. We are to dine together later, Ahara. I have invited
the ambassadors. We are having lobsters sent up from the
coast. Have you ever tasted a lobster? Ah, here is Shahr
Baraz. What do you mean by leaving the Queen alone?"

Shahr Baraz stood in the doorway. His face was expressionless. "My apologies, Sultan. It will not happen again."

"That's all right, Baraz. She's been playing with you I
think, my western doe." And in an aside to Heria: "He
looks so much like his terrible old father, and he's just as
stiff-necked. Keep him on the hop, my love, that's the way.
Well, I must be off. Wear the blue today, the stuff the
Nalbeni sent us. It sets off your eyes." And he was gone,
striding out of the room with his aides struggling to keep
up, his voice booming down the corridor beyond.

B Y the time Albrec had been brought to the new Queen's
chambers she had cast aside her sombre marriage garments and was swathed from head to toe in sky-blue silk,
a circlet of silver sat upon her veiled head and her eyes
were as striking as paint could make them. She reclined on
a low divan whilst around her half a dozen maids perched
on cushions. A tall Merduk of advanced years whom Albrec had never seen at the court before stood straight as a
spear by the door. The room's austere stone walls had been
hung with embroidered curtains and bright tapestries. Incense smouldered in a golden burner and several braziers
gave off a comfortable warmth, the charcoal within their
filigreed sides bright red. Three little girls kept the coals
glowing with discreet wheezes of their tiny bellows. The
contrast between the delicate sumptuousness of the chamber and the disfigured poverty of the little monk could not
have been greater.

Albrec bowed at a nudge from Serrim, the eunuch.

"Your Majesty, I believe I am to congratulate you on your wedding."

The Merduk Queen took a moment to respond.

"Be seated, Father. Rokzanne, some wine for our guest."

Albrec was brought a footstool to perch himself upon and a silver goblet of the thin, acrid liquid the Merduks chose to call wine. He did not take his eyes from the Queen's veiled face.

"I would have received you with less ceremony," Heria said lightly, "but Serrim here insisted that I begin to comport myself as befitting my newly exalted rank."

Albrec cast his eyes about the chamber, a cross between a barracks and a brothel. "Admirable," he muttered.

"Yes. Come, let me show you the view from the balcony." Heria rose and extended a hand to the little monk. He rose awkwardly off his low stool and took her fingers in what remained of his own hand. The women in the chamber whispered and murmured.

She led him out on to the balcony and they stood there with the fresh wind in their faces, looking down upon the ruin of the fortress. Already the Long Walls were demolished, and thousands of soldiers were working to dismantle their remnants and float the cyclopean granite blocks on flatboats across the Searil. The foundations for another fortress were being laid there on the east bank of the river. The tower in which Heria and Albrec stood would soon be all that remained of Kaile Ormann's great work. Even the dyke itself was to be dammed up and filled in through the labour of thousands of Torunnan slaves. The minor fortifications on the island would be rebuilt, and where the Long Walls had stood would be a barbican. Aurungzeb was constructing a mirror-image of the ancient fortress, to face west instead of east.

"Tell me about him, Father," Heria murmured. "Tell me everything you know. Quickly."

The maids and eunuchs were watching them. Albrec kept his voice so low the wind rendered it almost inaudible.

"I have heard it said that he is John Mogen come again. He sits high in the favour of the Torunnan Queen—it was no doubt she who made him commander-in-chief. This happened after I left the capital. He fought here, at the dyke, and in the south. Even the Fimbrians obey him."

"Tell me how he looks now, Father."

Albrec studied her face. It was white and set above the veil, like carved ivory. With the heavy paint on her eyelids she looked as though she were wearing a mask.

"Heria, do not torment yourself."

"Tell me."

Albrec thought back to that brief encounter on the road to Torunn. It seemed a very long time ago. "He has pain written on his face and in his eyes. There is a hardness about him." He is a killer, Albrec thought. One of those men who find they have an aptitude for it, as others can sculpt statues or make music. But he said nothing of this to Heria.

The Merduk Queen remained very still, the cold wind lifting her veil up like smoke. "Thank you, Father."

"Will you not come in from the balcony now, lady?" the eunuch's high-pitched voice piped behind them. "It becomes cold."

"Yes, Serrim. We will come in. I was just showing Father Albrec the beginnings of our Sultan's new fortress. He expressed a wish to see it." And to Albrec in a quick, hunted aside: "I must get you out of here, back to Torunn. We must help him win this war. But you must never tell him what I have become. His wife is dead. Do you hear me? *She is dead.*"

Albrec nodded dumbly, and followed her back into the scented warmth of the room behind.

FOURTEEN

IT was raining as the long column of weary men and horses filed through the East Gate, and they churned the road into a quagmire of shin-deep mud as they came. An exhausted army, straggling back over the hills to the north for miles—an army that had in its midst a motley convoy of several hundred waggons and carts, all brimming over with silent, huddled civilians, some with oilcloths pulled over their heads, others sitting numbly under the rain. Almost every waggon had a cluster of filthy footsoldiers about it, fighting its wheels free of the sucking muck. The entire spectacle looked like some strange quasi-military exodus.

Corfe, Andruw, Marsch and Formio stood by and watched while the army and its charges filed through the gate of the Torunnan capital. The guards on the city walls had come out in their thousands to watch the melancholy procession, and they were soon joined by many of the citizens so that the battlements were packed with bobbing heads. No-one cheered—no one was sure if the army was returning in defeat or victory.

"How many altogether, do you think?" Andruw asked.

Corfe wiped the ubiquitous rain out of his eyes. "Five, six thousand."

"I reckon they took another two or three away with them," Andruw said.

"I know, Andruw, I know. But these, at least, are safe now. And that army was crippled before we gave up the pursuit. We have delivered the north from them—for the time being."

"They are like a dog which cannot be trained," Formio said. "It lunges forward, you rap it on the muzzle and it draws back. But it keeps lunging forward again."

"Yes. Persistent bastards, I'll give them that," Andruw said with a twisted smile.

The army had virtually destroyed the Merduk force they had encountered outside Berrona, charging down on them while they were still frantically trying to form up outside their camp. But once they had been broken and hurled back inside the campsite the battle had degenerated into a murderous free-for-all. For inside the tents had been thousands of brutalised Torunnan women, inhabitants of the surrounding towns gathered together for the pleasure of the Merduk troops. Ranafast's Torunnans had run wild after the discovery, slaying every Merduk in sight. Corfe estimated the enemy dead at over eleven thousand.

But while the army had been embroiled in the butchery within the camp, several thousand of the enemy had managed to flee intact, and they had taken with them a large body of captives. Corfe's men had been too spent to follow them far, and snow had begun to drive down on the wings of a bitter wind off the mountains. The pursuit had been abandoned, and after digging four hundred graves for their own dead the army had re-formed for the long march south. The waggons had slowed them down, and they had shared their rations with the rescued prisoners. With the result that not a man of the army had eaten in the last three days, and half the Cathedrallers were now on foot. As their overworked mounts had collapsed, they had been carved up and eaten by the famished soldiers. Six hundred good warhorses were now mere jumbles of bones on the road behind them. But the campaign had been successful, Corfe reminded himself. They had done what he had set out to do. It was simply that he could take no joy in it.

"Beer," Andruw said with feeling. "A big, frothing mug of the stuff. And a wedge of cheese so big you could stop a door with it. And an apple."

"And fresh-baked bread," Marsch added. "With honey. Anything but meat. I will not eat meat again for a month. And I would sooner starve than eat another horse."

Corfe thought of the Queen's chambers, a bath full of steaming water and a roaring fire. He had not taken his boots off in a week and his feet felt swollen and sodden. The leather straps of his armour were green with mould and the steel itself was a rusted saffron wherever the red paint had chipped away. Only the blade of John Mogen's sword was bright and untarnished. He had Merduk blood under his nails.

"The men need a rest," he said. "The whole army needs to be refitted, and we'll have to send south for more horses. I wonder how Rusio has been getting on while we've been away."

"I'll wager his backside has not been far from a fire the whole time," Andruw retorted. "Send out some of those paper-collar garrison soldiers next time, Corfe. Remind them what it's like to feel the rain in their face."

"Maybe I will, Andruw. Maybe I will. For now, I want you three to go on inside the city. Make sure that the men are well bedded down—no bullshit from any quartermasters. I want to see them drunk by nightfall. They deserve it."

"There's an order easily obeyed." Andruw grinned. "Marsch, Formio, you heard the man. We have work to do."

"What about you, General?" Formio asked.

"I think I'll stand here awhile and watch the army march in."

"Come on, Corfe, get in and out of the rain," Andruw

cajoled. "They won't march any faster with you standing here."

"No, you three go on ahead. I want to think."

Andruw clapped him on the shoulder. "Don't philosophize too long. You may find all the beer drunk by the time you walk through the gate."

Andruw and Marsch mounted their emaciated horses and set off to join the column, but Formio lingered a moment.

"We did all we could, General," he said quietly.

"I know. It's just that it never feels as though it's enough."

The Fimbrian nodded. "For what it is worth, my men are content to serve under you. It seems that Torunna can produce soldiers too."

Corfe found himself smiling. "Go on, see to your troops, Formio. And thank you." He realised that he had just been given the greatest professional compliment of his life.

Formio set off in the wake of Marsch and Andruw without another word.

CORFE stood alone until the rearguard came into sight almost an hour later, then he mounted his horse and trotted down to join them. Two hundred Cathedrallers under Ebro and Morin, their steeds' noses drooping inches from the ground.

"What's the storey, Haptman?" he asked.

Ebro saluted. The pompous young officer Corfe had first met the previous year was now an experienced leader of men with the eyes of a veteran. He had come a long way.

"Five more horses in the last two miles," Ebro told him. "Another day and I reckon we'd all be afoot."

"No sign of the enemy?"

Ebro shook his head. "General, I do believe they're halfway back to Orkhan by now. We put the fear of God into them."

"That was the idea. Good work, Ebro."

The scarlet-armoured horsemen filed past in a muddy stream. Some of them looked up as they passed their commander and nodded or raised a hand. Many had shrivelled Merduk heads dangling from their pommels. Corfe wondered how few of his original galley slaves were left now. He sat his horse until they had all passed by and then finally entered the East Gate himself, the last man in the army to do so. The heavy wooden and iron doors boomed shut behind him.

IT was very late by the time he finally entered his chambers. He had visited the wounded in the military hospitals, racking his brains to try and address every man by his name, singling out those whom he had seen in battle and reminding them of their courage. He had gripped the bony fist of one wounded Cimbric tribesman as the man died then and there, in front of him. Those days in the open, eating horseflesh, rattling in agony in the back of a springless waggon, only to lose the fight when placed at last in a warm bed with clean blankets. The tribesman had died saying Corfe's name, understanding no word of Normannic.

Then there had been the dwindling horse-lines, seeing to it that the surviving mounts were well looked after, and then a half-dozen meetings with various quartermasters to ensure that the freed prisoners Corfe had brought south were being looked after. Most of them had been billeted with the civilian population. And at the last there had been a beer with Andruw, Marsch, Formio, Ranafast and Ebro, standing in a rowdy barracks and gulping down the tepid stuff by the pint, the six of them clinking their jugs together like men at a party whilst around them the soldiers did the same, most of them naked, having cast off their filthy clothes and rusted armour. Corfe had left his officers to their drinking and had staggered off towards the palace, both glad and reluctant to leave the warmth and comradeship of the barracks.

It seemed a crowd of people was waiting for him when he arrived, all bobbing and bowing and eager to lay hands on him. For once he was happy to have a crowd of flunkeys around, unbuckling straps, pulling off his boots, bringing him a warm woollen robe. They had built a blazing fire in the hearth and closed the shutters on the pouring rain beyond the balcony. They brought in ewers of steaming water and trays of food and drink. They would have washed him

too if he had let them. He ordered them out and performed
that task himself, but he was too tyred to use the towells
that had been left out and sat alone watching the flames
with his bare feet stretched out to the hearth, a puddle of
water on the flagged stone of the floor below him. His skin
was white and wrinkled and there was still dead men's
blood under his nails, but he did not care. He was too weary
even to pick at the tray of delicacies they had set out for
him, though he poured himself some wine and gulped it
down in order to warm his innards. So good to be alone,
to have silence and no immediate decisions to make. To
just feel the kindly wine warm him and hear the rain rattling
at the window.

"Hail, the conquering hero," a voice said. "So you are
back."

He did not turn round. "I'm back."

The Torunnan Queen came into the firelight. He had not
heard her enter the room.

"You look exhausted."

Odelia was dressed in a simple linen gown, and her hair
hung loose around her shoulders, shining in the firelight.
She looked like a young woman ready for bed.

"I waited for you," she said, "but they said you were
somewhere in the city, with the army."

"I had things to do."

"I'm sure you had. You have been nearly six weeks
away. Could you not have found time to visit your Queen
and tell her about the campaign?"

"I was going to leave it until the morning. I'm meeting
the High Command at dawn."

Odelia pulled a chair up beside him. "So tell me now,
plainly, without all the military technicalities."

He stared at the flamelight which the wine had trapped
scarlet in his glass. It was as though a little heart struggled
to beat in there.

"We found a Merduk army near Berrona, close to the
Searil, and destroyed it. They had been ravaging the whole
country up around there. They took the women and murdered the men. The entire region is littered with corpses,
depopulated. A wilderness. The march back to Torunn

was ... difficult. The waggons slowed us down and we went short of food. Half the horses are gone, but our casualties were very light, considering. I believe the Torrin Gap is secure again, at least for a while."

"Well, that is news indeed. I congratulate you, Corfe. Your band of heroes has done it again. How many Merduks did they kill this time?"

He thought of the unbelievable slaughter within the Merduk camp, all order lost, men squirming for their lives in the thick mud, shrieking. Ranafast's Torunnans had captured two hundred of the enemy as they tumbled out of their tents and cut the throats of every last one. No quarter. No prisoners.

"What news here, in the capital?" he asked, ignoring her question.

"Berza's fleet has defeated the Nalbenic ships in an action off the Kardikian coast. There will be no more shipborne supplies for Aurungzeb's armies. Fournier's spies tell us that the Sultan has found himself a wife. He demolished Ormann Dyke and married her in the ruins. She is rumoured to be a Ramusian."

Corfe stirred. "Ormann Dyke is—"

"No more. Yes. Kaile Ormann's walls have been cast down, and the Merduks are busy rearing up another fortress on the east bank of the river. It would seem they intend to stay."

"It could be a good sign—a signall that the Sultan is beginning to think defensively."

"I am glad to hear it."

"This wife of his. Why should he marry a Ramusian? He has a whole harem of Merduk princesses to bed, or so I had always heard."

"She is supposed to be a great beauty, that is all we know."

"Maybe she'll have an influence on him."

"Perhaps. I would not put too much store in the wiles of women! They are overrated."

"Coming from you, Your Majesty, that is hard to credit."

She leaned forward and kissed him. "I am different."

"That I believe."

"Come to bed, Corfe. I have missed you."

"In a moment. I want to feel my feet again, and remember what a chair feels like under my arse."

She laughed, throwing her head back, and in that moment he loved her. He shunted the feeling aside, swamped by guilt, confusion, even a kind of shame. He did not love her. He would not.

"Fournier has been busy in my absence, I take it."

"Oh, yes. By the way, did you ever meet a little deformed monk named Albrec?"

Corfe frowned. "I don't think so. No—wait. Yes, once, outside Torunn. He had no nose."

"That's the one. Macrobius has told me that the fellow went out to preach to the Merduks."

"There is a fool for every season, I suppose. What did they do, crucify him?"

"No. He is something of a fixture in the Merduk court, pontificating about the brotherhood of man and such."

"We seem very well informed about the doings of the Merduk court."

"That is what I have been leading up to. Fournier has planted a spy there, God knows how. He may be a weasely treasonous dastard, but he knows his business. Even I am not allowed to know our agent's name. Twice in the past month a Merduk deserter has come to the gates with a despatch hidden on him."

"He uses Merduks? A man for every message? He'll be caught soon. You can't keep that kind of thing secret for long. I take it there is no way to get a message to this agent?"

Odelia shrugged. "I fail to see how even Fournier can do that."

"What about your . . . abilities? Your—"

"My witchery?" The Queen laughed again. "They run a different road, Corfe. Do you know anything of the Seven Disciplines?"

"I've heard of them, that's all."

"A true mage must master four of the Seven. I know only two—Cantrimy and True Theurgy. I may be one step better than a common hedge-witch, but I am no wizard."

"I see. Then I would like to talk to these so-called Merduk deserters."

"So would I. There is something odd going on at the Merduk court. But Fournier has hidden them away as though they were a miser's hoard. He may even have disposed of them already."

"You are the Queen. Order him to produce them, or the despatches they carried at least."

"That would offend him, and then we might lose his co-operation entirely."

Corfe's eyes narrowed and a light kindled in them, red from the hearth glow. When he looked like that, Odelia thought, you could see the violence graven in him. She felt herself shiver, as though someone had walked over her grave.

"You mean to tell me," Corfe said softly, "that this blue-blooded son of a bitch will deliberately withhold information which could be vital to the conduct of this war, simply out of a fit of pique?"

"He is not one of your soldiers, Corfe. He is a noble, and must be handled with care."

"*Nobles.*" His voice was still soft, but the tone of it set the hair rising on the back of her neck. "I have never yet seen one who was worth so much as a bucket of warm spit. These deserters, or whatever they are, their knowledge of what goes on in the Merduk camps could be priceless to us."

"You cannot touch Fournier," Odelia snapped. "He is of the nobility. You cannot sweep aside the entire bedrock of a kingdom's fabric just like that. Leave him to me."

"All right then; if the kingdom's fabric is so important I will leave him alone."

What would he be like as a king? Odelia wondered. Am I mad to consider it? He has so much anger in him. He might save Torunna, and then tear it apart afterwards. If only he could be healed.

She set a hand on his brow. "What are you doing?" he demanded, still angry.

"Stealing your mind. What do you think? Now be quiet."

Very well, do it. Take that plunge. She was no mind-

rhymer, but she was a healer of sorts, and she loved him.
That opened the door for her. She stepped through it with
a fearful sort of determination.

It was like hearing distant thunder, a baying recklessness
of baffled hurt and fury. She dove past scenes of slaughter,
ecstasies of boundless murder. Corfe's trade, his vocation,
was the killing of his fellow man, and he was good at it—
but he did not enjoy it. That gave her a vast sense of relief.
His soul was not that of a bloodthirsty barbarian, but it was
savage nonetheless. He was possessed of a deep self-
loathing, a desire for redemption that surprised and touched
her.

There—that was Aekir, burning like the end of the
world. Go back further, to before that. And there was an
ordinary young man with kinder eyes and less iron certainty
in his heart. Wholly different, it seemed, and unexceptional.

She realised then that he must not be healed—not by
her. His suffering had made him what he was, had forged
a man out of the boy and rendered him steel-hard. She
found herself both in awe of him and pitying his pain.
There was nothing to be done here. Nothing.

She came out again, unwilling to look at the happiness
there had been before Aekir, the fleeting images of the
raven-haired girl who had been and would always be his
only love. But the youth who had married the silk merchant's daughter was no more. Only the general remained.
Yes, he could be King. He could be a very great king, one
that later centuries would spin legends around. But he
would never be truly at ease with himself—and that was
the mainspring, the thing that drove him to greatness.

She sat back in her chair and rubbed her eyes.

"Well?" he asked.

"Well, nothing. You are a muddle-headed peasant who
needs to get drunk more often."

His smile warmed her. There would never be passion
there, not for her, but he esteemed her nonetheless. That
would have to be enough.

"I think your magicks are overrated," he said.

"Magic often is. I am off to bed. I am an old woman
who needs her rest."

He took her hand. "No. Sit with me awhile, and we will go together."

She actually felt herself blushing, and was glad of the dimness of the room. "Very well then. Let us sit here by the fire and pretend."

"Pretend what?"

"That there are no wars, no armies. Just the rain on the window, the wine in your glass."

"I'll drink to that."

And they sat there hand in hand as the fire burnt low, as content with their common silence, it seemed, as some long-married couple at the end of a day's labour.

IT has become a bizarre habit for an old man, Betanza thought, this night-time pacing of wintry cloisters. I am getting strange in my twilight years.

Charibon's cathedral bells had tolled the middle of the night away, and the cloisters were deserted except for his black-robed shape walking up and down, the very picture of a troubled soul. He did this most nights of late, marching his doubts into the flagstones until he was weary enough to finally tumble into dreamless sleep. And then dragging himself awake in time for matins, with the sun still lost over the dark horizon.

The old need less sleep than the young anyway, he told himself. They are that much more familiar with the concept of their own mortality.

There had been a thaw, and now instead of snow it was a chill black rain that was pouring down out of the Cimbrics, flattening the swell on the Sea of Tor and rattling on the stone shingles of the monastery-city. It was moving slowly east, washing down the Torian plains and beating on the western foothills of the Thurians. In the morning it would be frowning over northern Torunna, where Corfe's army was still a long day's march away from their beds.

Betanza paused in his endless pacing. There was a solitary figure standing in the cloister ahead of him, looking beyond the pillars to the sodden lawn they enclosed and the black starless wedge of sky above it. A tall figure in a monk's habit. Another eccentric, it seemed.

As he drew close the man turned, and Betanza made out a beak of a nose and high forehead under the cowl. A hint of bristling eye-brows.

"God be with you," the man said.

"And with you," the Vicar-General replied politely. He would have walked on, not wanting to interrupt the solitary cleric's devotions, but the other spoke again, stalling him.

"Would you be Betanza, by any chance, head of the Inceptine Order?"

"I would." Impossible to make out the colour of the monk's habit in the darkness, but the material of it was rich and unadorned.

"Ah, I have heard of you, Father. At one time you were a duke of Astarac, I believe."

His curiosity stirred, Betanza looked more closely at the other man. "Indeed. And you are?"

"My name is Aruan. I am a visitor from the west, come seeking counsell in these turbulent times."

The man had the accent of Astarac, but there was an archaic strangeness to his diallect. He spoke, Betanza thought, like a character from some old history or romance. There were so many clerics from so many different parts of the world in Charibon at present, however. Only yesterday a delegation had arrived from Fimbria, of all places, with an escort of forty sable-clad pikemen.

"What part of Astarac do you hail from?" he asked.

"I was originally from Garmidalan, but I have not lived there for many years. Ah—listen, Betanza. Do you hear it?"

Betanza cocked his head, and over the hissing rain there came faint but clear a far-off melancholy howl. It was amplified by another, and then another.

"Wolves," he said. "They scavenge right into the very streets of the city at this time of year."

Aruan smiled oddly under his hood. "Yes, I'll warrant they do."

"Well, I must be getting on. I will leave you to your meditations, Aruan." And Betanza continued his interrupted walk. Something about the stranger unsettled him, and he did not care to be addressed in such a familiar fashion. But he was not in the mood to make an issue of it. He buried his cold hands in his sleeves and paced out the flagstones around the cloister once more, the familiar dilemmas doing the rounds of his mind.

—And he stopped short. The man Aruan was in front of him once again.

Startled, he actually retreated a step from the dark figure. "How did you—?"

"Forgive me. I am very light on my feet, and you were lost in thought. If you could perhaps spare me some of your time, Betanza, there are things I would like to discuss with you."

"See me in the morning. Now get out of my way," Betanza blustered.

"That is a pity. Such a pity." And something preternatural began to occur before Betanza's astonished eyes. The black shape of Aruan bulked out and grew taller, the hem of his habit lifting off the ground. Two yellow lights blinked on like candles under his cowl, and there was the sound of heavy cloth tearing. Betanza made the Sign of the Saint and backed away, struck dumb by the transformation.

"You are a capable man," a voice said, and it was no longer recognisable as wholly human. "It is such a shame. I like independent thinkers. But you do not have the abilities or the vulnerabilities I seek. Forgive me, Betanza."

A werewolf towered there, the habit shrugged aside in rent fragments. Its ears spiked out like horns from the massive skull. Betanza turned to run but it caught him, lifting him into the air as though he were a child. Then it bit once, deep into the bone and cartilage of his neck, nameless things popping under its fangs. Betanza spasmed manically, then fell limp as a rag, his eyes bulging sightlessly. He was set down gently upon the blood-spattered flagstones of the cloister, a puddle of black robes with a white, agonised face staring out of them.

Beyond the monastery, the wolves howled sadly in the rain.

FIFTEEN

"Aм I a fool? Do I look like a fool to you?" the Sultan of Ostrabar roared. "Do you expect me to believe that a host of fifteen thousand men constitutes a reconnaissance patrol? Beard of the beloved Prophet, I am surrounded by imbeciles! What is this? Some game of your own, Shahr Johor? Tell me how this could have happened, and explain why I was not informed!"

The lofty conference chamber within which Pieter Martellus had once planned the defence of Ormann Dyke was silent. The assembled Merduk officers kept their faces carefully blank. Shahr Indun Johor, commander-in-chief of the Merduk army, cleared his throat. A fine sheen of sweat varnished his handsome face.

"Majesty, I—"

"No elabourations or justifications. I want the truth!"

"I may have exceeded my orders, it is true. But I was told to conduct a reconnaissance in force of the Torrin Gap, and if practicable establish a garrison there to cut communications between Torunna and Almark."

"You are parroting the very text of my written orders. Very good! Now explain to me how they were disobeyed."

"Majesty, I did not disobey them—truly. But resistance was so minimal up there that I thought the time ripe to establish a firm foothold. That is . . . that is what the army of Khedive Arzamir was to accomplish. None of our patrols reported the presence of regular Torunnan troops. Not one! Still less those accursed red horsemen and their Fimbrian allies. So I—I exceeded my orders. I told Arzamir that if resistance did not stiffen he was to push on and try for Charibon. It was a mistake, I know." Shahr Johor drew himself up as if awaiting a blow. "I take full responsibility. I gambled, and I lost. And we are ten thousand men the poorer for it. I have no excuses."

The room was very still. It might have been populated by a crowd of armoured statues. On the riverbanks below they could hear a Merduk subadar haranguing his troops, and beyond that the regular clink of a thousand hammers as the last remnants of the Long Walls were demolished stone by stone.

Aurungzeb seemed to slump, the rage which had ballooned his frame leaking out of him. He ground his teeth audibly and then hissed, "What manner of man is he? Is he a magician? Can he read our minds? I would give half my kingdom to have his head on a spear. Batak!"

There was a leathery flapping sound, and a pigeon-sized homunculus swooped down from the rafters to land on the table in the middle of the room. Several of the officers present backed away from it; others wrinkled up their noses in disgust. The tiny creature folded its wings, cocked its head to one side, and spoke with the voice of a full-grown man.

"My Sultan?"

"Damn it, Batak, cannot you be here in person? How much longer must you hole up in that tower of yours with your abominations?"

"My researches are almost complete, my lord. How may I be of service?"

"Earn the gold that has been showered upon you. Rid me of this Torunnan general."

The homunculus picked up a discarded quill from the table, nibbled on it and then cast it away, spitting like a cat. The glow which infested its eyes wavered, then grew strong again.

"What you ask is no light thing, my Sultan. The assassins—"

"Have declined my offer. Apparently one of their number has been lost in Torunn already, and they have no wish to hazard more. No, you are the wizard, the great master of magic. Your late master Orkh had every confidence in you, else he would not have made you court mage after him. Now fulfil his confidence. I want this man dead, and soon. The final assault on Torunna will begin within weeks. I want this paladin of theirs cold in the ground ere it begins."

"I will see what I can do, my lord." The glow in the homunculus's eyes went out. It glared at the men who surrounded it, baring its miniature fangs. Then it took off, the wind from its wings sending papers flying from the table. It bobbed in midair for a moment, and then flew out of the open windows and disappeared.

"Such creatures are inherently evil, and should not be utilised by a follower of the Prophet," a voice said harshly.

Aurungzeb turned. It was Mehr Jirah, and beside him was Ahara, a vision of veiled midnight-blue silk. To their rear stood the austere figure of Shahr Baraz. Silent attendants closed the doors again behind the trio.

"In time of war, all means must be utilised," the Sultan mumbled uncomfortably. "Is there something we can help you with, Mehr Jirah? This is a closed indaba of the High Command. There is no place for mullahs here. And Ahara, my Queen, what brings you here at this time? We are a gathering of men. Women—even queens—do not appear at such gatherings. It is not fitting."

Ahara remained silent, but looked at her companion.

"We wish to speak with you, my Sultan—both of us," Mehr Jirah said. "Our matter, however, is of the greatest importance, not something to be blurted out in haste—thus it can wait until the indaba has run its course."

His calm certainty appeared to subdue Aurungzeb. He seemed about to speak, but thought better of it, and turned back to the table, one hand toying with the hilt of the curved dagger he wore tucked into his belt sash.

"We were nearly done, at any rate. Shahr Johor, you made a grave error of judgement, but I can see what led you to it. For that reason I am willing to be clement. I will give you one more chance, and one only. Tell me of your plans for the final campaign. A swift outline, if you please. I can see that Mehr Jirah and my Queen are impatient."

This last was said with obvious curiosity.

The Merduk khedive unrolled a large map on the table and weighted down its corners with inkwells. "The planning is already far advanced, Majesty, and is completely unaffected by our losses in the north. As you know, we have had to bring forward the date of our advance due to the loss of the seaborne supply line—"

"Nalbenic bombasts. They swore they could sweep the sea of Torunnan ships, and what happens? They lose half their fleet and keep the other half cowering in port."

"Quite. Our logistics are slightly more precarious than I could wish, which means that—"

"Which means that this is our last throw."

"Yes, Majesty. This is likely to be the last chance we will have to take the Torunnan capital. We simply do not have the resources, or the men, to continue this campaign for another year."

There was a long, almost reverent silence in the chamber at these words. They had all known this, of course, but to have it stated so baldly, and in the presence of the Sultan, brought it home to them. The Ramusians might view the Sultan's forces as illimitable, but the men around the table knew better. Too many troops had died in the heavy fighting since the fall of the dyke, and their lines of supply had been whittled down to a single major road: a slender thread for the fate of any army to hang upon. The reconstruction of a Merduk Ormann Dyke now seemed foresight, not pessimism, but for the victors of Aekir it was a bitter pill to swallow.

Finally Aurungzeb broke the stillness. "Go on, Shahr Johor."

The young Merduk khedive picked up a dry quill and began pointing at the unrolled map. Depicted upon it in some detail was the region between the Torrin river and the southern Thurians. Once a fertile and peaceful land, it had become the cockpit for the entire western war.

"The main army will advance in a body, here, down the line of the Western Road. In it will be the *Minhraib*, the *Hraibadar*, our new arquebusier regiments, the elephants, artillery and siege train—some hundred thousand men all told. This force will pitch into any enemy body it meets, and pin it. At the same time, the *Ferinai* and our mounted pistoleers, plus the remnants of the Nalbenic horse-archers—twenty-five thousand men in all—will set off to the north and advance separately."

"That second force you mention is entirely cavalry," Aurungzeb pointed out.

"Yes, Majesty. They must be completely mobile, and swift-moving. Their mission is twofold. Firstly, they will protect the northern flank of the main body, in case the red horsemen and their allies are still at large in that area. If this proves to be unnecessary—and I believe it will—they will wait until the main body has engaged the Torunnan army, and then come down upon the enemy flank or rear. They will be the hammer to our anvil."

"Why do you believe this enemy force in the north is no longer in the field?"

"They freed a large quantity of female captives that our troops had rounded up. I am certain they will escort these back to the Torunnan capital. It was, I believe, only due to the presence of these captives that any of Khedive Arzamir's army escaped intact at all."

"Hammer and anvil," Aurungzeb murmured. "I like it."

"It's how he caught the Nalbeni in the Torunn battle," one of the other officers said, an older man with a scarred face.

"Who?"

"This Torunnan general, Majesty. He halted them with arquebusiers and then threw his cavalry at their flanks. Decimated them. If it worked against troops as fleet as horsearchers I'll wager it will against Torunnan infantry."

"I am glad to see we are learning lessons from the behaviour of the enemy," Aurungzeb said wryly, but his brow was thunderous. "Very well. Shahr Johor, when will the army move out?"

"Within two weeks, Majesty."

"What if this vaunted general of theirs does not come out to meet us, but stands siege in Torunn? What then?"

"He will come out, my Sultan. It is in his nature. It is said he lost his wife in Aekir, and it has taught him to hate us. All his strategies, even the defensive ones, are based on the tactical offencive. These scarlet-armoured cavalry of his excel in it. He will come out."

"I hope you are right. We would win a siege, no doubt of that, but then the war would drag through the summer, perhaps later. The *Minhraib* must be returned to Ostrabar in time for the harvest."

"By harvest time, Your Majesty, you shall be using the throne of Torunna as a footstool. I stake my life upon it."

"You have, Shahr Johor—believe me, you have. This is very well. I like this plan. The Torunnan army numbers no more than thirty thousand. If we can pin them down in the open and launch the *Ferinai* into their rear, I cannot see how they will survive. If Batak's magicks do not put paid to him first, I shall have this Torunnan general in a captureyoke. I will walk him to Orkhan, where he will be crucified." Aurungzeb chuckled. "Having said that, if he meets his fate upon the field of battle, I shall not be unduly displeased."

A rustle of laughter flitted about the room.

"That will do for now. You will all leave, but for Mehr Jirah and his urgent errand. Ahara, my sweet, seat yourself. Shahr Baraz, are you a complete boor? Find my Queen a chair."

The Merduk officers filed out, bowing in turn to Aurungzeb and Ahara. The door clicked shut behind them.

"Well, Mehr Jirah. What is so urgent that you must enter

an indaba unannounced and, though I am not one to prate
about protocol, why is my Queen at your side?"

"Forgive me, Sultan. But when something momentous
occurs which impinges upon the very faith of our people
and the manner of their belief, then I deem it necessary to
bring it to your attention at once."

"You intrigue and alarm me. Go on."

"You recall the Ramusian monk who has come to us
from Torunn?"

"That madman. What about him?"

"Sultan, I believe he is not mad." Mehr Jirah's face grew
stern and he rose to his full height as though bracing himself. "I believe he speaks the truth."

Aurungzeb blinked. "What? What are you telling me?"

"I have been conducting researches in our archives for
the last two months, and I have had access—which you so
graciously granted—to all the documents that were saved
from the ecclesiastical and historical sections of the Library
of Gadorian Hagus in Aekir. They tally with a tradition that
my own *Hraib* hold to be true. In short, the Prophet Ahrimuz, blest be his name, came to us out of the west, and
it now seems certain that he was none other than the western Saint Ramusio—"

"Mehr Jirah!"

"Sultan, the Saint and the Prophet are the same person.
Our religion and that of the westerners are products of one
mind, worshipping the same God and venerating the same
man as His emissary."

Aurungzeb's swarthy face had gone pale. "Mehr Jirah,
you are mistaken," he barked hoarsely. "The idea is absurd."

"I wish it were, truly. This knowledge has shaken me to
the very core. The monk whom we deemed a madman is
in fact a scholar of profound learning, and a man of great
faith. He did not come to us out of a whim—he came to
tell us the truth, and he bore with him the copy of an ancient document which confirms it, having fled with it from
Charibon itself. The Ramusian Church has suppressed this
knowledge for centuries, but God has seen fit to pass it on
to us."

There was a pause. Finally Aurungzeb spoke, unwillingly it seemed.

"Ahara, what part have you in this?"

"I acted as interpreter for Mehr Jirah in his conversations with the monk Albrec, my lord. I am able to confirm what Mehr Jirah says."

"Do you not think, Sultan," the mullah continued, "that it is a strange twist of fate which has brought a western queen and a Ramusian scholar to you at this time? I see the hand of God at work. His word has been corrupted and hidden for long enough. Now is the time to finally let it see the light of day."

Aurungzeb's eyes flashed. He began pacing about the room like a restless bear. "This is all a tri`k`—some ruse of the Ramusians to divide us and mislead us in the very hour of our final victory. My Queen: she was once a Ramusian. I can see how she was taken in, wishing to reconcile the faith of her past and the true faith which she has had the fortune to be reborn into. But you, Mehr Jirah: you are a holy man, a man of learning and shrewdness. How can you bring yourself to believe such lies? Such a blasphemous falsehood?"

"I know the truth when I hear it," Mehr Jirah retorted icily. "I am not a fool, nor yet some manner of wishful thinker. I have spent my life pondering the words of the Prophet and reviling the teachings of the western imposter-saint. Imagine my shock when I look more closely at these teachings, and find in some cases the same phrases uttered by Ramusio and Ahrimuz, blest be his name, the same parables . . . even the mannerisms of the two men are the same! If this is a Ramusian trick, then it is one that was conceived centuries ago. Besides, the Ramusian texts I studied antedated the arrivall of our own Prophet. Ahrimuz was there! Before he ever crossed the Jafrar and taught the Merduk peoples, he was there, in Normannia, and he was a westerner. His name, my Sultan, was Ramusio."

Aurungzeb was manageing to look both frightened and furious at the same time.

"Who else knows of this discovery of yours?"

"I have taken the liberty of gathering together the mullahs of several of the closest *Hraib*. They agree with me—albeit reluctantly. Our concern now is in what manner we should disseminate this knowledge amongst the tribes and sultanates."

"All this was done without my knowledge. On whose authority—?"

Mehr Jirah thumped a fist on the table, making the map of Torunna quiver. "I am not answerable to you or anyone else on this earth for my actions or the dictates of my conscience! I am answerable to God alone. We do not ask your permission to do what we know to be right, Sultan. We are merely keeping you informed. We will not sit on the truth, as the Ramusians have for the past five centuries. Their current version of their faith is a stench in the very nostrils of God. Would you genuinely have me commit the same blasphemy?"

Aurungzeb seemed to shrink. He pulled himself up a chair and sat down heavily. "This will affect the outlook of the army—you realise that. Some of the *Minhraib* are unwilling to fight as it is. If it gets out that the Ramusians are some kind of—of co-religionists, why then—"

"I prefer to think of them as brothers in faith," Mehr Jirah interrupted grimly. "According to the Prophet, it is a heinous crime to attack one whose beliefs are the same as one's own. Eventually, Sultan, we may have to see the Ramusians as such. They may be riven with discord, but they revere the same Prophet as we do."

"Belief in the same God has not stopped men from killing one another. It never will. Take a close look at your brothers in faith, Mehr Jirah. They are busy cutting one another's throats as we speak. In Hebrion and Astarac—and even Torunna—they have been fighting civil wars incessantly, even while we hammer at their eastern frontier."

"I am not naïve, Sultan. I know the war cannot be halted in its tracks. But all I ask is that when the time comes to make peace—as it will—you keep in your mind what you have been told here."

"I will do so, Mehr Jirah. You have my word on it. When we have taken Torunn I will be merciful. There will be no sack, I assure you."

Mehr Jirah looked long and hard at his Sultan for several tense seconds, and then bowed. "I can ask no more. And now, with your permission, I will leave."

"Are you intent on disseminating this news amongst the troops, Mehr Jirah?"

"Not quite yet. There are many points of doctrine which remain to be clarified. I would ask you one favour though, my Sultan."

"Ask away."

"I would like the Ramusian monk released into my custody. I tyre of skulking around this fortress's dungeons."

"By all means, Mehr Jirah. You shall have your little maniac if you please. Tell Akran I said he was to be freed. Now you may leave me. Shahr Baraz, you also."

"Sultan, my lady—"

"Can do without her shadow for five minutes. Escort Mehr Jirah out, will you? Your mistress will be with you presently."

Mehr Jirah and Shahr Baraz both bowed, and departed. Heria had risen to her feet when Aurungzeb held up a hand. "No, please my dear. Sit down. There is no ceremony between Sultan and Queen when they are alone together."

As she resumed her seat he padded close until he hulked above her like a hill. He was smiling. Then one hairy-knuckled hand swooped down and ripped off her veil. The fingers grasped her jaw, their pressure pursing up her lips like a rose. When Aurungzeb spoke it was in a low, soft purr, like that of a murmuring lover.

"If you ever, ever do anything like this again behind my back, I will have you sent to a field brothel. Do you understand me, Ahara?"

She nodded dumbly.

"You are my Queen, but only because you have my son in your belly. You will be treated with respect because of him, and because of me—but that is all. Do not think that your beauty, intoxicating though it is, will ever make a fool of me. Do I make myself clear? Am I transparent enough for you?"

Again, the silent nod.

"Very good." He kissed the bloodred lips. As his hand

released her face it flushed pink, save for the white finger-marks.

"You will come to my bed tonight. You may be with child, but there are ways and means around that. Now put on your veil and return to your chambers."

WHEN Heria had returned to her suite in the austere old tower she let her maids disrobe her, sitting passively upon her dressing stool like a sculpture. Her evening robes donned, she dismissed them and sat alone for a long time, utterly still. At last there was a knock at the door.

"My lady," Shahr Baraz said. "Are you all right?"

She closed her eyes for a moment, and then said calmly, "Do come in, Shahr Baraz."

The old Merduk looked concerned. "His displeasure is like a gale of wind, lady. Soon over, soon forgotten. Do not let it trouble you."

She smiled at that. "What do you think of Mehr Jirah's findings?"

"I am surprised no-one else has noticed such things in the five centuries Merduk and Ramusian have co-existed."

"Perhaps they have. Perhaps the knowledge was always buried again. It will not be this time, though."

"Lady, I am not sure if you wish to set us all at each other's throats, or if you are genuinely crusading for the truth. Frankly, it worries me."

"I want the war to end. Is that so bad? I want no more men killed or women raped or children orphaned. If that is treason then I am a traitor to the very marrow of my bones."

"The Ramusians also do their share of killing," Shahr Baraz said wryly.

"Which is why the monk Albrec must be released and allowed to return to Torunn. They are sitting on this information there as they would like to do here."

"Men will always kill each other."

"I know. But they at least can stop pretending to do it in the name of God."

"There is that, I suppose. I would say this to you though: do not push Aurungzeb too far."

"I thought he was a gale of wind."

"He is, when he is crossed in what he thinks is a small thing, but he did not become Sultan by sitting on his hands. If anything threatens the foundation of his power, he will annihilate it without regret or remorse."

"Including me?"

"Including you."

"Thank you for your frankness, Shahr Baraz. It's strange. Since coming to live amongst the Merduks I have met more honest men than I ever did in my life before. There is you, Mehr Jirah, and the monk, Albrec."

"Three men are not so many. Were folk so dishonest in Aekir, then?" Shahr Baraz asked with a smile.

Her face clouded. She looked away.

"I'm sorry, lady. I did not mean to—"

"It's nothing. Nothing at all. I will get used to it in time. People can grow accustomed to all manner of things."

There was a pause. "I will be outside the door if you need me for anything, lady," Shahr Baraz said at last. He bowed and left the room, when what he wanted to do was take her in his arms. As he resumed his post outside her door he scourged himself for his weakness, his absurdity. She was too fine to be a Merduk broodmare, and yet he thought there could be a core of pure steel behind those lovely eyes. That fellow she had loved in Aekir, who had been her husband: he must have been a man indeed. She deserved no less.

SIXTEEN

BARDOLIN squatted on the stone floor and rubbed his wrists thoughtfully. The sores had dried up and healed in a matter of moments. The only evidence of his suffering that remained were the silver scars on his skin. He felt his shaven chin and chuckled with wonder.

"My God, I am a man again."

"You were never anything else," Golophin said shortly from his chair by the fire. Have yourself some wine, Bard. But go easy. Your stomach will not be used to it."

Bardolin straightened and rose from the floor with some difficulty, grimacing. "I'm not yet used to standing upright, either. It's been three months since I was able to stretch my limbs. God, my throat is as dry as sand. I have not talked so much in a year, Golophin. It is good to get it all out at last. It helps the healing. Even your magicks cannot restore me wholly in a moment."

"And your magicks, Bardolin: what of them? You should have recovered from the loss of your familiar by now. What about your own Disciplines? Are they still there, or has the change stifled them?"

Bardolin said nothing. He sipped his wine carefully and eyed the pile of junk at one side of the circular tower room. His chains lay there, with his blood and filth still encrusted upon them. And the splintered fragments of the crate they had transported him here within. Six brawny longshoremen terrified out of their wits as the thing within the crate roared and snarled at them and beat against the walls of its wooden prison. They had tumbled the crate off the end of their waggon and then urged the frightened horses into a gallop, fleeing the lonely tower with all the speed they could whip out of the beasts.

"It comes and goes without any reason or rhyme," he said finally. "As every day passes it grows more uncontrollable. The wolf, I mean."

"That will pass. In time you and the beast will mesh together more fully, and you will be able to change form at will. I have seen it before."

"I'm glad one of us is an expert," Bardolin said tartly.

Golophin studied his friend and former pupil for a while in silence. He had become a gaunt shade of a man, the bones of his face standing out under the skin, his eyes sunk in deep orbits, the flesh around them dark as the skin of a grape. His head had been shaven down to the scalp to rid him of the vermin which infested it, and it gave him the air of a sinister convict. The wholesome, hale-looking soldier-mage Golophin had once known seemed to have fled without a trace.

"You touched my mind once," the old mage said quietly. "I was scanning the west on the chance I might find some trace of you, and I heard you cry out for help."

Bardolin stared into the fire. "We were at sea, I think. I felt you. But then he came along and broke the connection."

"He is a remarkable man, if man is indeed the word."

"I don't know what he is, Golophin. Something new, as I am. His immortality has something to do with the black change, as has his power. I am beginning to fathom it all. Here in the Old World we always thought that a shifter could not master any of the other six Disciplines—the beast disrupted some necessary harmony in the soul. But now I think differently. The beast, once mastered, can lead one to the most intimate understanding of the Dweomer possible. A shifter is in essence a conjured animal, a creature owing its existence entirely to some force outside the normal laws of the universe. When a man becomes a lycanthrope, he becomes, if you like, a thing of pure magic, and if he has the will then it is all there waiting for him. All that power."

"You almost sound as though you accept your fate."

"Hawkwood brought me here thinking you could cure me. We both know you cannot. And perhaps I do not want to be cured any more. Golophin, have you thought of that? This Aruan is incredibly powerful. I could be too. All I need is time, time to think and research."

"This tower and everything in it is at your disposal, Bard, you know that."

"Thank you."

"But I have one question. When you unlock this reservoir of power, if you ever do, what will you do with it? Aruan is intent on establishing himself in the Old World, perhaps not tomorrow or this month or even this year, but soon. He intends some kind of sorcerous hegemony. He's been working towards it for centuries, from what you tell me. When that day comes, then it will be the ordinary kings and soldiers of the world versus him and his kind. Our kind. Where do the lines get drawn?"

Bardolin would not look at him. "I don't know. He has a point, don't you think? For centuries we've been persecuted, tortured, murdered because of the gift we were born with. It is time it was stopped. The Dweomer-folk have a right to live in peace."

"I agree. But starting a war is not the way to secure that right. It will make the ordinary folk of the world more fearful of us than ever."

"It is time the ordinary folk of the world were made to regret their blind bigotry," Bardolin snarled, and there was such genuine menace in his voice that Golophin, startled, could think of nothing more to say.

• • •

Hawkwood had not ridden a horse for longer than he could remember. Luckily, the animal he had hired seemed to know more about it than he did. He bumped along in a state of weary discomfort, his destination visible as a grey finger of stone shimmering in the spring haze above the hills to the north. There was another rider on the road ahead, a woman by the looks of things. Her mount was lame. Even as he watched, she dismounted and began inspecting its hooves one by one. He drew level and reined in, some battered old remnant of courtesy surfacing.

"Can I help?"

The woman was well-dressed, a tall, plain girl in her late twenties with a long nose and a wondrous head of fiery hair that caught the sunshine.

"I doubt it," and she went back to examining her horse.

His appearance was against him, Hawkwood knew. Though he had bathed and changed and suffered a haircut at the hands of Donna Ponera, Galliardo's formidable wife, he still looked like some spruced-up vagabond.

"Have you far to go?" he tried again.

"He's thrown a shoe. God's blood. Is there a smithy hereabouts?"

"I don't know. Where are you heading for?"

The girl straightened. "Not far. Yonder tower." She gave Hawkwood a swift, unimpressed appraisal. "I have a pistol. You'll find easier pickings elsewhere."

Hawkwood laughed. "I'll bet I would. It so happens I also am going to the tower. You know the Mage Golophin then?"

"Perhaps." She looked him over with more curiosity now. He liked the frankness of her stare, the strength he saw in her features. Not much beauty there, in the conventional sense, but definite character. "My name is Hawkwood," he said.

"I am Isolla." She seemed relieved when her name elicited no reaction from him. "I suppose we may as well travel the rest of the way together. It's not so far. Is Golophin expecting you?"

"Yes. And you?"

A slight hesitation. "Yes. You may as well dismount, instead of staring down at me."

"You can ride my horse if you like."

"No. I only ride sidesaddle anyway."

So she was well-born. He could have guessed that from her clothes. Her accent intrigued him, though. It was of Astarac.

"You know Golophin well?" he asked her as they walked side by side leading their mounts.

"Well enough. And you?"

"Only by reputation. He is looking after a sick friend of mine."

"Are you all right? You have a strange gait."

"I have not ridden a horse in a long time. Or walked upon solid earth for that matter."

"What, do you possess wings that take you everywhere?"

"No, a ship. She put in only this morning."

He saw a light dawn in her eyes. She looked him up and down again, this time with some wonder. "Richard Hawkwood the mariner—of course! I am a dunce. Your name is all over the city."

"The very same." He waited for her to give some fuller account of herself, but in vain. They strolled together companionably enough after that, the miles flitting by with little more conversation. For some reason Hawkwood was almost disappointed when they finally knocked on the door of Golophin's tower. There was something about this Isolla that finally made him feel as though he had come home.

I've been at sea too long, he told himself.

"CURIOSITY," Golophin said, annoyed. "In a man it is a virtue, leading to enlightenment. In a woman it is a vice, leading to mischief." He looked at Isolla disapprovingly, but she seemed unabashed.

"That's a saying dreamt up by a man. I am not some gossiping lady's maid, Golophin."

"You should not be behaving like one then. Ah, Captain Hawkwood, I thank you for delivering our princess safe and sound, since she was pig-headed enough to come out here."

"Princess?" Hawkwood asked her. Some absurd little hope died within him.

"It's not important," she said uncomfortably.

"You are looking at the next Queen of Hebrion, no less," Golophin said. "As if the world needed another queen. Make yourself useful, Isolla. Pour us some wine. There's a jug of it cooling in the study."

She left the room, undismayed by the old wizard's disapproval. And indeed, as soon as she had left the room a smile spread across his face.

"She should have been a man," he said with obvious affection.

Hawkwood disagreed, but kept his opinion to himself.

"So, Captain, we meet at last. I am glad you came."

"Where's Bardolin?"

"Asleep. It will speed his healing."

"Is he . . . has he—?"

"The beast is dormant for now. I have been able to help him control it."

"You can cure him, then?"

"No. No-one can. But I can help him manage it. He has been telling me of your voyage. A veritable nightmare."

"Yes. It was."

"Not many could have survived it."

Hawkwood went to the window. It looked out from the tower's great height over southern Hebrion, the land green and serene under the sun, the sea a sparkle on the horizon.

"I think we were meant to survive it—Bardolin was anyway. They allowed us to escape. I sometimes wonder if they even guided our course on the voyage home. Bardolin told you of them, I suppose. A race of monstrosities. He thinks some of them are in Normannia already, and more are coming. They have plans for us, the wizards of the west."

"Well, we are forewarned at least—thanks to you. What are your own plans now, Captain?"

The question took Hawkwood by surprise. "I hadn't thought about it. Lord, I've only been back on dry land a day. So much has happened. My wife died in Abrusio, my house is gone. All I have left is my ship, and she is in a sorry state. I suppose I was thinking of going to the King, to see if he had anything for me." He realised how that sounded, and flushed.

"You have earned something, that much is true," Golophin reassured him gently. "I am sure Abeleyn will not be remiss in recognising that. Your expedition may have been a failure, but it has also been a valuable source of information. Tell me, what think you of Lord Murad?"

"He's unhinged. Oh, not in a foaming-at-the-mouth kind of way, but something has gone awry in his head. It was the west that did it."

"And the girl-shifter, Griella."

"Bardolin told you of that? Yes, perhaps. That was a queer thing. He felt something for her, and she for him, but it harmed them both."

Isolla came back with pewter mugs of chilled wine. "Your Majesty," Hawkwood said as he took his, eyes dancing.

She frowned. "Not yet."

"Not for several weeks." Golophin grinned. "I think she grows impatient."

"With you, yes. Sometimes you are like a little boy, Golophin."

"Is that so? Abeleyn always thought of me as an old woman. I am a man for all seasons it seems."

Hawkwood dragged his gaze away from Isolla and set aside his tankard after the merest sip. "I'll be going. I just wanted to make sure all was well with Bardolin."

"I'll speak to the King on your behalf, Captain. We'll see you are recompensed for your losses, and your achievement," Golophin promised.

"That won't be necessary," Hawkwood said with stiff pride. "Look after Bardolin; he's a good man, no matter what that bastard wizard turned him into. I can take care of myself. Goodbye, Golophin." He bowed slightly. "Lady." And left.

"A proud man for a commoner," Isolla said.

"He is not a common man," Golophin retorted. "I was a fool to phrase it so. He deserves recognition for what he did, but he'll turn his back on it if he thinks it smacks of charity. And meanwhile Lord Murad is no doubt standing on his hind legs as we speak, relating the marvells of his expedition and reaping as much of the credit as he can. It's a filthy world, Isolla."

"It could be worse," she told him. He glanced at her, and laughed.

"Ah, what it is to be in love." Which made her blush to the roots of her hair.

"You'll make him a grand wife, if our stiff-necked Captain doesn't steal you away first."

"What? What are you saying?"

"Never mind. Hebrion has her King again, and will soon have a worthy Queen. The country needs a rest from war and intrigue for a while. So do I. I intend to immure myself here with Bardolin, and lose myself in pure research. I have neglected that lately. Too much of politics in the way. You and Abeleyn can run the kingdom admirably between you without my help. Just be sure to keep an eye on Murad, and that harpy, Jemilla."

"She's finished at court. None of the nobles will give her the time of day now."

"Don't be too sure. She still bears a king's child who, although illegitimate, will always be older than any you have."

"We had best hope she has a girl, then."

"Indeed. Now get back to the palace, Isolla. There is a man there who has need of you."

She kissed the old wizard on the cheek. In Hebrion she had found a husband, and a man who had become like a father. Golophin was right: the worst was over, surely. The country would have its rest.

PART TWO

DEATH OF A SOLDIER

Soon a great warrior
Will tower over the land,
And you will see the ground
Strewn with severed heads.
The clamour of blue swords
Will echo in the hills;
The dew of blood
Will lace the limbs of men.

Njal's Saga

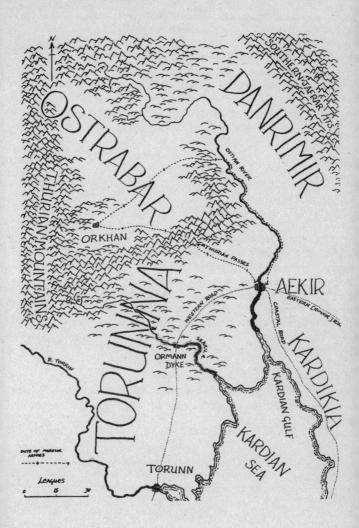

SEVENTEEN

THE Papal palace of Macrobius had once been an Inceptine abbey, and was now bursting at the seams with all manner of clerics and office-seekers, armed guards and inky-fingered clerks. Their numbers were augmented today by richly dressed Torunnan soldiers, a bodyguard fit for a queen. And in their midst, like a scarlet spearhead, eight Cathedrallers in all their barbaric glory. The military tailors had quickly run up some crimson surcoats for them—it would not do for them to tramp into the Pontiff's presence in their battered armour—and though they were, sartorially speaking, smarter than they had ever been before, their tattooed faces and long hair set them apart.

Queen Odelia and her commander-in-chief had come to call upon Macrobius, and they must needs be received with all the pomp and ceremony that embattled Torunn could muster. Two thrones had been set up—that reserved for the Queen noticeably less ornate than Macrobius's—and to one side there was a stark black chair for the sable-clad general.

Corfe was far and away the most sombre-looking member of the cavalcade that had made its way through Torunn's packed streets to the Papal palace, but it was he who elicited the most excitement from the gathered crowds. They cheered him to the echo, and some of the more effusive pushed through the cordon of troops to touch his stirruped boot or even stroke the flank of his restive destrier. Andruw, who rode at his side, thought it all immensely funny, but for himself he felt like a fraud. They called him the "Deliverer of his country," but that country was a hell of a long way from being delivered yet, he thought.

The cavalcade dismounted in the main square of the abbey. The balconies which surrounded the square were lined with cheering monks and priests—a weird and somewhat comical sight. Then Corfe took the Queen's arm, and to a flourish of trumpets they were ushered into the great reception hall of the palace, running the gauntlet of a throng of clapping notables. These were most of what remained of Torunna's nobility, and their greeting was markedly less enthusiastic than that of the crowds beyond the abbey walls. They eyed the tattooed tribesmen with distaste, the black-clad general with wonder and dislike, and the ageing Queen with guarded disapproval. Corfe's face was stiff as wood as he stood before the Papal dais and looked once more on the blind old man who was the spiritual leader of half the western world.

Monsignor Alembord had barely cleared his throat to announce the eminent visitors in his stately fashion when Macrobius cut him short by hobbling down from the dais and reaching out blindly.

"Corfe."

Corfe took the searching hand. It felt as dry as an autumn leaf in his grasp, frail as thistledown. He looked at the ravaged face and remembered the long cold nights on the Western Road on the retreat from Aekir.

"Holiness. I am here."

The chamber fell into silence, Alembord's proclamation strangling into a muted cough. All eyes swivelled to the general and the Pontiff.

Macrobius smiled. "It has been a long time, General."

"Yes. It has."

"I told you once your star had not yet stopped rising. I was right. You have come a long way from Aekir, my friend. On a long, hard road."

"We both have," Corfe said. His throat burnt. The sight of Macrobius's face brought back memories from another world, another time. The old man gripped his shoulder. "Sit beside me now, and tell me of your travells. We shall have more than burnt turnip to share this time."

The chair which had been set aside for Corfe was hurriedly moved closer to the Papal throne and the trio took their seats after Macrobius had greeted the Queen with rather more formality. Musicians began to play, and the crowd in the hall broke into a loud surf of conversation. Andruw remained standing at the foot of the dais with the Cathedraller bodyguards and found himself next to a man of about his own age in the robes of an Inceptine.

"What cheer, Father?" he said brightly.

"What cheer *your grace*, soldier. I'm a bishop, you know."

Andruw looked him up and down. "What shall I do— kiss your ring?"

Avila laughed, and took two brimming glasses of wine from an attendant who passed by with a tray. "You can kiss my clerical backside if you want. But have a drink first. These levees are liquid occasions, and I hear you've been working up quite a thirst in the north, you and your scarlet barbarians."

"I didn't know they made bishops so young these days."

"Or colonels either, for that matter. I came here from Charibon with . . . with a friend of mine."

"Wait! I know you, I think. Didn't we run into you and your friend? You were with a couple of Fimbrians on the Northern Road a few months back. Corfe stopped and talked to you."

"You have a good memory."

"Your friend—he was the one without a nose. Where's he today? Keeping out of the way of the high and mighty?"

"I . . . I don't know where he is. I tell you what though,

we'll drink to him. A toast to Albrec. Albrec the mad, may
God be good to him."

And they clinked their glasses together, before gulping
down the good wine.

"WE have reason to believe he is still alive, this errant
bishop of yours," Odelia said. "And what is more,
he is moving freely in the Merduk court, spreading his message. As far as we know, the Merduk mullahs are debating
this message even now."

Macrobius nodded. "I knew he would succeed. He has
the same aura of destiny about him as that I sensed in Corfe
here. Well, mayhap it is better this way. The thing is taken
out of our hands after all. I see no option but to broadcast
the news abroad here in Torunna also. The time for discussion and debate is past. We must begin spreading the
word of the new faith."

"Quite a revelation, this new faith of yours," Corfe said
quietly.

Odelia had told him what was engendering the rancour-
ous argument in the Papal palace. He had been as astonished as anyone, but had tended to think of it as a Church
affair. The Merduks were purportedly engaged in the same
debate: that gave it a different colour entirely. There might
be military ramifications.

The Pontiff, the Queen and Corfe were closeted in Macrobius's private quarters at the end of a long, tiring day
much given over to speech and spectacle. The whole oc-
casion had been a complete success, Odelia had been keen
to point out. Her coronation had been ratified by the
Church, and everyone had witnessed the Pontiff greet Corfe
like a long-lost friend. Anyone seeking to destabilise the
new order would think twice after seeing the rapturous welcome given to them by the crowds, and the apparent amity
between the Crown and the Church.

"If the Merduks take this Albrec's message to heart, will
it affect their conduct of the war?" Odelia asked.

"I do not know," the Pontiff told her. "There are men of
conscience amongst the Merduk nation, we have always

known that. But men of conscience do not often have the influence necessary to halt wars."

"I agree," Corfe put in. "The Sultan will keep fighting. Everything points to the fact that this campaign is meant to be the climax of the entire war. He means to take Torunn, and he will not let the mullahs get in his way—not now. But if we can survive through to the summer, it may be that a negotiated end to the war will be more feasible."

"An end to the war," Odelia said. "My God, could that be possible? A final end to it?"

"I spoke to Fournier yesterday. He is as insufferably arrogant as always, but when I persevered he deigned to tell me that the Merduk armies are completely overstretched, with desertions rising daily. If this next assault fails, he cannot see how the Sultan will continue. The *Minhraib* campaigned right through last year's harvest. If they do so a second year running, then Ostrabar will face famine. This is Aurungzeb's last throw."

"I had no idea," Odelia said. "I don't think of them as men with crops and families. To me they are more like . . . like cockroaches. Kill one and a dozen more appear. So there is hope at last—a light at the tunnel's end."

"There is hope," Corfe said heavily. "But as I say, he is betting everything on this last assault. We could be facing as many as a hundred and fifty thousand enemy in the field."

"Should we not then stay behind these walls and stand siege? We could hold out for months—well past harvest."

"If we did that he could send the *Minhraib* home and contain us with a smaller force. No. We need to make him commit every man he has. We have to push him to the limit. To do that, we will have to take to the field and challenge him openly."

"Corfe," Macrobius said gently, "the odds you speak of seem almost hopeless."

"I know, I know. But victory for us is a different thing from the kind of victory the Merduks need. If we can smash up their army somewhat—blunt this last assault—and yet keep Torunn from undergoing a siege, then we will have won. I believe we can do that, but I need some advantage, some chance to even things up a little. I haven't found it yet, but I will."

"I pray to God you do," Macrobius said. His eyeless face was sunken and gaunt, vivid testimony to what Merduks would do in the hour of their victory.

"If this happens, if you manage to halt this juggernaut of theirs, what then?" Odelia asked. "How much can we expect to regain, or lose by a negotiated peace?"

"Ormann Dyke is gone for ever," Corfe said flatly. "That is something we must get used to. So is Aekir. If the kingdom can be partitioned down the line of the Searil, then we will have to count ourselves fortunate. It all depends on how well the army does in the field. We'll be buying back our country with Torunnan blood, literally. But my job is to kill Merduks, not to bargain with them. I leave that to Fournier and his ilk. I have no taste or aptitude for it."

You will acquire one though. I will see to that, Odelia thought. And out loud she said: "When, then, will the army take to the field?"

Corfe sat silently for what seemed a long time, until the Queen began to chafe with impatience. Macrobius appeared serene.

"I need upwards of nine hundred warhorses, to replace our losses and mount the new recruits that are still coming in," Corfe said finally. "Then there are the logistical details to work out with Passifal and the quartermaster's department. This will be no mere raid. When we leave Torunn this time we must be prepared to stay out for weeks, if not months. To that end the Western Road must be repaired and cleared, depots set up. And I mean to conscript every able-bodied man in the kingdom, whatever his station in life."

Odelia's mouth opened in shock. "You cannot do that!"

"Why not? The laws are on the statute books. Theoretically they are in force already, except for the fact that they have never actually been enforced."

"Even John Mogen did not try to enforce them—wisely. He knew the nobles would have his head on a spear if he ever even contemplated such a thing."

"He did not have to do it at Aekir. Every man in the city

willingly lent a hand in the defence, even if it was only to carry ammunition and plug breaches."

"That was different. That was a siege."

Corfe's fist came hurtling down on to the table beside him with a crash that astonished both the Queen and the Pontiff. "There will be no exceptions. If I conscript them, then I can leave an appropriate garrison in the city and still take out a sizeable field army. The nobles in the south of the kingdom all have private armies—I know that only too well. It is time these privately raised forces shared in the defence of the kingdom as a whole. Today I had orders written up commanding these blue-bloods to bring their armed retainers in person to the capital. If my calculations are correct, the local lords alone could add another fifteen thousand men to the defence."

"You do not have the authority—" Odelia began heatedly.

"Don't I? I am commander-in-chief of Torunna's military. Lawyers may quibble over it, but I see every armed man in the kingdom as part of that military. They can issue writs against me as much as they like once the war is over, but for now I will have their men, and if they refuse, by God I'll hang them."

There was naked murder on his face. Odelia looked away. She had never believed she could be afraid of any man, but the savagery that scoured his spirit occasionally leapt out of his eyes like some eldritch fire. It unnerved her. For how many men had those eyes been their last sight on earth? She sometimes thought she had no idea what he was truly capable of, for all that she loved him.

"All right then," she said. "You shall have your conscription. I will put my name to your orders, but I warn you, Corfe, you are making powerful enemies."

"The only enemies I am concerned with are those encamped to the east. I piss on the rest of them. Sorry, Father."

Macrobius smiled weakly. "Her Majesty is right, Corfe. Even John Mogen did not take on the nobility."

"I need men, Father. Their precious titles will not be

worth much if there is no kingdom left for them to lord about in. Let it be on my head alone."

"Don't say such things," Odelia said with a shiver. "It's bad luck."

Corfe shrugged. "I don't much believe in luck any more, lady. Men make their own, if it exists. I intend to take an army of forty thousand men out of this city in less than two sennights, and it will be tactics and logistics which decide their fate, not luck."

"Let us hope," Macrobius said, touching Corfe lightly on the wrist, "that faith has something to do with it also."

"When men have faith in themselves, Father," Corfe said doggedly, "they do not need to have faith in anything else."

ALBREC and Mehr Jirah met in a room within Ormann Dyke's great tower, not far from the Queen's apartments. It was the third hour of the night and no-one was abroad in the vast building except a few yawning sentries. But below the tower thousands of men worked through the night by the light of bonfires. On both banks of the Searil river they swarmed like ants, demolishing in the west and rebuilding in the east. The night-black river was crowded with heavy barges and lighters full to the gunwale with lumber, stone and weary working parties, and at the make-shift docks which had been constructed on both sides of the river scores of elephants waited patiently in harness, their mahouts dozing on their necks. The Sultan had decreed that the reconstruction of Ormann Dyke would be complete before the summer, and at its completion it would be renamed *Khedi Anwar*, the Fortress of the River.

The chamber in which Albrec and Mehr Jirah sat was windowless, a dusty store-room which was half full of all manner of junk. Fragments of chain mail, the links rusted into an orange mass. Broken sabre blades, rotting Torunnan uniforms, even a box of moldy hardtack much gnawed by mice. The two clerics, having nodded to each other, stood waiting, neither able to speak the other's tongue. At last they were startled by the swift entry of Queen Ahara and Shahr Baraz. The Queen was got up like a veiled Merduk maid, and Shahr Baraz was dressed as a common soldier.

"We do not have much time," the Queen said. "The eunuchs will miss me in another quarter-hour or less. Albrec, you are leaving for Torunn tonight. Shahr Baraz has horses and two of his own retainers waiting below. They will escort you to within sight of the capital."

"Lady," Albrec said, "I am not sure—"

"There is no time for discussion. Shahr Baraz has procured you a pass that will see you past the pickets. You must preach your message in Torunna as you have here. Mehr Jirah agrees with us in this. Your life is in danger as long as you remain at Ormann Dyke."

Albrec bowed wordlessly. When he straightened he shook the hands of Mehr Jirah and Shahr Baraz. "Whatever else I have found amongst the Merduks," he said thickly, "I have found two good men."

Heria translated the brief sentence and the two Merduks looked away. Shahr Baraz produced a leather bag with dun coloured clothing poking out of its neck.

"Wear these," he said in Normannic. "They are clothes of a Merduk mullah. A holy man. May—may the God of Victories watch over you." Then he looked at Heria, nodded and left. Mehr Jirah followed without another word.

"I can still preach here too, lady," Albrec said gently.

"No. Go back to him. Give him this." She handed the little monk a despatch scroll with a military seal. "They are plans for the forthcoming campaign. But do not tell who gave them to you, Father."

Albrec took the scroll gingerly. "I seem to make a habit of bearing fateful documents. Was there no other way you could get this to Torunn? I am not much of a courier."

"Two men we have sent out already," Heria said in a low voice. "Merduk soldiers with Ramusian blood in them—Shahr Baraz's retainers. But we do not know if they got through."

Albrec looked at her wonderingly. "So he is in on it too? How did you persuade him?"

"He said his father would have done it. The Shahr Baraz who took Aekir would not have condoned a war fought in the way Aurungzeb fights it today. And besides, my Shahr Baraz is a pious man. He thinks the war should stop, since the Ramusians are brothers in faith. Mehr Jirah and many of the mullahs think likewise."

"Come with me, Heria," Albrec said impulsively. "Come back to your people—to your husband."

She shook her head, the grey eyes bright with tears above the veil. "It is too late for me. And besides, they would miss me within the hour. We would be hunted down. No, Father, go back alone. Help him save my people."

"Then at least let me tell him you are alive."

"No! I am dead now, do you hear? I am not fit to be Corfe's wife any more. This is my world now, here. I must make the best of it I can."

Albrec took her hand and kissed it. "The Merduks have a worthy Queen then."

She turned away. "I must go now. Take the stairs at the bottom of the passage outside. They lead out to the west court-yard. Your escort awaits you there. You will have several hours start—they won't miss you until after dawn. Go now, Father. Get the scroll to Corfe."

Albrec bowed, his eyes stinging with pity for her, and then did as he was bidden.

EIGHTEEN

ALL day they had been trooping into the city, a motley procession of armed men in livery all the colours of the rainbow. Some were armed with nothing more than halberds and scythes on long poles, others were splendidly equipped with arquebuses and sabres. Most were on foot, but several hundred rode prancing warhorses in half-armour and had silk pennons whipping from their lance heads.

Corfe, General Rusio and Quartermaster Passifal stood on the battlements of the southern barbican and watched them troop in. As the long serried column trailed to an end a compact group of five hundred Cathedraller cavalry came up behind them, Andruw at their head. As the tribesmen passed through the gateway below Andruw saluted and winked, then was lost to view in a cavernous clatter of hooves as he and his men entered the city.

"That's the last contingent will make it this week, General," Passifal said. He was consulting a damp sheaf of papers. "Gavriar of Rone has promised three hundred men, but they'll be a long time on the road, and the Duke of Gebrar, old Saranfyr, he's put his name down for four hundred more, but it's a hundred and forty leagues from Gebrar if it's a mile. We'll be lucky to see them inside a month."

"How many do we have then?" Corfe asked.

"Some six thousand retainers, plus another five thousand conscripts—most of them folk from Aekir."

"Not as many as we had hoped," Rusio grumbled.

"No," Corfe told him. "But it's a damn sight better than nothing. I can leave six or seven thousand men to garrison the city and still march out with—what? Thirty-six or seven thousand."

"Some of these retainers the lords sent are nothing more than unschooled peasants," Rusio said, leaning on a merlon. "In many cases they've sent us squads of village idiots and petty criminals, the dregs of their demesnes."

"All they have to do is stand on the battlements and wave a pike," Corfe said. "Rusio, I want you to take five hundred veterans and start training the more incapable. Some of the contingents, though, can be draughted straight into the regular army."

"What about their fancy dress?" Passifal asked, mouth twitching.

Many of the lords had clad their retainers in all manner of garish heraldry.

"It won't look so fancy after a few days in the mud, I'll warrant."

"And the lords themselves?" Rusio inquired. "We've half a dozen keen young noblemen who are set on leading their father's pet army into battle."

"Rate them as ensigns, and put capable sergeants under them."

"Their daddies may not like that, nor the young scrubs themselves."

"I don't give a stuff what they like. I won't hand men over to untried officers to be squandered. This is war, not some kind of parlour game. If there are any complaints, have them forwarded to the Queen."

"Yes, General."

Feet on the catwalk behind them, and Andruw appeared,

his helm swinging from one hand. "Well, that's the last of them," he said. "The rest are hiding in the woods or the foothills."

"Did you have any trouble?" Corfe asked him.

"Are you serious? Once they saw the dreaded scarlet horsemen they'd have handed over their daughters if we'd asked. And I very nearly did, mark you. Poor stuff, though, most of 'em. They might be all right standing atop a wall, Corfe, but I wouldn't march them out of here. They'd go to pieces in the field."

"What about the retainers?"

"Oh, they're better equipped than the regulars are, but they've no notion of drill at any level higher than a tercio. I'd rate them baggage guards or suchlike."

"My thoughts exactly. Thanks, Andruw. Now, what about these horses?"

"I have a hundred of the men under Marsch and Ebro escorting the herd. They'll be here in three or four days."

"How many did you manage to scrape up?"

"Fifteen hundred, but only a third of those are true destriers. Some of them are no better than carthorses, others are three-year-olds, barely broken."

"They'll have to do. The Cathedrallers are the only heavy cavalry we have. If we mount every man, we can muster up some . . ."

"I make it a little over two thousand," Passifal said, consulting his papers again. "Another batch of tribesmen arrived this morning. Felimbri I think, nearly two hundred of them on little scrub ponies."

"Thanks, Colonel."

"If this goes on half the damn Torunnan army will be savages or Fimbrians," Rusio said tartly.

"And it would be none the worse for that, General," Corfe retorted. "Very well. Now, how are the work gangs proceeding on the Western Road . . . ?"

The small knot of men stood on the windswept battlements and went through the headings on Passifal's lists one by one. The lists were endless, and the days too short to tackle half their concerns, but little by little the army was being prepared for the campaign ahead. The last campaign, perhaps. That was what they hoped. In the meantime billets had to be found for the new recruits, willing and unwilling; horses had to be broken in and trained in addition to men; the baggage train had to be inventoried and stocked with anything thirty-odd thousand soldiers might need for a protracted stay in a veritable wilderness; and the road itself, which would bear their feet in so few days' time, had to be repaired lest they find themselves bogged down in mud within sight of the city. Nothing could be left to chance, not this time. It was the last throw of the dice for the Torunnans. If it failed, then there was nothing left to stand between the kingdom and the horror of a Merduk occupation.

CORFE had been invited to dine that night at the town house of Count Fournier. He did not truly have the time to spare for leisurely dinners, but the invitation had intrigued him, so he dressed in court sable and went, despite Andruw's jocular warning to watch what he ate. Fournier's house was more of a mansion, with an arch in one wing wide enough to admit a coach and four. It stood in the fashionable western half of the city, within sight of the palace itself, and to the rear it had extensive gardens which ran down to the river. On the bank of the Torrin there was a small summerhouse and it was to this that Corfe was led by a crop-headed page as soon as he had left his horse with a young stable boy. Fournier met him with a smile and an outstretched hand. The summerhouse had more glass in it than Corfe had ever seen before, outside of a cathedral. It was lit by candle-lanterns, and a table within had been set for two. To one side the mighty Torrin gurgled and plopped in the darkness, its bank obscured by a line of willows. As Corfe looked around, something detached itself from one of the willows and flapped away with a beat of leathery wings. A bat of some sort.

"No escort or entourage, General?" Fournier asked with raised eye-brow. "You keep little state for a man of such elevated rank."

"I thought I'd be discreet. Besides, the Cathedrallers are mobbed every time they ride through the streets."

"Ah, yes, I should have thought. Have a seat. Have some wine. My cook has been working wonders tonight. Some bass from the estuary I believe, and wild pigeon."

Silver glittering in the candlelight upon a spotless white tablecloth. Crystal goblets brimming with wine, a gold-chased decanter and a small crowd of footmen, not one yet in his thirties. Fournier noted Corfe's appraising glances and said shortly, "I like to be surrounded by youth. It helps keep my—my energy levels high. Ah, Marion, the first course, if you please."

Some kind of fish. Corfe ate it automatically, his plate cleared by the time Fournier had had three mouthfuls. The nobleman laughed.

"You are not in the field now, General. You should savour my cook's work. He is an easterner as a matter of fact, a convert from Calmar. I believe he might once have been a corsair, but one should not inquire too thoroughly into the antecedents of genius, should one?"

Corfe said nothing. Fournier seemed to be enjoying himself, as if he possessed some secret knowledge which he was savouring with even more gusto than he did the food.

The plates were taken away, another course came and went. Fournier talked inconsequently of gastronomic matters, the decline in Torunn's fishing fleet, the proper way to dress a carp. Corfe drank wine sparingly and uttered the odd monosyllable. Finally the cloth was drawn and the two men were left with a dish of nuts and a decanter of brandy. The servants left, and for a while the only sound was the quiet night music of the river close by.

"You have shown commendable patience, General," Fournier said, sipping the good Fimbrian spirit. "I had expected an outburst of some sort ere the main course arrived."

"I know."

"Forgive me. I like to play my little games. Why are you here? What's afoot on this, the eve of great events? I will tell you, as a reward for your forbearance."

Fournier reached under his chair and set upon the table a bloodstained scroll of paper. Upon it was a broken seal, but enough of the wax remained for Corfe to make out the crossed scimitars of Ostrabar's military. Despite himself, he sat up straight in his chair.

"Do have a walnut, General. They complement the brandy so well." Fournier broke one open with a pair of ivory handled nutcrackers. There was blood on the nutcrackers also.

"Make your point, Fournier," Corfe said. "I do not have any more time to waste."

Fournier's voice changed: the bantering tone fled to be replaced by cold steel. "My agents made a capture today of some interest to us all. A Merduk mullah with two companions, out riding alone. The mullah was a strange little fellow with a mutilated face and no fingers on one hand. He spoke perfect Normannic, with the accent of Almark, and claimed to be one Bishop Albrec, fresh from the delights of the Merduk court."

Corfe said nothing, but the candlelight made two little hellish fires of his eyes.

"Our adventurous cleric was bearing this scroll on him. He took quite a deal of persuasion to give it up, I might add. After further persuasion he revealed that he had been charged with delivery of it to you, my dear General. You alone, and in person. Now, we have an agent in the enemy camp, that you already know. But would you believe that until tonight I did not know the identity of that agent? Strange, but true. Now I know everything there is to know, General. Or almost everything. Perhaps you could explain to me why exactly you are receiving despatches from someone at the very heart of the Merduk court?"

"I have no idea what you're talking about, Fournier. What is in this scroll?"

"That is of no matter for the moment. However, there is the rather alarming prospect of the Torunnan commander-in-chief being in clandestine communication with the enemy High Command. That, my dear Corfe Cear-Inaf, is treason in anyone's book."

"Don't be absurd, Fournier. It's come from this agent of yours you've been preening yourself over for weeks. What's in the damned scroll? And what have you done with this Albrec?"

"All in good time, General. You see, the interesting thing is that the scroll did not come from any agent of mine. It came, as my little misshapen bishop finally admitted, direct from the hands of the Merduk Queen herself. Perhaps you could explain this."

Corfe blinked, startled. "I have no idea—"

"Colonel Willem," said Fournier, raising his voice a fraction. And out of the darkness a group of men instantly appeared. The candles lit up the length of their drawn swords.

A shaven-headed man with a patch over one eye stepped into the summerhouse. Willem, one of Corfe's senior officers. Behind him was young Colonel Aras. Willem had a horse pistol cocked and ready, the match already smouldering on the wheel.

"Place General Cear-Inaf under arrest. You will take him to my offices down by the waterfront and hold him there."

"With pleasure, Count," Willem said, grinning to show broad gap-ridden teeth. "Get up, traitor."

Corfe remained in his seat. The amazement fled out of his mind in a moment. Suddenly many things had become clear. He took in the faces of the newcomers with a quick glance. All strangers to him but for Willem and Aras. They were not even in army uniform. He turned to Fournier, keeping his voice as casual as he could.

"Why not just have me shot now?"

"It's obvious, I would have thought. The mob would never wear it. You're their darling, General. We must discredit you before we hang you."

"You'll never convince the Queen," Corfe told him.

"Her opinion is as immaterial as her rule is unconstitutional. The line of the Fantyrs is at an end. Torunna must look elsewhere for her rulers."

"I'll wager she'll not have to look far."

Fournier smiled. "Willem, get this upstart peasant out of my sight."

THEY had a closed carriage waiting in the court-yard. Corfe was manacled and locked inside. Aras shared it with him, another pistol cocked and pointed at his breast, whilst Willem and the others rode pillion. The carriage lurched and bumped through the sleeping capital, for it was late—some time past the middle night, Corfe guessed. His mind was racing but he felt curiously calm. It was all in the open at last. No more intrigue: only naked force would work now.

He looked Aras in the eye. "When I saw you hold your ground in the King's Battle I never would have believed you could be a part of something like this."

Aras said nothing. The carriage interior was lit by a single fluttering candle-lantern and it was hard to see the expression on his face.

"This will mean civil war, Aras. The army will not stand for it. And the Merduks will be handed the kingdom on a plate. That is what he intends—to be governor of a Merduk province."

Again, silence but for the rumbling of the iron-bound wheels and the horses' hooves on the cobbles.

"For God's sake, man, can't you see where your duty lies?"

The carriage stopped. The door was unbolted and opened from without and Corfe was hauled outside. He could smell dead fish in the air, pitch and seaweed. They were down near the southern docks, on the edge of the estuary. Lightless buildings bulked up against the sky, and he could see the masts of ships outlined before the stars. He offered no resistance as they manhandled him. Willem wanted him dead at once, that was plain. Corfe would not give him an excuse to fire.

Swinging lanterns scattering broken light on the wet cobbles. Men in armour, arquebuses, pikes. The soldiers were all in strange liveries—part of the conscripted retainers that Corfe had brought into the capital. They had foxed him there. He had brought the enemy into the city himself. That was the reason for their confidence.

Inside. Someone boxing him on the ear for no reason. Down stone stairs with water running down the walls. Torchlight guttering here, a noisome stink that turned his stomach.

"Hold him," Willem's voice said, and men pinioned him.

The one-eyed colonel sized him up in the unsteady torch-light.

"Caught you by surprise, didn't we? You thought it was all signed, sealed and delivered. Well you thought wrong, you little guttersnipe—" and he brought the butt of his pistol down on Corfe's temple.

Corfe staggered, and at the second blow the world darkened and his legs went out from under him. He struggled, but the men about him held him fast as Willem rained blow after blow down on his head. No pain, just a succession of explosions in his brain, like a battery of culverins going off one by one. Somehow he remained conscious. His blood dappled the flags of the floor, gummed shut his eyes and nose. He heard his own breathing as though from a great distance, as stertorous as that of a dying consumptive.

Keys clinking, and then he was flung into a black cell, and the door clanged shut behind him. The footsteps outside retreated, laughter retreating with them.

His head felt like it belonged to someone else. The lights were sparkling through it like a twilit battle, and the tight manacles were already puffing up his hands. The floor was sodden and stinking.

Corfe sat up, and the pain began to seep in under the shock of it all. His ears were ringing, his mouth full of blood. He retched, heaving out a mess of bile on to the filthy floor.

"Who is that?" a voice asked in the darkness, an odd voice, something wrong with it.

"Who wants to know?" he rasped.

"My name is Albrec. I'm a monk."

He fought for breath. "We meet again, then. My name is Corfe. I'm a soldier." And then the blackness of the cell folded over his mind, and his face hit the floor.

B Y dawn the arrests had begun. Willem and his men went around in squads. Andruw and Marsch were picked up first, along with Morin, Ebro and Ranafast. Then Quartermaster Passifal and General Rusio were roused out of their beds and led away in chains. The Cathedrallers' barracks were surrounded by three thousand arquebusiers under Col-

onel Willem, while Colonel Aras led twenty more tercios
to confine Formio's Fimbrians. An order was issued to the
army in general, directing it to stay in barracks, and a curfew was imposed upon the entire city. Lastly, Fournier himself took fifty men and marched them into the palace,
demanding admittance to the Queen's chambers. Odelia
was placed under guard—for her own protection, naturally—and the palace was sealed off.

By noon the waterfront dungeons were crammed full
with almost the entire Torunnan High Command, and the
brightly clad retainers whom Andruw had mocked were in
control of three quarters of the city. The Cathedrallers had
made an abortive breakout attempt, but Willem's arquebusiers had shot them down in scores. The Fimbrians had
as yet made no move except to fortify their barracks with
a series of makeshift barricades. They had little or no ammunition for their few arquebuses, however, and their pikes
would be almost worthless in street fighting. They were
contained, for the moment. Fournier was confident they
would accept some form of terms and was content to leave
them be. As the afternoon wore round, however, he had
batteries of heavy artillery wheeled into position around
both them and the Cathedrallers, and Colonel Willem took
some twelve thousand of the Torunnan regulars out of the
city to the north. They had been told that a Merduk raiding
party was closing in on the city and their commander-in-
chief had ordered them to intercept it. Once they had left
Torunn, though, Willem led them off to the east, towards
the coast where they would be safely out of the way. The
rest of the regulars, leaderless and bewildered, remained in
barracks, while around them the populace were kept off the
streets by armed patrols and rumours of Merduk infiltrators
were circulated to keep them cowed. Thus, with a judicious
mixture of bluff, guile and armed force did Fournier tighten
his grip upon the capital.

He took over the chambers Lofantyr had used for meetings of the High Command in a wing of the palace, and by
the early evening the place was abuzz with couriers coming
and going, officers receiving new appointments and confused soldiers standing guard. After a frugal meal he dis-

missed everyone from the room and sat at the long table in the chair which King Lofantyr had once occupied, toying with the oiled point of his beard. When the clap of wings sounded at the window he did not turn round, nor did he seem startled when a homunculus landed before him amid the papers and maps and inkwells. The little creature folded its wings and cocked its head to one side.

"I must congratulate you," the beast said in a man's voice. "The operation proceeded even more smoothly than we had hoped."

"That was the easy part. Maintaining the facade for the next week will be harder. I trust you are keeping your master well informed."

"Of course. And he is mightily pleased. He wants Cear-Inaf kept alive, so that he may dispose of him at his leisure when he enters the city."

"And the Queen? What of her? She cannot live, you know that."

"Indeed. But Aurungzeb has this strange aversion to the execution of Royalty. He feels that kind of thing puts odd ideas into men's minds."

"It may be that she will simply disappear, then. She may escape and never be heard of again."

"I think that would be best."

"When does your master's army move?"

"It has begun to march already. In less than a week, my dear Count, you will be the new governor of Torunna, answerable only to the Sultan himself. The war will be over."

"The war will be over," Fournier repeated thoughtfully. "Cear-Inaf is an upstart and a fool. He has done well, but even his much-vaunted generalship could not prevail against a hundred and fifty thousand. What I have done is spare Torunna a catastrophic defeat. I have saved thousands of lives."

"Indubitably." Was it his imagination, or was there a sardonic sneer to the voice which issued out of the homunculus?

"Go now," he said sharply. "Tell your master I will hold Torunn for him. When the army arrives the gates shall be thrown open, and I shall see to it that the regulars are deployed elsewhere. There will be no resistance."

"What of Cear-Inaf's personal troops? Those tribesmen and the Fimbrians, not to mention the veterans from the dyke?"

"They are contained. They will be entirely neutralised within the next few days."

The homunculus gathered itself up for flight, spreading its bat-like wings. "I certainly hope so, my dear Count. For your sake." Then the creature paused in the act of springing into the air. "By the way, we have heard rumours that there is an agent of yours at work in the court. Is this true?"

"That is a rumour, nothing more. All my attempts to insert an agent close to Aurungzeb have failed. You may congratulate him on his security."

"Thank you. The homunculus will return in two days, to monitor your progress. Until then, Count, fare well." And the thing took off at last, and flapped its way out of the open window. Fournier watched it go, and when it had disappeared he took a handkerchief from his pocket and wiped the sweat out of his mustache.

W HEN Corfe woke he thought that the nightmare which had plagued his unconsciousness was still about him, cackling in the darkness. He raised a hand to his face and felt agony shoot through his wrists as its chained fellow came with it. His hands were swollen to the point of use-lessness. Another day in these manacles and he would lose them. His face, when he touched it gingerly, felt as though it did not belong to him. It was some misshapen caricature his fingers found strange to the touch. Despite himself, he groaned aloud.

"Corfe?" a voice said. "Are you awake?"

"Yes."

"What have they done? I've heard shooting."

"They're trying to take over the city, I should think."

"They've been bringing in other prisoners all morning. Dozens of them. I hear the doors."

Corfe found it hard to keep his thoughts together. His mind seemed wrapped in wool. "Fournier caught you," he said muzzily.

"Yes, on the way in. I had two companions. Merduks. He killed them after the torture. They would not speak." There was a sound like a sob. "I'm so sorry. I could not bear it."

"The scroll. What was in it?"

"The entire Merduk campaign plan and order of battle."

Corfe struggled to clear his mind, collect his thoughts. He fought against the urge to lay his head in the foul-smelling muck of the floor and go to sleep.

"The Merduk Queen—he said it was from her. Is that true?"

There was a silence. Finally Albrec said, "Yes."

"Why? Why would she do such a thing?"

"She is—she is a Ramusian, from Aekir. She wanted revenge."

"I honour her for it."

"Yes, though nothing will come of it now. What is Fournier going to do?"

"I think he means to surrender the city to the Merduks. He has done some deal. I have been an arrogant fool, such a fool."

Quiet descended upon the interior of the cell. Water was gurgling away somewhere, and they could hear the rush of the sewers below.

The sewers.

"Father," Corfe said with sudden energy. "Go over the floor of this place. There must be a drain somewhere, a grating or something."

"Corfe—"

"Do it!"

They began searching around in the fetid darkness with their hands, their fingers squelching into nameless things. Once, Corfe's fastened upon the wriggling wetness of a rat. He listened for the sound of the water, finally found it and tore heaps of rotting straw from around the grating. His half-numb fingers searched out its dimensions: eighteen inches square, no more.

A yank on the metal of the bars, but it would not budge. It was firmly set in mortar. He searched his pockets with awkward, fevered haste, and found there a folded clasp knife. Willem had taken his poniard, but had been too busy pistol-whipping him to search his pockets.

"Bastards!" Corfe spat in triumph. He unfolded the knife with his clumsy hands and began scraping at the mortar which held the grating fast. It was already crumbling in places, loosened by the wetness of the floor. He levered up clods and splinters of the stuff, stabbing with the little knife. There was a crack, and the point broke off. He hardly paused, but worked on in the smothering darkness by touch. Every so often the coruscating lights in his head came back, and he had to pause and fight the dizzying sickness they brought. It took hours—or what seemed like hours—but at the end of that time he had picked out every trace of the mortar from around the grating. He put the broken knife carefully back in his pocket. Something warm and liquid was trickling down his temples. Sweat or blood, he knew not.

"Over here, Father. Help me."

Albrec bumped into him. "I have only one good hand."

No matter. Three are better than two. Get a hold here." He positioned the monk's fingers for him. "Now, after three, pull like a good 'un."

They heaved until Corfe thought his head would burst. A slight shift, a tiny grating sound, no more. He collapsed on to his side on the floor.

Several minutes passed, and then they tried again. This time Corfe was sure one corner of the grating had shifted, and when he felt over it he found that it was raised above the level of the floor flags some half an inch.

A strange, unearthly time of blinding pain and intense physical struggle, all in pitch blackness. They tugged on one corner of the grating after another, their fingers slipping on slime. Finally Corfe was able to get the chain of his manacles under one corner and pull back, feeling as though his hands were about to be wrenched off at the wrists.

A squeal of scraped metal, and he fell over on his back, the heavy grating jerking free to smash into his kneecap with dazzling pain. He lay on his back, gasping for air. "We—we did it, Father."

They rested and listened in the blackness. No jailer approached, no alarm was raised.

"Are we going to go down there?" Albrec asked at last.

"We're on the waterfront. The sewers here lead straight into the river. It shouldn't be far—not more than a hundred yards. Come, Father Albrec. I'll have you breathing clean air inside fifteen minutes. I'll go first."

The sound of rushing water seemed very loud as Corfe squeezed himself into the drain. He retched once at the smell, but nothing came up. His stomach had long since rid itself of the last vestiges of Fournier's dinner.

His legs were dangling in a current of icy liquid. He felt a moment of black panic at the idea of venturing down there. What if there was no room to breathe? What if—?

His grip on the lip of the drain slipped and he scraped down through the short shaft and splashed into the sewer below. The current took him and buffeted him against rough brick walls. His head was under water. He could not breathe, was not even sure which way was up. His lungs shrieked for air. The tunnel was less than a yard wide; he braced himself against it, shearing the skin from his knuckles and knees. A moment's gasp of air, and then he had slipped and was being hurtled along again. His head smacked against the tunnel wall. He felt like screaming.

And then he was in midair, flying effortlessly before crashing into water again after a fall of several yards through nothingness. Clean, cold air. He was out. He was in the river, and it was night outside. The water was brackish here, this close to the estuary. He choked on it, struggled manically to keep his head up, his manacled hands flailing. The current was taking him downstream, out to sea. But there was a tree here, leaning low over the water. He grasped at a trailing limb, missed, was slashed in the face by another and caught hold of a third, his grip slicing down the leaves. He pulled himself up it as though on a rope, and found mud under his feet. He waded ashore, shuddering with cold, and took a second to collect himself. Then he remembered Albrec, and floundered about on the muddy bank until he had found a long stick, all the while watching the surface of the racing river. He waited then for a long time, but saw nothing. It was too cold to remain. Either Albrec had drowned, or he had remained in the cell. He could not wait any longer. The lights of Torunn were bright and yellow and the city wall towered like a monolith barely two hundred yards away. Corfe had been washed ashore on a little patch of wasteland just within the city perimetre, not far from the southern barbican. It was too exposed here. He had to move on.

There were reed-beds here at the riverside, filled with old rubbish and stinking with the effluent of the sewers. He crept along in them as quietly as he could, and then stopped. Something was crashing about in front of him. A man.

"Lord God," a voice whispered. "Oh, Lord—"

"Albrec!"

"Corfe?"

He moved forward again. The monk was caught in thigh-deep mud and looked like some glistening swamp denizen. Corfe hauled him out and then they lay there in the reeds for a while, utterly spent. Above them the clear sky was ablaze with stars from one horizon to the next.

"Come," Corfe said at last. "We have to get away. We'll die here else."

Wordlessly, Albrec staggered to his feet and the two of them lurched off together like a pair of mud-daubed drunks.

"Where are we going?" the monk asked.

"To the only man of importance I think Fournier will have left alone. Your master, Macrobius."

"What about the army?"

"Fournier will have it under control somehow. And he'll have neutralised all my officers. Maybe the Queen too. I have to get these damned manacles off before my hands die. How much shooting did you hear when you were in there?"

"A lot of volleys. But they lasted a few minutes, not more."

"There's been no major battle then. They must have my men bottled up. The Merduks are probably on the march already. Hurry, Albrec! We don't have time to waste."

NINETEEN

A S the ladies-in-waiting quaked, terrified, the Queen twitched and snarled in her chair, the whites of her eyes flickering under closed lids. She had been like this for almost two hours, and they longed to cry out to someone for help, a doctor or apothecary to be sent. But ancient Grania, who had been at the palace longer than any of the rest and whose dark eyes were unclouded by any vestige of senility, told them to hush their useless mouths and pretend nothing untowards was happening, else the guards posted outside might take it into their heads to come in. So the little flock of ladies embroidered and knitted with absent fervour, stabbing fingertips with monotonous regularity while brimming over with hiccuping little sobs for the predicament they had found themselves in: and Grania glanced towards heaven and helped herself to the wine.

None of them noticed when the black furred shape with ruby eyes crept back into the chamber through the smoke hood and took up its accustomed place in the centre of a

huge web that quivered sootily in the shadows of the rafters. The Queen sighed, and sagged in her chair. Then she
rubbed her eyes and stood up, putting a hand to the hollow
of her back. For several seconds she looked what she was:
a tyred woman in her sixth decade. As the ladies-in-waiting
chattered around her she took the goblet of wine that the
silent Grania offered and drained it at a draught.

"I am getting too old for this sort of thing," she said to
the aged woman who had once been her wet nurse.

"We all are," the crone retorted drily. And to the brightly
plumaged chatterers about her she snapped: "Oh shut up,
all of you."

"No," Odelia said, "Keep talking. That is an order. Let
the guards hear us gossiping away. Were we too silent, they
would be the more suspicious."

"How bad is it?" Grania asked the Queen as the surrounding women talked desperately of the weather, the
price of silk, all the while trying to spare an ear for the
Queen's words.

"Bad enough. They have massacred many of his Cathedrallers. The poor fools charged massed arquebusiers with
nothing more than sabres."

"And his Fimbrians?"

"Strangely supine. But something tells me that their commander, Formio, is not letting the grass grow under his feet.
The rest of the city is under curfew. Fournier has installed
himself in the East Wing. So sure of himself is he that he
has only fifty or sixty men around him. The rest patrol the
city. There are fires down by the dockyards, but I don't
know what they signify. Arach's vision is limited, and
sometimes hard to decipher."

"Sit, lady. You are exhausted."

"How can I sit?" Odelia exploded. "I do not even know
if he is alive or dead!" She passed a hand over her face.
"Pardon me. I am tyred. I was blind: I should have foreseen
this."

"No-one else did," Grania said bluntly. "Do not torment
yourself because you are no soothsayer."

The Queen sank back down upon her chair. "He cannot

be dead, Grania. He must not be dead." And she buried her
face in her hands and wept.

IT was a long, weary way from the waterfront to the Pontifical palace, and it took Corfe and Albrec most of the
remainder of the night to traverse it. Fournier's patrols were
easy to dodge. They spent as much time gawking at the
wonders of the great city as they did keeping an eye out
for curfew-breakers. They were, when it came down to it,
untutored men of the country awed by the size and sprawl
of the capital. Eavesdropping on their conversations as they
trooped past, Corfe realised that some of them did not even
know why they were here, except that it was some kind of
emergency engendered by the Merduk war.

Halted at the gates of the abbey by watchful Knights
Militant, Corfe and Albrec were eyed with astonished dis-
belief when they demanded to see Macrobius. They were
still fettered, and liberally plastered with mud and sewer
filth. But something in Corfe's eye made one of the gate
guards dash off at once to fetch Monsignor Alembord. The
portly Inceptine looked none too pleased to be dragged out
of his bed, but there was no denying that he recognised the
bedraggled pair straight away. They were ushered inside
the gates amid much whispering and brought to a little reception chamber where Corfe demanded a blacksmith or
armourer to cut off their manacles. Alembord waddled
away, looking thoroughly confused. He was almost entirely
unaware of the coup that had taken place: Fournier's men
had left the abbey alone, as Corfe had suspected they
would.

The yawning armourer arrived soon after with a wooden
box full of the tools of his trade. The fetters were cut from
the two prisoners' wrists, and Corfe had to clench his teeth
against the agony of returning circulation in his hands.
They were swollen to twice their normal size and where
the iron had encircled his wrists, deep slices had been
carved out of the puffed flesh. He let them bleed freely,
hoping it would wash some of the filth out of them.

Basins of clean, hot water, and fresh clothes were found
for the two men. The clothes turned out to be spare Incep-

tine habits, and thus it was dressed as a monk that Corfe finally found himself ushered into Macrobius's private suite. It still wanted an hour until dawn.

Private though the suite might nominally be, it was crowded with anxious clerics and alarmed Knights Militant. They and Macrobius listened in grim silence as Corfe related the events of the past thirty-six hours, Albrec narrating his own part in the storey. As he and Corfe had agreed, however, no mention was made of the spy at the Merduk court.

When they had finished, Macrobius, who had listened without a word, said simply: "What would you have me do?"

"How many armed men can the abbey muster?" Corfe asked.

"Monsignor Alembord?"

"Some sixty to seventy, Holiness."

"Good," Corfe said. "Then you must sally out at dawn with all of them, and go to City Square. Call a meeting, raise the rooftops—create a commotion that will get people out on to the streets. Fournier does not have enough men to clamp down on the entire city, and he will not be able to cow the population if they can be raised against him. Get the people on to the streets, Holiness."

"And you, Corfe, what will you do?"

"I'm going to try and get through to my men. If you can make enough of a commotion, Fournier will have to take troops away from their containment and then there will be a good chance I can break them out. After that, he will be defeated, I promise you."

"What of the Merduks?" Alembord asked with round eyes.

"I am assuming they are on the move even as we speak. If they force march, they can be here in four or five days at most. That does not give us much time. This thing must be crushed by tomorrow at the latest if we are to take the field in time."

"Very well," Macrobius said, his chin out-thrust. "It shall be as you say. Monsignor Alembord, rouse the entire abbey. I want everyone in their best habits, the Knights in full armour and mounted, with every flag and pennon they can find. We shall make a spectacle of it, give Fournier something to distract his mind. See to it at once."

As the unfortunate Alembord hurried away, Macrobius turned back to Corfe. "How do you intend to get through to your men?"

"With your permission, Holiness, I will retain the disguise I've been given. I will be a cleric desiring only to offer spiritual succour to the beleaguered soldiers. For that reason, I will go to Formio's Fimbrians first. The idea of a priest offering comfort to my Cathedrallers would not stand up."

"And will you go alone?"

"Yes. Albrec here is too easily recognizable, even by these bumpkins from the south. He will have to remain here in the abbey."

"And what about the Queen, Corfe?"

"She, also, will have to be left to her own devices for a while. For now it is soldiers I need, not monarchs."

COUNT Fournier's beard had been tugged from its usual fine point into a bristling mess. He paced the room like a restless cat while his senior officers stared woodenly at him.

"Escaped? Escaped? How can you be telling me this? The one man above all who must be contained, and you tell me he is at large. Exactly how could this have happened?"

Gabriel Venuzzi's handsome face was sallow as a whitewashed wall. "It seems he managed to lever up a grating and make his way into the sewers, Count. He and that noseless monk who was incarcerated with him."

"That is another thing. I specifically said that the prisoners were to be confined separately."

"There are not enough cells in the waterfront dungeons. By my last estimate, we have almost four-score prisoners down there. Some of them are even three to a cell now. Every officer above the rank of ensign is being picked up. Perhaps we could relax the rules a little."

"No! We must cut off the head if the body is not to crush

us. Every man on the lists must be arrested. Start using the common jails if you have to, but take every name on the list!"

"It shall be as you say."

"What of the Queen?"

"Still confined to her chambers."

"Have the guards look in on her every few minutes."

"Count Fournier!" Venuzzi was shocked. "She is the Queen. Do you expect common soldiers to tramp in and out of her chambers like gawking sightseers?"

"Do as I say, damn it. I don't have time for your lace-edged court niceties, Venuzzi. Our heads will all be on the block if this does not come off. How in the world could he have got away? Where would he go? To his men, obviously. But how to get through the lines? By subterfuge, naturally. Venuzzi, inform our officers that no-one—*no-one*—is to be allowed through the lines to the Fimbrians or the Cathedrallers. Do you understand me, Venuzzi? Not so much as a damned mouse."

"I am not an imbecile, Count."

"I thought that also until you let Cear-Inaf slip away. Now get out and set about your errands."

Venuzzi left, his formerly pale face flushed and furious. Fournier turned to a beefy figure who lounged by the door. "Sardinac, get some more men up here in the palace, and some artillery pieces."

The man called Sardinac straightened. "We don't have too many artillerists to spare, Count. These are hired retainers we're working with, remember, not Torunnan regulars."

"Don't I know it! Take some of the guns which they have deployed about the Fimbrian quarter. And send another courier in to treat with that ass Formio. His position is hopeless, and it's not his fight. Safe conduct out of the city—the same as the last one."

Sardinac bowed, and exited in Venuzzi's wake.

Fournier wiped his brow with a scented handkerchief. He was surrounded by fools, that was the problem. Such a beautiful plan, but it had to work in all things or it would work in none. There was so little margin for error.

Out on to the balcony his restless feet took him. You could see a corner of City Square from here. It was like glimpsing a slice of some odd carnival. He could see Knights Militant bedecked with banners, richly robed priests—and a milling crowd of several thousand of the city lowly who had braved the curfew to see what was going on. That also had to be contained. His men were like butter scraped across too much bread. Who would have thought Macrobius would issue out of his lair and get up on his hind legs to preach, the old fool?

There was a lit brazier in the room, the charcoal red and grey with heat. Fournier went to the table, unlocked a small chest and took out a battered scroll with the broken seal of the Merduk military upon it. He studied it for a moment thoughtfully, and seemed about to consign it to the brazier, but then thought better of it. He tucked it into the breast of his doublet and patted it with one manicured hand.

"SERGEANT! We've a priest here wants to go and talk to the Fimbrians," the young soldier said. "That's all right, ain't it?"

The sergeant, a corpulent veteran of many tavern brawls, marched ponderously over to the barricade where the black-robed Inceptine stood surrounded by half a dozen nervous young men with the slow-match smouldering balefully on the wheel-locks of their arquebuses. He drew a sabre.

"New orders, Fintan lad. No-one to go through the lines. Courier arrived just this minute. Father, your time has been wasted. You might want to say a prayer for us, though, out here facing those damned Fimbrians."

"By all means, my son." The priest, his face hidden in the cowl of his habit, raised his hands in the Sign of the Saint. As he did, the wide sleeves of his raiment fell back to reveal badly cut wrists. The soldiers had bowed their heads to receive his blessing, but they snapped upright when a clear young voice shouted out: "Sergeant! Bring that man to me at once!"

Colonel Aras was standing outside a nearby grain ware-house surrounded by a crowd of other officers and couriers.

He stalked forward. "The priest! Grab that priest and bring him here!"

The Inceptine tensed as he found the barrels of six arquebuses levelled at him. The sergeant looked him up and down quizzically.

"Looks like someone else is in need of a prayer, Father."

"It seems so, Sergeant," the priest said. "Be careful of those Fimbrians. They collect the ears of their enemies, I've heard."

"Bring him into my quarters, Sergeant, and be quick about it!" Aras barked, white-faced. "Enough chatter."

The Inceptine was escorted past the crowd of staring soldiers and into the cavernous interior of the warehouse. There was a little office within, divided off from the rest of the building. They left him there. Some young noblemen were bent over a map. They straightened and nodded at him, looking a trifle bewildered. Aras ordered the room emptied.

"You can throw back your hood now, General," he said when they had gone.

Corfe did as he was told. "I congratulate you, Aras. You have quick eyes."

The two men looked at one another in silence for a long moment, until Aras stirred and reached for a decanter. "Some wine?"

"Thank you."

They drank, each watching the other.

"What now?" Corfe said. "Will you turn me over to your master—and the kingdom over to the Merduks? Or will you remember your duty?"

Aras flopped down into a chair. "You have no idea what this has cost me," he whispered.

"To do what? Betray your country?"

The younger man sprang to his feet again, his face outraged. But it leaked out of him like water from a punctured skin. He stared into his wine.

"You were wrong," he said quietly. "Wrong to go about things the way you did. The great men of a kingdom cannot be trampled upon. They will not wear it."

"And in the end their own prestige is worth more to them

than the kingdom. You know me, Aras. If a man has ability
I couldn't care less whether he's a duke or a beggar. Look
at Rusio. I made him a general though he was one of my
bitterest enemies. But Fournier—he is motivated by more
than wounded pride, you must know that. He has his heart
set on ruling Torunna, even if it is only as a pawn of the
Merduks. You are all—all of you—merely his tools, to be
used and discarded."

"He's going to negotiate a peace, and end the war with
honour," Aras said.

"He is going to capitulate unconditionally, and feed off
the carcase that the Merduks leave behind."

Aras turned away. "What would you have me do?" he
murmured. "Betray him?"

"A traitor cannot be betrayed. These Fimbrians you are
besieging. They served under you in battle. They held their
line at your orders, and died where they stood because you
asked them to. They are your comrades, not your enemies.
When did Fournier ever set his shoulder beside yours, or
face a battle-line with you? Give it up, Aras. Do the honourable thing. Order your men to stand down and let me
save this city of ours."

Aras said nothing for a long time. When he spoke again
it was in a loud voice. "Haptman Vennor!"

A young man in the livery of one of the southern lords
put his head around the door. "Colonel?"

"The men are to stack arms and stand down. This priest
here is to be escorted through our lines to the Fimbrian
barracks. Dismantle the barricades. It is over."

Haptman Vennor gaped at him.

"Sir—on whose authority—?"

"Obey my orders, damn it! I command here. Do as I
say!"

The startled officer saluted and withdrew.

"Thank you," Corfe said quietly.

"I hope you will speak up for me at my court-martial,
sir," Aras said.

"Court-martial?" Corfe laughed. "Aras my dear fellow, I
need you in the ranks. As soon as we have this little mess
sorted out, we have a meeting with the Merduk army to

arrange. I cannot afford to lose an officer with your experience." He held out a hand. Aras hesitated, and then shook
it warmly. "I won't let you down, sir, not again. I am your
man until death."

Corfe smiled. "I think I knew that already, or part of me
did—else I would have bolted as soon as you recognised
me."

"What do you want me to do with these mercenaries?"

"They will remain under your command for now. Mercenaries or not, they are still Torunnans. As soon as Formio
and his men have shaken out, we'll march on the palace
together."

ODELIA stood on the balcony and watched the smoke
of war drift over the tortured city. Out by the North
Gate there were crackles of volley-fire rolling still, and the
waterfront was a mass of fire above which the smoke roiled
in billowing thunderheads. The masts of ships stood stark
and angular against the flames. Some of them had had their
moorings cut to save them from the inferno and they were
drifting helplessly down the estuary towards the sea.

Nearer at hand, the deafening roar of the artillery salvoes
had subsided at last, to be replaced by a chaotic storm of
gunfire and the massed roaring of men fighting for their
lives. The Fimbrians were storming the palace, and terrified
valets and maids had come running to her chambers to huddle in panic-stricken crowds, like rabbits fleeing a wildfire.
And Corfe was alive. He and Formio were retaking the
palace room by gutted room. Fournier had lost the gamble,
and would soon surrender his life as well. It warmed her
to think on it.

The doors crashed open and a knot of grimy soldiers
burst into the room, making the maids scream and cower.
Behind them came Count Fournier himself, along with Gabriel Venuzzi and a gaggle of the southern nobles' sons
who had marched into the city scant days before with such
pomp and heraldry. They were smoke-blackened or bloodstained now, with frightened eyes and drawn swords. Fournier, however, was as dapper as always. In fact he seemed
to have taken special care with his toilet, and was dressed

in midnight blue with black hose and a silver-hilted rapier. He held a handkerchief to his nose against the powder-smoke that eddied through the entire palace, but when he saw the Queen he pocketed it with a flourish and then bowed deeply.

"Your Majesty."

"My dear Count. What could possibly bring you here at this time?"

A crash of gunfire drowned his reply and he frowned, irritated. "Your pardon, Majesty. I thought it the merest good manners to come and make my farewells."

"Are you leaving us then, Count?"

Fournier smiled. "Sadly, yes. But my journey is not a long one."

The roar of battle seemed to be rageing just down the corridor. Fournier's companions took off towards it, yelling—except for Gabriel Venuzzi, who collapsed upon the floor and began sobbing loudly.

"Before I go," Fournier went on, "there is something I would like to give you. A parting gift which I hope will be of some use to the—ah, the new Torunna which will no doubt come into existence after my departure."

He reached into the breast of his doublet and pulled out a tattered scroll. It was bloodstained and ragged, with a broken seal upon it.

"You see, lady, despite what you may think, I never wanted harm to come to this kingdom. I simply could not see any way to save it except my own. Others may save it—that is quite possible—but in doing so they will also destroy it. If you do not see what I mean already, I am sure you will one day."

Odelia took the scroll with a slight inclination of her head. "I will see you hanged, Count. And your head I will post above the city gate."

Fournier smiled. "I am sorry to disappoint you, Majesty, but I am a nobleman of the old school who will take his leave of the world in the manner he sees fit. Excuse me."

He walked over to a table in the corner which had decanters of wine and brandy set upon it, ignoring the crash and roar of the fighting which was rageing a few doors

down. Pouring himself a goblet of wine, he sprinkled a
white powder into the glass from a screw of paper he had
palmed. Then he tossed off the liquid with one swift gulp.

"Gaderian. As good a vintage to finish with as any, I
suppose." He bowed perfectly. When he had straightened,
Odelia could see the sudden sweat on his forehead. He took
one step towards her, and then folded over and toppled to
the floor.

Odelia went to him and despite herself she knelt and
cradled his head in her hands.

"You are a traitor, Fournier," she said gently. "But you
never lacked courage."

Fournier smiled up at her.

"He is a man of blood and iron, lady. He will never make
you happy." Then his eyes rolled back, and he died.

Odelia shut the dead eyelids, frowning. The firing down
the passageway reached a crescendo, and there was the
clash of steel on steel, men shrieking, orders half lost in
the chaos. Then a voice she knew thundered out: "Cease
fire! Cease fire there! You—drop your weapons. Formio,
round them up. Andruw, come with me."

An eerie quiet fell, and then booted feet were marching
up the corridor, crashing on marble. Through the door came
Corfe and Andruw, with a bodyguard of Fimbrians and
wild-eyed Cathedrallers. Corfe's face was badly bruised
and black with powder, and one eye was swollen. The
Queen rose, letting Fournier's head thump to the floor.

"Good day, General," she said, aching with the need to
run to him, embrace him.

"I trust I see you well, lady?" Corfe replied, his eyes
scanning the room. Coming to rest on Fournier they narrowed. "The Count made good his escape, I see."

"Yes, just this moment."

"Lucky for him. I'd have impaled the traitor, had I taken
him alive. Lads, cheque the next suite. That yokel down
there says there's no more but we can't be too sure." Andruw and the other soldiers tramped off purposefully. Corfe
noticed the bedraggled heap of the weeping Venuzzi and
kicked him out of his way.

"The city is secure, Majesty," he said. "A force has been

sent out to bring in the head of Colonel Willem. He is holed up to the east with some of the regulars."

"What of the other conspirators?" the Queen asked.

"We shot them as we found them. Which reminds me." Corfe drew John Mogen's sword. There was a flash as swift as lightning, a sickening crunch, and Gabriel Venuzzi's head spun end over end, attached to the body only by a ribbon of spouting arterial blood. The ladies-in-waiting shrieked; one fainted. Odelia curled her lip.

"Was that necessary?"

Corfe looked at her with no whit of softness in his eyes. "He had eighty of my men shot. He's lucky to have died quickly." He wiped his sword on Venuzzi's body.

Odelia turned her back on him and walked away from the puddle of gore on the floor. "Clean up that mess," she snapped at one of the maids.

The view out the window again. Fully a quarter of the city was burning, most of it down by the river. But the gunfire had stopped. Macrobius was still preaching in City Square, as he had been doing since dawn. What was he talking about? she wondered absently.

Corfe joined her. He looked like a prizefighter who had lost his bout.

"Well, you have delivered the city, General," Odelia said, angry with him for all manner of reasons she could not name. "I congratulate you. Now all you have to do is save us from the Merduks." Was it possible that Fournier's last words had registered with something in her? That disgusting murder in cold blood—right in front of her eyes! What kind of man was he anyway?

"Marsch is dead," Corfe said quietly.

"What?"

"He was killed while leading the breakout attempt."

She turned to him then and saw the tears coursing down his cheeks, though his face was set as hard as marble.

"Oh Corfe, I'm so sorry." She took him into her arms and for a moment he yielded, buried his face in the hollow of her shoulder. But then he pulled away and wiped his eyes with his fingers. "I must go. There's a lot to do, and not much time."

She turned to watch him. He left the room blindly, tramping through Venuzzi's gore and leaving a trail of bloody footprints behind him.

T ORUNN'S brief but bloody agony ended at last as the regular army stamped out the last embers of the abortive coup. The fires were brought under control, thousands of the capital's citizens mobilised to form bucket chains. Safely perched on a cherry tree in the heights of the palace gardens, the homunculus watched the spectacle with unblinking eyes. As darkness fell, it took off and flapped northwards.

That night, on the topmost battlements of Ormann Dyke's remaining tower, Aurungzeb, Sultan of Ostrabar, hammered his fist down on the unyielding stone of the ancient battlement.

"Who is sovereign here? Who commands? Shahr Johor, you may be my khedive, but you are not irreplaceable. I have indulged your whims once before, and forgiven you for the failure which resulted. You will now indulge me!"

"But Highness," Shahr Johor protested, "to change a battle-plan when the army is only days away from contact with the enemy is—is foolhardy."

"What did you say?"

Hopelessly, Shahr Johor pinched the bridge of his nose. "Your pardon, my Sultan. I am a little tyred."

"Yes, you are. Get yourself some sleep ere the fight begins, or you will be of no use to anyone." Aurungzeb's voice lost its harsh edge. "I am not a complete child in military matters, Shahr Johor, and what I am suggesting is not a complete rewriting of the plan, merely a minor revision."

Shahr Johor nodded, too weary to protest further.

"Batak failed to have this Torunnan commander-in-chief neutralised. That traitor Fournier failed to deliver Torunn to me without a fight. Batak tells me that the coup has already been stamped out—in the space of two days! There has been too much intrigue, and all of it a mere waste of time. Enough of it. Brute force is all that will destroy the Torunnans—that, and a good battle-plan. I have made a study of your intentions." Aurungzeb's voice fell, became more reasonable. "Your plan is fine. I have no quarrel with it. All I am asking is that you strengthen this flank march of yours. Take ten thousand of the *Hraibadar* from the main body and send them along with the cavalry."

"I don't understand your sudden desire to change the plan, Highness," Shahr Johor said stubbornly.

"There has been a lot of coming and going between here and Torunn. I suspect"—here Aurungzeb lowered his voice further—"I suspect we may have a traitor in our midst."

Shahr Johor snapped upright. "Are you sure?"

Aurungzeb flapped one massive hand. "I am not *sure*, but it is as well to be suspicious. That mad monk escaped from here with the connivance of someone at the court, and who knows what information he might have in his addled pate? Make the change, Shahr Johor. Do as I wish. I shall not meddle further in your handling of this battle."

"Very well, my Sultan. I bow to your superior wisdom. The flank march we planned will be augmented, and with the best shock infantry we possess. And no-one shall know of it but you and I, until the very day they set out."

"You relieve my mind, Shahr Johor. This may well be the deciding battle of the war. Nothing about its conduct must be left to chance. Mehr Jirah has half the army convinced that the western Saint is also our Prophet, and the *Minhraib*, curse them, are simple enough to believe that it means an end to war with the Ramusians. It may be that this is the last great levy Ostrabar will ever be able to mobilise."

"I won't fail you, Highness," Shahr Johor said fervently. "The Unbelievers will be struck as though by a thunderbolt. In a few days, not more, you will sit in Torunn and receive the homage of the Torunnan Queen. And this much-vaunted general of theirs shall be but a memory."

TWENTY

THERE had been no time for councils of war, debates on strategy or any of the last-minute wrangles so beloved of high commands since man had first started wageing organised war. Before the fires which raged down on the waterfront of Torunn had even stopped smouldering, the army was on the move. Corfe was leading thirty-five thousand men out of the capital, and leaving four thousand behind to garrison it. Some of the men in both the garrison and the field army had lately been in arms against each other, but now that it was the Merduk they were to fight against, their former allegiances were forgotten. Care had to be taken, however, to keep the Cathedrallers away from the conscripts. The tribesmen had taken Marsch's death hard, and were not inclined to forgive or forget in a hurry.

Andruw commanded the Cathedrallers now, with Ebro as his second-in-command. Formio led the Fimbrians, as always, and Ranafast the dyke veterans. The main body of the Torunnan regulars were under General Rusio, with Aras as his second, and the newly arrived conscripts had been scattered throughout the veteran tercios, two or three to a company. Back in Torunn, the garrison had been left under the personal command of the Queen herself, which had raised more than a few eye-brows. But Corfe simply did not have the officers to spare. Many had died as they were broken out of the dungeons. In any case, if the field army were destroyed, Torunn would have no chance.

It was not the best-equipped force that Torunna had ever sent out into battle. Most of the conscripts did not even possess uniforms, and some were still unfamiliar with their weapons, though Corfe had weeded out the most unhandy and reserved them for the garrison. In addition, the baggage train was a somewhat haphazard affair, as many of the supplies destined to be carried by it had gone up in smoke along with the riverfront warehouses. So the men were marching forth with rations for a week, no more, and two hundred of the Cathedrallers were serving as heavy infantry for lack of horses. But tucked away in Corfe's saddlebags was something he hoped would tip the scales in their favour: the Merduk battle-plan which Albrec had brought away from Ormann Dyke, and which the Queen had had translated. He knew what part of the enemy army was going where, and even though their advance had been brought forward, he thought they would stick to their original plan—for it is no light thing to redesign the accepted strategy of a large army, especially when that army is already on the march.

Without that information, Corfe privately believed that there would have been little or no hope for his men, and in his mind he blest Aurungzeb's nameless Ramusian Queen.

No cheers to see them off, but the walls were thickly crowded with Torunn's population all the same. There was a headlong sense of urgency about the city. So much had happened in such a short space of time that the departure of the army for the decisive battle seemed but one more notable event amongst many. No time for farewells either. The regulars had an appointment to keep, and they marched out of the city gates knowing they were already late for it.

The army tramped eighteen miles that first day, and when the lead elements started to lay out their bivouacs the rearguard was still a league behind them. As was his wont, Corfe found himself a nearby knoll and sat his horse there, watching them trudge into camp. He was not seeing them, though. He was thinking of an ex-slave who had once sworn allegiance to him with the chains of the galleys still on his wrists. A savage from the Cimbrics who had become his friend.

Andruw and Formio joined him, the Fimbrian actually mounted on a quiet mare. The trio exchanged sombre salutes and then watched as the first campfires were lit below, until there was a constellation of them rivalling the brilliance of the first stars.

The darkness deepened. The trio sat their horses without sharing a word, but glad of one another's company. Then Andruw twisted in his saddle and peered north. "Corfe, Formio. Look there."

On the horizon, a ruddy glow like that of a burning town. Except that there were no towns for many leagues in that direction.

"It's their campfires," Corfe realised. "Like the lights of a city. That's the enemy, gentlemen."

They studied the phenomenon. It was, in its way, as awe-inspiring as the Northern Lights which could be seen in winter from the foothills of the Thurians.

"It doesn't seem as though it could be the work of man, somehow," Formio said.

"When there's enough of them, men can do just about anything," Andruw told him. "And they're capable of anything." His voice fell into something approaching a whisper. "But I've never known or heard of them fighting a war like this one. There has never been a pause in it, from the first assaults on Aekir until now. Ormann Dyke, the North More, the King's Battle, Berrona, and then the battle for the city itself. There's no end to it—in the space of a year."

"Is that all it's been?" Corfe wondered. "One year? And yet the whole world has changed."

They were all thinking of Marsch, though no-one mentioned his name.

"Sound officers' call as soon as the rearguard is bedded down," Corfe said at last. "We'll meet here. I have something to show you."

"Going to pull a rabbit out of a hat, Corfe?" Andruw asked lightly.

"Something like that."

They saluted and left him. Corfe dismounted, hobbled and unsaddled his horse and let it graze. Then he sat on a mossy boulder and watched the northern horizon, where the Merduk host was lighting up a Torunnan sky. One single year, and the deaths of untold thousands. He had begun it as a junior officer, obscure but happy. And he had ended it commander of Torunna's last army, his heart as black and empty as a withered apple. All in that one year.

FORMIO held a lantern over the map and the assembled officers kept down its corners with the toes of their boots. They crowded around the circle of light as though straining to warm themselves at a fire. Corfe pointed out features with a broken stick.

"We are here, and the enemy is . . . there, or thereabouts. You've seen the light of their camp for yourselves. I reckon they're less than half a day's march away. They number a hundred and twenty-five thousand, one fifth of them cavalry. The Merduk khedive, Shahr Johor, is going to send this cavalry out on a flank march to the north, to come in on our left flank when we've engaged the main body, and roll us up. Hammer and anvil—simple, but effective. His cavalry consist of *Ferinai*, horse-archers, and mounted infantry who've been taken out of the *Minhraib* and armed with horse-pistols. The *Ferinai* are the core of the force. If we cripple them, the rest will crumble. They number only some eight thousand, for they lost a third of their men in the King's Battle, attacking Aras and Formio."

"And I suppose you can tell us what they're going to have for breakfast in the morning," Andruw said with a raised eye-brow. "General, we seem remarkably well-informed as to the enemy's composition and intentions."

"That is because I have managed to get hold of a copy of their battle-plan, Colonel," Corfe said with a smile.

That raised a ripple of astonishment amongst the assembled officers. "Sir," Aras began, "how—?"

Corfe held up a hand. "It's enough that we¯possess it. Don't trouble yourselves about how we came by it. I intend to detach the commands of Colonel Cear-Adurhal and Adjutant Formio to deal with this flank march. Attached to them will be Ranafast's arquebusiers. This combined force will be under the overall command of Colonel Cear-Adurhal. It should be able to see the enemy cavalry off."

"Of course. It'll only be outnumbered three to one," someone muttered.

"The *Ferinai* will be in the van. Andruw, if you can cripple them, the rest will fold too. I have it on good authority that the *Minhraib*—over a third of the Merduk army—have no stomach for this fight. The Sultan will be keeping them in reserve to the rear. There's a good chance they'll remain skulking there if they see things going badly.

"This is the line of the main body's advance." He traced it out on the map with his stick. "As you can see, they're using the Western Road. What I intend to do is to take our own regulars up and, if we can, pitch into' them whilst they're still in march column; that way we'll deal with them piecemeal."

"Where do you think we'll contact them?" Rusio asked.

"About here, at this crossroads." Corfe peered more closely at the map. "Roughly where this little hamlet lies. Armagedir."

"That's an old name. It means *Journey's End* in Old Normannnic," said Andrew.

Corfe straightened. "Andruw, Formio and Ranafast— your task will be to rout the Merduk cavalry and then come in on the enemy flank, much as they were intending to do with us. On the success or failure of that manoevre the fate of the battle will hinge. Gentlemen, I can't emphasise enough that we must rely on speed. There can be no foul-ups, no delays. What we lack in numbers, we must make up for in . . . in—"

"Alacrity?" Aras suggested.

"Aye. That's the word. When we attack, we must follow up every enemy retreat, and give them no chance to reform. If they manage to bring their numbers to bear, then they'll swamp us. Those of you who were at Berrona will remember how we pitched into them while they were still struggling to get their boots on. We must do the same here. We cannot allow them a moment to take stock. This fact must be instilled all the way down the chain of command. Do I make myself clear?"

There was a collective murmur of assent.

"Good. I don't have to point out to you that we have little in the way of reserves—"

"As usual," someone said, and there was a rustle of laughter. Corfe smiled.

"That's right. The line must not break. If it does, then it's all over—for us, for your families, for our country. There will be no second chance."

The faces grew sober again as this sank in. Corfe studied them all. Andruw, Formio, Ranafast, Rusio, Aras, Morin, Ebro and a dozen others. How many fewer would there be after this battle, which he meant to make the last? For once, he felt the burden of their lives and deaths heavy on his conscience. He was sure of one thing though: they were not fighting so that after the war lords in gilt carriages could dictate the running of their country. If they accomplished this feat, if they saved Torunna, then there would be many things that needed changing in this country. And they would have earned the right to make those changes.

"Very well, gentlemen. Reveille is two hours before dawn. Andruw, Formio and Ranafast: you know your orders. General Rusio, in the morning the main body will shake out straight into battle-line, and advance in that fashion. Mounted pickets out in front."

Rusio nodded. Like the others, he was white-faced and determined. "When do you reckon we'll run into them, sir?"

Corfe studied the map again. In his mind's eye he saw the armies on the march, on a collision course. Like two shortsighted titans bent on violence.

"I reckon we'll hit them just before noon," he said.

Rusio nodded. "I wish you joy of the encounter, sir."

"Thank you. Gentlemen, you know speech-making isn't my bent. I don't have to inspire you with rhetoric or inflame your spirits. We're professionals at the end of the day, and we have a job ahead of us that cannot be shirked. Now go to your commands. I want your junior officers briefed, and then you can get some sleep. Good luck to all of you."

"May God be with us," someone said. Then they saluted him and filed away one by one. At last only Andruw remained. There was none of the accustomed levity on his face.

"You're giving me the army, Corfe. Our army."

"I know. They're the best we've got, and they've been given the hardest job."

Andruw shook his head. "It should be you leading them then. Where are you going to be? Stuck in the main body with the other footslogging regulars? Baby-sitting Rusio?"

"I need to keep an eye on him. He's capable, but he's got no imagination."

"I'm not up to it, Corfe."

"Yes, you are. You're the best man I have."

They faced each other squarely, without speaking. Then Andruw put out his hand. Corfe clasped it firmly. In the next instant they were embracing like brothers.

"You take care out there tomorrow," Corfe said roughly.

"Look for me in the afternoon. I'll be coming out of the west, yelling like a cat with its tail afire." Then Andruw punched him playfully on the stomach and turned away. Corfe watched him retreating into the night, until he had disappeared into the fire and shadows of the sleeping army. He never saw Andruw alive again.

H E did the rounds of the camp that night, as he always did, having quiet words with the sentries, nodding to those soldiers who were lying staring at the stars, unable to sleep. Sharing gulps of wine with them, or old jokes. Once even a song.

For the first time in a long while, it was not cold. The men slept on grass, not in squelching mud, and the breeze that ruffled the campfires was not bitter. Corfe could almost believe that spring was on its way at last, this long winter of the world finally releasing its grip on the cold earth. He had never been a pious man, but he found he was silently reiterating a formless sort of prayer as he walked between the crowded campfires and watched his men gathering strength for the ordeal of the day to come. Though killing was his business, the one thing in which he excelled, he prayed for it to end.

ON the topmost tower of Torunn's Royal palace four people stood in the black hour before the dawn and waited for the day to begin. Odelia Queen of Torunn, Macrobius the Pontiff, and Bishops Albrec and Avila.

When at last the sky lightened from black to cobalt blue to a storm-delicate green, the boiling saffron ball of the sun soared up out of the east in a fierce conflagration of colour, as though the scattered clouds on the world's horizon had caught light and were being consumed by the heat of some vast, silent furnace which burnt furiously at the edge of the earth. The foursome stood there as the morning light grew and waxed and took over a flawless sky, and the city came to life at their feet, oblivious. They watched the thousands of people who climbed the walls and stood waiting on the battlements, the packed crowds hushed in the public squares. The very church bells were stilled.

And finally, faint over the hills to the north, there came the long, distant thunder of the guns, like a rumour from a darker world. The last battle had begun.

TWENTY-ONE

The final clash between Merduk and Ramusian on the continent of Normannia took place on the nineteenth day of Forialon, in the year of the Saint 552.

The Merduks had a screen of light cavalry out to their front. These Corfe dispersed by sending forward a line of arquebusiers, who brought down half a dozen of the enemy with a swift volley. The rest fled to warn their comrades of the approaching cataclysm. The Torunnan advance continued, lines of skirmishers out to flanks and front, the main body of the infantry sweating and toiling to maintain the brutal pace Corfe had set. The line grew ragged, and sergeants shouted themselves hoarse at the men to keep their dressing, but Corfe was not worried about a few untidy ranks here and there. Speed was the thing. The Merduks had been warned, and would be struggling to redeploy their forces from vulnerable march-column into battle-line. But that would take time, as did all manoevres involving large numbers of men. Had he possessed more cavalry, he might have sent forward a mounted screen of his own, strong enough to wipe out the Merduk pickets and take their main body totally by surprise—but there was no point wishing for the moon. The Cathedrallers had been needed on the flank, and there were simply no more horsemen to be had.

He turned to Cerne, who with seven other tribesmen had remained with him as a sort of unofficial bodyguard.

"Sound me double march."

The tribesman put his horn to his lips, closed his eyes and blew the intricate yet instantly recognizable call. Up and down the three mile line, other trumpeters took it up. The Torunnans picked up their feet and began to run.

Over a slight rise in the ground they jogged, panting. Corfe cantered ahead of the struggling army, and there it was. Perhaps half a mile away, the mighty Merduk host was halted. Its battlefront was as yet less than a mile wide, but men were sprinting into position on both flanks, striving to lengthen it before the Torunnans struck. Back to the rear of the line, a mad chaos of milling men and guns and elephants and baggage waggons stretched for as far as the eye could see. At a crossroads to the left rear of the Merduk line, the hamlet of Armagedir stood forlornly, swamped by a tide of hell-bent humanity. There were tall banners flying amid the houses. The Merduk khedive seemed to have taken it as his command post.

They had chosen their ground well. The line was set upon a low hill, just enough to blunt the momentum of an infantry charge. There was a narrow row of trees to their rear which some long-dead farmer had planted as a windbreak. Corfe could see a second rank falling into position there. The Merduk khedive had been startled by the unlooked-for appearance of the Torunnans, but he was collecting his wits with commendable speed.

Corfe looked west, to the moorland which rolled featurelessly to the horizon. Andruw was out there somewhere, hunting the Merduk cavalry. It would be a few hours yet before he could be expected to arrive. If he arrived at all, Corfe told himself quickly, as if to forestall bad luck.

The army was running past him now, and his restive

horse danced and snorted as the great crowd of men passed by. He thought he could feel the very vibration of those tens of thousands of booted feet through his saddle. He heard his name shouted by short-of-breath voices. Equipment rattling, the smell of the match, already lit, the stench of many bodies engaged in hard labour. A distilled essence of men about to plunge into war.

Then the thumping of hooves on the upland turf, and Rusio had reined in beside him accompanied by a gaggle of staff officers.

"We've got them, General! We're going to knock them flying!" he chortled.

"Get your horse batteries out to the front, Rusio. I want them unlimbered and firing before the infantry go in. First rank halts and gives them a volley: the other ranks keep going. You know the drill. See to it!"

Rusio's grin faded. He saluted and sped off.

Galloping six-horse teams now pulled ahead of the infantry, each towing a six-pounder. The artillery unlimbered with practised speed and their crews began loading frantically. Then the first lanyard was pulled, the first shell went arcing out of a cannon muzzle—you could actually follow it if you possessed quick eyes—and crashed into scarlet ruin in the ranks of the deploying Murduks. A damn good shot, even at such close range. The cannon barrels were depressed almost to the horizontal, so close were the gunners to the enemy.

Twenty-four guns were deployed now, and they began barking out in sequence, the heavy weapons leaping back as they went off. Those gunners knew their trade all right, Corfe thought approvingly.

Some of the first salvo was long; instead of hitting the Merduk front line it landed in the rear elements, sowing chaos and slaughter—but that was just as good. The gunners had orders to elevate their pieces to maximum once their own infantry passed them by, and keep lobbing shells on an arc into the Merduk rear. That would disrupt the arrival of any reinforcements.

Four salvoes, and then the infantry was running past the guns. They were in a line a league long and four ranks deep, a frontage of one yard per man—and despite his quip the night before, Corfe had kept back some three thousand veterans as a last-ditch reserve, in case disaster struck somewhere. These three thousand were in field-column, and formed up beside him as he sat his horse surrounded by his bodyguard and a dozen couriers.

The first Torunnan rank halted, brought their arquebuses into the shoulder, and then fired. Six thousand weapons going off at once. Corfe heard the tearing crackle of it a second after he had watched the smoke billow out of the line. The enemy host was virtually hidden by a cliff of grey-white fumes. The other three Torunnan lines charged through the first and disappeared into the reek of powder-smoke, a formless roar issuing from their throats as they went. It would be like a vision of hell in there as they came to close quarters with the enemy.

That was it: the army was committed, and had caught the Merduks before they had properly deployed. The first part of his plan had worked.

ANDRUW reined in his horse and held up a hand. Behind him the long column of men halted. He turned to Ebro. "Hear that?"

They listened. "Artillery," Ebro said. "They're engaged."

"Damn, that was quick." Andruw frowned. "Trumpeter, sound battle-line. Morin, take a squadron out to the north. Find me these bastards, and find them quick."

"It shall be so." The tribesman grinned. He shouted in Cimbric, and a group of Cathedrallers peeled off and pelted away after him northwards.

"We should have run across them by now," Andruw fretted. "What are they doing, hiding down rabbit holes? They must be making slower time than we'd thought. Courier, to me."

A young ensign pranced up, unarmoured and mounted on a long-limbed gelding. His eyes were bright as those of an excited child. "Sir!"

"Go to General Cear-Inaf. Tell him we still have not located the enemy cavalry, and our arrival on the battlefield may be delayed. Ask him if our orders stand. And make it quick!"

The courier saluted smartly and galloped off, clods of turf flying in the wake of his eager horse.

"Twenty-five thousand horsemen," Andruw said irritably. "And we can't find hide nor hair of them."

"They'll turn up," Ebro said confidently. Andruw glared at him, and realised how easy it was to be confident when there was a superior around to make the hardest decisions. Then, "Hear that?" he said again.

Arquebus fire, a rolling clatter of it to the south of them.

"The infantry has got stuck in," he said. "That's it—they can't break off now. They're in it up to their ears. Where the hell is that damned enemy cavalry?"

CORFE sat his horse and watched the battle rage before him like some awesome spectacle laid on for his entertainment. He hated this—watching men dying from a distance with his sword still in its scabbard. It was one of the burdens of high rank he thought he would never get used to.

What would he be doing if he were the Merduk khedive? The first instinct would be to shore up the sagging line. The Torunnans had pushed it clear back to the row of trees, but there the Merduks seemed to have rallied, as men often will about some linear feature in the terrain. Their losses had been horrific in those first few minutes of carnage, but they had the numbers to absorb them. No—if the khedive was second-rate he would send reinforcements to the line; but if he were any good, he would tell the men there to hang on, and send fresh regiments out on the flanks, seeking to encircle the outnumbered Torunnans. But which flank? He had his cavalry out on his right somewhere, so the odds were it would be the left. Yes, he would build up on his left flank.

Corfe turned to the waiting veterans who stood leaning their elbows on their gun rests and watching.

"Colonel Passifal!"

The white-haired quartermaster saluted. "Sir?"

"Take your command out on our right, double-quick.

Don't commit them until you see the enemy feeling around the end of our line. When you do, hit them hard, but don't join our centre. Keep your men mobile. Do you understand?"

"Aye, sir. You reckon that's where they'll strike next?"

"It's what I would do. Good luck, Passifal."

The unearthly din of a great battle. Unless it had been experienced, it was impossible to describe. Heavy guns, small arms, men shouting to encourage themselves or intimidate others. Men screaming in agony—a noise unlike any other. It coalesced into a stupendous barrage of sound which stressed the senses to the point of overload. And when one was in the middle of it—right in the belly of that murderous madness—it could invade the mind, spurring men on to inexplicable heroism or craven cowardice. Laying bare the very core of the soul. Until it had been experienced, no man could predict how he would react to it.

Passifal's troops doubling off, a dark stain on the land. En masse, soldiers seen from a distance looked like nothing so much as some huge, bristling caterpillar slithering over the face of the earth. Men in the centre of a formation like that would see nothing but the back of the man in front of them. They would be treading on heels, cursing, praying, the sweat stinging their eyes. The heroic balladeers knew nothing of real war, not as it was waged in this age of the world. It was a job of work: sheer hard drudgery punctuated by brief episodes of unbelievable violence and abject terror.

There! Corfe felt a moment of intense satisfaction as fresh Merduk regiments arrived to extend the line on the right, just as he had thought they would. They were getting into position when Passifal's column slammed into them, all the weight of that tight-packed body of men. The Merduks were sent flying, transformed from a military formation into a mob in the time it took for a man to peel an apple. Passifal re-formed his own men into a supported battle-line, and they began firing, breaking up attempts by the enemy to rally. He might be a quartermaster, but he still knew his trade.

Corfe looked back at the centre. Hard to make out what was going on in there, but Rusio still seemed to be ad-

vancing. That was the thing: to keep the pressure on, to
deny the enemy time to think. So far it was working well.
But men can only fight for so long.

He turned his face towards the deserted moors in the
north. Where was Andruw? What was going on out there?

"I find them, Ondruw! I find them!" Morin crowed, his
horse blowing and fuming under him, sides dank with
sweat.

"Where?"

Morin struggled to think in Torunnan units of distance.
"One and a part of a league east of here, in long—" He
grasped for the word, face screwed up in concentration.

"Line? Like we are now?"

The tribesman shook his head furiously.

"Column, Morin, are they in column, like along a road?"

Morin's face cleared. "Column—that is the word. But
they have their *Ferinai* out to front, in—in line. And they
have men on foot, infantry, coming behind."

Formio came trotting up on his long-suffering mare. He
had taken to horseback for the sake of speed, but he clearly
did not relish it any more than she did. "What's afoot, Andruw?"

"Morin sighted them, thank God," Andruw breathed.
"That was good work. Spread the word, Formio. We're
going to pitch into 'em as we are. Cathedrallers on the right,
Fimbrians in the middle, Ranafast's lads to the rear." Then
he hesitated. "Morin, did you say infantry?"

"Yes, men on foot with guns. Behind the horsemen."

Formio's face remained impassive, but he rode up close
to Andruw and spoke into his ear. "No-one said anything
about infantry. I thought it was just cavalry we were facing."

"It's probably just a baggage guard or suchlike. No need
to worry about them. The main thing is, we've located them
at last. If I have to, I'll face the arquebusiers about and
we'll make a big square. Let them try charging Fimbrian
pike and Torunnan shot, and see where it gets them."

Formio stared at him for a moment, and then nodded. "I

see what you mean. But we have to destroy them, not just hold our own."

It was Andruw's turn to pause. "All right. I'll hold the Cathedrallers back. When the time is ready, they'll charge and roll them up. We'll hammer them, Formio, don't worry."

"Very well then. Let's hammer them." But Formio looked troubled.

The army redeployed towards the east. The Fimbrians led the advance while the Cathedrallers covered the flanks and the Torunnan arquebusiers brought up the rear. Just over seven and a half thousand men in all, they could hear the distant clamour of the battle rageing around Armagedir and marched over the upland moors with a will, eager to come to grips with the foe.

Thirty-five thousand Merduk troops awaited them.

BACK at Armagedir, the morning was wearing away and the Torunnan advance had stalled. Rusio's men had been halted in their tracks by sheer weight of enemy numbers. The line of trees had changed hands half a dozen times in the last hour and was thick with the dead of both armies. The battle here was fast degenerating into a bloody stalemate, and unlike the Merduk khedive, Corfe did not have fresh troops to feed into the grinder. He could hold his own for another hour, perhaps even two, but at the end of that time the army would be exhausted. And the Merduk khedive had fully one third of his own forces as yet uncommitted to the battle. They were forming up behind Armagedir, molested only by stray rounds from the Torunnan artillery. Something had to be done, or those thirty thousand fresh troops would be coming around Corfe's flank in the next half-hour.

Where the hell was Andruw? He ought to at least be on his way by now.

Corfe made up his mind and called over a courier. He scribbled out a message while giving it verbally at the same time.

"Go to the artillery commander, Nonius. Have him limber up his guns and move them forward into our own battle-line. He is to unlimber there in the middle of our infantry and give the enemy every charge of canister he possesses. When that happens, Rusio is to advance. He is to push forward to the crossroads and take Armagedir. Repeat it."

The courier did so, white-faced.

"Good. Take this note to Nonius first, and then to General Rusio. Tell Rusio that Passifal's men will support his right flank. He is to break the Merduk line. Do you hear me? He is to break it. Here. Now go."

The courier seized the note and took off at a tearing gallop.

Something had happened to Andruw, out in the moors. Corfe could feel it. Something had gone wrong.

Then another courier thundered in, this one's horse about to founder under him. He had come from the north. Corfe's heart leapt.

"Compliments of Colonel Cear-Adurhal sir," the man gasped. "He has still not found the enemy. Wants to know if his orders stand."

"How long ago did you leave him?" Corfe asked sharply.

"An hour, maybe. No sign of the enemy out there, sir."

"God's blood," Corfe hissed. What was going on?

"Tell him to keep looking. No—wait. It'll take you an hour to get back to him. If he hasn't found anything by then, he's to come here and attack the Merduk right. Throw in everything he's got."

"Everything he's got. Yes, sir."

"Get yourself a fresh horse and get going."

Corfe tried to shake off the apprehension that was flooding through him. He kicked his horse into motion and cantered southwards, to where Passifal's men were standing ready out on the right. They were the only reserve he had, and he was about to throw them into the battle. He could think of nothing else to do.

ANDRUW'S command charged full-tilt into the enemy with a shouted roar that seemed to flatten the very grass. The *Ferinai*, the elite of Merduk armies, came to meet them, eight thousand men on heavy horses dressed in armour identical to that worn by the Cathedrallers. And the tribesmen spurred their own mounts into a headlong gallop, drawing ahead of the Fimbrians and Torunnans.

There was a tangible shock as the two bodies of cavalry met. Horses were shrieking, some knocked clear off their feet by the impact. Men were thrown through the air to be trampled by the huge horde of milling beasts. Lances snapped off and swords were drawn. There was a rising clatter, like a preternatural blacksmith's shop gone wild, as troopers of both sides hammered at their steel-clad adversaries. The struggle became a thousand little hand-to-hand combats as the formations ground to a halt and a fierce melee developed. The Cathedrallers were pushed back, hopelessly outnumbered though fighting like maniacs. But then the Fimbrians came up, their pike-points levelled. They smashed a swathe through the halted enemy cavalry, their flanks and rear protected by Ranafast's arquebusiers. The combined formation was as compact as a clenched fist, and seemed unstoppable. Andruw led the Cathedrallers back out of the battle-line, and re-formed them in the rear. Many of them were on foot: others had dismounted comrades clinging on behind them or were dragged out by the grasp of a stirrup. Andruw had lost his helmet in the whirling press of men and horses, and seemed infected by a wild gaiety. He joined in the cheer when the *Ferinai* fell back, their retreat turning into something resembling a rout as the implacable Fimbrians followed up. The plan was working after all.

Then there was a staggering volley of arquebus fire that seemed to go on for ever. The Fimbrians collapsed by the hundred as a storm of bullets mowed them down, clicking through their armour with a sound oddly like hail on a tin roof. They faltered, their front ranks collapsing, men stumbling backwards on their fellows with the heavy bullets blasting chunks out of their bodies, cutting their feet from under them, snapping pike shafts in two. The advance ground to a halt, its furthest limit marked by a tideline of con torted bodies, in places two or three deep.

To the rear of the *Ferinai* had been a huge host of infantry, ten thousand of them at least. They had lain down

in the rough upland grass and the wiry heather, and the
retreating Merduk cavalry had passed over them. Then
when the pike-men had approached, they had risen to their
feet and fired at point-blank range. It was the same tactic
Corfe had used on the Nalbenic cavalry in the King's Battle. Andruw stared at the carnage in the Fimbrian ranks with
horror. The Merduks had formed up in five lines, and when
one line fired it lay down again so that the one behind it
could discharge the next volley. It was continuous, murderous, and the Fimbrians were being decimated.

Andruw struggled to think. What would Corfe do? His
own instinct was to lead the Cathedrallers in a wild charge,
but that would accomplish nothing. No—something else.

Ranafast cantered up. "Andruw, they're on our flanks.
The bastards have horse-archers on our flanks."

Andruw tore his eyes away from the death of the Fimbrians to the surrounding hills. Sure enough, massed formations of cavalry were moving to right and left on the
high ground about them. In a few minutes his command
would be surrounded.

"God Almighty!" he breathed. What could he do? The
whole thing was falling to pieces in front of his eyes.

Hard to think in the rising chaos. Ranafast was staring
at him expectantly.

"Take your arquebusiers, and keep those horse-archers
clear of our flanks and rear. We're pulling out."

Ranafast was astonished. "Pulling out? Saint's blood,
Andruw, the Fimbrians are being cut to pieces and the enemy is all over us. How the hell do we pull out? They'll
follow and break us."

But it was becoming clear in Andruw's mind now. The
initial panic had faded away, leaving calm certainty in its
place.

"No, it'll be all right. Get a courier to Formio. Tell him
to get his men the hell out of there as soon as he can. He
must break off contact. As he does, I'll lead the Cathedrallers in. We'll keep the enemy occupied long enough for
you and Formio to shoot your way clear. I'm making you
second-in-command now, Ranafast. Get as many of your
and Formio's men out as you can. Take them to Corfe."

Ranafast was white-faced. "And you? You've no chance, Andruw."

"It'll take a mounted charge to make an impact in there. Besides, the Fimbrians are spent, and your lot are needed to keep the horse-archers at bay. It'll have to be the tribesmen."

"Let me lead them in," Ranafast pleaded.

"No, it's on my head, all this mess. I must do what I can to remedy it. Get back to Corfe, for God's sake. Leave another rearguard on the way if you have to, but get there with as many as you can and pile into the enemy flank. He can't hold them unless you do."

They shook hands. "What shall I tell him?" Ranafast asked.

"Tell him . . . Tell him he made a cavalryman out of me at last. Goodbye, Ranafast."

Andruw spun his horse around and galloped off to join the Cathedrallers. Ranafast watched him go, one lone figure in the middle of that murderous turmoil. Then he collected himself and started bellowing orders at his own officers.

THE Fimbrians withdrew, crouching like men bent against a rainstorm, their pikes bristling impotently. As they did, the *Hraibadar* arquebusiers confronting them gave a great shout, elated at having made a Fimbrian phalanx retreat. They began to edge forward, first in ones and twos, then by companies and tercios, gathering courage as they became convinced that the enemy retreat was not a feint. Their carefully dressed lines became mixed up, and they began firing at will instead of in organised volleys.

An awesome thunder of hooves, and then the Cathedrallers appeared on one flank: a great mass of them at full, reckless gallop, the tribesmen singing their shrill battle-paean. Andruw was at their head, yelling with the best of them. The *Hraibadar* ranks seemed to give a visible shiver, like the twitch of a horse under a fly, just at the moment of impact.

And the heavy cavalry plunged straight into them. Fifteen hundred horsemen at top speed. Ranafast watched them strike from his position in the middle of the dyke veterans. The *Hraibadar* line buckled and broke. He saw one massive warhorse turn end over end through the air. Its fellows trampled the enemy infantry as though they were corn. He felt a surge of hope. By God, Andruw was going to do it. He was going to make it.

But there were ten thousand of the *Hraibadar*, and while the tribesmen had sent reeling fully one third of the Merduk regiments, the remainder were pulling back in good order, redeploying for a counter-attack. The success of the charge was temporary only, as Andruw had known it would be. But it had opened a gap in the encirclement, a gap that Ranafast's own men were widening, blasting well-aimed volleys into the harassing horse-archers. The Fimbrians had completely disengaged now, and were surrounded by Torunnan arquebusiers. The formation resembled nothing so much as a great densely packed square. Lucky the enemy had no artillery—the massed ranks would have made a perfect target. Ranafast bellowed the order, and the square began to move southwards, towards Armagedir, sweeping the Nalbenic light cavalry out of its way as a rhino might toss aside a troublesome terrier. Behind it, the Cathedrallers fought on in a mire of slaughter, surrounded now, but battling on without hope or quarter.

A knot of Fimbrians were carrying something towards Ranafast. A body. The Torunnan dismounted as they approached. It was Formio. He had been shot in the shoulder and stomach and his lips were blue, but his eyes were unclouded.

"We've broken free," he said. There was blood on his teeth. "I suggest we counter-attack, Ranafast. Andruw—"

"Andruw's orders were to keep going and to join Corfe," Ranafast said, his voice harsh as that of an old raven. Not Formio too.

"I intend to obey him. There is nothing we can do for the tribesmen now. We must make the most of the time they've bought us."

Formio stared at him, then bent forward and coughed up a gout of dark gore which splashed his punctured breastplate. Some inhuman reserve of strength enabled him to

straighten again in the arms of his men and look the Torunnan in the eye.

"We can't—"

"We must, Formio," Ranafast said gently. "Corfe is fighting the main battle; this is only a sideshow. We must."

Formio closed his eyes, nodded silently. One of his men
wiped the blood from his mouth, then looked up.

"He's almost gone, Colonel." The Fimbrian's visage was
a set mask.

"Bring him with us. I won't leave him here to become
carrion." Then Ranafast turned away, his own face a bitter
gnarl of grief.

THE Torunnan infantry had lunged forward once more,
clawing for the ground under them yard by bloody
yard. Rusio's troops now occupied the line of trees which
had been the rallying point for the enemy. Out on the left,
Aras had his standard planted in the hamlet of Armagedir
itself, and fifteen tercios had grouped themselves around it
and were holding against twenty times their number. The
thatch on the roofs of the houses there was burning, so that
all Corfe could glimpse were minute red flashes of gunfire
crackling in clusters and lines, sometimes the glint of armour through the dense smoke.

Nonius was moving his guns forward with the infantry,
but it was slow work. Many of the horses had been killed,
and the gunners were manhandling the heavy pieces over
broken ground that was strewn with corpses. The Merduk
artillery was still embroiled in the hopeless tangle of men
and equipment which backed up on the Western Road for
fully five miles to their rear.

The insane roar of the battle went on without pause, a
barrage of the very senses. Along a three-mile stretch of
upland moor the two opposing lines of close-packed men
strove to annihilate one another. They fought for possession
of a line of trees, a burnt-out cluster of houses, a muddy
stretch of road. Every little feature in the terrain took on a
great significance when men struggled to kill each other
upon it. Untold thousands littered the field of battle already,
and thousands more had become pitiful maimed wrecks of

humanity that swore and screamed and tried to drag themselves out of the holocaust.

Over on the right, Passifal had fully committed his men
to the line. That was it—the bottom of the barrel. Corfe
had nothing left to throw into the contest. And on the Merduk right, opposite Aras's hard-pressed tercios, the enemy
was massing for a counter-attack. When the Merduk general was ready he would launch some thirty thousand fresh
men into the battle there, and it would all be over.

Strangely, Corfe found the knowledge almost liberating.
It was finished at last. He had done his best, and it had not
been good enough, but at least now there was nothing more
to worry about. Something had happened to Andruw, that
was clear. The last two couriers that Corfe had sent out
seemed to have been swallowed up by the very hills. It was
as though all those men had simply disappeared.

There. Large formations moving through the smoke,
pointed towards Armagedir. The Merduk general had finally launched the counter-attack. Aras was about to be
crushed. Corfe looked about himself. He had with him his
eight Cathedraller bodyguards, and another ten youthful ensigns who acted as aides and couriers. Not much of a re-
inforcement, but better than nothing.

He turned to one of the young officers.

"Arian, go to General Rusio. Tell him he is to hold the
line at all hazards, and if he deems it practicable he is to
advance. Tell him I am joining Colonel Aras's men. They
are about to be hit by the enemy counter-attack. Go now."

The young officer saluted smartly and galloped off. Corfe
watched him go, wondering if he had ever been that earnest. He missed his friends. He missed Andruw and Formio. Marsch and the Cathedrallers. It was not the same,
fighting without them. And he realised with a flash of insight or intuition that it would never be the same again.
That time was over.

Corfe kicked his horse savagely in the belly and it half
reared. He did not fear death, he feared failure. And he had
failed. There was nothing more to be afraid of.

He drew Mogen's sword for the first time that day and
turned to Cerne, his trumpeter. "Follow me."

Then the group of riders took off after him as he rode full tilt up the hillside, into the smoking hell of Armagedir.

HUNDREDS of men lay wounded to the rear of the line here, making it hard for the horses to pick their way over them. The fuming roar of the battle was unbelievable, astonishing. Corfe had never before known its like, not even in the more furious assaults upon Ormann Dyke. It was as though both armies knew that this was the deciding contest of the century-old war. For one side complete victory beckoned, for the other annihilation. The Torunnans would not retreat because, like Corfe, they had ceased to be afraid of anything except the consequences of failure. So they died where they stood, fighting it out with gunstocks and sabres when their ammunition ran out, struggling like savages with anything that came to hand, even the very stones at their feet. They were dying hard, and for the first time in a long while Corfe felt proud to be one of them.

His party dismounted as they approached the ruins of the hamlet around which Aras's men had made their stand. The ground was too choked with bodies for the horses to be ridden further, and even the war-hardened destriers were becoming terrified by the din.

Aras's command stood at bay like an island in a sea of Merduks. The enemy had poured around its left flank and was pushing into the right, where it connected with the main body of the Torunnan army. They were trying to pinch off the beleaguered tercios from Rusio's forces, isolate and destroy them. But their assaults on the hamlet itself broke like waves on a sea cliff. Aras's troops stood and fought in the ruins of Armagedir as though it were the last fortress of the western world. And in a way it was.

The Torunnans looked up as Corfe and his entourage pushed their way through the choked ranks, and he heard his name called out again and again. There was even a momentary cheer. At last he found his way to the sable standard under which Aras and his staff officers clustered. The young colonel brightened at the sight of his commander-in-chief, and saluted with alacrity. "Good to see you, sir. We were beginning to wonder if the rest of the army had forgotten about us."

Corfe shook his hand. "Consider yourself a general now, Aras. You've earned it."

Even under grime and powder-smoke he could see the younger man flush with pleasure. He felt something of a fraud, knowing Aras would not live long enough to enjoy his promotion.

"Your orders, General?" Aras asked, still beaming. "I daresay our flank march will be arriving any time now."

Corfe did not have to lower his voice to avoid being overheard; the rageing chaos of the battle was like a great curtain.

"I believe our flank march may have run into trouble, Aras. It's possible you will not be reinforced. We must hold on here to the end. To the end, do you understand me?"

Aras stared at him, the dismay naked across his face for a second. Then he collected himself, and managed a strangled laugh. "At least I'll die a general. Don't worry, sir, these men aren't going anywhere. They know their duty, as do I."

Corfe gripped his shoulder. "I know," he said in almost a whisper.

"Sir!" one of the staff officers shouted. "They're coming in—a whole wave of them."

The Merduk counter-attack rolled into Armagedir like some unstoppable juggernaut. It was met with a furious crescendo of arquebus fire which obliterated the leading rank, and then it was hand to hand all down the line. The Torunnan perimetre shrank under that savage assault, the men crowded back on to the blazing buildings of the hamlet they defended. And there they halted. Corfe shoved his way to the forefront of the line and was able to forget strategy, politics, the worries of a high-ranking officer. He found himself battling for his life like the lowliest ranker, his Cathedraller bodyguards ranged about him and singing as they slew. The little knot of scarlet-armoured men seemed to draw the enemy as a candle will moths at twilight. They were more heavily armoured than their Torunnan comrades, and stood like a wedge of red-hot iron while the lightly armed warriors of the *Minhraib* crashed in on them to be hewn down one after another. Armagedir became cut off from the rest of the army as the Merduks swamped the Torunnan left wing. It became a murderous cauldron of insane violence within which men fought and killed without thought of self-preservation or hope of rescue. It was the end, the apocalypse. Corfe saw men dying with their teeth locked in an enemy's throat, others strangling each other, snarling like animals, eyes empty of reason. The *Minhraib* threw themselves on the Cathedrallers like dogs mobbing a bear, three and four at a time sacrificing themselves to bring down one steel-clad tribesman and cut his throat on the blood-sodden ground. Corfe swung and hacked in a berserk rage, sword blows clanging off his armour, one ringing hollow on his helm, exploding his bruised face with stars of agony. Something stabbed him through the thigh and he fell to his knees, bellowing, Mogen's sword dealing slaughter left and right. He was on the ground, buffeted by a massive scrum of bodies, trampled by booted feet. He fought himself upright, the sword blows raining down on him. Aras and Cerne were at his shoulders, helping him up. Then a blade burst out of Cerne's eye, and he toppled without a sound. The detonation of an arquebus scorched Corfe's hand. He stabbed out blindly, felt flesh and bone give way under the Answerer's wicked edge. Someone hacked at his neck, and his sight erupted with stars and spangled darkness. He went down again.

A sunlit hillside above Aekir in some age of the world long past, and he was sitting on crackling bracken with Heria by his side, sharing wine. His wife's smile rent his heart.

Andruw laughing amid the roar of guns, a delight in life lighting up his face and making it into that of a boy.

Barbius's Fimbrians advancing to their deaths in terrible glory at the North More.

Berrona burning low on a far horizon.

A smoky hut in which his mother wept quietly and his father stared at the earthen floor as Corfe told him he was going for a soldier.

Dappled sunlight on the Torrin river as he splashed and swam there one long summer afternoon.

And the roar and blare of many trumpets, the beat of heavy drums rising even over the clamour of war. The press of bodies about him eased. He was hauled to his feet and found himself looking through a film of blood at Aras's slashed face.

"Andruw has come!" he was shouting. "The Fimbrians have struck the Merduk flank!"

And raising his heavy head he saw the pikes outlined against the fuming sky, and all about him the men of Armagedir were cheering as the Merduks poured away in absolute panic. The dyke veterans were lined on a hillside to the north, blasting out volley after volley into the close-packed throng of the enemy. And the Fimbrians were cutting them down like corn, advancing as relentlessly as if they meant to sweep every Merduk off the edge of the world.

Corfe bent his head and wept.

TWENTY-TWO

T HE levee had gone very well, Murad thought. Half the
kingdom's remaining nobility seemed to have been
present, and they had listened, agog, as Murad had told
them of his experiences in the west. It was good of the
King to have allowed him to do it. It announced that the
Lord of Galiapeno had returned indeed it and, what was more,
enjoyed the Royal favour. But it had also been a draining
experience.

Traveller's tales. Is that all they thought he had to tell?
Empty-headed fools.

The King had limped down from his throne and was now
mingling with his subjects. He had a genius for gestures
like that, Murad thought, though it was hardly fitting, not
so soon after these same men who were now fawning about
him had been conspiring to take the throne away from him.

If it were I wearing that crown, Murad thought, I'd have
executed every last one of them.

His head was swimming. He had been able to keep down

nothing but wine since stepping off the ship. I am back in my own world, he thought. And what a little world it is. Time to retire. He craved a dreamless slumber, something that would restore the weariness of his very soul. Oblivion, without the bloody pictures that haunted his sleep.

"Lord Murad," a woman's voice said. "How very honoured I am to meet you."

She was a striking, dark-haired lady with intelligent eyes and a low-cut bodice. She was also very pregnant. Murad bowed. "I am flattered. Might I ask—?"

"I am the lady Jemilla. I have a feeling you probably know of me already."

He did indeed. Abeleyn had told him everything. So this was the woman who bore the King's child, who had tried to set up a regency. Murad's interest quickened. She was a beauty, no doubt of that. Why was she at liberty? Abeleyn was so damned soft. She ought to be hidden away somewhere, and the brat strangled when it was born.

"I believe," she went on, fluttering her fan under her chin, "that you now enjoy the happy distinction of being the man closest by blood to the King himself."

"I am," Murad said, and smiled. It would be nice to bed her. It was obvious what she was doing: fishing for a new puppet to play against the King.

"It is so hot in here, lady," he said. "Would you care to take a turn with me outside in the gardens?"

She took his arm. Her eyes had suddenly lost their coy look. "What woman could refuse such a gallant adventurer?"

SHE gasped and squealed and moaned as he thrust into her, pulling her hips towards him with fistfuls of her dress. Murad clenched his teeth as he spent himself within, gave her one last savage thrust and pulled away with the sweat running down his face. Jemilla sank to her side in the deeper shadows under the tree. Twilight was fast sinking into darkness and her face was a mere livid blur. The gardens were alive with the birds' evensong, and he could still hear the buzz and laughter of the chattering guests in the reception hall. Murad refastened his breeches and leaned on one elbow in the resinous-smelling dimness under the cypress.

"You have a direct way of approaching things," he told Jemilla.

"It saves time."

"I agree. You have hopes for your child, obviously, but what exactly is your fascination with me? I am no young girl's dream. And I have been away from court a long time."

"Precisely. You are not tainted by the events which have been transpiring in Abrusio. Your hands are clean. We could be useful to one another," Jemilla said calmly.

Murad brushed the dead leaves from his shoulders. "I could be useful to you, you mean. Lady, your name is mud at court. The King tolerates you out of some outdated chivalric impulse. Your child, when it is born, will be shunted off to some backwater estate in the Hebros, and you with it. What can you offer me, aside from the occasional roll in the grass?"

She leaned closer. Her hand slid down his belly and over the brim of his breeches. He flinched minutely as her hot fingers gripped his flaccid member.

"Marry me," she said.

"What?" Murad actually chuckled.

"I could not then be shunted off, as you put it. And my son's claims would be all the stronger." Her hand started to work up and down on him. He began to harden again in her grasp.

"This may be true, but I ask again: what do I get out of it?"

"You become the legal guardian of the King's heir. If something were to happen to the King after my son is born, he would be too young to be crowned. And you would be regent automatically."

"Regicide? Is that your game?" He wrenched her hand out of his breeches. "Lady, if something were to happen to the King, I would be next in line anyway, have you thought of that? I would have no need to play uncle to your bastard."

"You may be the King's cousin, but you are not of the

Hibrusid house. You might find some difficulty persuading
the rest of the nobles that your claim is preeminent. With
myself as your wife, the King's only son as your legal
ward, your position would be unassailable. Call yourself
regent if you would: you would be King in everything but
name."

"And what would you be—a dutiful little wife? I'd
sooner share my bed with a viper."

She sat up, and shrugged. Her bodice had come down
and her heavy, dark-nippled breasts were bare. She took his
hand and set it upon one of them, squeezed his fingers in
on the ripe softness.

"Think on it awhile," she said, her voice a low purr.
"Abeleyn is a travesty of a man held together by sorcery
alone. He will not make old bones."

"I may be many things," Murad said, "but I am not yet
a traitor."

"Think on it," she repeated, and rose to her feet, tugging
up her dress, shaking grass out of her hair. "By the way,
your ship was piloted by one Richard Hawkwood, was it
not?"

"Yes. So?"

Her voice changed. She lost some of her assured poise.
"How is he? I have a lady's maid who wishes to know."

"A lady's maid with a yen for a mariner? He's well
enough, I suppose. Like me, he survived. There is not much
more to be said."

"I see." She became her assured self again, and bent forward to kiss Murad's scarred forehead. "Think on my offer.
I am staying in the West Wing—the guest apartments. You
can visit me when you like. Come and talk to me. I am
lonely there." She brushed one delicate finger along the scar
that convulsed the skin of his temple, then turned and
walked away across the garden towards the lights of the
palace, her fan fluttering all the way.

Murad watched her go. A peculiar hunger arose within
him. There was something about the lady Jemilla which
challenged his pride. He liked that. Her schemes were dangerous daydreams—but he would visit her, of that he was
sure. He would make her squeal, by God.

He left the shadow of the tree and looked up at the first stars come gleaming in the spring sky. Abrusio. He was home at last. And that murderous nightmare he had left behind him could be forgotten. His venture had been a failure, but it had taught him many things. He had information now that could one day prove useful.

Tomorrow he would visit the city barracks and see about getting back his old command. And he needed a new horse, something bad-tempered and spirited from the Feramuno studs. Something he would enjoy breaking down.

There were many things he was going to enjoy breaking down. Murad lifted his face and laughed aloud into the starlit sky. It was good to be alive.

EPILOGUE

SPRING, it seemed, had come at last. There was a fresh-
ness to the air, and primroses had come out in bright
lines about the margins of the Western Road. Corfe stood
on the summit of the tower and watched the light tumble
cloud patterns over the hills. If he turned his head, he could
see the sea glimmering on the world's horizon. A world at
peace.

"I thought I would find you here," a woman's voice said.
She touched him lightly on the arm, her long skirts whispering around her. She wore a crown.

An aged woman. She looked old enough to be his grandmother, and yet she was about to become his wife.

"It looks so quiet," he said, still staring out at the empty
hills beyond the city walls. "As if it had all been a dream."

"Or a nightmare," Odelia retorted.

He said nothing. The great burial mounds of Armagedir
were too far away for him to see, but he knew he would
always feel them there, somewhere at his shoulder. Andruw

lay in one of them, and Morin and Cerne and Ebro and Ranafast and Rusio—and ten thousand other faceless men who had died at his bidding. They were one monument he would never be able to forget.

"It's time, Corfe," the Queen said gently.

"I know."

If he looked east, towards the sea, he would find a large, ornate encampment pitched there, gay with the silk pennons and horsetail standards of the Merduks. The enemy had come calling in the aftermath of defeat, not exactly cap in hand but with a certain strained humility all the same. Corfe had given leave for the Merduk Sultan and a suitable escort to pitch their tents within sight of the city walls. His representatives had been permitted into the city this very morning, entering in peace the place they had squandered so much blood to take. They wanted to witness the crowning of Torunna's new King, the man with whom they would be treating in the days to come. It was too bizarre for words. Andruw would have found it so immensely funny.

Corfe blinked away the heat in his eyes. It was hard, harder than he could have imagined.

"He died well," Odelia said gently, "the way he would have wished. They all did."

Corfe nodded. He, too, would have been happy to die that day, knowing the battle was won.

"There is still the peace," Odelia said with that disquieting prescience of hers. "It remains to be achieved. What you do today is part of that."

"I know. I'm not sure it is the way I would have chosen, though."

"It is the best way," she said, pressing his arm. "Trust me, Corfe."

He limped away from the parapet with her hand still on his arm and turned back towards the city below. From this height, Torunn looked like some fairy-tale metropolis. The streets were packed with people—it was said a quarter of a million had gathered in City Square—and every house seemed to be flying some flag or banner. The citizens crowded upper-floor windows like tiers of house martins in

their nests, and Torunnan regulars in full dress were stationed at every corner.

"Let's get it over with," Corfe said.

FORMIO had drawn up an honour guard of pike-stiff Fimbrians in the court-yard of the palace, and as Corfe and
Odelia appeared they snapped to attention like automatons.
The Fimbrian adjutant saluted his commander with a rare
smile, one arm still in a sling. He looked pale and somewhat ethereal, but had insisted on leaving his sickbed for
this day. The chill in Corfe warmed a little. Aras was there
too, the huge scar in his face nearly healed. The Queen had
worked tyrelessly in the aftermath of Armagedir, saving
countless lives and wearing herself down to a shadow in
the process. "Give you joy, sir," Aras ventured.

"Thank you, General."

Corfe and Odelia climbed into the open barouche that
awaited them, and set off out of the palace flanked by fifty
mounted Cathedrallers—all that had survived. As soon as
they appeared at the palace gates a great roar went up from
the waiting crowds. They trundled through the cobbled
streets with the Cathedrallers raising a clattering din of
hooves about them and the people cheering madly. The air
was full of blossoms that spectators were scattering from
the windows overhead.

"Wave, Corfe," Odelia said out of the corner of her
mouth. "They're your people. They are what you won the
war for."

The cavalcade halted before the steps of the city cathedral and there they got out in a cloud of footmen, digni-
taries and whirling blossom. There was a salute of massed
trumpets. They paused on the stone steps, Odelia smiling
and nodding graciously at the Merduk ambassador, one
Mehr Jirah, Corfe giving him a cold glance before they
walked on, pageboys lifting the Queen's train and the hem
of Corfe's long cloak.

And into the cathedral, its pews stuffed to overflowing
with what nobility the kingdom still possessed, their numbers augmented by the great and the good of Torunna.
Corfe's eye was caught by Admiral Berza, near the aisle.

The old admiral winked at him as he passed by, his face as stiff as wood. There was Passifal's white head amongst the assembled military. Corfe recognised no-one else. He limped up the aisle staring straight ahead, expressionless.

Up at the altar Macrobius stood ready, smiling his blind smile. He was flanked by Bishops Albrec and Avila, who each bore velvet cushions. On one rested the crown of Torunna. On the other was a pair of plain gold wedding rings. One led to the other: both were deemed necessary for the well-being of the country.

Corfe and the Queen came to a halt before the Pontiff. As they did, Albrec caught Corfe's eye—he seemed strangely troubled. For a moment Corfe wondered if the little cleric was about to speak, but had thought better of it. The moment passed.

Another blare of trumpets. Incense, heady as powder-smoke, writhing in ribbons within the shafted sunlight of the high windows. The stained glass threw down a maelstrom of colour upon the flagstones, dimming the serried candle flames, raising painful glitters off the gold and gems that sparkled everywhere, even on Corfe's clothing.

Pictures pelting through his mind like rain. His first marriage, in a small chapel near Aekir's South Gate. Heria had held a posy of primroses. It had been spring, as it was today. They had been married two years when the siege began.

Sitting in the mud under a wrecked ox waggon on the Western Road with this same man who was about to crown him, gnawing on a half-raw turnip and wiping the rain out of his eyes.

Sharing a skin of wine with Marsch and Andruw on the battlements of Hedeby, after their first battle together. Drunk with victory and the comradeship that had enriched it, momentarily believing that all things were possible.

"Yes, I will," he answered when Macrobius asked him the question. And he had the cold gold slipped upon his finger. Odelia looking into his eyes, the years come crowding into her face at last. When he set the other ring in place she clenched her fist around it as if to prevent it ever slipping off. Her kiss was dry and chaste as a mother's. A few moments later the crown was set upon his head. It was surprisingly light, nothing like the weight of a helm. It might have been made of tinsel and feathers for all Corfe felt it.

When he straightened, the sunlight caught the precious metals of his crown and set it aflame, and all the bells of Torunn's cathedral began tolling at once in peal after jubilant peal, and outside he could hear the massed crowds of people who were now his subjects set up a mighty roar.

And it was done. He had a wife once more, and Torunna a King.

THE Merduk ambassador was first in line at the levee that afternoon. Corfe and the Queen received him in the huge audience hall of the palace, flanked by guards and palace functionaries. The new steward was present—none other than Colonel Passifal, appointed by Royal decree. He stood to one side of the trio of thrones looking uncomfortable but oddly determined. General Aras, also present, had been elevated to commander-in-chief of the army, with Formio as a de facto second-in-command. The Fimbrian was Corfe's first choice, but as Odelia had made very clear even a King had to think twice before placing the national army under the command of a foreigner.

Corfe needed familiar faces about him, and they were becoming increasingly hard to find. The third throne on the dais was occupied by another one, that of Macrobius. Standing beside him was Albrec and a gnomish old cleric named Mercadius, who could speak fluent Merduk. Corfe shared a history with almost all these familiar faces: he had fought side by side with Aras, Formio and Passifal. He had saved Macrobius's life. He had escaped from Fournier's dungeons with Albrec. The war had cost him his wife, and the best comrades he had ever known, but had it not been for the war he would never have known the friendship of men like these, like Andruw and Marsch, and he would have been the poorer for it.

Mehr Jirah entered the audience chamber without ceremony, flanked only by a pair of Merduk clerics who looked surprisingly similar to Ramusian monks, albeit without tonsures. Mercadius of Orfor translated his speech into Normannic for the assembled listeners.

"These are the words I was bade to say to the King of Torunna by my master the Sultan of Ostrabar.

"We send greetings to Torunna's new King, and congratulate him on his unexpected elevation. Truly, God has been kind to him. We will suffer ourselves to speak to him now as one soldier to another, in terms as plain as we can make them. The slaughter of our young men has gone on long enough. We have carpeted the world with the bodies of our dead, and in the name of God and His Prophet we offer the Torunnan King this chance to end the killing. In our generosity we will withhold the wrath of our mighty armies and suffer the kingdom of Torunna to survive, if King Corfe will merely acknowledge the suzerainty of Aurungzeb the Great, Sultan of Ostrabar, conqueror of Aekir and Ormann Dyke. He has to but bend his knee to us and this war will come to an end, and we shall have peace between our peoples for all time. What says Torunna's monarch?"

There was an angry stir from the assembled Torunnans as Mercadius translated the words, and Aras took a step forward, his hand going to where his sword should have been. But no-one bore arms in the audience chamber save the King alone. Corfe stood up, eyes flashing.

"Mehr Jirah, you are known to some of us here. I have been told you are a man of integrity and honour, and so I ask you to remember that what I say now is not directed at you or the faith you profess—a faith we know to be almost the same as our own. This is to Aurungzeb, your lord.

"Tell him that Torunna will never submit to him, not if he brings ten times the armies he possesses in front of her walls. At Armagedir he tried to destroy us, and we defeated him. If we have to, we will defeat him again. We will never surrender, not if we must fight to the last man hiding in the hills. We will fight him until the world cracks open at doomsday.

"Peace we would have, yes, but only if he takes his beaten armies and leaves Torunna's soil for ever. If he does

not, I swear by my God that I will drive him out. His people
will never know a moment of rest while I live. If it takes
twenty years, I will throw him back beyond the Ostian
river. I will slay every Merduk man, woman and child who
falls into my hands. I will burn his cities and salt his soil.
I will make of his kingdom a howling wilderness, and wipe
the very memory of Ostrabar and its sultan from the face
of the world."

A cheer erupted in the chamber. Mehr Jirah looked
shocked for a moment, but quickly regained his dignified
poise.

"That is our answer. Take it back to your master, and
make it clear to him that there will be no second chance. I
am King here now, and I will not hesitate to mobilise every
able man in my kingdom to back my words. He no longer
fights an army, but an entire people. This is his choice, now
and only now—peace, or a war that will last another hundred years. Tell him to think carefully. His decision will
alter the very fate of the world for him and all those who
come after him. Now you may go."

Mehr Jirah bowed. He nodded at Albrec, and then turned
on his heel and left. Corfe took his seat once more. "Passifal, our next supplicant, if you please." He had to raise
his voice to make himself heard above the surf of talk in
the hall.

Odelia leaned over the arm of her throne and whispered
fiercely in his ear.

"Are you out of your mind? Have you no notion of diplomacy at all? We had a chance to halt the war, but you
are set on starting it again."

"No. I may be no diplomat, but I have some military
insight. He can't fight on. We've beaten him, and he has
to be told that. And I didn't fight Armagedir so that I could
place my neck in a Merduk yoke. He thinks he knows what
war is; he has no idea. If he is stupid and proud enough to
keep fighting, I will show him how war can be waged."

There was such contained ferocity about Corfe as he
spoke that Odelia's retort died in her throat. At that moment
she realised she had overreached herself. She had thought
that Corfe, once King, would be content to lead armies and

fight wars while she negotiated the treaties and dictated policy. She knew better now. Not only would he rule, and rule in all things, but other rulers would want to deal with him and him alone, not with his ageing Queen. It was he who had won the war, after all. It was he whom the common people mobbed in the streets and cheered at every opportunity. Even her own attendants looked first to him.

She uttered a bitter little laugh that was lost in the next fanfare. All her life she had ruled through men. Now one had come to power through her, and reduced her to a cipher.

AURUNGZEB received Mehr Jirah in silence. In the sumptuous ostentation of his tent he had Corfe's words relayed to him by the mullah and listened patiently as his officers and aides expressed outrage at the Ramusian's insolence. His Queen sat beside him, also silent. He took her cold hand, thinking of his son in her belly and what world he might be born into. He had the makings of it here, at this moment. And for the first time in his life he was afraid.

"Batak," he said at last. "That little beast of yours flits about the Torunnan palace day and night. What say you in this matter?"

The mage pondered a moment. "I think his words, my Sultan, are not empty. This man is not a braggart. He does what he says."

"We have all realised that, I think," Aurungzeb said wryly. "Shahr Baraz?"

The old Merduk shrugged. "He's the best soldier they've ever produced. I believe he and my father would have had much in common."

"Is there no-one around me who can give me some wisdom in their counsell?" Aurungzeb snapped. "I am surrounded by platitude-mouthing old women! Where is Shahr Johor?"

The occupants of the tent looked at one another. Finally Akran, the chamberlain, ventured: "You—ah—you had him executed, Majesty."

"What? Oh, yes of course. Well, that was inevitable. He should have died with his men at Armagedir. Blood of God,

what happened there? How did he do it? We should have
won!"

"We did, at least, destroy those accursed red horsemen,
Majesty," Serrim the eunuch offered.

"Yes, those scarlet fiends. And we slew ten thousand
more of his army, did we not? He must be as severely
crippled as we are! How does he come to be making
threats? What manner of maniac is he? Does he know nothing of the niceties of negotiation?"

The gathering of attendants, advisors and officials said
nothing. In the quiet they could hear the crowds of Torunn
still cheering, less than half a league away. The noise grated
on Aurungzeb's nerves. Why did they cheer him? He had
led so many of their sons and fathers to their deaths, and
yet they loved him for it. The Torunnans—there was a collective madness about them. They were a people unhinged.
How did one deal with that? When Aurungzeb spoke again
the petulance in his voice was like that of a child refused
its treat.

"I asked him for safe conduct, the reception of an ambassador—*I opened negotiations with the bastard!* He must
give something in return! Isn't that right, Batak?"

"Undoubtedly, sire. But remember that he is reputed to
be nothing more than a common soldier, a peasant. He has
no idea of protocol, or the basic courtesies that exist between monarchs. The conventions of diplomacy are beyond
him. He speaks the language of the barrack room only."

"That may be no bad thing," Shahr Baraz rumbled. "At
least if he gives his word, you can be sure he'll keep it."

"Don't prate to me about the virtues of soldiers," Aurungzeb growled. "They are overrated."

Once more there was silence in the tent. The members
of the court had never seen the Sultan so unsure, so needful
of advice. He had always been one to follow his own counsell, even if it meant flying in the face of facts.

"The war must end," Mehr Jirah said at last. "Of that
there is no question. Thirty thousand of our men died at
Armagedir. Our army can fight no more."

"Then neither can his!"

"I think it can, Sultan. The Torunnans are not striving

for conquest, but for survival. They will never give up, especially with this man leading them. Armagedir was the last chance we had to win the war at a stroke, and every one of our soldiers knows it. They also know that this is no longer a holy war. The Ramusians are not infidels, but co-believers in the Prophet—"

"You and your damn preachings have done that," Aurungzeb raged.

"Would you deny the tenets of your own faith?" Mehr Jirah asked, unintimidated.

"No—no, of course not. All right then. It seems I have no choice. We will remain in negotiation. Mehr Jirah, Batak, Shahr Baraz, the three of you will go to Torunn in the morning and offer to broker a treaty. But no backsliding, mind! God knows I have grovelled enough for one day. Ahara, you were once a Ramusian. What say you? Are they right in this thing? Will this new soldier-king fight us to the end?"

Heria did not look at him. She placed a hand on her swollen abdomen. "You will have a son soon, my lord. I would like him to grow up in peace. Yes, this man will never give in. He . . . Father Albrec told me that he had too much iron in him. But he is a good man at heart. A decent man. He will keep his word, once given."

"Perhaps," Aurungzeb grunted. "I must say, I have a perverse hankering to meet him, face to face. Perhaps if we sign a treaty we may pay him a state visit." And he laughed harshly. "The times are changing, indeed."

No-one noticed how white Heria's face had gone. The veil was good for that much at least.

THE war between the Merduks and the Ramusians had begun so long ago that no-one except the historians was sure in what year the two peoples had first come to blows. But everyone knew when it had ended: in the first year of the reign of King Corfe, the same year the Fantyr dynasty had ceased to be.

And five and a half centuries after the coming of the Blessed Saint who had also been the Prophet, the dual nature of Ramusio was finally recognised and the two great religions he had founded came together and admitted their common origin. All this was written into the Treaty of Armagedir, a document it took soldiers and scholars several weeks to hammer out in a spacious tent which had been erected halfway between the walls of Torunn and the Merduk encampment especially for that purpose.

The Merduks agreed to make the River Searil the border of their new domain. Khedi Anwar, which had once been Ormann Dyke, became the southernmost of their settlements, and Aekir was renamed Aurungabar and designated the Ostrabarian capital. The cathedral of Carcaseon was transformed into the temple of Pir-Sar, and both Merduks and Ramusians were to be allowed to worship there, since it had been made holy by the founder of both their faiths. Those Aekirian refugees who wished to return to their former home were free to do so without fear of molestation, and the monarchs of Torunna and Ostrabar exchanged ambassadors and set up embassies in each other's capitals.

But much of that was still in the future. For now, the gates of Torunn were thrown open for the treaty-signing ceremonies, and the war-weary city made ready to receive a visit from the man who had tried to conquer it. For Corfe, it had the surreal quality of a dream. He and Aurungzeb had negotiated through intermediaries, the Sultan considering it beneath his dignity to haggle over the clauses of a treaty in person. Today he would see the face of—perhaps even shake the hand of—the man he had striven so long to destroy. And his mysterious Ramusian Queen, whose contribution to the winning of the war only Corfe and Albrec knew of. Corfe wondered how the history books would view the event. He had come to realise that the facts and history's perception of them were two very different things.

He stood in his dressing chamber with the summer sunshine flooding in a glorious stream through the tall windows whilst half a dozen valets stood by, disconsolate. They held in their arms a bewildering array of garments which dripped with gems, gold lace and fur trimmings. Corfe had refused them all, and stood in the plain black of a Torunnan infantryman. He wore no crown, but had been persuaded to place on his head an ancient circlet of silver which at one time

Fimbrian marshals had worn at the court of the Electors. Albrec, of all people, had dug it up for him out of some dusty palace coffer. It had once belonged to Kaile Ormann himself, which Corfe thought rather fitting.

Trumpets ringing out down by the city gates, heralding the approach of the Sultan's cavalcade. It seemed to Corfe he had heard more damned trumpets blown in the past few weeks than he had heard in all his life upon battlefields. Torunn had become one vast carnival of late, the people celebrating victory, peace, a new King—one thing after another. And now this, the last of the state occasions which Corfe intended to preside over for a long time.

He'd like to take Formio and Aras out into the hills and go hunting for a while, sleep under the stars again, stare into a campfire and drink rough army wine. The war had been hellish, but it had possessed its moments of sweetness too. Or perhaps he was merely a damned nostalgic fool, destined to become a dissatisfied old man for whom all glory was in the past. Now there was a concept. The very idea made him smile. But as one of the more courageous of the valets stepped forward for the third time with the ermine-trimmed robe the smile twisted into a frown.

"For the last time, no. Now get out of here, all of you."

"Sire, the Queen insisted—"

"Bugger off."

"My lord, that is hardly the language a king is expected to use," Odelia said, sweeping into the room with a pair of maids behind her.

He limped about to meet her eyes. Despite her ministrations, he suspected that his Armagedir wound had marked him permanently. He would be lame for the rest of his life. Well, many had come out of the war with worse souvenirs.

"I always thought that kings could use what language they chose," he said lightly. Odelia kissed him on the cheek, then drew back to survey his plain attire with mock despair.

"The Sultan will mistake you for a common soldier, if you're not careful."

"He made that mistake before. I doubt he will again."

Odelia laughed, something she had begun to do more

often of late. The bright sunlight was not kind to the lines
on her face. Whatever magicks she had once applied to
maintain her youthful appearance were still being used on
the wounded of the army. Her newfound age still perturbed
him sometimes. So he took her hand and kissed it.

"Are they at the walls yet?"

"Just entering the barbican. Perched upon a column of
elephants, if you please. It looks like a travelling circus is
coming to town."

"Well then, lady, let us go down and greet the clowns."

Her hand came up and touched his temple briefly. "You
have gone grey, Corfe. I never noticed before."

"That was Armagedir. It made an old man of me."

"In that case, you will not mind taking an old woman's
arm. Come. We have a dais set out for us hung with lilies,
and they're beginning to wilt in the sun. Its height has been
carefully calculated: just high enough to make Aurungzeb
look like a supplicant, yet not so high that he can feel insulted."

"Ah, the subtleties of diplomacy."

"And of carpentry."

The crowd gave a massive roar as they appeared side by
side and climbed into a carriage which would transport
them to the dais just beyond the palace gates. Once there,
Odelia had a final, critical look at the arrangements, and
they sat down upon the thrones that awaited them. Behind
them Mercadius stood, blinking like an owl in the sunlight
and looking half asleep on his feet: he was to interpret the
proceedings. A dozen Cathedrallers, their armour freshly
painted and shining, stood about the sides of the dais like
scarlet statuary.

Corfe found himself looking down a wide avenue from
which the crowds were held back by two lines of Torunnan
regulars. The noise was deafening and the sun hot. Odelia's
hand was cold as he gripped it, however. It felt as insub-
stantial as straw within his own strong fingers.

Albrec mounted the dais, his face dark with some unknown worry. He bowed. "Your pardon, Majesties. I would
count it an honour if you allowed me to be present at this
time. I will stay out of the way."

Odelia looked as though she was about to refuse, but Corfe waved him closer. "By all means, Father. After all, you're better acquainted with the Merduk Sultan than we are." Why did the little monk look so troubled? He was wiping sweat off his face with one sleeve.

"Albrec, are you all right?" Corfe asked him quietly.

"Corfe, I must—"

And here the damnable trumpets began sounding out again. A swaying line of palanquin-bearing elephants approached, painted and draped and bejewelled until they seemed like beasts out of some gaudy legend. Atop the lead animal, which had been painted white, Corfe could make out the broad, turbaned shape of the man who must be Aurungzeb, and beside him under the tasselled canopy the slighter shadow of his Queen.

The play-acting part of it was scheduled to last no more than a few minutes. In the audience hall of the palace two copies of the treaty waited to be signed—that was the real business of the day. Then there would be a banquet, and some entertainments or other which Odelia had dreamt up, and it would be done. Aurungzeb would not be staying in Torunn overnight, treaty or no treaty.

Formio and Aras appeared at the foot of the dais. Corfe had thought it only fair that they be here for this moment. The two had become fast friends despite the odds. The Aras Corfe knew now was a long way from the pompous young man he had first encountered at Staed. What was it Andruw had said? All piss and vinegar—yes, that was it. And Corfe smiled. I hope you can see this, Andruw. You made it happen, you and those damned tribesmen.

So many ghosts.

The lead elephant halted, and then went to its knees as smoothly as a well-trained lap-dog. Silk-clad attendants appeared and helped the Sultan and his Queen out of the high palanquin. A knot of people, as bright as silk butterflies, fussed around the couple. Corfe looked at Odelia. She nodded, and they both rose to their feet to greet their guests.

The Sultan was a tall man, topping Corfe by half a head. The fine breadth of his shoulders was marred somewhat by the paunch that had begun to develop under the sash which belted his middle. He had a huge beard, as broad as a besom, and his snow-white turban was set with a ruby brooch. The eyes under the turban's brim were alight with intelligence and irritation. Clearly, he did not like the fact that, thanks to the dais, Corfe and Odelia were looking down on him.

Of Aurungzeb's Queen, Corfe could make out little, except that she was heavily pregnant. She was clad in blue silk, the colour of which Corfe immediately liked. Her face above the veil had been garishly painted, the eye-brows drawn out with stibium, kohl smeared across the lids. She did not look up at the dais, but kept her gaze fixed resolutely on the ground. Directly behind her stood an old Merduk with a formidable face and direct glance. He looked like an over-protective father.

The Sultan's chamberlain had appeared at one side to announce his master's appearance, but Aurungzeb did not wait for the diplomatic niceties to begin. Instead he clambered up on to the dais itself, which caused Corfe's Cathedraller bodyguard to half draw their swords. Corfe held up a hand, and they relaxed.

The Sultan loomed over him. "So you are the man I have been fighting," he said, his Normannic surprisingly good.

"I am the man."

They stared at one another in frank, mutual curiosity. Finally Aurungzeb grinned. "I thought you would be taller."

They both laughed, and incredibly Corfe found himself liking the man.

"I see you have your mad little priest here as well—except that he is not mad, of course. Brother Albrec, you have turned our world upside-down. I hope you are pleased with yourself."

Albrec bowed wordlessly. The Sultan nodded to Odelia. "Lady, I hope you are good . . . well. Yes, that is the word." He took Odelia's hand and kissed it, then scrutinized the nearest Cathedraller, who was watching him warily.

"I thought we had killed them all," he said affably.

Corfe frowned. "Not all of them."

"You must be running short of *Ferinai* armour for them.

I can perhaps send you a few hundred sets."

"There is no need," Odelia said smoothly. "We captured several hundred more at Armagedir."

It was the Sultan's turn to frown. But not for long. "My manners have deserted me. Let me introduce Queen Ahara. Shahr Baraz, help her up here. That's it."

The old, severe-looking Merduk helped the Merduk Queen up on the dais. Around the little tableau of figures, the crowds had gone quiet and were watching events unfold as if it were some passion play laid on for their entertainment.

"Ahara was from Aekir," the Sultan explained. "She will soon give me a son. The next Sultan of Ostrabar will have Ramusian blood in him. For that reason at least, it is good that this long war finally comes to an end."

Albrec laid a hand on Corfe's shoulder, surprising him. The little monk was staring intently at him. Half amused, half puzzled, he took the Merduk Queen's hand to kiss, raised it to his lips. "Lady—"

Her eyes were full of tears. Corfe hesitated, wondering what was wrong, and in that instant, he knew her.

He knew her.

Albrec's grip on his shoulder tightened bruisingly.

"It may be that one day our children will even play together," Aurungzeb went on, oblivious. He seemed to enjoy showing off his command of Normannic. "Imagine how we will be able to improve our respective kingdoms, if there is no war to fight, no frontier to maintain. I foresee a new era with the signing of this treaty. Today is a famous day."

So much, in one terrible moment. A whole host of impulses come roaring at him, only to be beaten back. His life shipwrecked beyond hope or happiness. Albrec's grip on his shoulder anchoring him to reality in a world which had suddenly gone insane.

Her eyes had not changed, despite the paint that had been applied about them. Perhaps there was a wisdom in them now which had not been there before. Her fingers clasped his hand as they hovered below his lips, a gentle pressure, no more.

Something broke, deep within him.

Corfe shut his eyes, and kissed the hand of the woman who had been his wife. He held her fingers one moment more, and then released them and straightened.

"I hope I see you well, lady," he said, his voice as harsh and thick as a raven's croak.

"I am well enough, my lord," she replied.

One second longer they had looking at one another, and then the madness of the world came flooding back in on them. The day must be seen through, and the thing they had come here for must be done. Had to be done.

"Are you all right?" Odelia whispered to Corfe as they led the Merduk Royal couple down from the dais to the carriages that awaited.

He nodded, grey in the face. Albrec had to help him into the carriage; he was as unsteady as an old man.

The crowds found their voices at last, and began to cheer as the carriages trundled the short distance to the open doors of the great audience hall, where rank after rank of Fimbrian pikemen were drawn up alongside Torunnan regulars and a small, vermilion line of Cathedrallers. Aras and Formio rode alongside the carriage.

"Wave, Corfe," Odelia said to him. "This is supposed to be a glad day. The war is over, remember."

But he did not wave. He stared out at that sea of cheering people, and thought he saw faces he knew in the crowd. Andruw and Marsch, Ebro, Cerne, Ranafast, Martellus. And at the last he saw Heria, the woman who had once been his wife, with that heartbreaking smile of hers, one corner of her mouth quirking upwards.

He closed his eyes. She had joined the faces of the dead at last.